BODY AND SOUL

Erin stared straight up into his face and drank in all the details: the sheen of beard stubble glinting metallic gold in the light from the corridor outside. The shadows beneath his brilliant eyes, the sharp line of his jutting cheekbones. How was it possible for a mouth to be so stern, and yet so sensual?

And his piercing eyes saw right into her soul.

She lost herself in it. She wanted to touch his face, to trail her fingers over every masculine detail, to feel the warmth of his skin. She wanted to press herself against his lean, solid bulk. She wished she had something to feed him, whether he was hungry or not.

Connor reached behind himself and shoved the door shut without breaking eye contact. She needed so badly for someone to know how lonely and lost she felt. Her mother was adrift in despair. Most of her friends were avoiding her. Not out of unkindness so much as sheer embarrassment, she suspected. But that didn't help the loneliness.

Connor saw it all, and it didn't embarrass him. His gaze didn't shy away. She didn't shy away, either, when he reached for her.

His touch was so careful and delicate, she could barely believe it was happening. Her eyes welled up. He smoothed away the tears that spilled over with a brush of his thumb, and folded her into his arms.

SHANNON McKENNA

STANDING IN THE SHADOWS

KENSINGTON PUBLISHING CORP.
http://www.kensingtonbooks.com

> *For Nicola*
> *ti amo*

BRAVA BOOKS are published by

Kensington Publishing Corp.
850 Third Avenue
New York, NY 10022

All Kensington Titles, Imprints, and Distributed Lines are available at special quantity discounts for bulk purchases for sales promotions, premiums, fund-raising, and educational or institutional use. Special book excerpts or customized printings can also be created to fit specific needs. For details, write or phone the office of the Kensington special sales manager: Kensington Publishing Corp., 850 Third Avenue, New York, NY 10022, attn: Special Sales Department, Phone: 1-800-221-2647.

Brava Books and the Brava logo Reg. U.S. Pat. & TM Off.

First Brava Books trade paperback printing: August 2003
First Brava Books mass market printing: August 2004

10 9 8 7 6 5 4 3 2 1

Printed in the United States of America

Prologue

*T*he windowless room was dark. The only light came from banks of machines that flickered, and made soft, intermittent beeping sounds.

The door opened. A woman entered the room and flipped on a lamp. The light revealed a man who lay upon a narrow mattress made of high-tech black latex foam. His sallow, wasted body bristled with hair-fine needles attached to wires, which fed into the machines behind him.

The woman shut and locked the door behind herself. She was middle-aged, dressed in a white lab coat, with steel-gray hair and an imposing jaw. Her thin lips were painted a bright, cruel red.

She removed the needles from his body with movements both brisk and delicate. She anointed her hands with oil, breathed deeply, and performed preparatory energetic exercises to stimulate the power and heat in her large, thick-fingered hands. She then proceeded to massage him expertly, front and back, from his feet to his balding scalp. She massaged his face, her brow a scowling mask, fearsomely intent.

That done, she took several blood samples. She measured his blood pressure, his pulse. She reapplied the complex pattern of needles, made adjustments in the machines. She replenished the nourishment and medications provided by the plastic bag that dangled from the IV rack. Then she cupped his face in her hands. She kissed him on both cheeks, then on his half-open mouth.

The kiss was prolonged and passionate. When she lifted her head, her eyes were glowing, her face flushed. Her breath was rapid, and the marks of her lipstick against his pale skin made him look as if he had been bitten.

She flicked off the light and left him, locking the door behind her.

Once again, the darkness was broken only by colored lights that flickered and pulsed, and soft, intermittent beeping.

Chapter

1

The silver cell phone that lay on the passenger seat of the beige Cadillac buzzed and vibrated, like a dying fly on a dusty windowsill.

Connor slouched lower in the driver's seat and contemplated it. Normal people were wired to grab the thing, check the number, and respond. In him, those wires were cut, that programming deleted. He stared at it, amazed at his own indifference. Or maybe amazed was too strong a word. Stupefied would be closer. Let it die. Five rings. Six. Seven. Eight. The cell phone persisted, buzzing angrily.

It got up to fourteen, and gave up in disgust.

He went back to staring at Tiff's current love nest through the rain that trickled over the windshield. It was a big, ugly town house that squatted across the street. The world outside the car was a blurry wash of grays and greens. Lights still on in the second-floor bedroom. Tiff was taking her time. He checked his watch. She was usually a slam-bam, twenty-minutes-at-the-most sort of girl, but she'd gone up those stairs almost forty minutes ago. A record, for her.

Maybe it was true love.

Connor snorted to himself, hefting the heavy camera into

place and training the telephoto lens on the doorway. He wished she'd hurry. Once he'd snapped the photos her husband had paid McCloud Investigative Services to get, his duty would be done, and he could crawl back under his rock. A dark bar and a shot of single malt, someplace where the pale gray daylight could not sting his eyes. Where he could concentrate on not thinking about Erin.

He let the camera drop with a sigh, and pulled out his tobacco and rolling papers. After he'd woken up from the coma, during the agonizing tedium of rehab, he'd gotten the bright idea of switching to hand-rolled, reasoning that if he let himself roll them only with his fucked-up hand, he'd slow down and consequently smoke less. Problem was, he got good at it real fast. By now he could roll a tight cigarette in seconds flat with either hand, without looking. So much for that pathetic attempt at self-mastery.

He rolled the cigarette on autopilot, eyes trained on the town house, and wondered idly who had called. Only three people had the number: his friend Seth, and his two brothers, Sean and Davy. Seth for sure had better things to do on a Saturday afternoon than call him. The guy was neck-deep in honeymoon bliss with Raine. Probably writhing in bed right now, engaged in sex acts that were still against the law somewhere in the southern states. Lucky bastard.

Connor's mouth twisted in self-disgust. Seth had suffered, too, from all the shit that had come down in the past few months. He was a good guy, and a true friend, if a difficult one. He deserved the happiness he'd found with Raine. It was unworthy of Connor to be envious, but Jesus. Watching those two, glowing like neon, joined at the hip, sucking on each other's faces, well . . . it didn't help.

Connor wrenched his mind away from that dead-end track and stared at the cell phone. Couldn't be Seth. He checked his watch. His younger brother Sean was at the dojo at this hour, teaching an afternoon kickboxing class. That left his older brother, Davy.

Boredom tricked him into picking up the cell phone to check the number, and as if the goddamn thing had been lying in wait for him, it buzzed right in his hand, making him jump and curse. Telepathic bastard. Davy's instincts and timing were legendary.

He gave in and pushed the talk button with a grunt of disgust. "What?"

"Nick called." Davy's deep voice was brusque and business-like.

"So?"

"What do you mean, so? The guy's your friend. You need your friends, Con. You worked with him for years, and he—"

"I'm not working with him," Connor said flatly. "I'm not working with any of them now."

Davy made an inarticulate, frustrated sound. "I know I promised not to give out this number, but it was a mistake. Call him, or I'll—"

"Don't do it," Connor warned.

"Don't make me," Davy said.

"So I'll throw the phone into the nearest Dumpster," Connor said, his voice casual. "I don't give a flying fuck."

He could almost hear his older brother's teeth grinding. "You know, your attitude sucks," Davy said.

"Stop trying to shove me around, and it won't bother you so much," Connor suggested.

Davy treated him to a long pause, calculated to make Connor feel guilty and flustered. It didn't work. He just waited right back.

"He wants to talk to you," Davy finally said. His voice was carefully neutral. "Says it's important."

The light in the town house bedroom went off. Connor lifted the camera to the ready. "Don't even want to know," he said.

Davy grunted in disgust. "Got Tiff's latest adventure on film yet?"

"Any minute now. She's just finishing up."

"Got plans after?"

Connor hesitated. "Uh . . ."

"I've got steaks in the fridge," Davy wheedled. "And a case of Anchor Steam."

"I'm not really hungry."

"I know. You haven't been hungry for the past year and a half. That's why you've lost twenty-five goddamn pounds. Get the pictures, and then get your ass over here. You need to eat."

Connor sighed. His brother knew how useless his blustering orders were, but he refused to get a clue. His stubborn skull was harder than concrete. "Hey, Davy. It's not that I don't like your cooking—"

"Nick's got some news that might interest you about Novak."

Connor shot bolt upright in his seat, the heavy camera bouncing painfully off his scarred leg. "Novak? What about Novak?"

"That's it. That's all he said."

"That filthy fuck is rotting in a maximum security prison cell. What news could there possibly be about him?"

"Guess you better call and find out, huh? Then hightail it over here. I'll mix up the marinade. Later, bro."

Connor stared at the phone in his hand, too rattled to be annoyed at Davy's casual bullying. His hand was shaking. Whoa. He wouldn't have thought there was still that much adrenaline left in the tank.

Kurt Novak, who had set in motion a chain of events that effectively ruined Connor's life. Or so he saw it on his self-pitying days, which were happening way too often lately. Kurt Novak, who had murdered Connor's partner, Jesse. Who was responsible for the coma, the scars, the limp. Who had blackmailed and corrupted Connor's colleague Ed Riggs.

Novak, who had almost gotten his vicious, filthy claws into Erin, Ed's daughter. Her incredibly narrow escape had given him nightmares for months. Oh, yeah. If there was one magic word on earth that could jolt him awake and make him give a shit, it was Novak.

Erin. He rubbed his face and tried not to think of the last time he'd seen Erin's beautiful face, but the image was burned indelibly into his mind. She'd been wrapped in a blanket in the back of the patrol car. Dazed with shock. Her eyes had been huge with horror and betrayal.

He had put that look in her eyes.

He gritted his teeth against the twisting ache of helpless anger that went along with that memory, and the explosion of sensual images. They made him feel guilty and sick, but they wouldn't leave him alone. Every detail his brain had recorded about Erin was erotically charged, right down to the way her dark hair swirled into an elfin, downward-pointing whorl at the nape of her neck when she pulled it up. The way she had of looking at the world with those big, thoughtful eyes. Self-possessed and quiet, drawing her own mysterious conclusions. Making him ache and burn to know what she was thinking.

And then *bam*, her shy, sweet smile flashing out unexpectedly. Like a bolt of lightning that melted down his brain.

A flash of movement caught his eye, and he yanked the camera up to the ready. Tiff had already scuttled halfway down the steps before he got in a series of rapid-fire shots. She shot a furtive glance to the right, then to the left, dark hair swishing over her beige raincoat. The guy followed her down the steps. Tall, fortyish, balding. Neither of them looked particularly relaxed or fulfilled. The guy tried to kiss her. Tiff turned away so the kiss landed on her ear. He got it all on film.

Tiff got into her car. It roared to life, and she pulled away, faster than she needed to on the rainy, deserted street. The guy stared after her, bewildered. Clueless bastard. He had no idea what a snake pit he was sliding into. Nobody ever did, until it was too late.

Connor let the camera drop. The guy climbed his steps

and went back inside, shoulders slumped. Those pictures ought to be enough for Phil Kurtz, Tiff's scheming dickhead of a husband. Ironically, Phil was cheating on Tiff, too. He just wanted to make sure that Tiff wouldn't be able to screw him over in the inevitable acrimonious divorce.

It made him nauseous. Not that he cared who Tiff Kurtz was sleeping with. She could boff a whole platoon of balding suits if she wanted. Phil was such a whiny, vindictive prick, he almost didn't blame her, and yet, he did. He couldn't help it. She should leave Phil. Make it clean, honest. Start a new life. A real life.

Hah. Like he had any right to judge. He tried to laugh at himself, but the laugh petered out with no breath to bear it up. He couldn't stomach the betrayal. Lying and sneaking, slinking around in the shadows like a bad dog trying to get away with something. It pressed down on his chest, suffocating him. Or maybe that was just the effect of all the unfiltered cigarettes he was sucking on.

It was his own fault for letting Davy talk him into helping out with the detective agency. He hadn't been able to face going back to his old job after what happened last fall, but he should've known better. After putting a colleague behind bars for setting you up to die, well, following cheating spouses around wasn't exactly therapeutic. Davy must figure that Tiff was just the kind of stultifying no-brainer that even his washed-up little brother would have a hard time fucking up.

Oh, man. The pity party was getting ugly. He clenched his teeth and tried to adjust his attitude by sheer brute force. Davy unloaded Tiff and her ilk onto him because he was bored with them, and who could blame him. And if Connor couldn't take it, he should shut up and get another job. Security guard, maybe. Night shift, so he wouldn't have to interact with anybody. Maybe he could be a janitor in some huge industrial facility. Shove a push broom down miles of deserted corridors night after night. Oh, yeah. That ought to cheer him right up.

It wasn't like he was hurting for money. His house was paid for. The investments Davy had forced him to make had done fine. His car was a vintage '67 Caddy that would not die. He didn't care about expensive clothes. He didn't date. Once he'd acquired the stereo and video system that he liked, he hardly knew what to spend the interest dividends on. With what he had socked away, he could probably scrape by even if he never worked again.

God, what a bleak prospect. Forty-odd years more of scraping along, doing nothing, meaning nothing to anyone. It made him shudder.

Connor fished the unsmoked cigarette out of his coat pocket. Everything got dirty and stained, everything broke down, everything had a price. It was time to accept reality and stop sulking. He had to get his life back. Some kind of life.

He'd liked his life once. He'd spent nine years as an agent in the undercover FBI task force that his partner Jesse had dubbed "The Cave," and he'd been good at feeling his way into the parts he played. He'd seen his share of ugly stuff, and yeah, he'd been haunted by some of it, but he'd also known the bone-deep satisfaction that came from doing what he was born to do. He'd loved being in the middle of everything, wired to a taut web of interconnected threads; touch one, and the whole fabric rippled and hummed. Senses buzzing, brain working overtime, churning out connections, deductions, conclusions. He'd loved it. And he'd loved trying to make a difference.

But now the threads were ripped. He was numb and isolated, in free fall. What good would it do to hear about Novak? He couldn't help. His web was cut. He had nothing to offer. What would be the point?

He lit the cigarette and groped around in his mind for Nick's number. It popped up instantly, blinking on the screen inside his mind. Photographic memory was a McCloud family trait. Sometimes it was useful, sometimes it was just a dumb parlor trick. Sometimes it was a curse. It kept things eternally fresh in his brain that he would prefer to forget. Like that white linen halter top that Erin had worn at the Riggs family Fourth of July picnic, for instance. Six goddamn years ago, and the memory was as sharp as broken glass. She'd been braless that day, so it was by far the best view he'd ever gotten of her beautiful tits. High and soft and tenderly pointed, bouncing every time she moved. Dark, taut nipples pressed hard against the thin fabric. He'd been amazed that Barbara, her mother, had allowed it. Particularly after Barbara had caught him staring. Her eyes had turned to ice.

Barbara was no fool. She hadn't wanted her innocent young daughter hooking up with a cop. Look how it had turned out for her.

He knew better than to try to shove memories away. It just made them stronger, until they were huge and muscular, taking over his whole mind. Like the image of Erin's dark, haunted eyes behind the patrol car window. Full of the terrible knowledge of betrayal.

He sucked smoke into his lungs and stared at the cell phone with unfriendly eyes. He'd thrown away the old one after what happened last fall. If he used this one to call Nick, then Nick would have the new number. Not good. He liked being unreachable. It suited his mood.

He closed his eyes, recalling last Christmas, when Davy and Sean had given him the damn thing. It was from Seth's hoard of gizmos, which meant that it had a bunch of high-tech bells and whistles, some useful, some not. He'd leafed through Seth's sheaf of explanatory paperwork, putting on a show of interest so as not to hurt everybody's feelings. He vaguely remembered a function that blocked the incoming number from the display. He flipped through the pages in his mind, found the sequence. Keyed it in, dialed.

His stomach knotted painfully as it rang.

"Nick Ward," his ex-colleague answered.

"It's Connor."

"No shit." Nick's voice was stone cold. "Had a good sulk, Con?"

He'd known this was going to be bad. "Can we skip this part, Nick? I'm not in the mood."

"I don't care about your goddamn mood. I'm not the one who sold you out. I don't appreciate being punished for what Riggs did to you."

"I'm not punishing you," Connor said defensively.

"No? So what have you been doing for the last six months, asshole?"

Connor slumped lower in his seat. "I've been kind of out of it lately. You'd be stupid if you took it personally."

Nick let out an unsatisfied grunt.

Connor waited. "So?"

"So what?"

Nick's tone set his teeth on edge. "Davy said you had some news for me," he said. "About Novak."

"Oh. That." Nick was enjoying himself now, the snotty bastard. "I thought that might get your attention. Novak's broken out of prison."

Adrenaline blasted through him. "What the fuck? When? How?"

"Three nights ago. Him, and two of his goons, Georg Luksch and Martin Olivier. Very slick, well planned, well financed. Help from the outside, probably the inside, too. Nobody got killed, amazingly enough. Daddy Novak must've been behind it. You can do a lot with billions of dollars. They're already back in Europe. Novak and Luksch have been spotted in France."

Nick paused, waiting for a reaction, but Connor was speechless. The muscles in his bum leg cramped up, sending fiery bolts of pain through his thigh. He gripped it with his fingers and tried to breathe.

"I just thought you should know. Considering that Georg Luksch has a personal bone to pick with you," Nick said.

"Ever since last November when you smashed all the bones in his face."

"He was under orders to hurt Erin." Connor's voice vibrated with tension. "It was less than he deserved."

Nick paused. "He never touched her. We have only Ed's word that he was planning to, and Ed's credibility is worth shit. Ed was trying to save his own skin, but did you think of that before you charged off to the rescue? Oh no. You had to be the big hero. For the love of Christ. It's lucky you weren't on active duty. You would have been crucified."

"Georg Luksch is a convicted assassin," Connor said, through clenched teeth. "He was ready to hurt her. He's lucky he's not dead."

"Yeah. Sure. Whatever you say. Anyhow, your hero complex aside, I just wanted you to watch your back. Not that you give a shit, or need anybody's help. And you've got better things to do than talk to me, so I won't waste any more of your valuable time—"

"Hey, Nick. Don't."

Something in Connor's voice made Nick pause. "Oh, what the hell," he said wearily. "If things get weird, call me, OK?"

"Yeah, thanks," Connor said. "But, uh . . . what about Erin?"

"What about her?"

"Novak hasn't forgotten about her," Connor said. "No way has he forgotten. Somebody should be assigned to guard her. Immediately."

Nick's long silence felt ominous. "You are seriously hung up on that chick, aren't you, Con?"

He clenched his teeth and counted until he had his temper under control. "No," he said, in a low, careful voice. "It's just obvious to anybody with half a brain that she's going to be on his hit list."

Nick sighed. "You haven't been listening, have you? You're lost in your own fantasy world. Wake up. Novak is in France. He was spotted in Marseilles. He's a monster, but he's not an idiot. He's not thinking about Erin. And don't make me regret keeping you in the loop, because you don't deserve to be there."

Connor shook his head. "Nick, I know this guy. Novak would never—"

"Let it go, Con. Move on with your life. And watch your back."

Nick hung up abruptly. Connor stared down at the phone in his shaking hand, ashamed of having blocked the number. He disabled the function and hit redial. Quick, before he could change his mind.

"Nick Ward," his friend said tersely.

"Memorize this number," Connor said.

Nick let out a startled laugh. "Whoa. I'm *so* honored."

"Yeah, right. See you, Nick."

"I hope so," Nick said.

Connor broke the connection and let the phone drop onto the seat, his mind racing. Novak was filthy rich. He had the resources and the cunning to do the smart thing, to buy a new identity, a whole new life. But Connor had been studying him for years. Novak wouldn't do the smart thing. He would do whatever the fuck he pleased. He thought he was a god. That delusion had flushed him out before. And that same delusion was what made him so deadly when his pride was stung.

Particularly to Erin. Christ, why was he the only one who could see it? His partner Jesse would have understood, but Jesse was long gone. Novak had tortured him to death sixteen months ago.

Erin had slipped through Novak's fingers. He would consider that a personal insult. He would never let it go for the sake of expediency.

His leg was cramping again. He dug his fingers into the muscles and tried to breathe into it. He and his brothers had each other for protection, but Erin was wide open, laid out on the sacrificial altar. And Connor was the one who had put

her there. His testimony had sent her dad to jail. She had to
hate his guts for it, and who could blame her?

He covered his face with his hands and groaned. Erin
would be at the very center of Novak's twisted thoughts.

Just like she was always at the center of his own.

He tried to think it through logically, but logic had nothing to do with these impulses. He had to feel his way through
it. If the Feds wouldn't protect her, then he had to step into
that empty space and protect her himself. He was so goddamn predictable. Erin was so innocent and luscious, calculated to push all his lamebrain, would-be hero buttons. And
all those years of hot, explicit sexual fantasies about her didn't
help either, when it came to thinking clearly.

Still, the thought of having a real job to do, a job that
might actually mean something to somebody, jerked his
mind into focus so laser-sharp it was painful. It rolled back
the fog that had shrouded him for months. His whole body
was buzzing with wild, jittery energy.

He had to do this, no matter how much she hated him.
And the thought of seeing her again made his face get hot,
and his dick get hard, and his heart thud heavily against his
ribs.

Christ, she scared him worse than Novak did.

Subject:	Re: New Acquisitions
Date:	Sat, May 18, 14:54
From:	"Claude Mueller"
To:	"Erin Riggs"

Dear Ms. Riggs:

Thank you for forwarding me a copy of your master's thesis. I was intrigued with your theories on the
religious significance of bird imagery in La Tene period Celtic artifacts. I just acquired a third century
B.C.E. La Tene battle helmet with a bronze mechani-

cal raven perched on top (see attached JPG). I look forward to discussing it with you.

In addition to the helmet, I have several other new items to show you. I will be passing through Oregon en route to Hong Kong, staying at the Silver Fork Bay Resort tomorrow. I am arriving late in the evening and leaving the following day. This is short notice, and I understand if you cannot make it, but I went ahead and arranged an e-ticket for the SeaTac-Portland shuttle for you tomorrow. A limo will be waiting in Portland to take you to the coast. We can examine the pieces together Monday morning, and then have lunch, if time permits.

I hope you do not find me presumptuous. Please come. I look forward to meeting you in person, since I continue to have the strangest feeling that I know you already.

I trust the same economic arrangement as before will be acceptable. JPGs of the items that I want you to examine are attached.

Sincerely yours,
Claude Mueller
Quicksilver Foundation

Erin leaped out of her chair and hopped for joy. The walls of the studio apartments in the Kinsdale Arms were too thin to permit herself howls of triumph, so she pressed her hand to her mouth to muffle the howls into ecstatic squeaking noises. She reread the e-mail on the screen again and again, just to make sure it still said the same thing.

This job was going to save her sorry butt, and in the nick of time, too. She was probably knocking the rotten ceiling plaster onto the head of her cantankerous downstairs neighbor with her jumping, but she didn't care. Maybe the great Whoever had decided she'd had enough piss-poor luck lately, and it was time to give her a breather.

Edna demanded an explanation for this unseemly excitement with a disapproving meow. Erin picked her up, but she cuddled the finicky cat too tightly. Edna leaped out of her arms with a disgusted *prrrt*.

Erin spun around in a goofy dance step. Her luck was finally turning. Her eyes fell on the cross-stitch that hung over her computer, which read: "You Shape Your Own Reality Every Day." For the first time in months, it didn't make her feel as if someone were asking her, in the snootiest of tones, *"And is this the best you can do?"*

She'd stitched the damned thing four months ago, right after getting fired from her job. She had been so angry, she could barely see straight, and the project had been an effort to channel all that negative, destructive energy into a positive direction. She'd written it off as a failed experiment, though. Especially since every time she looked at the thing she wanted to rip it off the wall and hurl it across the room.

Oh, well. It was the effort that counted. And she had to at least try to think positively. With Dad in jail, Mom crumbling in on herself, and Cindy acting out, she couldn't afford one instant of self-pity.

She printed out Mueller's e-mail and the e-ticket itinerary attached to it. First class. How lovely. Not that she would've minded economy. A Greyhound bus would've been fine. Hell, she'd have cheerfully agreed to hitchhike down to Silver Fork, but being pampered was such a balm to her bruised ego. She glanced around the water-stained walls of the dismal studio apartment, the single window that looked out at a sooty, blank brick wall, and sighed.

First things first. She grabbed her organizer, riffled through it until she found today's To Do list, and added: *Call temp agency. Call Tonia to feed Edna. Call Mom. Pack.* She dialed the temp agency.

"Hello, this is Erin Riggs, leaving a message for Kelly. I won't be able to make it in to Winger, Drexler & Lowe on Monday. I have a last-minute business trip tomorrow. I'm caught up on all the current case transcriptions, so all they'll need is someone to cover their phones. Of course, I'll be back in on Tuesday. Thanks, and have a nice weekend."

She forcibly suppressed her guilt about missing a day's work with no notice as she hung up the phone. Her fee for one of these consulting jobs equaled almost two weeks' pay from the temp agency at thirteen bucks an hour. And wasn't that what temping was all about? Less commitment from both parties, right? Right. Like one of those relationships where you were free to see other people. Not that she was an expert on those. Or any other kind of relationship, for that matter.

The easy-come, easy-go temp concept was hard to get used to. She liked to fling herself into her work and give two hundred percent. Which was why it had hurt so badly when they had fired her from the job she'd gotten out of grad school. She'd been the assistant curator for the growing Celtic antiquities collection at the Huppert Institute.

She had worked her butt off for them, and she'd done an excellent job, but Lydia, her boss, had trumped up an excuse to get rid of her during the media furor surrounding Dad's trial. She claimed that Erin was too distracted by her personal problems to do her job, but it was clear that she considered Erin a liability for the museum's image. Bad for future funding. "Unappetizing" had been the word Lydia had used, the day she'd fired her. Which, coincidentally, had been the same day that a pack of bloodthirsty journalists had followed Erin to work, demanding to know how she felt about the videos.

Those celebrated X-rated videos of her father and his mistress, which had been used to blackmail him into corruption and murder. The videos which, God alone knew how or why, were now available on the Internet for all to enjoy.

Erin tried to shove the memory away, using her shopworn sanity-saving mantras: *I have nothing to be ashamed of; Let it go; This too shall pass* . . . None of them worked worth a damn anymore, not that they ever had. Lydia had all but blamed Erin personally for the whole thing.

To hell with Lydia, and with Dad, too, for getting them into this sordid, public mess. Her anger felt like poison running through her body, making her guilty and sick. Dad was paying the highest price he could for what he'd done. Being sour and pissy wouldn't change things, and she had no time to mope. Busy was better.

That phrase was another sanity saver. The best of the lot. It was dorky and uncool, but she was already a lost cause when it came to cool. Look up *uncool* in the dictionary, and you'd find a photo of Erin Riggs. Busy, busy, busy Erin Riggs.

She sharpened a pencil and crossed off *Call temp agency*. Sure, it was stupid to put items on her list just to immediately cross them off. Grasping for a cheap, fleeting sense of accomplishment. She didn't care. Every little bit of accomplishment helped. Even the cheap kind.

Mom's bills still headed the list. The scariest, most depressing item. She decided to stall for a couple more minutes, and dialed her friend Tonia's number. Tonia's machine clicked on. "Hi, Tonia? I got a last-minute job from Mueller, and I have to go to the coast tomorrow. Just wondering if you could pass by to feed Edna. Let me know. Don't worry if you can't, I'll find another solution. Talk to you later."

She hung up, her belly fluttering with anxiety as she gathered together Mom's checkbook, bank statements, her calculator, and the stack of unopened mail that she'd collected from beneath the mail slot on her last visit home. Throwing away junk mail cut the pile down to half, but many of the remaining envelopes had *FINAL NOTICE* stenciled across them in scary red block print. *Brrr.* Special pile for those.

She arranged them neatly in piles. Unpaid property taxes, due months ago. Threatening letters from collection agencies. Past due mortgage payments. Past due phone bills. Medical bills. Credit card bills, big ones. A letter from the bursar's office of Endicott Falls College, "regretting the necessity of withdrawing Cynthia Riggs's scholarship, based on poor academic performance." That one made Erin close her eyes and press her hand against her mouth.

Moving right along. No point in dwelling on it. Organization was calming. It put things in perspective. She piled collection agency letters in one pile, past due notices in another, and made three columns in her notebook: *Urgently Overdue, Overdue,* and *Due.* She totaled the sums, and compared it to what was left in Mom's account. Her heart sank.

She couldn't cover the shortfall in the *Urgently Overdue* column, not even if she drained her meager checking account dry. Mom had to get a job; it was the only solution, but Erin hadn't had much luck even getting Mom out of bed lately, let alone out into the workforce.

But it was that, or lose the house she had moved into as a bride. That would push Mom over the edge for sure.

Erin let her face drop down against the neat piles of bills and fought the urge to cry. Sniveling was not constructive. She'd done enough of it in these past few months, so she should know. She needed fresh ideas, new solutions. It was just so hard to think outside the box, all by herself. Her tired, lonesome brain felt like it was padlocked inside a box. With chains wrapped around it.

This job from Claude Mueller was a godsend. He was a mysterious figure, a reclusive, art-loving multimillionaire, the administrator of the enormous Quicksilver Fund. He had found her in a random Internet search on Celtic artifacts, which had landed him on one of her articles, posted on the website she'd designed when she started her own consulting business. He'd begun to e-mail her, complimenting her on her articles, asking questions, even requesting a copy of her doctoral thesis. Oh, boy. The ultimate ego rush for an antiquities nerd like her.

But then he had asked her to come to Chicago to authenticate some new acquisitions, and he hadn't blinked an eye at her fee. Or rather, his staff hadn't. He had been in Paris at the time. She hadn't met him on that or any of the three subsequent jobs, the fees for which had been providential. The first had paid for her move from the apartment on Queen Anne to this far cheaper room in the run-down Kinsdale Arms. The second and third, in San Diego, had covered the insurance deductibles of Mom's recent medical bills. The Santa Fe job had paid two of her mother's past due mortgage payments. And this one, hopefully, would almost cover the *Urgently Overdue* column.

Working for Mueller had been so dignified. First class, all expenses paid. It had been lovely to be treated with deference and respect. Such a pleasant break from the squalid grind of her daily life; arguing with the bank over missed mortgage payments, begging her landlord to call the exterminator, spending all of January with no hot water. And the sordid details of Dad's trial, surfacing one after the other, until nothing could shock her anymore. Well, almost nothing. Those videos had been quite a jolt.

Enough. Moving right along. So Claude Mueller wanted to meet her in person, did he? How gratifying. She was curious about him, too. She paper-clipped the bills together, put them into the *Mom's Bills* folder in her file cabinet, and turned her attention to the Mueller e-mail.

She had to hit the perfect tone for her reply. Warm, enthusiastic, but not puppyish or, God forbid, desperate. Reserved, but with just a flash of extra personal interest showing through at the end. Looking forward to it . . . pleased to have the opportunity to meet you at last, etc. Referrals from Mueller could set her highly specialized consulting business on its way. And she was finished in Seattle with museum work, since the Huppert had fired her. She would have to change cities to get away from the dark cloud that hung over her, and she couldn't possibly leave her mother and Cindy when they were both so unstable.

She had gleaned all the info she could on Mueller from the Internet. He was publicity-shy, though he'd been cited in museum journals for his generous donations to the arts. Her grant-writing and development colleagues were forever swooning over the largesse of the Quicksilver Fund. He was in his early forties, and lived on a private island off the coast of southern France. That was all she knew.

She read over her response and hit SEND. Who knew? Maybe Mueller would prove to be attractive and charming. His e-mails were faintly flirtatious. He was intellectual, erudite. Wealthy, too, not that she cared, but it was an interesting fact to file away. He appreciated the sensual, enigmatic beauty of Celtic artifacts, which were her passion. He was a collector of beautiful objects.

Nothing at all like Connor McCloud.

Ouch. Damn. And here she'd been quietly patting herself on the back for not thinking of Connor for hours. She tried to wrestle her mind away from him, but it was too late. His hair had grown out, as shaggy and wild as a Celtic warrior the last time she'd seen him, at the Crystal Mountain nightmare last fall. He'd leaned on his blood-spattered cane while Georg was loaded onto a stretcher behind him, staring at her. His face had been so hard and fierce, his eyes boring into hers. Blazing with barely controlled fury. The image was indelibly marked on her memory.

That was the day that her life had begun to unravel. And Connor had been the one to haul Dad into custody. Her father, the traitor and murderer. God, when was this going to hurt a little less?

She'd had a knee-trembling crush on Connor McCloud for ten years, ever since Dad had brought the recruits he was training for the new undercover unit home to dinner when she was sixteen. One look at him, and something had gone hot and soft and stupid inside of her. His tilted eyes, the translucent green of a glacial lake. His lean, foxy face, all planes and angles. The sexy grooves in his cheeks when he grinned. His beard stubble, glinting gold. He'd always been quiet and shy when he ate at their house, his mile-a-minute partner Jesse doing most of the talking, but his laid-back, sexy baritone voice sent shivers through her body whenever he spoke. His hair was a shaggy mane, a crazy mix of every possible color of blonde. She wanted to touch its thick, springy texture. To bury her face in it and breathe him in.

And his body had been the focus of her most feverish erotic dreams in the privacy of her bed for years. He was so tall and lean and muscular. Whipcord tough, every muscle defined, but as graceful and agile as a dancer. She'd loved it when he pushed up his sleeves so she could sneak peeks at his thick, ropy forearms. His broad shoulders and long, graceful hands, those powerful legs, that excellent butt that looked so fine in his faded jeans. He was so gorgeous, it made her head spin.

She'd been tongue-tied and fluff-brained in his presence for years, but any romantic dreams she might have had about finally catching his interest when she grew a bosom, or got up the nerve to talk to him, had evaporated forever that day at Crystal Mountain. When she discovered that Dad was collaborating with a vicious criminal. That Georg, the guy who'd been coming on to her at the ski lodge, was an assassin who was hovering over her in order to control Dad.

That it had been Dad's betrayal that had gotten Jesse killed, and almost cost Connor his life.

She covered her face, trying to breathe through the burning ache in her chest. Boy, had that ever put a damper on her secret fantasy life.

Her own stupidity made her sigh. She had bigger problems than unrequited lust. Beginning with her mother's finances. Busy was better, she repeated as she dialed Mom's number. Busy was much better.

We're sorry, but the number you have dialed has been disconnected . . . Oh, God. It seemed like just last week that she'd had Mom's phone turned back on. She couldn't leave town without checking on Mom.

She reached for her keys before she could stop herself.

Her car had been repossessed months ago. She still hadn't broken the habit. She ran down the stairs, shoved open the door, and raised her face to the sky. The clouds were clearing. A star glowed low on the horizon.

"Hi, Erin."

That low voice sent a shock of intense awareness through her body. She stumbled back against the door.

Connor McCloud was standing right there, staring at her.

Chapter

2

He was slouched against an ancient, battered beige Cadillac, parked in a tow zone. The stub of a glowing cigarette was pinched between his thumb and forefinger. He sank into a crouch and stubbed it out. His face was hard, and grim with what looked like controlled anger. He straightened up, looming over her. She'd forgotten how tall he was. Six foot three, or something ridiculous like that.

Her hand was pressed hard against her open mouth. She forced herself to drop it. *Head up, shoulders back, don't lock your knees,* she told herself silently. "Why are you lurking in front of my building?"

His dark brows twitched together. "I'm not lurking," he said. "I was just having a smoke before I rang your bell."

His tawny hair was longer and wilder than it had been at Crystal Mountain. His chiseled, angular face was even leaner. His green eyes were so brilliant against the smudges of weariness beneath them. Wind ruffled his hair around his broad shoulders. It blew across his face, and he brushed it back with his hand. The one with the brutal burn scar.

He could have been a barbarian Celtic warrior heading

into battle, with that hard, implacable look on his face. Stiffen his hair with lime, give him a bronze helm, a torque of twisted gold around his neck, chain mail—except that most Iron Age Celtic warriors had disdained armor to show their contempt for danger, the fussy scholar inside her reminded. They'd run naked into battle, screaming with rage and challenge.

Oh, please. Back off. Don't go there.

She didn't want that image in her head, but it was too late. She was already picturing Connor's big, hard, sinewy body. Stark naked.

Her eyes dropped, flustered. She focused on the cigarette butts that littered the ground beside his battered boots. Three of them.

She glanced up. "Three cigarettes? Looks like lurking to me."

His face tightened. "I was just working up my nerve."

"To ring my doorbell?" She couldn't keep the sarcasm out of her voice. "Oh, please. I'm not that scary."

His lips twitched. "Believe me, you are. For me, you are."

"Hmm. I'm glad I have that effect on somebody, because the rest of the world doesn't seem too impressed with me these days," she said.

His eyes were so unwavering that the urge to babble was coming over her. "Why do you need to work up the nerve to talk to me?"

"Your last words to me were less than cordial," he said wryly. "Something along the lines of 'Get away from me, you sick bastard.' "

She bit her lip. "Oh, dear. Did I really say that to you?"

"It was a bad scene," he conceded. "You were upset."

"I'm sorry," she said. "For the record, you didn't deserve it."

His eyes were so intensely bright. How could such a cool color give out such an impression of heat? It scorched her face, made something clench up low and hot and tight in her body. She wrapped her arms around herself. "There were extenuating circumstances."

"Yeah, there sure as hell were. Are you OK, Erin?"

Wind gusted around them, setting his long canvas coat flapping around his knees. She shivered and clutched her thin denim jacket tightly around her. No one had asked that question in such a long time, she'd forgotten how to answer it. "Is that what you waited three whole cigarettes outside my building to ask?" she hedged.

A quick, hard shake of his head was her answer.

"So . . . what, then?"

"I asked my question first," he said.

She looked down, away, around, anywhere else, but his gaze was like a magnet, pulling her eyes back and dragging the truth right out of her. Dad used to say that McCloud was a goddamn psychic. It had made Dad nervous. Rightly so, as it happened.

"Never mind," Connor said. "Shouldn't have asked. I need to talk to you, Erin. Can I come up to your place?"

The thought of his potent male presence filling her dingy little apartment sent shivers all down her spine. She backed up, and bumped into the wrought iron railing. "I'm, uh, on my way to visit Mom, and I'm in kind of a hurry, because the bus is about to come, so I—"

"I'll give you a ride to your mom's house. We can talk in the car."

Oh, great. That would be even worse. Stuck all alone in a car with a huge barbarian warrior. She couldn't bear his burning scrutiny when she felt so weepy and shaky and vulnerable. She shook her head and backed away from him, toward the bus stop. "No. Sorry. Please, Connor. Just . . . stay away from me." She turned, and fled.

"Erin." His arms closed around her from behind. "Listen to me."

His solid heat pressed against her body nudged her shaky

nerves toward what felt like panic. "Don't touch me," she warned. "I'll scream."

His arms tightened around her ruthlessly. "Please. Don't," he said. "Listen to me, Erin. Novak's broken out of prison."

A cloud of black spots danced in front of her eyes. She sagged, and was abruptly grateful for his strong arms, holding her upright. "Novak?" Her voice was a wispy thread of sound.

"He broke out the other night. With two of his goons. Georg Luksch was one of them."

Her fingers dug into his rock-hard forearms. Her head spun, and her stomach with it. "I think I'm going to be sick," she said.

"Sit down, on the steps. Put your head down." He crouched beside her and rested his arm across her shoulder. His touch was light and careful, but the contact reverberated through her entire body.

"I hate to scare you," he said gently. "But you had to know."

"Oh yeah?" She looked up at him. "What good does it do me?"

"So you can take steps to protect yourself." He sounded as if he were stating something too obvious to put into words.

She dropped her face down against her knees. She shook with bitter laughter, like a dry coughing fit. Protect herself. Hah. What could she do? Hire an army? Buy a cannon? Move into a fortress? She'd been trying so hard to put this nightmare behind her, but she'd just swung around in a big circle and smacked into it again, face-first.

She lifted her face, and stared into blank, empty space. "I can't deal with this," she said. "I don't want to know. I've had enough."

"It doesn't matter what you want. You have to—"

"I'll tell you what I have to do, Connor McCloud." She

wrenched herself away from him and rose up onto unsteady feet. "I have to go to my mother's house to pay her bills and mortgage, and get her phone turned back on because she won't get out of bed. Then I have to call Cindy's school and beg them not to withdraw her scholarship. I take the bus because I lost my job and my car got repossessed. I'll worry about homicidal maniacs another time. And here comes my bus. So thank you for your concern, and have a nice evening."

Connor's face was stark with misery. "I didn't want you to get hurt, Erin. I would've done anything to stop it."

The look on his face made her chest hurt and her throat swell shut. The bus groaned to a halt, a suffocating cloud of diesel fumes rising around them. The door sighed and opened its maw for her.

She laid her hand against his broad chest, and yanked it right back, shocked by her own boldness. His body was so hard and warm.

"I know it wasn't your fault," she said. "What happened to Dad. He did it to himself. I knew he was in trouble, but he wouldn't let anyone help him. And none of us knew how bad it was."

"Miss!" the driver bellowed. "You on or off?"

"It wasn't your fault," she repeated. She scrambled into the bus, and clutched the pole as it pulled away, watching Connor's tall form recede into the dusk. Wind whipped his shaggy hair around his stern, sculpted face. The canvas coat flapped. His penetrating eyes held hers, tugging at her, until the bus turned the corner and he was lost to sight.

She collapsed into a seat. Her eyes darted from passenger to passenger, as if Georg would suddenly pop out of nowhere and flash her that seductive smile that had so perplexed her at Crystal Mountain six months ago. She'd been surprised and gratified to be pursued by a guy like that. Almost tempted to give him a whirl just to break the spell of her self-imposed celibacy—but something had held her back.

Her friends had been so impatient with her. *What the hell*

do you want in a guy, Erin? He's smart, he's built, he's charm-
ing, he's got a sexy accent, he looks like a GQ cover model,
and he's warm for your form! Stop acting like a friggin' nun!
Go get you some, girlfriend!

She'd tried to explain that the easy warmth that Georg ex-
uded didn't warm her. It was sort of like the way her taste
buds could not be fooled by saccharine or Nutrasweet. The
sweetness didn't follow through, it didn't satisfy. Her girlfriends had shrugged that off as unconvincing. They told her
she was too fussy. Or just plain chicken.

The fact that she hadn't gone to bed with that awful man
had been her one small, private satisfaction and comfort afterwards, when her world lay around her in ruins.

Nobody in the bus was the right size or build to be Georg.
Every time the bus lumbered to a stop, she held her breath
until she saw who boarded. A teenage Goth girl with black
lips and a pierced face. A portly Latina lady. A young urban
professional woman in a suit, coming home from working
Saturday at some high-powered job, like she herself so often
had, back in the dear old days of steady employment. No Georg.
Not that she would necessarily recognize his face, after what
Connor had done to it. The memory of that bloody duel
made her queasy again.

She was being stupid, really. If Novak really was bothering to think of her, it wouldn't be Georg that he would send.

It could be anybody.

Novak read the e-mail on the screen of the laptop and
typed a response. His hands were deft on the keyboard even
with the use of only his right hand plus the thumb and middle finger of his left. He stared at the text as he rubbed the
stumps of his maimed hand.

A constant, throbbing reminder of the debt he was owed.

The wind on the terrace made his eyes tear up. They burned
and stung, unused to the colored lenses, and he pulled the case

out of his pocket and removed them. The glues and the custom-made prosthetics that changed the shape of his features were uncomfortable, but temporary. Just until he could organize a final bout of cosmetic surgery.

He gazed out over the city. Such a pleasure, after months of staring at the walls of a prison cell, to cast his gaze out toward ranges of ragged mountains that hemmed in the jewel-toned greens and blues and silver grays of Seattle. He hit SEND, and took a sip of cabernet out of a splendid reproduction of a second-century B.C.E. Celtic drinking cup. It was fashioned from a real human skull, decorated with hammered gold. A fanciful indulgence, but after his prison experience, he was entitled.

He had Erin to thank for this expensive new caprice. Odd, that he had not developed a taste for blood-drenched Celtic artifacts until now. Their penchant for ritual murder resonated in his own soul.

The sacrifice that he had planned was blessed by the gods. He knew this was so because Celia had come to him in a vision. He was always moved when one of his angels visited him. They had come to him in the hospital where he lay near death, and they had comforted him in prison. Souls he had liberated, forever young and beautiful. Their shades had fluttered around him, distressed to see him suffering. Belinda had come, and Paola, and Brigitte, and all the rest, but when Celia came, it was special. Celia had been the first.

He savored his wine, his pulse leaping at the memory of the night that had marked his life. He had taken Celia's lovely body, and as he spent himself inside her, the impulse rose up like a genie from a bottle, huge and powerful. The urge to place his thumbs against the throbbing pulse in her throat, and press.

She had thrashed beneath him, her face turning color, protruding eyes full of growing awareness. Celia could not speak, she could only gasp, but he had sensed her passionate assent. They had been linked, a single mind. She was an angel, offering herself to him.

The fanged gods had claimed him as their own that night. And he had understood what tribute the gods demanded to confer power and divinity. They had marked him, and he would prove himself worthy.

Celia had been a virgin, too. He had found that out afterwards, when he washed himself. How poignant. It was a curse to be so sensitive. Doomed to grasp for the spontaneous perfection of Celia's sacrifice, over and over. Never quite reaching it.

The door to the terrace opened. He felt the red, throbbing glow of Georg's energy without turning. "Have a glass of wine, Georg. Enjoy the pleasures of freedom. You refuse to relax. This puts us at risk."

"I don't want wine."

Novak looked at him. The thick, shiny pink scar that marred Georg's cheek was flushed scarlet over his prison pallor. His beautiful yellow hair had been shorn to stubble on his scalp, and his eyes were like glowing coals. "Are you sulking, Georg? I hate sulking."

"Why won't you let me just kill them?" Georg hissed. "I will be a fugitive for the rest of my life anyway. I don't care if—"

"I want better than that for you, my friend. You cannot risk being taken again."

"I have already made arrangements," Georg said. "I will die before I go back to prison."

"Of course you have. I thank you for your dedication," Novak replied. "But you will see, when you are calmer, that my plan is better."

Georg's face was a mask of agony. "I cannot bear it. I am dying." The words burst out in the obscure Hungarian dialect they shared.

Novak rose from his chaise and put down his wine. He

placed the scarred stumps of his maimed hand against Georg's ruined face. His cosmetic surgeons would improve matters, but the young man's youthful perfection was gone forever. Another score to settle.

"Do you know why the butterfly must struggle to escape its chrysalis?" he asked, sliding into dialect himself.

Georg jerked his face away. "I am not in the mood for your fables."

"Silence." The nails of his left thumb and middle finger dug into Georg's face. "It is the act of struggling that forces out the fluid from the butterfly's body and completes the development of its wings. If the butterfly is released prematurely, it will lurch around, swollen and clumsy, and soon die. Never having flown."

Georg's lips drew back from his gaping, missing teeth with a soundless hiss of pain. "And what is this supposed to mean to me?"

"I think you know." He let go. Blood welled out of the red marks that his nails had left. "Struggle is necessary. Punishment exalts."

"Easy for you to talk of punishment. You did not suffer as I did, with your father's money to protect you."

Novak went very still. Georg cringed away, sensing that he had gone too far.

Georg was wrong. His father had taught him about punishment. That lesson was frozen in his mind, dead center. A tableau in a globe of imperishable crystal. He turned away from the memory and held up his left hand. "Does this look as if I know nothing of punishment?"

Georg's eyes dropped in shame, as well they ought.

A gull shrieked in the darkening sky. Novak looked up, and exulted in the wild creature's freedom. Soon he would be reborn, with no father, no mother. He would be spotless, surrounded by gods and angels. He would be free at last, and he would never look back.

He jolted himself back to the present. "Be grateful that you have been chosen as my instrument to make this sacrifice, Georg. My gods are not for cowards, or weaklings."

Georg hesitated. "I am not weak," he said sourly.

"No, you are not." He patted Georg's shoulder. The younger man flinched at the contact. "You know my tastes just as I know yours. I would rip their throats out with my teeth and drink their blood, if I had that luxury. But I cannot compromise this new identity before I have even established it. You know exactly what it will cost me to step aside and let you play . . . while I watch."

Georg nodded reluctantly.

"I have chosen you to tear them to pieces for me, Georg," Novak said gently. "And still, you cannot wait. You whine. You complain."

Georg's eyes narrowed. "Do you plan to give it up, then?"

"Give up what? Drinking the blood of innocents?" Novak toasted Georg with the skull goblet and smiled. "You know me too well to ask such a stupid question."

Streaks of purplish red appeared on Georg's cheeks. The flush faded almost instantly to ghostly pallor. "I will help you," he said.

"I know you will, my friend," Novak said. "And you will be rewarded for your loyalty. You must be patient, and trust me."

The terrace door opened, and Tamara and Nigel stepped out. Nigel looked uncomfortable, but that was his natural state of being.

Tamara smiled, stunning in her brief, ice-green dress. She'd changed her chestnut hair to red and her golden eyes to green since he had sent her to monitor the household of Victor Lazar, his old friend and nemesis. He suspected that she had done her duty there with a fraction too much zeal. Perhaps he was being unfair.

In any case, red suited her, and after six months of enforced celibacy, it suited him, too. She was astonishingly beautiful. He would settle for nothing less in his bed. And her ability to hack into computer databases and change the nature of reality to suit his whims was nothing short of magic. She was immensely talented.

Nigel cleared his throat. "The courier has just delivered the blood samples from Switzerland," he announced.

Novak nodded his approval. Plans were proceeding with orderly smoothness. "Excellent. You know what needs to be done. See to it."

"The switch is arranged," Nigel said. "I have identified a technician at the DNA laboratory named Chuck Whitehead who is perfect for our purposes. I will arrange for him to do the switch late Sunday night. According to my statistical analysis, that's the period when the laboratory is most deserted. I will dispose of him afterwards myself."

"I have some good news, as well," Tamara said. "We won't need to bait the trap after all. The transponder on McCloud's car shows him parked outside Erin Riggs's apartment for thirty-five minutes this afternoon. He then followed her to her mother's house."

His eyes wandered over her body, appreciating how the sheath set off her long, perfect legs. "Wonderful. Stalking the poor girl already."

Tamara's smile widened. What a remarkable creature. Wanted all over the world for computer crimes and fraud, and her sexual skills were just as prodigious. She would do absolutely anything.

In fact, now that he thought about it, her lack of squeamishness was almost inhibiting. A touch of disgust or fear was like a pinch of salt that brought out the flavor of a dish. After so long without sex, he had been less discerning than usual, but his natural high standards were quickly reasserting themselves.

He was irritated. He wondered if she were doing it deliberately. Unacceptable, that one of his servants should presume to manipulate him. How *dare* she.

Georg stirred restlessly, his fists clenching. "So the police must have told McCloud that we are free," he said.

Tamara turned her brilliant smile upon him. "It would seem so."

"Then Erin knows that I am coming for her."

Tamara's smile faltered at the concentrated malevolence in Georg's voice. Then the smile quickly reappeared . . . and gave him an idea.

"No, Georg," he said. "Don't be obtuse. Erin knows nothing of the sort. I have spent a great deal of money to arrange for reports of our sighting in France."

"I am dying," Georg moaned, in dialect. "I suffer."

Novak sighed. Georg could be so tedious. The poor man was a volcano of festering anger from his traumatic prison experience.

Perhaps he should offer Tamara to Georg, and observe the results. He could gauge her loyalty and commitment, and at the same time, siphon off some of Georg's restless, dangerous energy.

"Stay and help us celebrate, my dear," he said. "Georg, would you care to indulge? Let Tamara ease your torment."

Georg's ruined mouth twisted in a feral smile.

Novak studied Tamara's reaction. Her expression did not waver, but he sensed the tightening in her jaw as the smile froze into place.

His loins stirred. *Yes*. This was what had been missing. Delicious.

He smiled at Nigel. "Nigel, you may stay. Tamara likes to be watched, no? Did you learn to love it during your time with Victor?"

Her smile was like a neon sign, bright and empty. "Of course, boss," she said, without missing a beat.

Nigel's face paled, but he knew better than to decline. Poor, sexless Nigel. This would be good for him. He was less manually skilled as an assassin than Georg, but the mask he presented to the world was impeccable. He was a dried-up, forgettable, middle-aged gray man, whereas Georg had lost his ability to blend. Georg was now no more than a deadly weapon to be kept hidden until violence was called for.

Georg wrenched Tamara's fragile dress down. The shoulder straps broke, and she stood naked on the terrace, the chilly evening breeze making her dark nipples tighten. She waited, unsure of what was expected of her. It was rare, to see her at a loss. Arousing.

Nigel grimaced, afraid to look away. Georg unbuttoned his pants.

He settled back on his chaise, lifted the skull goblet to his lips, and gestured for them to begin.

It occurred to him, as he watched the spectacle, that he could liberate Tamara after her usefulness was done. The danger to his new identity would be minimal. Tamara was estranged from what family she had. She barely existed on paper. The contacts through which he had found her would not ask questions. Her body would never be found.

Perhaps she had been offered to him just for this purpose.

Georg was being very rough. Novak sipped his wine and thought about reining him in. He did not want Tamara damaged, at least not yet. But then again, the show suited his mood, just as it was.

The ancient Celts believed that the skulls of their victims had potent magical powers. Perhaps he would make a new drinking goblet out of Tamara, decorated with hammered gold. What he had planned for Erin Riggs and Connor McCloud was a gift for his fanged gods.

But Tamara would be all for him. A special treat.

The earthy, rhythmic sounds of the act taking place on the terrace were drowned out by the voices of his angels in his head, like the wind in the leaves. Tamara would soon join their ranks.

Punishment exalted. His angels knew this. And the word

they whispered, over and over, was always *"Never . . . never . . . never . . ."*

In every language on earth.

Mom's car was in the driveway, but the house was dark. Erin was surprised to discover that her heart could actually sink any lower.

She approached the handsome Victorian house where she'd grown up. The overgrown rhododendrons wreathed the porch in shadow. The Fillmores next door had mowed a surgically neat line where their lawn ended, to accentuate the ragged forlornness of the Riggs's lawn and make their silent protest plain.

She rummaged through her purse for the keys and let herself in, deliberately making a lot of noise. She switched on the porch light. Nothing happened. She peered up at it, and realized that the bulb was gone. Very strange. If Mom had removed it, she would have replaced it.

It was as dark as a tomb inside, with the blinds drawn. She flipped on the floor lamp in the living room. Nothing. She tried to tighten the bulb. There was no bulb.

She tried the track lighting in the dining room. Nothing. Maybe the power was out . . . no. The lights had been on at the Fillmores'.

"Mom?" she called out.

No response. She felt her way slowly, toward the utility closet where the lightbulbs were kept. She grabbed three, and stumbled back. She screwed a bulb into the living room lamp and flipped it on.

The sight jolted her rattled nerves. The rolling table that held the television was dragged away from the wall. The cables that connected it to the power strip were torn away. The cable box lay on the ground. Her first thought was of burglars, but nothing seemed to be missing.

Her dread intensified. "Mom? Is something wrong with the TV?"

Still no response. She threaded a bulb into the hanging lamp over the dining room table. The room looked normal. She climbed onto a chair to replace the bulb in the kitchen ceiling lamp.

The light revealed a cluttered mess. She peeked in the empty refrigerator, sniffed the milk. It had turned to cheese. She would load the dishwasher and set it running before she left. Maybe do some grocery shopping, but that would leave her no money to travel with.

She headed for the stairs, and gazed, tight-lipped, at the new pile of untouched mail below the mail slot.

There was still a bulb in the wall sconce on the stairs, thank goodness. She started to climb, passing photos of herself and Cindy, her grandparents, and her parents' wedding portraits. The four of them, skiing together in Banff on that vacation they had taken five years ago.

She knocked on the door to the master bedroom. "Mom?" Her voice sounded like a frightened child's.

"Honey? Is that you?" Her mother's voice was froggy and thick.

Her relief was so intense, tears sprang into her eyes. She opened the door. Her mother was sitting on the bed, blinking in the light from the stairs. The room smelled stale.

"Mom? I'm turning the light on," she warned.

Barbara Riggs gazed up at her daughter, her eyes dazed and reddened. Her usually meticulous bed was wildly disarranged, half of the mattress showing. A terrycloth bathrobe was draped over the television. "Mom? Are you OK?"

The shadows under her mother's eyes looked like bruises. "Sure. Just resting, sweetie." She turned her gaze away, as if looking her daughter in the eye were an activity too effortful to sustain.

"Why is the bathrobe over the TV?" Erin asked.

Her mother's neck sank into her hunched shoulders like a

turtle retracting into its shell. "It was looking at me," she muttered.

Those five words scared Erin more than anything else had that day, which was saying a hell of a lot. "Mom? What do you mean?"

Barbara shook her head and pushed herself up off the bed with visible effort. "Nothing, honey. Let's go have a cup of tea."

"Your milk's gone bad," Erin said. "You hate it without milk."

"So I'll just have to cope, won't I?"

Erin flinched at her mother's sharp tone. Barbara's eyes softened. "I'm sorry, sweetie. It's not you. You're an angel. It's just . . . everything. You know?"

"I know," Erin said quietly. "It's OK. Let me make up this bed."

She tucked and straightened the bed, but when she grabbed the bathrobe to pull it off the TV, her mother lunged to stop her. "No!"

Erin let go of it, but the robe was already sliding onto the floor with a plop. "What is it?" she asked. "What is it with the TV?"

Her mother wrapped her arms around her middle. "It's just that I've, ah . . . I've been seeing things."

Erin waited for more, but Mom just shook her head, her eyes bleak and staring. "What things?" Erin prompted.

"When I turn on the TV," her mother said.

"Most people do," Erin observed. "That's what it's for."

"Do not be snotty with me, young lady," Barbara snapped.

Erin took a deep breath and tried again. "What do you see, Mom?"

Barbara sank back down on the bed. "I see your dad, and that woman," she said dully. "In those videos. Every channel. Both TVs."

Erin sat down heavily on the bed. "Oh," she whispered. "I see."

"No. You don't. You can't." Barbara's voice trembled. She wiped her puffy eyes, and groped for the bedside box of Kleenex. "The first time, I thought it was a dream. But then it started happening more often. Now it's all the time. Every time I touch the thing. Today it turned itself on. I swear, I didn't even touch it today, and it turned itself on."

Erin had to try several times before she could choreograph her voice into being low and soothing. "That's not possible, Mom."

"I know it's not," her mother snapped. "Believe me, I know. And I know that it . . . that it isn't a good sign. That I'm seeing things."

Their eyes met, and Erin glimpsed the depths of her mother's terror. The yawning fear of losing her grip on reality itself.

She reached for the controls on the TV.

"No!" her mother cried out. "Honey, please. Don't—"

"Let me show you, Mom," she insisted. "It'll be perfectly normal."

An old *Star Trek* episode filled the room. She changed channels, to a rerun of *M.A.S.H.* And again, to the evening news. She changed that channel quickly, in case news of Novak's escape should be announced. That was all Mom needed to hear tonight. She left it on a perky commercial for floor wax. "See? Nothing wrong with the TV."

Her mother's brow furrowed into a knot of perplexity. A chorus line of dancing cartoon mops high-kicked their way across a gleaming cartoon floor. "I don't understand," she whispered.

"Nothing to understand." Erin tried to sound cheerful. It felt forced and hollow. She flipped off the TV. "Come on downstairs, Mom."

Barbara followed her, with slow, shuffling steps. "I don't know whether to be relieved, or even more frightened that it was normal."

"I vote for relieved," Erin said. "In fact, I vote that we celebrate. Get dressed, and we can go out to the Safeway. Your fridge is empty."

"Oh, that's OK, honey. I'll do it myself, tomorrow."

"Promise?"

Barbara patted her daughter's anxious face. "Of course I will."

A teabag dangled inside the teapot, fluffy with mold. "How long has it been since you ate, Mom?" Erin demanded.

Barbara made a vague gesture. "I had some crackers a while ago."

"You have to eat." Erin rummaged through the clutter for the dish soap. "Did you know about Cindy's scholarship?"

Barbara winced. "Yes," she murmured. "They called me."

"And?" Erin scrubbed the teapot with soapy water, and waited.

No reply was forthcoming. She looked over her shoulder, frowning. "Mom? What's happening? Tell me."

"What do you want me to say, hon? The conditions are clear. The scholarship is only valid if Cindy keeps up a 3.0 average. It was 2.1 last semester. Her midterms this semester were a disaster. There's no money for tuition if she loses that scholarship."

Erin stared at her in blank dismay. "Cindy can't just quit school."

Barbara's shoulders lifted, and dropped.

Erin stood there, frozen. Her soapy hands dripped onto the floor.

Mom looked so defeated. Now would be the moment to pull a rabbit out of a hat, but there was no money for tuition at a private college. Not even fees from her new client could solve a problem of that size. The CDs were cashed in. The new mortgage had gone to pay for Dad's defense.

Erin wiped her hands on her jeans. She groped for something positive to say as she gazed at her mother. The impulse sagged and faded into silence. Barbara Riggs had always been so well dressed and perfectly made up. Now her face was puffy, her eyes dull, her unwashed hair snarled into a crooked halo.

Suddenly the messy kitchen was too depressing to endure. "Let's go into the living room, Mom."

Barbara flinched. "I don't want to look at the—"

"There's nothing wrong with the TV. Once I hook it back up, I'll show you that it's as normal as the one upstairs. There's no space on this table for me to open your mail. Come on, let's go."

Erin scooped up the mail on her way in, trying not to notice her mother's stumbling, shambling gait behind her. She flipped on the lamp in the living room. Something was odd. She hadn't noticed it before, distracted as she'd been by the disheveled state of the TV. "Why is the clock turned to the wall? And Grandmother Riggs's mirror?"

Her mother's blank, startled gaze lit on the stained wooden backing of the antique mirror. The wire that held it to the hook barely cleared the ornate gilded frame. Her eyes widened. "I never touched it."

Erin dropped the mail on the couch, and lifted the mirror off the wall. It was incredibly heavy. She turned it around.

The mirror was shattered.

Cracks radiated out of an ugly hole, as if someone had bashed it with a blunt object. Glinting shards of mirror glass littered the carpet. Her mother's horror-stricken face was reflected in the jagged pieces.

Their eyes met. Mom held up her hands, as if to ward off a blow. "It wasn't me," she said. "I would never do that. Never."

"Who else has been in the house?" Erin demanded. "How on earth could you not have heard the person who did this?"

"I . . . I've been sleeping a lot," her mother faltered. "And a couple of times, I, ah, took some Vicodin for my headaches and my back pain. And when I take a Vicodin, an army could troop through here and I wouldn't hear them. But God knows, if there's one thing I would never forget, after everything that's happened, it's to lock the doors!"

Erin laid the mirror carefully upright on the floor against the wall and wrapped her arms around herself.

Seven years of bad luck. As if they hadn't had their quota.

Another thought struck her. She glanced at the grandfather clock, another of the treasures that had come with Grandmother Riggs from England at the end of the nineteenth century. She turned it around.

The face of the antique clock was shattered.

She drifted to the couch and sat down. The pile of mail beside her suddenly seemed much less important than it had minutes before.

"Mom, maybe you should talk to someone," she whispered.

Barbara's reddened eyes swam with desperate tears. "Honey. I swear. I did not do this. Please believe me."

A heavy silence fell between them. Silence that was like darkness, teeming and writhing with terrible possibilities.

Erin shook herself and got to her feet. "I'm going to clean up that broken glass. Then I'm taking the frame and clock to Cindy's room until we can repair them. And then we're going to clean up your kitchen."

"Don't worry about it, sweetie. I'll do it."

"No, you won't," Erin said.

Barbara tightened the sash of her bathrobe with an angry tug. "Do not take that tone with me, Erin Katherine Riggs."

Her mother's sharp response made her feel better, oddly enough.

She murmured a garbled apology and hefted the mirror, shaking as much glass as she could out onto the floor. Busy was better. Activity blocked thinking, and she didn't want to think. She preferred to scurry around, hauling the mirror and clock upstairs, gathering up slivers of glass from the carpet and putting them into a plastic bucket.

That was better than chewing on the two possibilities

available to her: Mom had done it and didn't remember doing it, or Mom hadn't done it. Which meant that someone else had.

She wasn't sure which notion terrified her more.

She shouldn't leave Mom at a time like this, but she couldn't afford not to go to Silver Fork. They needed that money so badly. Her mind ran over the problem the way the vacuum cleaner was running over the rug. Each time she thought she was done, she heard another little *ting*. Always more of them, hidden in the deep pile carpet like tiny, cruel teeth awaiting unwary bare feet.

Barbara ran a sink full of hot, soapy water, and was washing the dishes when Erin came back in from emptying the garbage. It was bad enough to have admitted to those hallucinations, or whatever they were, but to have her daughter think she was so far gone as to smash family heirlooms . . . that was unthinkable. Heaven knew, if she were to smash a Riggs family heirloom, she would damn well remember doing it.

Erin leaned against the porch doorway. Barbara's heart ached at the pinched, anxious look in her daughter's face.

"Thought I'd get to work on this mess," she said awkwardly.

Erin looked relieved. "Great idea."

"I'll just load up this dishwasher and set it running. Maybe we can nuke a couple of Budget Gourmets. Have you eaten?"

"I should get home. I have to pack for my trip tomorrow. Let's put one in for you." Erin peered into the freezer. "Swiss steak and chicken teriyaki are your choices, Mom."

Barbara's stomach lurched unpleasantly at the thought of food. "Leave them for now, hon. I'll have one later. What's this trip of yours?"

"I'm going to the coast. Another consulting job for Mueller."

"Oh, that's lovely! You see? Cream always rises to the top, no matter what happens. You're going to do just fine, sweetie."

"We all will, Mom," Erin said. "But you've got to stay on top of your mail, and we've got to work out a plan for paying the bills. And you've, uh, got to cool it with the Vicodin. You need to be more alert. If . . . if somebody is coming into the house."

Barbara nodded, and tried to smile. "Of course."

"I'll help as much as I can, but I can't do it alone." Erin's voice shook.

"Yes, I know," Barbara hastened to say. "I'm sorry I scared you, baby. I'll pull myself together, and we'll all be fine. You'll see."

"Cindy, too. Maybe we could set up a meeting with the scholarship committee, convince them to give her another chance. She can't just quit school. I'll call her tonight."

"Yes. You do that. She looks up to you," Barbara encouraged. "I appreciate your help, hon. I really do."

Erin pulled on her jacket and hesitated, gazing at her mother with big, worried eyes. "Are you sure you're going to be OK, Mom?"

"More than sure," Barbara assured her. "You go and get packed. Have a good trip. Call when you get there, OK?"

"I can't," Erin said. "Your phone's cut off."

Barbara flinched. "Oh, God. Well, don't worry about it, hon. I'll take care of it right away."

"I'll do it when I get back, Mom," Erin offered. "I don't mind."

"Don't worry. Run along and get ready. You have to be at your best tomorrow," Barbara urged.

Erin gave her a tight, lingering hug and a kiss, and left.

Barbara peered out the window and watched Erin run down the sidewalk, light-footed and graceful. She turned the corner and was lost to sight.

Barbara straightened up and looked around with a new sense of purpose. She twitched the crocheted throw on the loveseat back into place and rearranged the pictures on the mantel. She gathered up the mail and rifled through the envelopes with a semblance of her old efficiency, shaking her head at all the past due notices.

It was time to stop moping and working herself into a state. Making her little girl worry herself sick. For heaven's sake.

She stared at the TV with hostile eyes, and finally knelt down, plugged in the power strip, reattached the cables, and pushed it back to its place against the wall. She took the remote in her trembling hand and held it out in front of her like a weapon, challenging the blank screen. The mail crumpled against her chest in her shaking hand.

Enough foolishness. What she had seen was the result of too many sedatives. And it would be nice to watch the evening news.

She turned it on.

Gleaming, naked bodies, grunts and moans . . . the film flickered, but the images were horribly clear. Her husband. His mistress. She stabbed at the remote. The TV did not respond. She stabbed at the off button on the TV itself. Nothing. The thing was possessed.

She knocked the appliance onto the floor, but the bodies kept on grunting and heaving, lewd and bestial. Cackling, demonic laughter echoed in her head. She lunged for the fire iron by the fireplace and smashed it down against the screen. It sparked and popped, spraying glass all over the carpet. The demon TV was finally silenced.

Barbara Riggs stared at the fire iron protruding from the TV's shattered belly. She lifted her hands to her face. Envelopes fluttered down around her like snow, forgotten.

She sank to her knees. A high-pitched mewling sound was coming from her mouth. Shards of glass ground themselves into her knees. She barely felt them. Her heart pounded. Her lungs wouldn't take in air. She was coming apart. Shaking to pieces.

The terror filled her mind like black smoke, bearing her under.

Chapter

3

The car pulled to a stop beside Erin. She jumped and cowered back against the ivy-covered stone wall until she heard Connor's voice coming out of the dark interior of the vehicle. "It's just me."

Relief, anger, and excitement all mixed and fizzed in her belly. She brushed herself off and groped for her dignity. "You scared me!"

"Yeah, I noticed. Pretty spooked, aren't you?"

She could think of no reply to such an obvious statement, so she just started walking again.

The car followed her slowly. "Come on, Erin," he cajoled. "I'll give you a ride home. You're safe with me. Get in."

She glanced down at her watch. The next bus wouldn't pass for twenty minutes. "It makes me nervous to be followed around," she snapped.

"That's tough. It makes me nervous to see you alone on the street at night," he replied. "Get in."

She got in. The window whirred shut, the locks snapped down, and she was alone in a car with Connor McCloud. The fierce barbarian warrior who had played a starring role in her sexual fantasies for years.

"You need a full-time bodyguard until Novak's back in custody," he said sharply. "You can't wander around by yourself. It's not safe."

"A bodyguard?" She snorted in derision. "On my budget? I can barely afford to feed my cat."

"I'm not asking for pay."

"You?" She stiffened. "Good God, Connor, you can't—"

"Put your seatbelt on, Erin."

Her stiff, chilly fingers struggled with the belt. "I don't want a bodyguard," she said nervously. "I particularly don't want you for a bodyguard. Nothing personal, but I don't want to have anything to do with the Cave. I don't want to see Dad's ex-colleagues ever again."

"I'm not with the Cave anymore," he said. "Haven't been for months. They don't think you need protection. I do. This is my idea, and I'll take responsibility for it."

"Oh. Uh . . ." She searched desperately for words. "I, um, really appreciate the thought, Connor, but—"

"You don't take me seriously," he said. His voice was sharp with frustration. He flipped on his turn signal, and turned onto her street.

"Novak is probably busy plotting to take over the world by now," Erin said. "I'm sure he has better things to do than bother with the likes of me. And how do you know where I live, anyway?"

"Phone book."

"That's not possible. I'm not in the book yet."

He slanted her a wry glance. "You're in the database, Erin, even if you're not in the book. Anyone could find you." He parked in front of the decaying facade of the Kinsdale Arms and killed the engine. "This place is grim. What happened to your apartment on Queen Anne?"

Another surprise. "How did you know about—"

"Ed bragged about you when you got that hotshot job at the museum and moved into your own place," he said. "We all knew."

She winced at his mention of her father, and stared down at her lap. "This place is cheaper," she said simply. "Thanks for the ride."

His car door slammed, and he followed her into the lobby. "I'll walk you up to your apartment."

"That's not necessary, thank you," she told him.

Her words were futile. He fell into step behind her as she started up the staircase. She had no idea how to deal with him. He was so stubborn and determined, and she didn't want to be rude to him.

Six flights took forever, with his huge, quiet presence behind her. She stopped in front of her door. "Good night," she said pointedly.

He stuck his hands in his pockets and stared down at her with unnerving intensity. "Erin. I really didn't want you to get hurt."

"I'm all right," she whispered. It was a lie, but she couldn't resist the impulse to comfort him. She'd always been a hopeless softie. She found herself staring at the hollows under his cheekbones. The sensual shape of his lips, bracketed by harsh lines. It had been so long since she'd seen his gorgeous, radiant grin.

The words flew out of her mouth. "Do you, um, want to come in?"

"Yeah," he said.

Her stomach did a terrified back flip. She unlocked her door.

He followed her into her apartment. She flipped on the floor lamp she'd found at a rummage sale years ago, with a wicker laundry basket she had rigged for the lampshade. It cast a strange pattern of warm, reddish slices of light and shadow around the cramped room.

"It's not much," she said hesitantly. "I had to sell most of my stuff. Here, let me move this pile of books. Sit down. I can make you some coffee, or tea, if you'd like. I'm afraid I haven't got much to offer in the way of food. A can of tuna and some toast, maybe. Or cereal."

"I'm not hungry, thanks. Coffee would be fine." He wandered around, studying her pictures, scanning the titles of the books piled against the wall with evident fascination. Edna jumped down from her favorite perch on the bookshelf and stalked over to investigate him.

Connor crouched down to pet her cat, and Erin hung up her jacket and put the kettle on. His eloquent silence unleashed too much dangerous speculation in her mind. She turned around.

The chitchat she'd been rehearsing froze in her throat. The raw force of his gaze sent a shock wave of feminine awareness through her. He was staring at her body, measuring her with intense interest. She felt naked in her jeans and T-shirt. "You're thinner," he observed.

Her instinct was to back away, but the sink was already pressed against her back. The room was terribly small with him in it. "I, uh, haven't had much of an appetite, the past few months," she said.

"Tell me about it," he murmured.

Edna arched and purred beneath his hand, which was very odd. Edna was a nervous, traumatized ex-alley cat. She'd never let anyone but Erin touch her, and now look at her, flinging herself onto her back. Writhing with pleasure beneath Connor's long, stroking fingers.

Erin wrenched her gaze away from the unsettling spectacle. "This has been the one time in my life I've managed to lose weight without trying," she babbled. "And I'm too stressed out to enjoy it."

"Why did you ever try? Your body is gorgeous."

His tone was not flattering or flirtatious, just a flat request for information. "Well, I, uh . . . I've always been a little too—"

"Perfect." He rose to his feet with sinuous grace, still

studying her body. "You've always been perfect, Erin. You don't need to lose weight. You never did. Try not to lose any more."

She was completely flustered. "Ah . . . OK."

A sweet, brief smile transformed his lean face as he sat down in the chair she'd cleared for him. Edna promptly leaped into his lap.

Erin scooped coffee into the filter with trembling hands. Busy, busy, busy—

"Erin, can I ask you something personal?"

Her skin prickled at his tone. "That depends on the question."

"Last fall. At Crystal Mountain. That guy, Georg. Tell me the truth. Did you go to bed with him?"

She froze into agonized stillness, keeping her back to him. "Why does it matter to you?" Her voice was small and tight.

"It just does."

His question brought all the burning shame rushing back. She turned, and lifted her chin. "If I say yes, that means you'll lose all respect for me, right?" She flung the words at him.

"No," he said quietly. "It means that when I hunt him down and start beating him to death, this time I'll finish the job."

The kettle began to warble. She couldn't respond to it. She was paralyzed by the bleak intensity of his eyes. The warble rose to a shriek.

Connor jerked his chin toward it.

Erin grabbed the kettle with shaking hands. "I think you'd better leave," she said. "Right now."

Her voice sounded tight, breathless. Not authoritative at all.

Connor's gaze did not waver. "You promised me coffee."

His face was implacable. He would leave when it suited

him, and not before. And she had no one but herself to blame for inviting him in.

Connor placed Edna gently on the ground. He got up and wandered over to her desk, studying the photos and cards pinned to the corkboard. The travel itinerary and the printed-out Mueller e-mail lay on the desk in plain view. He picked them up and examined them. "Going someplace?"

"Just a work thing."

He frowned. "Didn't you say you lost your job?"

"I work for myself now. I've started my own consulting business."

"And you're getting by?" His gaze swept the tiny, wretched room.

"I'm not supporting myself with my business yet," she said stiffly. "I'm temping to make ends meet. But I have high hopes."

He held the e-mail up to the light and read it.

"Excuse me, Connor, but those are my private papers, and I did not invite you to look at them."

He ignored her, his gaze fixed on the page. "So Claude is delighted to meet with you at last, huh?" he said softly. "Who is this Claude?"

"None of your business. Put those down. *Now.*"

He glanced up, and took in the steaming mug in her hand. His eyes went right back to the e-mail. "I take it black," he said absently.

"Put those papers down, Connor." She tried to make her voice steely and commanding. It just sounded scared.

"So old Claude feels like he knows you already. Isn't that sweet." He laid the papers on her desk, and walked to the table, staring at her with narrowed eyes. "So, this Claude. You've never met him?"

She set his coffee down in front of him. "He's a client of mine. Not that it's any of your business."

"Art appraisal?"

"Authentication," she corrected. "Mr. Mueller recently developed an interest in Iron Age Celtic artifacts, which are my specialty."

He sipped his coffee, frowning. "How recently?"

"I've never discussed that with him," she said. "It's not—"

"What do you know about this guy, Erin?"

She bristled at the challenge in his voice. "Everything I need to know. He treats me like a professional. He pays well, and on time."

"But you've never met him?" His eyes probed her, merciless.

"I've met members of his administrative staff," she said. "He runs a charitable foundation called the Quicksilver Fund."

"So why haven't you met him yet?" he persisted.

"Because he's always had other pressing engagements," she retorted. "He's a busy man."

"Is he now," Connor said. "Isn't that interesting."

Coffee sloshed over the table as she slammed down her mug. "What the hell are you insinuating, Connor?"

"Do you know anyone personally who has met this guy?"

She pressed her lips together. "I know people whose arts organizations have received grants from him. That's enough for me."

"No, it's not enough. You can't go on this trip, Erin."

She jerked onto her feet, jarring the table painfully with her thigh. "The hell I can't! I am hanging on by my fingernails, Connor. That client is the best thing that's happened to me in the last six months! I will not jeopardize my business just because you are paranoid!"

"Erin, Novak is out there somewhere," Connor said. "I've been hunting him for years. I know his smell, and I'm smelling it now. He lives to fuck people up. You're Ed Riggs's daughter. You were in his sights. He won't forget you. Count on it."

Erin sank down into her chair. "Mueller can't possibly have anything to do with Novak," she said coldly. "Novak has been in a high-security prison ever since he was released from the hospital. Mueller started hiring me four months ago. We made plans to meet on two other occasions. Once in San Diego and once in Santa Fe."

"But he never showed up?"

She lifted her chin. "He had unexpected business."

"I just bet he did," Connor said. "I need to check this guy out."

"Don't you dare!" she flared. "Don't even think about messing with the last good thing I've got going. Everything else in my life has gone straight to hell. Don't you think you've done enough?"

Connor's mouth tightened to a grim line. He put down his cup, stood up, and headed for the door. His limp was just a barely perceptible, hitching stiffness in his leg. And it still broke her heart.

"Connor," she said. "Wait."

He pushed the door open, and waited, motionless.

"I'm sorry I said that." She got up and took a step toward him. "I know it's not your fault. It's been . . . a really awful time."

"Yeah." He turned and looked at her. "I know what you mean."

It was true. He did know how bad it was. She saw it in his eyes. He'd been betrayed and set up to die. He'd lost his partner, Jesse. He'd lost months of his life in a coma, suffered the shattered leg, the burns.

Connor had lost far more than she in this awful business.

An impulse from deep inside kept her feet moving until she stood right in front of him. His scent was a mix of soap and tobacco, resiny and sweet. Pine, wood smoke, and rainstorms. She stared straight up into his face, like she'd always wanted to do, and breathed him in. She drank in all the details: the sheen of beard stubble glinting metallic gold in the light from the corridor outside. The shadows beneath his brilliant eyes, the sharp line of his jutting cheekbones. How was it possible for a mouth to be so stern, and yet so sensual?

And his piercing eyes saw right into her soul.

She lost herself in it. She wanted to touch his face, to trail her fingers over every masculine detail, to feel the warmth of his skin. She wanted to press herself against his lean, solid bulk. She wished she had something to feed him, whether he was hungry or not.

Connor reached behind himself and shoved the door shut without breaking eye contact. She needed so badly for someone to know how lonely and lost she felt. Her mother was adrift in despair. Most of her friends were avoiding her. Not out of unkindness so much as sheer embarrassment, she suspected. But that didn't help the loneliness.

Connor saw it all, and it didn't embarrass him. His gaze didn't shy away. She didn't shy away, either, when he reached for her.

His touch was so careful and delicate, she could barely believe it was happening. Her eyes welled up. He smoothed away the tears that spilled over with a brush of his thumb, and folded her into his arms.

He pressed her face against the canvas of his coat. His hands stroked the length of her spine as if she were made of blown glass. He tucked her head under his chin. His breath warmed the top of her head.

She squeezed her eyes shut. He'd hugged her before, at her graduation party, at holiday gatherings, but not like this. Quick, nonsexual, brotherly hugs, but even so her heart had almost exploded out of her chest, it beat so fast and hard. His broad frame felt harder than she remembered, his muscles like tempered steel.

He'd been concentrated into the pure, potent essence of himself.

She wondered if the way she felt about him was written all over her face. He held her so carefully, vibrating with tension. Maybe he was afraid of hurting her feelings, or that she would misunderstand his friendly gesture and demand something he didn't want to give. All those years of romantic fantasies, all that heat, all that pent-up hunger, he had to feel it. Dad had said that he was psychic.

He'd seen everything: how lonely she felt, how needy. He stroked her hair, as if he were petting a wild animal that might bolt, or bite.

She didn't want careful, or gentle. She wanted him to push her onto the narrow futon cot, to pin her down with his big, strong body and give her something else to think about. Something hot and scary and wonderful. She could scream, she wanted it so bad. She wanted to wrap her arms around his neck, pull him closer, and just gobble him up.

God, how could he *not* pity her?

That thought stung her. It gave her the strength to jerk away. She dug in her pocket for a Kleenex. "Sorry about that," she mumbled.

"Any time." His voice sounded thick. He cleared his throat.

She kept her face averted. He had to leave, and fast, before she burst into tears and covered herself with glory. "Um, I have to pack. I've got lots to do, so, uh . . ."

"Erin—"

"Don't start." She backed away, shaking her head. "I'm going on this trip, and I don't want a bodyguard, thanks for the offer. Thanks for the ride, thanks for the advice, the sympathy and the . . . the hug. And now, I really, really need to be alone. Good night."

He made a sharp, frustrated sound. "You need better locks. Hell, you need a new door. It's a waste to put a good lock on a door like this. I could kick the hinges in with my bad leg." He scanned her apartment, scowling. "I'll call my friend Seth. He can install something that—"

"And how am I supposed to pay him?"

"I'll pay for it myself, if you're short on cash," he said impatiently. "Seth'll give me a good deal. It's important, Erin. You're not safe here."

"Thanks, but I can take care of myself. Good night, Connor."

"Does your mother have an alarm system?"

She thought of the shattered mirror and clock. An eddy of sickening fear swirled in her belly. "Yes. Dad insisted."

"Then maybe you should go stay with her for a while."

She bristled. "And maybe you should mind your own business."

He frowned, and pulled a matchbook out of his jeans pocket. "Give me a pen," he demanded.

She handed him a pen. He scribbled on the matchbook and handed it to her. "Call me. Anything happens, day or night, call me."

"OK," she whispered. The matchbook was warm from his pocket. Her fingers tightened over it until it crumpled in her hand. "Thanks."

"Promise me." His voice was hard.

She tucked it into her jeans pocket. "I promise."

One last, searching look, and he finally walked out the door.

A sharp knock made her jump. "Use the deadbolt," he ordered from outside. "I'm not leaving until I hear you do it."

She pushed in the bolt. "Good night, Connor."

He was silent for a few seconds. "Good night," he said quietly.

She put her ear to the door, but could not hear any footsteps. She waited a moment, opened the door and checked. No one was there.

She was finally alone. She slammed the door shut. After his bullying and lecturing and intimidating her with that overwhelming macho charisma, she'd thought his departure would be a relief.

Instead, she felt bereft. Almost piqued at him, for letting her drive him away so easily. Yikes, how clingy and passive-aggressive of her. She was in worse shape than she'd thought.

But how incredibly sweet of him to care.

* * *

Connor leaned his hot face against the steering column. He couldn't drive in this condition. He would kill himself.

His heart was thudding, his ears roaring. He was on the verge of coming in his pants. If she'd leaned just one breath closer to him, she'd have felt his hard-on, pressing against his jeans like a club. Those amazing, liquid brown eyes that a guy could get lost in, Jesus. Her eyes on his face had felt like an embrace. He'd wanted to grab her and kiss her so bad, his muscles were cramping from the effort of holding back.

Maybe she would have melted against him and kissed him back.

Yeah, and pigs had wings and hell had a skating rink. The closer he stuck to harsh reality, the less liable he was to screw up.

It was so ironic. Right before the huge fuck-up that had landed him in a coma and killed Jesse, he'd been working up the nerve to ask Erin Riggs out for dinner and a movie. Ever since she'd turned twenty-five. That had struck him as the magic number. She'd attained the status of fair game. He was nine years older than her, which wasn't all that excessive, but when she was seventeen and he was twenty-six, he'd known damn well it would've been sleazy to hit on her. Once she hit her twenties, he'd been really tempted. She was so juicy and innocent—but Ed would've ripped his head off if Connor had gotten anywhere near his precious baby girl. There was that to consider.

But the main reason he hadn't made a move was because she'd been gone so much, on study-abroad programs and archeological digs; six months in France, nine months in Scotland, a year in Wales, etc. He'd had some casual girlfriends in the meantime, some of them nice women, but he'd always pulled back when they started talking about the future. He'd braced himself to hear about Erin getting engaged.

Didn't happen. She'd finished grad school, gotten her curator job, moved out of the group house with her college girlfriend and into her own apartment. Twenty-five years old, and amazingly, she didn't have a boyfriend. It was time. All was fair in love and war, and all that crap. If Ed didn't like it, he could shove it.

But the shit had hit the fan before he ever got a chance to follow through. When he woke up from the coma and found out that he'd been betrayed, and Jesse murdered, he had no energy to spare for romance. He'd loved his partner like he loved his own brothers. He'd thrown everything into getting back on his feet so he could hunt down Lazar and Novak, flush out the traitor and avenge Jesse.

All of which had culminated in hauling Ed Riggs into custody.

Damn, he couldn't help but think that putting a girl's dad in prison for murder pretty much wrecked his chances of getting a date with her on a Saturday night. Particularly considering the shape he was in these days. He glanced into the rearview mirror, and winced.

He'd always been lean, and he forced himself to work out hard to compensate for the bum leg. He'd built back all the muscle mass that he'd lost in the coma, but he had no fat left on him at all. He could see every individual muscle and tendon moving under his skin when he looked at himself in the bathroom mirror. A goddamn walking anatomy poster. The burn scars didn't help much, either. Neither did the limp.

He wasn't much of a prize. Working for his older brother, snapping pictures of unfaithful spouses. He had no future. He barely had a present. All he had was a past, and everything in it nixed his chances of getting into Erin Riggs's bed.

What an idiot. Lusting after an ivory tower princess behind a wall of goddamn thorns. He wanted so badly to claw his way into that tower, and find out what went on behind those big, serious eyes. He wanted to make her smile. She hadn't smiled tonight. Not even once.

With that bracing thought, he put the car in gear and headed toward his brother Davy's lair, down on Lake Washington. Davy would be pissed at him for showing up three hours late, but he would just grumble and throw a steak on the grill. His stomach twitched with approval, one of the first signs of life he'd gotten from that quarter in a long while. Davy and Sean had taken up the practice of calling him at regular intervals and reminding him to eat. Annoying, but he guessed he was lucky that somebody cared. Otherwise he would be lost in space.

His younger brother Sean's Jeep was parked in the driveway. He was going to get lectured from both sides. They were talking on the back porch as he opened the door. Their voices suddenly ceased.

Two pairs of green eyes almost identical to his own scrutinized him as he stepped out onto the deck.

"You're late," Davy said. "We ate."

"Novak's busted out," Connor told them. "With two of his goons. One was that guy I roughed up last November. Georg Luksch."

They listened to the water lapping against the pebbles under the deck for a long moment.

"You think he's going to want to play with us?" Davy asked.

Connor sank into a chair, bone tired. "It's what he lives for."

Sean buried his face in his hands. "God. I'm swamped trying to get this business off the ground. I don't have time to play with Novak."

"I'm less worried about us than I am about Erin," Connor said.

Davy and Sean's gazes narrowed in on him, like a couple of laser beams. He bore it stoically.

"What about Erin?" Davy's deep voice was low and wary.

Connor folded a scrap of paper he'd found on the table into an origami unicorn. One of his bored-out-of-his-mind-in-rehab activities that had evolved into a full-blown nervous habit. "He had Erin in his clutches once. I pulled her loose. He's not going to forget that. Georg Luksch won't forget it, either. She's pretty, and young, and clueless. He goes for that. And he's going to want to punish Riggs for failing him."

"Erin is not your problem," Davy said. "You did your best for her. You didn't get much thanks for it. The most you can do is warn her."

"I already did."

Davy and Sean exchanged meaningful glances.

"You talked to her?" Sean demanded. "Tonight?"

Connor braced himself. "I went to her place," he admitted. "Followed her to her mom's house. Gave her a ride home."

Sean winced. "Uh-oh. Here we go again."

Davy took a swig of beer, his hard, lean face impassive. "How's she doing?" he asked.

"Not well," Connor said. "Like hell, actually. Since you asked."

"Look, Con," Sean began. "Don't bite my head off, but—"

"How about you don't even start?" Connor suggested.

Sean barged on, undaunted. "I know you've been carrying a torch for that chick for years, but your testimony put her dad's ass in jail. You cannot be her hero, dude. You're just going to get hurt."

Sean's words made him feel bleak and sad, not angry. "Thank you for sharing your opinion," he said. He unfolded the unicorn, and scribbled Claude Mueller's name, e-mail address, and the flight information that he'd memorized onto the paper. He pushed it across the table toward Davy. "Would you check these out for me?"

Davy picked it up and examined it. "Who is this guy?"

"This is the mysterious millionaire who has recently developed a passionate interest in Celtic artifacts. Erin's flying down to Portland, to be met and driven to Silver Fork Resort, where she will proceed to authenticate a mess of priceless relics for him."

"And what is it exactly that bothers you about this?" Sean asked.

"Neither she nor anybody she knows has ever actually seen the millionaire," he said. "He's always been too busy to meet with her since he started hiring her. Four months ago."

"Ah." Davy's voice was thoughtful.

"Find out who's paying for those flights," Connor told him. "And find out everything you can about the Quicksilver Foundation."

"I'll see what I can do."

"She's leaving tomorrow. I told her she needed a body-guard, and she spit in my eye," Connor said. "Threw me out of her apartment."

"I don't blame her," Sean said. "A guy who looks like you is not a good fashion accessory for a bodacious babe."

"Bite me," Connor said wearily. He pulled his tobacco and papers out of his pocket.

"Did it occur to you to shave, or brush your hair before you inflicted yourself on her?" Sean lectured. "Jesus, Con. You barbarian."

Connor nodded toward his older brother. "Davy's got beard stubble. Bug him for a while."

"Davy's another story." Sean's voice was elaborately patient. "Davy irons his shirts. Davy eats. Beard stubble is a very different fashion statement on Davy."

Davy stroked his stubble and gave Connor an apologetic shrug.

Connor looked at Davy. "Speaking of food. You promised me a steak."

Davy looked startled. "You mean, you actually want some?"

"I'm hungry," Connor said.

Sean's jaw sagged. "So having Erin Riggs spit in your eye stimulates your appetite, huh?" He sprang to his feet. "One rare T-bone coming right up. I'll nuke you a baked potato, if you want."

"Make it two," Connor said. "Lots of butter and sour cream and chives. And don't forget the black pepper."

"Don't push your luck." Sean's grouching was belied by his huge grin. He kicked open the screen door and bounded toward the kitchen.

"When do you need the Mueller info?" Davy asked.

"Tomorrow morning. I'm taking a road trip down to Portland."

Davy's face darkened. "To meet her plane? Oh, Christ. Forget the hero routine just this once. Call Nick. They're the ones who should—"

"I already tried Nick. They think Novak's back in Europe."

"They probably have good reason to think so," Davy growled.

"I've got a bad feeling," Connor said. "She can't go meet this guy all alone. If Ed were around, it would be his job to look after her, but—"

"But Ed's not around," Davy cut in. "And that is not your fault."

"It's not Erin's fault, either." Connor avoided his brother's gaze as he finished rolling the cigarette. "And I don't blame myself."

Davy slammed his beer bottle onto the table, a rare show of temper for his self-contained brother. "The hell you don't. You can't save the whole world, lamebrain. Get your own life back on track before you go racing off to rescue some damsel in distress."

"I didn't ask for your opinion on my love life," Connor retorted.

Davy's lowering eyebrows shot up. "Whoa," he said. "Back up two steps. Who said anything about your love life?"

Connor cupped the cigarette in his hand and lit it. He took a deep drag and exhaled, to calm himself down before he dared to speak.

"Leave it alone, Davy," he said.

"Watch it, Con," Davy said. "You're treading on shaky ground."

Sean burst through the screen door and passed Connor a cold beer. "Food'll be out in a few," he announced.

"Thanks," Connor muttered.

Sean looked from one brother to the other. His eyes narrowed. "Did I miss something?"

"No," Davy and Connor said, in unison.

Sean scowled. "I *hate* it when you guys do that," he snapped. He slammed the screen door behind him, hard.

Connor finished his cigarette in grim silence. Davy for once had the good sense to nurse his beer and keep his mouth shut.

Sean kicked open the door a few minutes later and placed a loaded plate in front of Connor. He dug into it without hesitation.

His two brothers silently watched him consume a twelve-ounce steak, two big baked potatoes, a sliced tomato, and three big hunks of hot, toasted French bread slathered with garlic butter.

Connor finally noticed their fixed stares. "Cut it out, you guys," he protested. "Quit watching me eat, already. You're inhibiting me."

Davy crossed his arms over his barrel chest. "Give us a break. We haven't seen you eat like that for sixteen months."

"It's awesome." Sean's face was unusually serious. "That's a week's worth of calories for you, Con. All in one meal. Check you out."

Connor mopped up the last of his steak juice with a hunk of bread. He felt a vague stab of guilt. "You guys shouldn't worry. I'm fine."

Davy snorted. "We'll see how fine you feel when you get back from Portland."

Sean frowned. "What's this about Portland?"

"He's going to be Erin's welcoming committee when she goes to meet the mysterious millionaire who may or may not be Novak," Davy told him. "He wants to guard her luscious body. Personally."

"Oh, Christ. You don't say. Well, finish your dinner, then. You're going to need your strength. What hardware you taking?" Sean asked.

"Just the SIG. And the Ruger SP-101, for backup."

"Want some company?" Sean asked.

Connor glanced at him, startled. "I thought you were busy."

"I'm not too busy to watch my brother's back," Sean said.

Connor's mouth twitched. "Think I need a baby-sitter, huh?"

"Interpret it however the fuck you want."

Connor finished the final swallow of beer. "I'm OK on my own," he said. "Thanks. I'll let you know if I change my mind."

"You want Erin all to yourself, huh?"

Connor ignored his younger brother's taunting with the ease of long practice. "Would you guys contact Seth and Raine about Novak?"

"I'm on it," Sean said promptly.

"I'll go get to work on this info," Davy said. "Get some sleep, Connor. You look beat. Crash here, and I'll give you the rundown over breakfast. The bed's already made up for you on the side porch."

"Thanks." He got to his feet and stared at his brothers, struck by the bizarre urge to say something sentimental to them.

Sean read it in his eyes, took pity on him, and headed him off. "Get a goddamn haircut if you're looking to get laid, Con."

Connor winced. "You are such a pig."

"Sure, but at least I look good," was Sean's parting shot.

Connor flopped onto the bed, staring out at the mass of tree branches that swayed outside the glassed-in side porch. The chair next to the bed had a towel, washcloth, and a pair of Davy's folded sweats lying on it, presumably for him to sleep in. He was exhausted, but his mind was buzzing. He closed his eyes, and his photographic memory promptly served up the image of Erin puttering around in her kitchen, her sweet, curvy body delicious in the faded jeans and T-shirt.

Fresh fodder for his sexual imagination. He'd fantasized about sneaking into her bedroom at Ed and Barbara's house for years. He'd imagined himself, a big, blundering bull in that feminine world of ruffles and lace, puffy pillows, perfume bottles, lingerie. And Erin, backing up toward her bed, her eyes heavy with excitement as he locked the door.

That fantasy had infinite variations, all of them red hot and X-rated, but tonight the setting changed by itself, unguided by his conscious mind. The ultra-femme bedroom of his fantasies gave way to the crowded studio apartment in the Kinsdale. Painfully neat and organized, the braided rug brightening up the scarred linoleum floor, the crazy quilt covering the narrow cot. Heaps of books piled against the wall. Alphabetized, for God's sake. How cute. Every detail lit by the patterned glow of the basket lamp and charged with erotic heat.

The Kinsdale room didn't make him feel clumsy and alien like the fantasy bedroom did, but it was even more alluring, because Erin was all over it. Her practicality and tidiness, her whimsical sense of humor, her refusal to give in to self-pity. Bright colors, indomitable spirit. That room was sexier than any place he could have dreamed up on his own.

He buried his face in the coarse wool army blanket and let the fantasy unfold. He kissed the salty tears off her cheeks, and she opened and clung to him as he devoured her tender mouth. He knelt down and nuzzled the warmth of that velvety strip of skin between the T-shirt and the waistband of her jeans that had so tantalized him tonight. He popped the buttons of the jeans open and tongued her navel as he dragged those jeans and panties down over her curvy hips, her round ass. Slowly, inch by precious inch, reveling in her hot female smell: baby powder and flower petal and ocean salt. He breathed it, in big, greedy gulps. He peeled every scrap of clothing away until she was naked, arms held out to him, her eyes soft with trust.

Yeah. Trust. He shoved away the derisive voices in his head. This was his fantasy, and he'd run it how he damn well pleased.

She trembled as he put his arms around her from behind and explored the exquisite, plump fullness of her breasts. Vivid details were imprinted in his mind as if they were memories, not fantasies. Her nipples puckered against his hand, tender buttons of flesh aching to be tongued and suckled. Her hair clip pulled loose, and her glossy hair tumbled and slid across her shoulders like a swath of dark satin.

He slid his hand over the rounded swell of her belly, delving into her dark thatch, searching for hidden treasure in the wet, secret heat of her cleft. She tightened around his fingers and flung her head back against his shoulder, squirming and whimpering with pleasure.

He pushed her down onto the bed and pushed her soft thighs until they sprawled apart. He cupped her rosy ass cheeks, kissed and tongued the folds and hollows between her legs, the electric fuzz of dark hair. He opened her like a dripping fruit with his tongue, sliding it along the glistening, succulent folds of her labia, wallowing in her colors and flavors. Lazy and slow, taking his time. Suckling her clit, flicking and lashing it with his tongue. He would bury his head between her thighs and thrust his tongue deep. He would make her buck and writhe and press her cunt against his face, until she jerked and sobbed and came.

And then he would do it all again.

Usually he finished himself off with the next logical step; clambering over her damp body and shoving himself into her quivering depths, sliding deeper and slicker with each thrust until his orgasm thundered through him. Tonight, he didn't get that far. He came along with her imagined orgasm, the pillow muffling his cry as he spurted into the washcloth. He pressed his face against the pillow, breath heaving.

When he lifted his head, he was startled to find his face wet with tears. That was weird. He wiped his cheek and stared at his wet hand for over a minute, but he was too tired to be overly freaked out about it.

He cleaned up in the back bathroom, dragged the blanket over himself and sank like a stone into real, honest-to-God sleep.

Chapter

4

"Sure, I can drop by and take care of kitty. No problem," Tonia said. "I have to come by really early, though. That OK?"

"Sure. I always wake up at the crack of dawn anyway when I have to catch a plane. Thank you so much, Tonia. You're an angel."

"I know. Get some sleep, *chica*. You have to look gorgeous for the zillionaire. I'm so excited that you're finally meeting him. 'Night, then. See you bright and early tomorrow morning."

Erin hung up, crossed *Call Tonia to feed Edna* off the To Do list, and proceeded to pace around the room like a caged animal. Every dish was washed, every crumb wiped up, every doable item on the To Do list was crossed off, except for *Pack,* which rated its own separate list.

Her rolling carry-on was small, so she'd been forced to eliminate several items, the latest of which was the little black dress she'd thought to take in case Claude Mueller proved to be interesting. For some reason, the brief, devastating encounter with Connor had taken all the fizz out of that possibility. As long as she had this stupid crush on him, every man she met would suffer by comparison.

Not that she hadn't tried. With Bradley, years before.

Something tightened up inside at the thought of Bradley. Ouch. Cancel that thought. If there was a fancy meal, she would wear her black pants and her silk blouse. Neat and sensible, and no chance that anyone could think she was hoping to attract romantic attention. She had no stomach for it. Which left room for the sewing kit, which she hated to leave. You always needed a sewing kit when you didn't bring one.

She was climbing the walls. She needed to laugh, or cry, but if she started crying she might never stop. She needed sleep, so she could wow them with her professional fabulousness. She needed to stop thinking about the way Connor could melt her into a puddle of terrified yearning with one exquisitely gentle hug.

She needed distraction. Packing and neatening were not enough. She'd promised Mom that she would call Cindy tonight. Now there was a worthy problem. She had to save Cindy's future from being derailed.

She dialed the group house where Cindy lived with her college girlfriends in Endicott Falls. "Hello?" responded a breathy voice.

"Hi. Victoria, right? It's Erin, Cindy's sister. Is she there?"

"No, she's down in the city with Billy," Victoria told her.

"Billy?" Erin's stomach fluttered with unease. "Who's Billy?"

"Oh, he's her new boyfriend. He's a really cool guy, Erin. Don't worry, you'll like him. He's, like, totally hot."

"What's she doing in the city? Don't you guys have finals?"

Victoria hesitated. "Um, I don't know Cindy's exam schedule," she hedged, uncomfortable. "But I'll tell her to call you when she gets back. Or you could try her cell phone."

"Cell phone? Since when does Cindy have a cell phone?"

"Billy gave it to her," Victoria bubbled. "He's so cool. He gives her designer clothes, too. He drives a Jag, and Caitlin told me that Cindy told her that it's not the only awesome car he's got. Plus, he's got a—"

"Victoria. Would you please give me Cindy's cell phone number?"

"Sure. It's right here on the message board."

Erin wrote it down with white-knuckled fingers. She barely heard herself as she thanked Victoria and got off the phone. She sat there on the bed, trying to reason away the dread that sat inside her like a cold stone. She was just spooked, she told herself. This news about Novak, the strange scene with Mom, the unsettling episode with Connor, it had thrown her off balance, and she was seeing everything as sinister. There was no reason to panic yet. Maybe this Billy was a perfectly nice guy.

Uh-huh. Sure. A perfectly nice guy who happened to drive a Jaguar. Who showered a nineteen-year-old girl with expensive clothes and electronic toys and lured her away from school during finals week.

It was strange. It was scary. It stank.

Her parents' reasoning behind encouraging Cindy to go to a private college in the small town of Endicott Falls was in the hopes that she would have more guidance and supervision than she might find in a big, sprawling public university. The thoughtless, impressionable Cindy was so eager to be liked. Willing to be led anywhere, just to be cool. The opposite of her shy, cautious older sister. And so pretty, too. Much prettier than Erin. Walking bait. Erin already hated Billy and his Jag. She hated him more with every number she pressed.

She was startled when the phone actually rang.

"Hello?" said Cindy's bright voice.

"Hi, Cindy. It's Erin."

"Oh. Um . . . hi. How did you get this number?"

Erin gritted her teeth. "Victoria gave it to me."

"What a ditz. I'm gonna have to kill her."

Her breezy tone put Erin's nerves on edge. "Why wouldn't you want me to have it, Cindy?"

"Don't even start," Cindy said, giggling. "You're such a little old lady. I didn't want you to worry, that's all."

"Worry about what?" Erin's voice was getting sharper.

"About me staying in the city with Billy for a while."

"Staying where, Cin?"

Cindy ignored her question. "I was going nuts in that sleepy town. Nobody does anything but study during exam week, so I—"

"What about your exams?" Erin burst out. "Why aren't you studying, too? Your scholarship was contingent on keeping your GPA—"

"See? I told you. This is why I didn't call. I knew you'd get all self-righteous on me. Billy offered to take me—"

"Who is this Billy?" she demanded. "Where did you meet him?"

"Billy is great," Cindy snapped. "He's the best thing that's happened in my shitty life since Dad got thrown in jail. I'm just taking a break from that tight-ass place and having some fun—"

"Cin, what kind of fun?" Her voice was a nervous squeak.

Cindy giggled. It was a trilling, mindless sound, so unlike her normal laughter that it made Erin's flesh creep. "Like, please," she said. "As if you'd know what fun was if it pinched you on the butt. Take a chill pill, Erin. I'm with Billy. I'm safe, I'm fine. I'm over the moon."

Erin was bewildered by the wall that had suddenly risen up between her and her sister. "Cin, we have to talk. We've got to figure out how you can stay in school. Your scholarship—"

"Oh, don't worry." Cindy giggled again. "My financial problems are at an end. That scholarship is, like, so minor, Erin."

"What the hell are you talking about?" Panic was clutching at her chest, making her heart pound. "Cindy, you can't just—"

"Don't get your panties in a wad. There are lots of ways to make money. More than I ever thought, and Billy is showing me how to—huh? What? Oh . . . yeah, totally. Billy says to tell you that college is overrated. A big fat waste of time and money. Who cares about Chaucer or counterpoint or Freud or the Industrial Revolution, anyhow? I mean, like, get real. It's all just theory. Life is to be lived. In the moment."

"Cindy, you're scaring me to death."

"Relax already. I'm just trying my wings. It's so normal. Just because you never wanted to party doesn't mean I can't, does it? Don't say anything to Mom, though, OK? She'd go ballistic for sure."

"Listen, I need to talk to you about Mom, too—"

" 'Bye, Erin. Don't call me, I'll call you. And don't worry! Everything will be totally cool." The connection abruptly broke.

Erin redialed the number. The prerecorded message informed her that the party she was trying to call was unreachable.

Like she didn't already know.

She slammed the phone down and curled up on her bed. She fished the matchbook that had Connor's phone number written on it out of her pocket, and stared at it.

Anything happens, anything at all, call me, he'd said. *Promise me.*

She was so tempted to call him and sob out all her problems to him. He was so warm and strong. He beckoned like a lighthouse in a storm. She wiped tears angrily away. Not an option. Connor was the last person she should turn to for help. No matter how terrified she felt.

*   *   *

Oh, Christ. There were at least a dozen big, scary-looking vitamin pills lying on the table next to a tall glass of fresh-squeezed orange juice when Connor stumbled out of the back bathroom in the morning. Davy had the imperturbable macho-zen act down to a high art, but he still insisted on treating his younger brother like a goddamned invalid.

Davy glanced at him, jerked his head toward the vitamins, and narrowed his eyes, as if to say, Don't even *think* of struggling.

"I start with coffee, not orange juice," Connor grumbled.

"This is my house. I am boss in my house. If you swallow them all down without giving me any shit, I will give you some coffee," Davy said. "And then we'll go over the Mueller stuff."

That snapped his mind to instant alertness. "Find anything interesting?"

Davy gave him an oblique look. "Want some breakfast?"

Connor yawned. "Hell, yes." His stomach was groaning.

Davy blinked. "I'll be damned. I'll go put on some eggs and ham for you. Two eggs or three?"

"Four," Connor said.

A grin split Davy's stern face. He vanished into the kitchen.

Connor was frowning at a weird transparent amber pill when Sean wandered out onto the porch. "What is this crap?" he asked plaintively. "It looks like a congealed glob of oil."

"It *is* a congealed glob of oil, you ignorant slob. Four hundred ECU of vitamin E in a gel capsule. Good for skin, nails, hair, and scar tissue. Take it. You need all the help you can get." Sean placed a mug of coffee in front of him. "Davy says if the pills are gone, you can drink this."

Connor studied his brother's sartorial splendor with wondering eyes. Sean always looked well-groomed, even when he just rolled out of bed. Some recessive gene that Connor had utterly failed to inherit.

Sean was decked out in a wine-red sweater that showed off all his muscles. Tight designer jeans. Hair mussed into perfect stylish disorder. A whiff of expensive aftershave drifted over and assailed Connor's nose.

He closed his eyes against Sean's blinding glory and swallowed down the gummy capsule. "What are you still doing here?"

Sean grimaced. "Woman trouble. Julia is camping out in her car in front of my condo. I told her from the start not to get all intense on me, that I'm not looking to commit right now. Didn't work. Never does. So I figured if I don't come home till morning for a few nights, she'll figure I'm boffing someone else and get a clue."

"You slut," Connor said. "Someday you'll pay up, big time." He picked up the last vitamin, a big, yellowish brown pill. "This is the one that makes your piss turn chartreuse, right?"

Sean glanced over at it. "That's the one. B complex. Great stuff."

"It looks like a rabbit pellet," Connor complained. "And it smells like horseshit. Why do you guys torture me with this crap?"

"Because we love you, asshole. Shut up and eat the pill."

Connor froze, startled by the edge in Sean's voice. Sean stared out at the water. A muscle twitched in his sharp, clean-shaven jaw.

For a moment, he caught a glimpse of the depths of his brothers' worry for him, and a hot ache swelled up in his throat. He covered by shoving the evil-smelling pill into his mouth, and choking it down with a gulp of coffee. "Jesus. I've got yellow skid marks on my esophagus."

"Suffer," was Sean's succinct rejoinder.

They sipped their coffee. This tense, meaningful silence was too much for him to take first thing in the morning. He had to knock it down to the level of bullshit banter, so they could both breathe again.

"So, uh . . . Julia," he ventured. "Is she the aerobics instructor with thighs like a vise?"

Sean seized onto the change of subject with evident relief. "Hell, no. That was Jill. You missed Kelsey, Rose and Caroline."

"Ah. I see," Connor murmured. "So what's with this Julia?"

Sean winced. "Curly blonde hair, big blue eyes, five-inch heels. I met her at a club a few weeks ago. It was fun for a while, and then *bam,* out of nowhere, she mutates into this gigantic bloodsucking insect."

Connor winced. "Shit. I hate it when that happens."

"Me, too. Lurking in the dark outside my condo all night, brrr. Creeps me out. Next thing I know, she'll be boiling my bunny."

Connor made sympathetic sounds. "Sounds painful."

The screen door flew open, kicked by Davy's massive booted foot. He laid two plates before his brother. Thick slabs of grilled ham, a heap of scrambled eggs full of melted cheddar. Four pieces of toast, dripping with butter. A pile of fresh honeydew, cantaloupe, and pineapple chunks with a big scoop of cottage cheese perched on top.

Connor blinked. "Whoa. So, uh . . . where's my damask napkin and my lemon-scented finger bowl?"

Davy shrugged, unembarrassed. "You need protein."

No arguing with that. He dove in, ignoring his rapt audience. A few minutes later, he pushed back two highly polished plates. "Let me have it," he said. "What's up with Claude Mueller?"

Davy flipped open a manila folder full of computer printouts. "There's not as much as I would've expected, for such a rich guy," he said. "Born in Brussels in '61. Mother Belgian, father Swiss, a big shot industrialist. Outrageously wealthy. Claude was sickly as a child, suffers from some weird form of hemophilia, now more or less under control. A reclusive loner type. He studied art and architecture at the Sorbonne from '80 to '83 and then gave it up due to ill health. In 1989, his parents were killed in a car accident. Claude was the sole heir to a fortune of around a half billion or so."

Connor choked on his coffee, and wiped his mouth. "Jesus," he said. "Hard to wrap your mind around that much money."

Sean gave him an evil grin. "My mind is stretchier than yours."

"Poor Claude was traumatized by his parents' deaths," Davy went on. "From that point on, he secluded himself on a tiny private island off the south of France. Never married, no children. All he cares about are antiquities. He had a collection of medieval reliquaries, weapons, Viking and Saxon artifacts, and of course Celtic stuff. He's a big presence on the 'Net. Spends lots of time in art history chat rooms and message boards. He administers the Quicksilver Fund, which he established in the early nineties. It's a stinking pile of money that he doles out to arts organizations. All of whom suck his virtual toes."

"Photos?" Connor asked.

"I couldn't find a recent one. These are over sixteen years old." Davy shoved a pile of color printouts across the table to him.

Connor pushed aside his plate and leafed through them.

Claude Mueller was thin, nondescript, neither handsome nor ugly. Bland features, olive skin, blue eyes, thinning brown hair. The clearest of the lot was a passport photo taken two decades ago. A chubbier version of the same man, with a mustache and goatee.

Connor studied them, letting his mind float open like a net, scooping for images, connections, snags, feelings. Nothing jumped out, nothing flashed by. All he felt was a prickling, restless unease. "Novak could pass for this guy," he mused. "Same height and build."

Davy and Sean's swift glances clearly continued a conversation they must have started last night after he'd gone to bed.

Davy shook his head. "I got into the database of the Quicksilver Fund last night. I found the transactions for the plane tickets Mueller bought for Erin in the past few months. The pressing business that kept Mueller from meeting Erin in Santa Fe was ill health. I saw the medical records. Two days before she was scheduled to go to Santa Fe, Mueller was admitted to a posh private clinic in Nice for a bleeding ulcer."

Something tightened steadily in Connor's stomach. Even though he knew this news should be making him feel better.

"I hacked into the clinic's records," Davy continued. "He couldn't make it to the meeting because he was vomiting blood, Con. Not because he was sitting in jail, plotting Erin's downfall."

Connor set down his cup. Davy's tone was flat, his voice unreadable. "Since when do you read French?" he demanded.

"I hung out in northern Africa for a while after Desert Storm, remember? They speak a lot of French in Egypt and Morocco. I picked it up. It's not hard, if you already know Spanish."

Connor stared into his coffee. So Davy knew French. His brother was full of surprises. "Wasn't it a little too easy, finding all this info?"

"Yeah, it was easy," Davy said slowly. "It's possible that it's an elaborate, fiendish plot. Anything's possible. But spending untold amounts of money to put together a cover story this complicated, all for Erin Riggs's benefit? Come on, Con. Sure she's a cute girl, but—"

"I'm not suggesting that it would be all for Erin's benefit," Connor snarled. "It's to Novak's benefit to have another identity."

Davy looked away. "It's like Nick said, Con. Novak's run home to hide under Daddy's wing. It's the smart thing to do."

"But he's insane." Connor looked from Davy to Sean. Both his brothers avoided his gaze. "He doesn't reason like a normal human."

"You have to face reality, Con." Sean's mouth was tight.

Connor clenched his jaw. "And what is your version of reality?"

Sean looked like he was bracing himself. "That you hate the idea of this girl you've always wanted going to meet a filthy rich guy who goes nuts for Celtic art. Nobody could blame you for hating it."

The food in Connor's belly congealed to a cold lump.

"Let her go, Con." Davy's voice was heavy. "Move on."

Connor rose to his feet and snatched the sheaf of paper from the table. "Thanks for your help. If you'll excuse me, I've got stuff to do."

"Yo, Con," Sean said, as Connor shoved open the door.

Connor jerked around with a this-had-better-be-good expression.

"The guy may have more money than God, but hey . . . he urps blood," Sean pointed out. "Bleeding ulcers are not sexy. Take what comfort you can from that."

Connor slammed the porch door so violently that it rattled in its frame. They braced themselves. *Slam* went the front door, too.

Sean dropped his head down and bonked his forehead against the table. "Shit, shit, shit. Just shoot me now. Put me out of my misery."

"Yeah, that was brilliant." Davy's voice was dour. "You always hit a nerve. Straight on, bull's eye."

"It's a family trait." Sean raised resentful, narrowed eyes.

"You were the one begging to be put out of his misery," Davy observed. "Not me."

Sean slumped down into his chair. "I didn't think things could suck any worse for him than they already did. I was wrong."

"Things can always get worse," Davy pointed out. "Always."

"Aw, shut up," Sean muttered. "Goddamn pessimist."

Chapter

5

It was sunset in the woods. She was naked beneath her gauzy dress. Her hair was loose, her breasts swayed beneath the fabric. Currents of warm air caressed her skin. Golden light slanted through the trees. They swayed and shivered in the soft, perfumed breeze.

Connor was following her, with a patient, measured gait through eons of dream time. His eyes were full of longing, and the realization grew so gradually inside her, when she finally understood, it was as if she had always known. He would never close the distance between them as long as her back was turned to him.

She stopped in a circle of trees, fragrant grass below and open sky above, hesitated for one last, trembling moment . . . and turned around.

His face lit up with triumphant joy. The wind rose as he approached her, whipping her hair around her face. She had solved the riddle, and finally they could claim what had always been theirs.

The air hummed like honeybees. Sweet, shimmering overtones filled the air. He placed his hands on her shoulders, pushed the dress off. It slid over her body to the fragrant grass below. There were no words. It was a ceremonial dance, a magical binding.

Incoherent yearning fountained up inside her, and she reached for him. She offered him all her need, all her secret heat and softness. He kissed her with a rough urgency that mirrored her own, and bore her to the ground. He gave her his heat and his hunger, the sinuous power of his body, the blazing energy that illuminated the dark places inside her, burning away fear and shame as the sun burned away fog.

Power rose through her like sap, and thousand-petaled flowers of every hue burst into bloom in her sex, her heart, her head. The grass was their soft, fragrant bed as he surged into her, deep and desperate—

The alarm shrilled. Erin jolted upright in bed. She slapped the alarm into submission and covered her face with shaking hands. The alarm had cut her off at the good part, and left her high and dry. What rotten, cruel timing. She could hardly breathe, she was so turned on.

She'd been having that dream for years. Connor's garb varied according to what she was researching at the time; sometimes he wore jeans and a T-shirt, sometimes he was a Celtic warrior, sometimes a Roman soldier. The details didn't matter. The dream always left her writhing in bed, quivering thighs clenchd tight around a pool of liquid heat. Distracted by lust. The last thing she needed to cope with today.

She tried to be objective, adult. Dreams were messages from the subconscious mind. This was fine and good, and she appreciated the courtesy. But what could this dream indicate, with her life the way it was? She'd never had sex with Connor. She'd barely ever managed to have sex with anybody, at least not successfully, so why should her subconscious mind use sex to make its point? To get her attention?

She hugged her knees to her chest, still shaking. If that was the intent, it had worked. Just a dream, she repeated. Just a dream.

She glanced at the clock. Seven o'clock. Time to make

some tea and calm herself down with something busy and constructive, but horror of horrors, there was nothing left to do. The apartment was already painfully tidy. Everything that could be alphabetized was. Every surface that could be scrubbed shone. Her packing was done, her travel clothes laid out, down to the last hairpin. If this went on, she would be reduced to cleaning off the gunk that accumulated on the computer keyboard with cotton swabs and alcohol. Coping mechanisms gone wild.

The intercom buzzed. Her first thought was that it might be Connor, and she stumbled across the room, electrified. "Who is it?"

"It's me, silly. Tonia. Don't tell me Ms. Perfect is still in bed?"

"Oh, hi, Tonia. The elevator's still broken. Take the stairs."

She pulled on some sweats while she waited for Tonia's knock. She opened the door and gave her friend a grateful hug. "You are such a sweetheart for helping me. I hate leaving Edna at the pet hotel."

Tonia tossed her black curls. "No big deal. Sorry I had to bug you so early. Shall I take Edna home with me, or just take your keys?"

"Whatever's more convenient for you," Erin said. "And I am taking you out to dinner as soon as I get back."

"Oh, stop." Tonia rolled her artfully made-up eyes. "I'll take Edna home, then. She can chase some of the neighbor cats around. She's such a warmongering bitch, she must feel stir-crazy in this tiny place."

Erin was all too aware of how the fussy Edna hated being cooped up in an efficiency apartment. But life was tough all around.

"I'm sure it'll be a nice treat for her," she said tightly.

Tonia lifted up a Starbucks bag. "I brought us some sticky buns, plus a couple of double-shot lattes. You need a stiff dose of caffeine."

Erin devoured a gooey bun while Tonia pawed through

Erin's suitcase. "You can't go meet an eligible zillionaire dressed like this," Tonia protested. "You don't have a single thing that shows off your chest, and you have a fine chest, girl! What am I going to do with you?"

Erin shrugged. "I'm going for professional, not sexpot."

"The two are not incompatible." Tonia wagged an admonishing finger at her. "When you come back, we are going shopping, and I will personally show you how to reconcile them."

"I'm broke," Erin said. "No shopping until my ship comes in."

Tonia rolled her eyes. "That's what I love about you, Erin. So naïve. Let me lay out the plan for you. Step One, borrow my clothes to make that all-important first impression. Step Two, get passionately friendly with the zillionaire. And then, *then* we will go shopping."

"Oh, stop it. This is a work thing. And besides, I . . ." Her voice trailed off, and she started to blush.

Tonia blinked. "Don't tell me you're blowing off this opportunity because you're hung up on that guy who ruined your life!"

"My life is not ruined, for your information," Erin snapped. "Connor came to see me yesterday."

"Here?" Tonia's jaw dropped. "In your apartment? What did he do? Did he come on to you? I'll shoot him if he came on to you."

"No! He didn't! He came to tell me that Novak and Georg Luksch broke out of prison. He's worried about my safety. He tried to persuade me not to go on this trip." No need to mention that intense hug, since it had been completely platonic. At least on his part, if not hers. "Actually, I thought it was sweet of him," she said hesitantly. "To warn me."

"Sweet?" Tonia snorted a derisive sound. "He wants into your pants. Sure, he saved you from the evil henchman of the big bad criminal, but you told me yourself that all that Georg did to you was flirt. And McCloud turned him into hamburger right in front of you. Maybe some girls go for that sort of thing, but you're not one of them."

It was painful to hear the facts laid out in Tonia's merciless style, but Erin nodded. "It was horrible."

"Watch out, Erin. This guy is violent, and wild, and dangerous. He's got a grudge against your dad, and he's way, *way* too interested in you. And you keep making excuses for him, like he's got some weird power over you, or something!"

"That's not true." She laid down the half-eaten sticky bun. Her appetite had faded away. "I don't think he means me any harm."

"No? He's insane if he tries to stop you from going on this trip. Anything that interferes with this client is harmful to you."

"I know." Erin stared out the window at the soot streaks on the wall of the adjoining building with hot, brimming eyes.

Tonia sighed. "I know it's hard. The whole clinic nursing staff was gooey about your devotion. Every single day, there you were to read to him. Like *Lassie Come Home*, or something. It was adorable."

Tonia's choice of metaphors was an uncomfortable one. "Tonia—"

"It broke our hearts, it was so romantic," Tonia barged on. "But it wasn't meant to be. He's just not good enough for you, Erin."

Erin shook her head. None of her friends or family knew that she'd visited Connor every day that he'd lain in a coma, but there had been no way to hide it from the nursing staff.

Her friendship with Tonia had begun one day when Tonia had found Erin crying in the ladies' room. Tonia had given her a tissue and a hug, and led her down to the café outside for coffee. For the first time ever, Erin had let it all pour out, and confessed her unrequited love, her longing and heartache. Her terror that Connor might never wake up.

"Sore subject, isn't it?" Tonia's taunting tone dragged her back to the present. "Truth hurts, don't it?"

Erin breathed through the urge to snarl until it was controllable. "Let's not talk about Connor anymore," she said evenly. "I turned down his offer. I'm going on my trip. I told him to leave me alone. I did all the right things, so there's no reason for you to scold me like this."

Tonia looked abashed. "You're so right. I am such a bitch sometimes. Forgive me?" She fluttered her long lashes.

Erin smiled reluctantly. "Of course."

"OK. Good. Let's move on to your wardrobe. If you take a cab to the station instead of a city bus, you will buy yourself just enough time to come home and raid my wardrobe before you go. Consider it an investment. If you land this guy, you will spend the rest of your days in the lap of luxury, shopping with your good friend Tonia. I have got the perfect suit and blouse for you. Wine-red, short skirt, and a tantalizing hint of that kick-ass cleavage you never take advantage of."

Erin smiled. "Thanks, but the zillionaire will just have to cope with the real me. I've just got to be true to my inner dowdiness."

Tonia made a frustrated sound. "Well, then, I'll be on my way. Help me get that cat of yours into the pet carrier, OK?"

"Remember her ear drops," Erin said anxiously. "It's four drops of vitamins in the wet food, plus one pill crushed up and sprinkled over her dry food, twice a day. She's already eaten this morning's pill."

Tonia rolled her eyes. "Next time you pick up a pet from the pound, try to pick a healthy one, would you?"

"But the healthy ones have a better chance of finding homes," Erin protested. "The sickly ones are doomed. I've got a soft spot for the underdog. Or undercat, as the case may be. Come on, Edna, let's go."

Edna hid under the bed, hissing and spitting. Erin finally managed to push her into the pet carrier and latch the door.

Tonia made a face. "I've got you now, my pretty, and I'm taking you to my lair where I'll make cat soup out of you." She gave Erin a hug. "Don't rule out what our mothers always told us, *chica*. It's as easy to fall in love with a rich man as an unemployed scumbag. 'Bye!"

Erin closed the door with a sigh. Tonia was the only one who knew about her feelings for Connor, but sometimes it seemed like Tonia enjoyed exploiting that tender spot. As if it gave her special power, to be the only one who knew. She poked at it, just to make Erin jump.

She reminded herself that Tonia was a good friend. It was she who had found her this apartment, it was she who had helped Erin move. Her other friends had drifted away when things got so grim, but Tonia had been right there, like a rock.

In spite of her strange personality quirks.

Connor eased the Cadillac into a parking space on the airport skyway level, and glanced at his watch. Erin's plane wasn't due to land for twenty minutes. It would take ten minutes or so for her to disembark and make her way to the luggage claim, where Mueller's limo driver was supposed to meet her.

Over his dead body.

His eyes fell on the sheaf of info that Davy had gleaned on Claude Mueller, scattered across the passenger seat. He'd memorized every fact. He should be relieved that Erin's mystery client checked out, but the ghost hand was squeezing his throat even harder. His instincts had never played him false before—but he'd never been in such a fucked-up state before, either. Even Sean and Davy thought he was going off the deep end. That made him feel so alone.

But he couldn't let it go. Not if Erin was at stake.

The only plan he'd come up with so far was to spirit her away from the airport without making a scene. A neat trick, considering that the old you-are-in-mortal-danger-and-only-I-can-save-you line had fallen pretty flat last night. He'd never been that smooth with the ladies. That was Sean's special talent, not his.

Thinking about Sean made him glance self-consciously into the rearview mirror. He'd made an effort today, but it hadn't done a whole lot of good. He'd put on the nicest shirt he could find, a rough-weave beige designer thing, a Christmas gift from the ever-hopeful Sean. The shirt still had creases from the packaging, and his chinos were crumpled from their sojourn at the bottom of the clean laundry basket, but that was too bad. There were some lengths to which he would not go, and ironing was one of them.

But he'd shaved. He'd combed his unruly blond mane, forced it to lie as smoothly as possible in a thick ponytail. His hair had always had a mind of its own. He should probably just chop it all off. Problem with cutting your hair, though, was that then you had to keep on cutting it. All the time. Big pain in the ass.

Oh, Christ, enough already. This wasn't a goddamn beauty contest. If he'd come here sporting his usual Clan of the Cave Bear hairdo, the airport National Guardsmen would've hauled him away before he even got in the door. Even decently groomed, dragging a beautiful, protesting young woman through an international airport was a delicate undertaking. The trick would be in that fateful split second that Erin caught sight of him.

He'd be lucky if she didn't scream.

He let his breath out slowly. He felt so damn nervous. He'd looked death in the face plenty of times and kept his cool, but one quiet, self-possessed girl scared him to death. Maybe he really was losing it. Interpol was dead sure that Novak was in Europe. Nick was convinced that Novak was no threat to Erin. Her mystery client checked out. There was no reason he could put his finger on to follow her around and hassle her. So why?

Fuck it. He just had to. It was one of those bone-deep feelings that could not be reasoned with. He shoved the Mueller papers into the glove compartment and got out of the car.

He could torture himself all day, and he would just keep limping along, following marching orders from an authority deep inside himself. His conscience, maybe. Davy and Sean called it his hero complex. He himself sometimes referred to it as dumber than shit, particularly when it almost got him killed.

It didn't really matter what it was called. Fact #1, he was doing a stupid, self-destructive thing that could prove to be dangerous, not to mention embarrassing. Fact #2, there wasn't a damn thing he could do to stop himself. Conclusion?

Go for it.

First he checked out the shuttle carousel in the luggage claim, to see who was waiting for Erin. Sure enough, a big, dark-haired, Spanish-looking guy in a uniform was holding a sign that read "Erin Riggs." Connor scanned the rest of the crowd. His plan would only work if Erin hadn't checked her luggage. Chances were good she just had a carry-on, but with women, you never knew.

And she wouldn't take kindly to being separated from her bag. Hell hath no fury like a woman deprived of her toiletries.

He took the escalator back up. There was a quivery feeling in his belly. He glanced at his watch. Eight minutes. He sauntered over to the Coffee People booth in the mall, bought a cup, drank it down faster than he should. He fingered the bag of tobacco in his pocket. He should have had the presence of mind to have a quick smoke outside. Damn smoke-free environments.

Three more minutes to wait. Coffee had been a big mistake. He studied the people around him. A woman with a baby and a four-year-old boy jumping up and down, waiting for his dad to come home. An elderly couple, their faces creased with smiles as they waited for their grandkids. Finally, the shuttle passengers started trickling out. One minute . . . two . . . and there she was, dressed in a deep green suit. Hair swept up, gleaming. Gold earrings dangled beneath her ears. She looked so gorgeous, he wanted to kick himself for not at least attempting to iron the shirt. It wouldn't have killed him to try.

Too late for regrets. She was wheeling a carry-on suitcase behind her, thank God. Time to put his half-assed plan into action.

His heart slammed against his ribs like a jackhammer as she came through the gate. She still hadn't caught sight of him. He chose a diagonal collision course that brought him right up behind her, and grabbed her arm. "Hey, sweetheart."

She spun around. He took full advantage of her shocked confusion and yanked her closer, staring down into wide, startled gold-brown eyes. Her mouth was moist with tinted lip gloss, hanging open in adorable confusion.

"Good to see you again, babe." He scooped her close and tight against his body, and kissed her.

She stiffened, latching onto his upper arms for balance. She made a soft, frightened sound against his mouth.

He deepened the kiss, sliding his arm to the deep flare of her hip, splaying his hand over her beautiful ass. He hadn't planned on kissing her. The impulse had sneaked up on him, but it was perfect. Inspired. It all looked like lovers' play, and that soft, luscious mouth of hers was too busy to complain.

Then her scent rose up around him, like a hot pink cloud, and his mind went blank. It was spring-like and tangy and sweet. Intensely female. A secret weapon that he was unprepared for. He wanted to gasp in huge, gulping lungfuls of it, like a man who'd been trapped underwater and had finally reached air.

Her scent blended with her taste, just as silky sweet, and a confusion of soft, unbelievable textures, the yielding tenderness of her lips, the satiny wisps of hair at the nape of her neck, her baby-smooth skin. His senses were overwhelmed.

She vibrated in his arms, a delicate tremor like a trapped bird. He forgot about Novak, about the airport, about the National Guardsmen. He forgot everything but his own desperate, clawing need to coax her mouth to open, to taste more of her.

She flung her head back, gasping for air. A stain of wildrose pink was burned into her cheeks, startling against the delicate gold tone of her skin. Her pupils were black wells ringed with jewel-toned agate brown. Sunset, honey, and chocolate. Her dark, curling lashes fluttered with dazed confusion.

She licked her lips. "Connor? What . . . what are you—"

He shifted to keep her off balance and slanted his mouth across her lips again. He slid his hand down her graceful spine and pressed her against his lower body as he cupped the nape of her neck. He dove deep into one of those waves-crashing-on-the-beach kisses, sweet and devouring and desperate. When he finally released her, he was trembling harder than she was.

She dragged in a deep, hitching breath. He leaned his hot forehead against hers, making a cage of privacy with his cupped hands around their faces. "Shhh," he murmured. He grabbed the suitcase out of her hand. "Let's go."

He wrapped his arm around her shoulder and pulled her along with him. She had to scurry to keep up. "Go where?" Her voice was still soft and uncertain. Not yet an attention-getting bellow of outrage. "Connor, please. I—"

This time he bent her over backwards so that she had to cling to his neck to stay on her feet. He moved his mouth across her lips, muffling her protests until finally she was just holding on, swaying. He pressed soft kisses over her face, her throat, and nuzzled the perfumed, tickling wisps at her neck.

"Shhh," he urged. "Trust me."

Into those big revolving doors, and he'd be home free.

"Trust you?" Her voice shook as he swept her into movement once again. "About what? Connor, I'm supposed to meet someone at baggage claim! Slow down!"

She was starting to splutter and struggle in his grasp, but they were out the revolving door, and he was hustling her across the skyway. No airport security. Just travelers going about their business, shooting them the occasional curious glance.

Erin dug in her heels and dragged him to a halt. "Wait a goddamn minute, Connor McCloud, and—no! Don't you dare kiss me again!" She shrank away. "That's a dirty trick! That's not fair!"

"I never claimed to be fair." He stared at her tender, reddened lips and realized that he was panting. Openmouthed, like an animal. He grabbed her hand and yanked her along. "Hurry."

"To what? For what? What the hell are you doing here?"

They were in the parking garage elevator well, bells were pinging, doors were about to open, and she was gathering her breath to yell at him again. He wrapped his arms around her and slid his tongue into her mouth.

A tiny squeak, and a speechless gasp, and she went limp.

So far this had gone more smoothly than his wildest hopes. The only trick would be getting himself to stop kissing her. She was so sweet. He could get lost in the sensual world of her moist, yielding mouth. He could get sucked in. Forget his own name.

He waited until the elevators emptied and the people had cleared out before he dared to release her. He cupped her face in his hands, stared into her eyes. Trying to communicate his urgency with all the force of his will. It actually seemed to work. He took her by the arm. She stumbled after him, unresisting.

He popped open his trunk, flung in her stone-heavy suitcase, and slammed it shut. "Let's go."

She wrenched herself out of his grasp. "Wait I'rr not going anywhere with you, Connor. Explain yourself to me. Right now."

Whatever spell the kiss had cast was short-lived. He backed her up against the Cadillac and boxed her in with his arms.

"I'm driving you to the coast," he said. "I'm booking us a room in a different hotel. Tomorrow I'll accompany you to that meeting. Afterwards, I'll drive you home. Any questions?"

"Connor, I told you last night I didn't want a body-guard—"

"Too bad."

She shoved against his chest. "I refuse to be pushed around. You have no right. You can't—oh!"

"Watch me." He shoved her back against the car, bending her over backwards. She blinked up at him, her chest heaving.

He knew it wasn't fair to intimidate her with his size and his strength. It didn't work in the long term anyway; it was just a quick and dirty temporary solution, but she was so warm, her tits straining against her blouse. He felt every tremor that rippled through her soft, pliant body. And her scent was a low-down, nasty trick. A drug that went straight to his head and made him stupid.

Her thick eyelashes swept down, veiling her eyes. She wiggled against him, unintentionally sensual. "Connor," she whispered. "Please. This isn't right."

"I'm holding your suitcase hostage, Erin. I mean business."

"I am not your responsibility, Connor." Her voice had a stern, lecturing tone that was strangely at odds with the vulnerable pose of her body. "You have no right. I can decide for myself—"

"I have to do this," he broke in. "You know why?"

He waited to answer his own question until her eyes flicked up to his. "Because this is what your dad would've done," he said flatly. "He had the right to shove you around, but he's not here."

Her mouth opened. Nothing came out. He seized her chin and forced her to meet his eyes again. "You've got no clue, Erin. No clue what Novak is capable of. Do we understand each other?"

She licked her lips, her throat bobbing. "But it's so rude!"

He was totally lost. "Rude? Who? Me?"

Her mouth tightened. "Yes, you, now that you mention it, but I wasn't referring to you. There's a driver waiting for me. It's rude to just not show up without even calling them!"

He was so startled, he laughed out loud. "Is that all? Who cares if Mueller's flunky waits at the airport? He won't get his feelings hurt."

She frowned. "If I had wanted to change the travel arrangements, I should've notified them in advance! I can't just—"

"So call them when we get to the coast. Tell them you had a change of plans. You met someone, you brought someone. Tell them your boyfriend decided to come along at the last minute."

"Boyfriend?" She shrank back.

"Why not?" He couldn't keep his eyes from her breasts, which were straining the buttons of her blouse to their utmost. "Don't you think they'd buy it? A woman like you, and a lowlife like me?"

She shoved him away, clearing just enough space for her to stand up. "Stop acting like a lowlife, Connor McCloud, if you don't want to be taken for one!"

"You're pissed at me because I kissed you?" His voice was dangerously unsteady. "I dared to touch the princess with my rude hands. Is that what's bothering you?"

She made a break for it, trying to duck out from under his arm. He blocked her. She straightened up, adjusted her jacket, tugged her skirt into place. She wasn't up to a physical tussle with him. She couldn't win it, and dignity was more important to her.

"To be perfectly truthful, no," she said stiffly. "That's not what's bothering me at all. It's just not very flattering to have a man kiss you only because he wants to shut you up."

He pulled that statement to pieces in an instant, looking at it from every side. Then he waited until curiosity compelled her eyes to flick up again. He stroked her exquisitely soft cheek with his thumb until the pink stain deepened to wild rose. He looked around. No one to see or hear. No reason at all to shut her up.

He kissed her again.

He wasn't sure what he expected. Maybe for her to stiffen up, shove him away. Anything but the roar of heat swelling inside him, the dazzling explosion of sparks. She clutched his upper arms; for balance, to pull him closer, he couldn't tell, he didn't care. He coaxed her mouth open. He wanted to touch that succulent pink tongue, to dance with it. He didn't mean to stick his hand inside her jacket, he just found his calluses snagging her blouse as he explored the exquisite heft of her tits, the small nipples, tightening under his palm. He had no deliberate intention of pressing the aching bulge of his crotch against her.

Jesus. What was he thinking? They were in an airport parking garage. He'd come down here to protect her.

Fucking her was not part of the plan.

He pulled away, with enormous effort. "I wasn't trying to shut you up that time," he said raggedly. "You feel flattered now?"

Chapter

6

She lifted her hand, touched her swollen mouth. She was lost in Connor's eyes. The pupils were dilated wells of deep, infinite black, bordered with pure mountain water green. She was speechless.

He wrenched the passenger side of the Cadillac open. "Get in."

Her legs weren't holding her up anyhow. She slid into the seat, boneless. The door swung shut with sharp finality. Connor got into the driver's side. He looked at her, looked away, rubbed his face. She panted, short, sharp gasps that were terribly audible in the quiet car.

"Aw, fuck it," he muttered. He slid toward her. She grabbed him and wrapped her arms around his neck so he couldn't change his mind.

They slid down the slippery leather seat, clenched together. Her fantasies didn't even come near to the raw reality of him. He was so strong and hard and solid. His mouth coaxed, then demanded. She opened to him, tasted coffee and smoke and heat. Salty and male. His tongue flicked against hers. Probed. Then thrust.

He hauled her up onto his lap so that she straddled him, and his hands slid up her thighs, shoving her skirt up around her hips. He gripped her waist and pulled her down, so that the hot, soft glow in her crotch was pressed hard against the bulge in his pants. She whimpered with excitement before she could stop herself. She'd never felt anything like this. She was melting between her legs, becoming a pool of hot syrup. A quivering glow that ached and wept for deeper contact.

And he would give it to her, here and now. She read the silent question in his eyes. If she didn't hurry up and answer it, her body would answer for her, and she would find herself having wild, public sex in the middle of a busy airport parking garage.

And maybe even liking it. Dear God.

She pushed at his chest until she was upright, but that was a mistake, because now they could both see her splayed hips, her sensible white panties pressed against his erection. He circled the tip of his finger against her mound, staring into her eyes. "Erin?"

She slid off of him and clambered to the other side of the car. Tugging her skirt down with trembling fingers, straightening her hair.

He flung his head back against the seat, clenched his fists. "I'm sorry," he said. "I swear, I didn't mean to do that."

"It's OK," she whispered. "It's not your fault."

He shot her a puzzled, ironic glance. "Whose fault is it, then?"

She shook her head and stared down at her lap.

He started up the car. "I didn't come down here to take advantage of you," he said roughly. "You need protection, Erin. I don't have any choice, and neither do you. But I promise I won't touch you again."

"There are always choices," Erin said.

"Not this time. Put on your seat belt."

The sharp authority in his voice reminded her of her father. The tone that signaled that there would be no bargaining, no back talk.

It was a mistake to think of her father. She strapped herself in, making herself small on the seat. Her mouth felt puffy. She peeked in the mirror and gasped in dismay. Her hair was falling down, her face was rosy red, and her mouth . . . it didn't even look like her mouth.

Connor flipped on the radio, turned the dial until he found some classic blues. "Change it if you want."

"This is fine." That was all she managed to say to him.

She just sat there, squeezing her quivering thighs tightly around the hot ache. Her panties were wet. She wanted to stop at the first hotel, drag him into it, and make him finish what he'd started. She wanted to jump out of the car and run screaming. She'd been split into pieces, and each piece wanted something different.

She peeked at his grim profile, and the images that rose up in her mind made her blush again. Herself naked against his long, hard body, limbs entwined. She thought of the unyielding bulk of his erection pressing against her panties. Imagined him penetrating her. Her breath hitched in her chest. She felt almost faint, her heart raced so hard.

She was so sick of celibacy. She was almost twenty-seven, away from home, and climbing the walls. No one would ever know if she did something so crazy as to have sex with Connor McCloud.

At least she wasn't a virgin, although Bradley hardly counted. Ironically enough, the main reason she'd been attracted to Bradley in the first place was because he bore a superficial resemblance to Connor. He was tall, lean, blond. Just graduated from Princeton, already accepted at Harvard Law. He'd been sharp and witty, had made her laugh. And he had persuaded her that he was the perfect stud to relieve her of the crushing burden of her virginity.

The memory unrolled in her mind no matter how she pushed it away. She had felt absolutely nothing when they finally did the deed. Just embarrassment, at the appraising comments he had made about her body, and in bed, an uncomfortable sense of being invaded. A powerful urge to shove him off, which she had controlled. After all, she had agreed to all that intimacy. Bradley didn't deserve to be shoved.

But she had felt so bleak and alone staring up at his face. His eyes squeezed shut, his teeth clenched in a grimace, lost in his own world as his hips pumped into her more or less numb body.

Afterwards he'd been so pleased with himself. Don't worry, he told her. She'd get the hang of it soon, and he'd give her lots of opportunities to practice. First item on the lesson plan: fellatio. Bradley thought it was a huge joke that she'd reached the ripe old age of twenty-one without ever having given head. "It's time, babe, it's definitely time," he'd said. "Let's get some pizza. As soon as I recover you can embark on your maiden voyage. I'm a great teacher, believe me."

She had excused herself and gone home before he recovered, afflicted by lingering sadness. After all the buildup, that was all?

She knew objectively, both from Bradley's own proud assertions as well as what she had read in romance novels and erotica, that Bradley wasn't technically a bad lover. He'd done everything he could think of to give her an orgasm; he'd paid careful attention to her breasts, which just felt irritated and ticklish at his touch, though she had feigned enjoyment. He'd stimulated her between her legs. But he hadn't concealed his impatience when she was slow to respond.

Finally one night, he'd flopped over onto his back and told her that if even he couldn't get her off, then she was one hurting puppy. Sorry, babe. Face the facts. The truth will set you free. She was a lousy lay. A tab of Ecstasy might loosen her up. Did she want to give it a try?

She hadn't. He'd gone off to Harvard and never called her again, to her relief. And her mother's disappointment.

Knowing for a fact that she was bad at sex had made it hard to contemplate trying again. She cringed at the thought of risking that empty, shamed sense of failure again. It was easier to throw herself into her research. That was something she knew for sure she was good at.

She'd almost convinced herself that she was fine alone when she found out about the deadly trap that Connor had fallen into. He and Jesse had been following a lead on Novak. Connor had been boarding a boat when it blew up and flung him into the icy waters of the Sound. He'd been burned, his leg smashed. By the time help arrived and fished him out, he was in a coma. And Jesse had been murdered.

She'd faced the truth, then, in one hard, horrible blow. She loved Connor McCloud. She wanted him, and only him. It had been no hardship to go to the clinic to read to him. The hard part had been to leave him every day, so still and quiet.

When he woke up, she'd been dizzy with joy, but she'd still hesitated to declare herself. It seemed hardly fair to inflict her adolescent yearnings on a man who was dazed with shock and grief, in severe physical pain. Weeks had gone by. Her resolve had faltered. The weeks had turned to months, and then Crystal Mountain had happened. Novak, Georg, Dad, and Connor, and a violent tornado of revenge and betrayal that had blown her whole life to pieces.

She'd been trying ever since to put it behind her, but she hadn't anticipated getting a chance like this, to find out once and for all if her erotic fantasies about Connor had any basis in reality. No one would ever know unless she told them, and she would never tell. She would hug this secret close to herself, precious and painful to the same degree. The one time that busy, sensible, practical Erin Riggs gave in to folly and did something wild and crazy.

She sneaked a glance at his profile again. He caught her doing it, and she looked away, color flaring in her face.

Connor's kisses alone turned her on more than anything that Bradley had ever done.

Her life felt so cold and bleak. His heat was irresistible.

Connor checked the directions before he pulled off the highway. He didn't trust himself at all today, not even his ironclad memory. He wasn't sure what scared him more: losing control and jumping all over a woman uninvited, or her response. She'd grabbed him, kissed him. Melted against him, red-hot and willing, just like his wildest fantasies.

Guarding her, that was what he was signed up for. Seducing her was out of the question. She would end up hating him for it, and he would deserve it. Even he wasn't capable of that much self-delusion. He could see how it would look to Nick's eyes. Connor goes to a lonely, vulnerable girl's apartment at night, tells her the bad guys are out to get her. Then he kidnaps her, bullies her, sequesters her suitcase, sticks his tongue down her throat, gropes her tits, shoves up her skirt. He'd been a heartbeat away from laying her out on the hood of his car and having at her, in front of God and everyone.

What a fucking hero.

She was huddled as far away from him on the seat as she could get, her fingers hiding her rosy, reddened lips. Probably wondering if he was going to leap on her like a wild animal.

"Almost there," he said.

Her face was pale gold again, except for faint rosy stains high on her delicate cheekbones. She nodded and looked swiftly away.

He pulled into the parking lot of the Crow's Nest Inn. It was a rustic place, covered with weathered gray shingles. Each of the rooms had a deck with an ocean view. He'd stayed here a few years back on a road trip, and had liked the place. "It's not as fancy as the millionaire's resort hotel," he told her. "But at least here you're on your own turf."

She got out of the car. "I'm on your turf, Connor. Not mine."

Her uppity tone stung him. "Do you think I'm making this stuff up, Erin?" he demanded.

Somehow she looked down her nose at him even though he was a head taller than she. "It's impossible for me to believe that Claude Mueller could have anything to do with Novak. Four times I've gone out on consulting jobs for him. Every time I've been treated with courtesy and respect. Which is more than I've gotten from anyone else lately."

"Like me?" he demanded.

"Yes, you," she said haughtily. "I didn't ask for your help. The only reason I am allowing you to force it on me is because I genuinely appreciate your concern, and—"

"Gee, thanks," he growled.

"—and I believe that it is sincere, *if* completely unnecessary—"

"Unnecessary, my ass!"

"—and I insist that you stop yelling. It's embarrassing."

He glanced around. She was right. People were gawking.

The next challenge to his self-control proved to be the check-in clerk, a gangly, pimpled kid who was hot to do his promotional spiel.

"A double room is eighty-five, but the Crow's Nest Suite is available. It's got a king-sized bed and a Jacuzzi," he informed them. "It's ten dollars more than the double, and we offer a complimentary—"

Connor slapped down two fifties. "Give me a room with two double beds," he said curtly. "Non-smoking."

The kid's spotted forehead furrowed in perplexity. "But the Crow's Nest Suite is only ten dollars more. Don't you want the Jacuzzi?"

He pictured Erin in a Jacuzzi, her dark hair spread out like a lily pad. Then, rising out of the water in a soft-focus cloud of steam, her hair clinging to every curve and contour of her flushed body, her skin beaded with drops of water, her breasts—

"No, I do *not* want the goddamn Jacuzzi," he snarled.

The kid jerked away from the counter at his tone.

Erin followed him to the elevator after he filled out the forms. Her eyes were downcast, her lashes casting fanlike shadows on her cheeks. It drove him nuts that he couldn't tell what she was thinking.

It was a nice room, large and fresh smelling, with a picture window and deck overlooking the beach. He bolted the door behind them, and mounted one of the squealers Seth had given him onto the door. Erin drifted over to the window and stared down at the sea foam pulsing over the gleaming sand. Seagulls strutted on it, as big as geese, leaving delicate tracks that washed away with every wave.

He stared at her back. She had such a proud way of holding her head, her back elegantly straight. Like a princess. Gleaming locks of loosened hair dangled below her chin. His body cramped with lust.

It was hard to believe that mind-blowing kiss in the parking garage had really happened. Here, staring at her upright dark silhouette against the gray ocean, the memory had the feel of a wishful dream.

"Uh, sorry you have to share a room with me," he said gruffly. "But if I'm going to guard you, I have to—"

"Of course," she said, cool as a cucumber.

He floundered on. "Look. I really don't intend to take advantage of the situation. What happened at the airport, I, uh . . . just lost my head. But it won't happen again."

"It's all right. Please don't give it another thought." She gave him a brief, dismissive smile, the equivalent of a pat on the head to calm down an overeager dog. She turned back to the window.

The subject was definitively closed.

He gritted his teeth. This had seemed so straightforward

back in Seattle. Now he felt like he was walking a tightrope over boiling lava.

He needed a smoke. He sat down on a bed and pulled out his stash. When he finished rolling the cigarette, she was watching him, her expression disapproving.

"It's a non-smoking room," she reminded him.

"Yeah, I know. I'll smoke it out on the deck," he told her.

Her dark eyebrows flicked together. "It's raining out there," she said. "And you must know those are terribly bad for you."

He grunted, and flicked open the lock on the sliding door. The wind off the ocean hit him like a slap. His coat billowed and snapped around his legs. The near impossibility of getting a cigarette lit under those conditions was a welcome challenge.

Anything to distract him from the way she had of putting him right in his place. One more of those regal, intergalactic-princess looks from her, and he would be ready to sit, lie down, roll over, and beg.

Don't give it another thought, his ass. He could almost laugh.

Like anything in life was ever that easy.

Erin hugged herself as she stared out the window. Connor cupped his hand against the wind and lit his cigarette after a few tries. He draped himself across the weathered wooden banister as he smoked it, scowling to the right and the left as if expecting attack from every side.

Oh, God, he was handsome. Everything about him was sexy. Even the way he smoked was sexy, and she deplored smoking. She wanted to snoop through the battered duffel he had flung on the bed. She wanted to see what toothpaste he used, to smell his shirts, to peek at the picture on his driver's license. She was out of her mind.

So he didn't intend to take advantage of the situation.

Well, then. Too bad for him. She would just have to take advantage of the situation herself. He was all alone with her. At her mercy. If that kiss in the car was any indication, he probably wouldn't object too strenuously to being used for sex. Her girlfriends had told her that men usually didn't.

Yes. Using him for sex. That was the only way to do this and come out of it intact. She had to use him before he could use her. She had to stay detached, keep the upper hand. Calm, cool, no big deal. Happened every day. Her girlfriends boasted about it.

Oh, God. Her head spun, and she sat down hard on the bed.

How could she be calm? She was scared to death. Bradley had told her she was as frigid as Greenland's icy mountains. But frigid meant that you didn't want sex, and that certainly wasn't her case. She wanted Connor so badly, she was frozen with fear.

But then again, wasn't that what frigid literally meant? Frozen. No matter what the cause, the end result was the same. Maybe they would both be in for a painful disappointment.

The sight of her organizer sticking out of her purse gave her an unpleasant shock. She'd gotten so carried away thinking about sex, she'd forgotten the purpose of her trip. She should take advantage of this moment alone to conduct some damage control. She flipped open her organizer, dialed the Silver Fork Resort and asked for Nigel Dobbs.

"Hello?" came Dobbs's clipped, snooty voice.

"Mr. Dobbs? This is Erin Riggs."

"Ms. Riggs! At last! We were quite worried about you."

"I appreciate your concern, and I'm so sorry I didn't have a chance to call and . . ." Her voice trailed off. Connor slid the glass door open with a resounding thud and stalked in, leaving it wide open. He stood inches in front of her, glaring. Cold, wet salt air swirled around him.

"Hello? Hello? Ms. Riggs, are you still there?"

"Ah, yes, I am. Excuse me. It must be a bad connection," she said hastily. "Ah, I'm so sorry. I'm, ah . . ."

"Are you all right? Are you in some kind of trouble?"

Oh, you have no idea. "Not at all," she assured him. "I'm fine."

"Do you need someone to come and pick you up?"

"No, thank you. That's why I called. I wanted to apologize for not notifying you in time to stop the driver from going to the airport in Portland. I had a change of plans and—"

"Tell them your boyfriend came along," Connor said.

She stared up at him, mouth working uselessly.

Dobbs's impatient sigh was audible. "Ms. Riggs? Do you intend to inform me of the nature of your change of plans at some point?"

She swallowed hard. "My . . . my boyfriend came along."

There was a long silence. "I see."

"He met up with me in Portland, and gave me a ride, and we've already checked into another hotel, so I—"

"Then I take it you will be unable to dine with Mr. Mueller. He will be very disappointed. Mr. Mueller's time is in extremely high demand."

"But I didn't know Mr. Mueller was going to be at the hotel this evening," she faltered. "I thought he was arriving very late tonight!"

"He changed his plans when he received your e-mail." Dobbs's voice was gelid. "He is arriving this afternoon. What a pity, hmm?"

Erin closed her eyes and mouthed a silent curse. "Well, um . . . maybe I can—"

"No." Connor's voice was hard and carrying. "No way. No dinner with that guy tonight. Forget it."

Nigel Dobbs coughed. "Ahem. Perhaps it would be for the best if you resolved your personal problems at a safe distance. I will inform Mr. Mueller of your change of plans when he arrives."

"Thank you," she said miserably.

"And should Mr. Mueller risk using your professional services another time, I would consider it a tremendous favor if you would give us prior notice of these changes. Mr. Mueller took an earlier flight from Paris expressly for the purpose of dining with you. If you had called to tell us of your change of plans, I would have advised you of this."

"Oh, God," she murmured. "I'm so sorry."

"I will send the car for you tomorrow. What is your address?"

She groped for the notepad by the phone. "Just a moment. It's on the stationery—"

She squeaked as Connor wrenched the phone out of her hand and blocked the receiver. "Don't give him the address," he said.

"Connor!" She lunged for the phone.

He held it out of her reach. "I will drive you to the resort tomorrow. Start to give him the address, and I rip the phone out of the wall." He wrapped his fingers around the cord and narrowed his eyes. "Nod, Erin. Show me that we understand each other."

She nodded. He handed the phone back. "Mr. Dobbs? I'd rather not put your driver to the trouble—"

"It's no trouble, Ms. Riggs."

"Really, it's fine. We'll drive ourselves to the resort."

"If you insist. When shall we expect you? Would eleven be acceptable? That way Mr. Mueller can rest."

"Eleven would be fine," she said. "And please give my apologies to Mr. Mueller. I truly didn't mean to—"

"Yes, yes, of course," Dobbs snapped. "Good evening."

Erin hung up the phone. She felt sick. Her stomach was clenched up tight with dismay. She pressed her shaking hand against it.

She took a deep, shuddering breath and stood up, facing him down. "Connor," she said. "That was beyond paranoid. That was my most valuable client. Are you deliberately trying to sabotage me?"

He shrugged. "You were about to tell that guy the address. Which cancels out any advantage that coming here might have given you."

She stalked over to the window and slid it violently shut. "And what possessed you to make me say that you were my boyfriend?"

"It draws less attention than saying I'm your bodyguard. It explains why I stick to you like a burr and give dirty looks to any man who gets near you. It's the standard jealous boyfriend act. Most women have dumped at least one of those losers and then put out a restraining order on him."

"I never have," she snapped.

"Don't worry, Erin. I was an undercover cop for nine years. I'm a good actor. You're not required to fuck me to make it convincing."

Her jaw dropped at his crude words. "Oh! Thank you, Connor! I am so comforted and reassured by that thoughtful remark!"

"I'm not aiming to reassure you," he retorted.

"That's pretty damn obvious!" she yelled back. "Do you have any idea how bad this makes me look? Mueller took an earlier flight from Paris specifically to meet with me tonight!"

"Oh, God, no." His face was a caricature of dismay. "The disappointed billionaire, eating his caviar all alone in the flickering candlelight. Poor Claude. You're breaking my heart."

She lifted her chin. "That's it." She grabbed her suitcase. "I was wrong to humor you. You have no respect for my work, and you are completely out of your mind. I am leaving—oof!"

He spun her around. "You're not going anywhere."

"Yes, I am." She backed away, but he was gripping her shoulders. "I've had enough of your—Connor!" The world tipped and spun, and she landed on the bed, bouncing. The bouncing stopped when he landed on top of her, pinning her down with his big, hard body.

"No," he said calmly, as if lying on top of her were no big deal. "You're not going anywhere, Erin."

She forced herself to close her mouth. Her heart thudded so hard, she was sure he could feel it against his chest. She struggled beneath his solid weight, and the movement felt . . . sensual.

She went motionless. "Connor. Don't," she whispered.

He cupped her face in his big hands. "Novak should've been taken out back when we had a chance. Same with Georg. I should've finished him off, but I let the system take care of him. Which was stupid, because the system is rotten with holes. Jesse fell through one of them and died. I fell through another one. I'm alive out of sheer, dumb luck. Novak and Georg escaped out of another hole. Are you following me?"

She gave him a tiny nod.

"I'm not going to let you fall through one of those holes, Erin. I won't leave you alone. I won't disappear. Is that understood?"

She dragged in another tiny breath. "Can't breathe."

He lifted himself up onto his elbows, still pinning her. "Let me tell you something about Kurt Novak."

She shook her head. "Please, don't. I don't want to think about—"

"Tough shit. Look at me."

She winced, and slowly, reluctantly met his gaze.

"His dad is a big guy in the Eastern European *mafiya*. Hungarian. Probably one of the richest men in the world. He arranged to send his boy to college in the States. I imagine the plan was to groom him to go legit, to broaden the power base, but Kurt, well, he was kind of a funny guy. Weird things started to happen at the dorm. It culminated in a girl getting strangled to death during sex."

Erin squeezed her eyes shut. "Connor, I don't—"

"Lucky for our boy Kurt, this girl wasn't rich, or the daughter of a politician or a general. Her mom was a widowed research librarian who didn't have the resources to fight the big fight. Or maybe it wasn't luck, maybe Kurt thought it through, at the tender age of nineteen. The thing was hushed up and paid off, and Kurt gets whisked back to Europe, to recover from the unpleasantness on the ski slopes of the Alps."

She turned her face away, but his hand forced it back until she met his eyes again. "Look at me when I talk to you, Erin."

How dare he order her. She wanted to say something sharp to put him in his place, but the intensity of his eyes wiped her mind blank.

"Do you know, if a normal, well-behaved dog starts to chase sheep and brings one down, he'll never stop. He can't forget the thrill, the taste of blood in his mouth."

"No. I didn't know that," she whispered.

"Well, why would you? You're a city girl. But anyhow, the dog has an excuse. He's just reverting back to what nature originally programmed him to do. But Novak, he discovered his true passion in life that night. Murdering young women is an expensive vice for him, like fine cocaine. Or collecting priceless Celtic artifacts."

She shook her head. "It's not possible, Connor. Mueller is—"

"Do you see why I'm freaked out by this? Please, Erin. Tell me that at least one person gets it. I'm dangling all alone out here. There's a guy loose who gets off on snuffing beautiful girls, and he knows your name. Tell me I have a right to be nervous for you!"

The desperate appeal in his voice made her want to put her arms around him and agree to anything, if only it would make him feel better. She stopped herself just in time. A nervous giggle escaped her. "I'm not such a prize. Novak could do better than me in the beauty department."

He looked incredulous. "Huh?"

"Cindy's the beauty, Erin's the brain," she babbled. "That's what my mother always says. It never occurs to her that it makes Cindy feel stupid and me feel ugly. But she means well. She always means well."

He frowned. "You are kidding, right? Tell me you're kidding."

She bit her lip. Her eyes slid away from his.

"Jesus," he said. "You are gorgeous. You must know that."

Color flooded into her face. "Please don't be ridiculous."

"I'm not the ridiculous one." He shifted so that his leg lay between hers. Her skirt was shoved up practically to her bottom.

"Connor." She stopped, and tried to calm the quiver in her voice. "Don't tell me any more about Novak. I don't want to dwell on violence and evil. I'm trying to think positively. I don't want to know."

"You can't run away from the truth."

She shoved at his chest. "I've faced enough ugly truths!"

"You don't get to decide when it's enough," he said. "None of us gets to decide. You can't control it. Ever."

"I can try," she snapped.

"Sure, you can try. But you'll just hurt yourself."

The bleak look in his eyes made the words she had wanted to say evaporate. Her chest was heaving, as if she'd been running.

"Please, Erin." His voice was low, impassioned. "I'll try to behave. I won't ruin your life. Just play along with me. Let me do my thing."

All this protective intensity, all for her. Yearning twisted her heart.

Connor had faced a lot of harsh truths, and he was still fighting. Still trying heroically to do the right thing. She wanted to grab him and say, *Oh yes. Save me from the big bad world. And while you're at it, kiss me senseless. And for God's sake, don't stop there.*

She gathered up every last scrap of her self-control. "Um,

maybe I could be more lucid and reasonable about all this if you weren't lying on top of me, squashing me flat and ruining my suit. Do you mind?"

His face tightened. He lifted himself off of her instantly.

She kicked off the shoe that still clung to her foot, sat up, and curled her legs up beneath her. Connor hunched on the edge of the bed with his back to her. Silently waiting.

Her dream flashed through her mind: the way he followed her with such stubborn patience. Never losing sight of her, never giving up. She wanted to drape herself across his broad shoulders and hug him.

The decision made itself, sudden and irrevocable. "OK," she said.

He turned his head, his eyes wary. "OK, what?"

"OK, you can do your thing. If you're serious about trying not to ruin my life, that is. And, um . . . thank you for caring."

He stared at her for a moment. "You're welcome."

His eyes flicked down over her body. Heat bloomed between her legs again, and she squeezed her thighs together and tried to smooth her hair back. Her blouse was disheveled. He watched her straighten and button and tuck with intense fascination. The longer the silence stretched, the more fraught with meaning it became.

"So?" She shot for a cheerful, let's-move-on sort of smile, but had no idea if she hit anywhere close to the mark. "Now what?"

He glanced down at his watch. "You hungry?"

She had been too worked up to think food, but all she'd eaten all day was a pecan sticky bun. "I could eat something," she admitted.

"Let's go to the restaurant downstairs. It's got excellent seafood."

"OK. I'll, um, just pop into the bathroom and freshen up."

She was too flustered to pick out what she needed while he watched. She just grabbed the whole suitcase and lugged it into the bathroom. She closed the lid on the toilet, sat down and doubled over, shaking with a silent combination of laughter and tears.

It was impossible, planning a seduction under these conditions.

Chapter

7

Connor dropped his face into his hands and listened to the water rushing in the sink. He was in deep trouble. Everything about her challenged and aroused him. He wanted to make that practical façade of hers dissolve into molten heat, to hear that cool, sensible voice sobbing with pleasure. Begging for more.

The bathroom door opened and Erin stepped out. She'd changed into a simple white blouse and a denim skirt that hit her just above her cute, dimpled knees. She laid her suit out on the bed. "This needs to be ironed," she murmured. "I'll, ah, steam it later."

Her face was flushed and dewy. She'd woven her hair into a loose, swinging braid that reached the small of her back, and she'd reapplied some lip gloss that highlighted the shape of her full, sensual lips.

Lip gloss was diabolical stuff, calculated to make a guy think about sex. Moist, lush lips, ready for kissing, for licking, for—

Whoa. Down, boy. He looked away quickly, rubbed his face.

"Are you all right?" she asked. "You look a bit strange."

He transformed a harsh laugh into a cough. "Headache," he lied.

"Would you like a painkiller? I've got Excedrin, Advil, and Tylenol."

"I just need some dinner, that's all."

"You're sure?" She looked disappointed, that she couldn't solve his problem with one of her pills. How innocent. Solving his problem would be a much bigger job than that. It would involve a long, sweaty night in the saddle, taking him from above, from below, from the back. Deep and hard and prolonged.

Come to think of it, it would probably take more than one night.

"Well, then. Let's go get you something to eat," she said briskly. "You probably just have low blood sugar."

"Yeah, that must be it." He stuck his hand in the pocket of his chinos and tented it out to give his boner some privacy as he disabled the squealer. He played it very cool in the elevator, keeping his dick jammed against his thigh. Once they were seated, had checked out the menu and discussed the relative merits of stuffed or deep-fried prawns, and pan-fried oysters versus au gratin, the conversation lagged.

Erin finally took matters into her own hands. "Connor, if I ask you a question, do you promise not to get mad?"

"Nope," he told her. "I can't promise anything of the kind, if I don't know what you're asking."

Her lips tightened. She ripped open a bag of oyster crackers and nibbled on them.

He couldn't stand it any more. "OK, fine. Now I'm curious," he said. "You have to tell me now, whether I get mad or not. Out with it."

"I just wanted to know about Claude Mueller." Her gaze flicked up, delicately cautious. "Did you, um . . . do a background check?"

"My brother Davy ran a check, yeah," he admitted. He braced himself for the lecture.

She just waited, expectant. "And?"

"And what?"

"Tell me what he found. I don't know much about Mueller, either."

"There's not a lot to tell," he said. "He looks fine on paper. He's got a sickening amount of money. He donates to the arts. He doesn't get out much. He buys lots of museum quality antiquities."

She looked puzzled. "So even though he checks out, you still—"

"On paper is not good enough! You've never seen this guy, Erin!"

"Keep your voice down, please." She reached across the table and touched the back of his hand with her fingertip, light and soothing. Like a kiss. "I was just curious. Please don't get all wound up again."

"I am not all wound up," he snarled.

At that fortuitous moment, his steak and prawns and Erin's pan-fried oysters arrived. He was fascinated with her perfect table manners: dabbity-dab with the napkin after every tidy bite. The quintessential good girl. Out of nowhere, he pictured himself crawling under the table. Spreading her legs wide, and pushing aside the gusset of her white cotton panties. Burying his face between her thighs, his tongue licking, lashing, probing, all while she tried to keep her cool and eat her dinner like nothing was out of the ordinary. Oh, yeah. What a perverse, sicko fantasy. It made his mouth water and his cock throb.

"What's the matter?" she asked. "Don't you like your meal?"

Nah, just want to dip you in drawn butter like a juicy prawn and then lick you all over. "I'm fine," he muttered. "Food's great."

She eyed him as she chewed another careful bite. "So, your brother Davy. Is he in law enforcement as well?"

He sliced off a chunk of steak. "Private investigator," he corrected.

"Older or younger?"

"Two years older."

"Do you have any other brothers or sisters?"

"Another brother, four years younger. Sean is his name."

"And where is your family from?" she inquired politely.

He hesitated, a fried prawn halfway to his mouth. "How much do you know about my family?" he asked. "Did Ed ever talk about me?"

Her eyes slid away from his, and her color deepened. "Sometimes," she said. "He had theories about all of his colleagues, and he talked about them with Mom. But he never talked about them with me. I just overheard. Or eavesdropped, I suppose I should say."

"So what was his theory about me?"

She looked trapped. "Um . . . once I heard him say that the reason you were so good undercover was because you'd been undercover all your life. But I never knew what he meant by that. And when I asked him, he told me it was none of my damn business."

He started to grin. "You asked him about me?"

Her eyelashes swept down. She cut an oyster into perfect quarters and daintily ate one. "I was curious. What did he mean, anyway?"

He stared down at his steak. "Well, uh, it's a long story."

She popped another oyster quarter into her lush, sexy mouth and gave him an encouraging smile.

He took a swig of beer and groped around for a logical beginning place. "Well . . . my mom died when I was eight, and Davy was ten—"

Her fork clattered onto her plate. "Oh, my God, I'm sorry," she said. "How awful for you."

"Yeah, it was bad," he admitted. "The twins were only four—"

"Twins?" Her eyes widened. "You didn't mention twins."

"I used to have three brothers," he explained. "Sean had a twin. His name was Kevin. He died ten years ago. Ran his truck off a cliff."

Her eyes widened in horrified dismay. She lifted her napkin to her mouth. "God, Connor. I didn't mean to bring back painful memories."

"And I didn't mean to freak you out with a Shakespearean tragedy, either," he said grimly. "I started out wrong. Sorry. Rewind. Let me try this again. So Dad and the four of us lived way out in the hills behind Endicott Falls. Don't know if you're familiar with the area."

She nodded. "I know Endicott Falls. Cindy goes to college there."

"I see. So anyhow, when Mom died, my dad went kind of nuts. He was a Vietnam vet, and I don't think the war experience did a lot for his mental stability to begin with. But when he lost her, he lost his grip. He home-schooled us, since the school bus didn't get within twenty miles of our place. Dad's curriculum was very . . . personalized."

He stopped, surprised. Usually he avoided talking about his strange childhood. The inevitable stupid questions and snap judgments irritated him. But the glow of interest in Erin's eyes made it easier.

"Dad was convinced that the end of civilization was at hand," he went on. "He was preparing us for the breakdown of the world order. So, along with reading and writing and math, it was hand-to-hand combat, social and political history, gardening, hunting, tracking. We learned how to build a lethal bomb out of ordinary stuff. How to dry meat, tan skins, eat grubs, sew up a wound. Everything a guy might need to know after the crash. Survival in the midst of anarchy."

"That's amazing," she said.

He dug into his steak. "A social worker came out to check on us once. Dad hid us in the woods, told her he'd sent us to live with his folks in upstate New York. Then he told her what was in store for her after the crash. Traumatized the poor woman. She ran away."

"What did you and your brothers think of all this?"

He shrugged. "Dad was a charismatic guy. Very convincing. And we were so isolated, no TV, no radio. Dad didn't want us brainwashed by mass media. For a long time we bought the whole story. But then Davy decided he wanted to go to high school. Told Dad he was going on a recon mission into enemy territory, but he was just desperate to meet some girls." He smiled at the memory; then his smile faded. "That was close to the end for Dad. He had a stroke later that year."

She reached across the table and placed her hand on his. Electricity sparked, and she jerked her hand back with a soft murmur.

He stared down at his hand, wishing she had left hers on top of it. "That's probably what Ed was referring to," he said. "Blending in, after growing up on another planet. You learn survival skills quick."

"So what happened when your father died?" she asked.

"We buried him out there on the land. I don't think that's legal, but we didn't know that. Davy got a job at the mill. We stuck together until I got through high school, and then Davy joined the Navy and I took over at the mill." He shrugged. "We got on with it."

"How old were you when he died?"

"Davy was eighteen, I was sixteen. Kevin and Sean were twelve."

Erin bit her lip. She was getting teary-eyed. It alarmed him.

"Look, you don't have to feel sorry for me," he assured her. "It was a strange way to grow up, but not a bad one. It was a beautiful place. I had my brothers for company. I don't regret learning what Dad taught us. If Mom hadn't died, I would've called myself lucky."

She mopped her eyes, a quick, furtive gesture, and smiled at him. "What was she like?" she asked.

He thought about it for a moment. "I was really small when she died," he said. "I've lost a lot of details. But I remember her laughing. My dad was a silent, moody type, but she could make him laugh. She was the only one who could. After she died, he never laughed again."

"How did she . . ." Her voice trailed off. "Uh, sorry," she murmured. "Never mind. I didn't mean to—"

"Tubal pregnancy," he said. "We were too far from the hospital. It was January. Three feet of snow. She bled to death."

She looked down and lifted her napkin to her mouth.

"I'm OK," he said helplessly. Christ, he hadn't meant to make her cry. "Don't get all worked up. It was almost thirty years ago."

She sniffed, and looked up at him with a soggy, embarrassed laugh. Her golden brown eyes were swimming with tears.

He didn't decide to do it, it just happened. He reached out to touch the fine-textured skin of her cheek, capturing the tear on his finger. He lifted his hand to his lips and tasted it.

A salty drop of distilled compassion.

The hunger simmering in his body roared up into something huge. She swayed away from him, her tear-bright eyes wide with feminine caution. There was a clatter, a spreading wetness. His hands had clenched on the tablecloth, knocking over a long-stemmed water glass. "Whoa," he muttered. He threw his napkin on top of the puddle. "Sorry about that."

"It's all right," she whispered.

They took a time-out, concentrating on the food left on their plates. Forks clinking in the heavy silence made him think of his father. Eamon McCloud had not tolerated frivolous chatter at the table. He had believed in keeping your mouth shut unless you had something relevant to say. Davy was almost as taciturn as Dad had been, but that mandatory silence had been pure hell on Sean, the born chatterbox.

But Erin hadn't been raised by Eamon McCloud. She

didn't know how to cope with enormous silences like he did. She took a deep breath and tried again. "So, what are your brothers like?" she asked brightly.

Her determination made him smile. "They're unique."

"I don't doubt it," she said fervently. "Are they married?"

"No," he said. "Davy was married once, back when he was in the service. We only knew about it because he got drunk one night and told us in a moment of weakness. She made a big impression on him, though. He doesn't want another wife ever again. Davy never learned how to have fun. He had little brothers to look after when he should've been out raising hell, and as soon as I was old enough to look after Sean and Kevin, he got shipped out to the Persian Gulf. The world according to Davy is a grim, dangerous place."

"And Sean?" she prompted. "What's he like?"

Connor smiled. "The polar opposite of Davy. He's a basket case, but in a good way. He's got a wild streak, and he's too handsome for his own good. A chick magnet since he was thirteen. Incredibly smart, like Davy, but he's got some problems with impulse control. And he gets into serious trouble when he's bored. The world according to Sean is a big playground, and everything in it is a joke. What are you smiling at?"

"You," she said. "I can see how much you love your brothers from the way you describe them."

He stared down at his plate, wondering what the hell a guy was supposed to say after a comment like that.

Erin propped her elbows on the table and steepled her fingers together under her chin. "So if the world according to Davy is grim and dangerous, and the world according to Sean is a playground, then what's the world according to Connor?"

He finished off the last swallow of beer, his eyes fixed on her lush, gleaming lips. "The vote's not in on that yet."

The waitress arrived and started collecting their dishes. "The special dessert tonight is fresh baked Dutch apple pie with homemade vanilla ice cream," she informed them.

They looked at each other. "Go for it," Connor said.

"Only if you do," she replied.

Connor grinned at the waitress. "Two," he said.

The pie proved to be delicious. The apples were tangy and sweet and buttery, the crust was crisp and crumbling, blending with the melting ice cream into a goopy, fabulous mess.

Erin closed her eyes and moaned with pleasure every time she puckered her beautiful lips around the dessert spoon, sucking it so it came out of her mouth hot and shiny clean, polished. Everything about her was turning him on, every little innocuous thing.

And it was going to get worse. He was going to see her in her nightgown. He was going to watch her sleep. See her tousled and sleep-flushed in the morning. He was going to press his face into her sheets when she went into the bathroom. Inhale her scent, absorb her warmth as he pictured the water streaming down over her soft, curvy body.

His head might explode before dawn, to say nothing of his balls.

The only solution was to escape into the shower and spend a minute or two trying to relieve the pressure with his fist.

Erin peeked at him in the elevator, daunted by the grim look on his face. Her decision to seduce Connor McCloud was signed and sealed but the actual execution of the seduction was still a scary question mark. She'd thought to make some progress when he opened up about his family, but when she started bawling like a ninny, he clammed right up again. Just thinking about his mother made her throat tighten up.

He looked tense, almost angry, a muscle pulsing in his jaw. He preceded her to the door, gestured for her to wait, and pulled out a gun from the back of his chinos. He checked the room before he let her come in, and silently reattached the weird devices onto the door and window.

"What are those?" she asked.

"Alarms. I got them from my friend Seth. He calls them squealers."

"What a fortress," she murmured.

His eyes hardened. "They can't hurt." He flipped a switch, and a tiny red light on the device attached to the window began to blink.

She felt so shy. She would never work up the courage to come on to him when he looked so fierce.

He threw his coat on the bed. "Do you need the bathroom for the next few minutes? I want to take a quick shower."

"Go ahead," she said.

He disappeared into the bathroom. She listened to the water run. He hadn't locked the bathroom door. If she really were a bold, naughty seductress, she would just shuck her clothes and join him.

And then? She had all kinds of fantasies, but so little practical experience. The shower pounded, like the rain that pounded against the picture window, the surf that pounded on the beach below. She buried her face in her hands and moaned in frustration. His big, gorgeous body was stark naked and soaking wet in there. And she was sitting out here.

A few minutes later Connor came out, dressed in jeans and a T-shirt, his hair tangled around his shoulders. He rummaged through his duffel, pulling out a fine-tooth comb with at least a third of the teeth missing. He dragged it through his hair. Erin flinched in protest at the sound of hairs stretching and snapping. "Ouch! Stop that!"

He looked startled. "Stop what?"

"Stop torturing your hair! You'll ruin it!"

He gave her a doubtful look. "Uh, my hair is used to it, Erin."

She shook her finger at him. "You have dry, split ends because you stretch it and break it with that awful comb. I've had long hair all my life. I know how to treat long hair. And how not to."

"But it's tangled. What am I supposed to do? Leave it in dreads?"

"Have you ever seen a hair conditioner commercial on TV?"

"I never did get into the habit of watching TV," he admitted.

She slid off the bed and unzipped her suitcase. "You need a deep conditioning pack. And you're in luck, because I've got some with me."

His eyes narrowed. "Uh, Erin. I don't know how to tell you this, but I'm really not the deep conditioning pack type."

"Then it stands to reason that you're not the long hair type, either," she said. "Want me to cut it short? I brought my good scissors."

"Oh, God," he muttered.

"Choose," she said briskly. "One or the other."

He took a step back. "You're scaring me."

She pulled her toiletries case out of the suitcase. "Don't be afraid, Connor. Just give in. You can't control everything, remember? You'll just hurt yourself." She pulled the scissors out with a flourish. "Voila!"

"That's not fair. Don't throw my words back in my face."

"Oh, don't be silly." She felt more centered now that she had a goal to accomplish. It let her natural bossiness spring to the fore. "Putting goop on your hair will only make it softer and shinier. It will have no discernible effect upon your virility."

"Promise?" he said.

"Yes," she said rashly. "I promise."

There was a hot flash in his eyes. "Want to put it to the test?"

The scissors dropped from her suddenly numb fingers

and thumped onto the bed. *Yes*, she wanted to say, *let's test it right now*.

The words wouldn't come out. The silence just got heavier.

He broke eye contact. "Sorry," he said. "Forget I said that."

He sat down on the bed. She stared at his broad back, at the thick, tangled mass of water-darkened blond hair that she'd always dreamed of touching. She wanted so badly to fuss over him and care for him. Just some small, comforting thing, no matter how insignificant.

"Connor. Let me do this," she pleaded. "Let me fix your hair."

He hesitated, and let out a long sigh. "Oh, what the hell."

"Excellent." Erin sprang into action, gathering scissors, shampoo, conditioner, plastic ice bucket, and comb. She kicked off her shoes and flung open the bathroom door. "Come on in here. We'll get started."

He waited in the bathroom doorway while she set the water running to warm it up. She folded a towel and draped it so that the chilly porcelain tub wouldn't touch his back.

"I can do this myself." His voice was tense. "Just tell me how."

"No, I want to," she fussed. "Take your shirt off. It'll just get wet."

He hesitated for so long that she looked up at him, puzzled.

His face was tight and miserable. He was clutching the bottom of his T-shirt like a bashful little boy.

She smoothed the towel into place. "Connor? What's the matter?"

He would not meet her eyes. "I don't look so good right now. The scars. They, uh . . . look like hell."

Dear God, how ironic. He was insecure about his body. She covered up a rush of startled tears with a forced laugh.

She went over to him, seized the bottom of his T-shirt and tugged it up.

He seized her hands. "Erin, I—"

"Shhh," she soothed. "Up with your arms."

He let her peel the shirt off. Her breath stuck in her lungs. He was incredibly beautiful. Racehorse lean and broad and sinewy, his ropy muscles were thick and tough, every finely cut detail showing beneath his smooth, pale golden skin. The burn scar blazed down over his ribs, left shoulder, arm, and hand. It chilled her to see how close he had come to death. "God, Connor," she whispered.

"Told you." His voice was colorless. "Pretty bad, huh?"

She brushed her fingertips across his shoulder. He jerked away.

"I'm sorry. Does it still hurt?" she asked anxiously.

He shook his head. He still wouldn't meet her eyes.

She wanted to memorize every dip and curve with her hands and mouth. The scar intensified his masculine beauty, by poignant contrast.

She could lean forward right now, press her lips against his hard chest. Nuzzle that whorl of flat, dark blond hair. Take that taut male nipple between her teeth and suckle it. She took an unsteady step backwards. "Sit by the tub and lean your head back." Her voice shook.

He did so, leaning his head back and stretching his long legs out in front of him. She stepped into the tub and sat down next to him.

"I'm going to shampoo your hair first," she told him.

He lifted his eyebrows. "I just washed it."

"Not with my good shampoo you didn't." She picked up the ice bucket and poured hot water slowly over his hair. "Scoot back further so I can hold your head in my hands."

He arched his back with a sigh and closed his eyes.

Shampoo lather foamed, dripping off his head, off her hands. It plopped into the hot water that lapped her ankles and floated there like whipped cream, like cumulus clouds.

Heat and steam and the slick, moist sounds of her hands caressing his hair put her in a sensual trance. She could have gone on caressing his beautifully shaped head forever. Admiring his ears, the thick hair that slid between her fingers, his dark, gold-tipped lashes. His sharp cheekbones, the grim lines that bracketed his mouth. Flinging his head back like that made the tendons stand out in his sinewy neck.

She could lean down and kiss him right now. It would be so easy. A perfect lead-in. The thought circled in her mind, teasing, dancing in almost close enough to spur her into action, then retreating.

She scooped up hot water with the ice bucket, rinsed the lather out of his hair. Squeezed the water out. Connor opened his eyes. His eyebrows lifted, questioning.

She smiled shyly and squeezed conditioner onto her palm. The stuff had cost a fortune, and it was almost used up. She wasn't going to be buying hair-care products with that kind of price tag for a very long time, but what the hell. Connor was worth it. She squeezed until the tube was empty and flung it aside. "I'm going to work this stuff into your hair, and you're going to leave it on for ten minutes."

He looked aggrieved. "Ten minutes?"

"A half hour would be better," she said sternly. "I really should wrap your hair in a hot towel to help it penetrate. But I think that would be pushing my luck." She massaged conditioner into his hair.

Connor seized one of her slippery hands and held it to his face. "Wow," he murmured. "My hair's going to smell like that?"

"Yes, and you will live." She stared at the brutal scarring on his long, graceful hand. "So don't whine."

He stroked her hand, as if the conditioner were a massage oil. "I finally know the secret."

She was half-hypnotized by his caressing hands. "What secret?"

"Why your hair is so pretty." A lazy smile played over his

mouth. "I always wondered how you made it so shiny and perfect. So this is how it's done. Hours in the bathroom, and sweet-smelling goop slathered all over you. I could get used to this."

Time warped and slowed even more in that silent, enchanted bathroom. The only sound was the hollow drip of the faucet plopping rhythmically into the bathtub. The room was a blur of fragrant mist.

She stared at his big, caressing hands and tried not to pant.

Connor's eyes flicked up to her face. He grinned. "You're rosy red, Erin. Are you hot? Or are you just blushing?"

"I'm hot," she said in a tiny voice. "I think it's time to rinse."

"Has it been ten minutes? Damn. Feels like ten seconds."

She had absolutely no idea. It could've been ten seconds, it could've been three hours. "At least ten minutes," she murmured.

He dropped his head into her hands with a growl of pleasure. "I feel like a sultan getting pampered by his beautiful bath attendant."

She giggled at the rush of erotic images his words provoked. Her eyes slid down the length of his body—and stopped at his groin.

He had an erection. A large erection. Not that she had much basis for comparison, but it was much larger than she'd expected.

Here it was, proof positive that if she came on to him, he wouldn't object. At least his body wouldn't. She could just reach down and . . . and what? Stroke him through his jeans, or would it be better to unbutton them? Her hands were goopy and wet. Maybe he would think it was vulgar and crass. Maybe he would be offended.

Or worse, amused. She was so goddamned chicken.

She rinsed his hair carefully and stood up. "Time to comb

and trim," she announced. "Sit up on the edge of the tub, please."

He grimaced. "Do I have to?"

"You've come this far. Don't choke at the finish."

He lifted himself up. "You're not going to make me look like a poodle, are you?" he grumbled. "It has to be long enough for a ponytail. And all one length, for God's sake. Otherwise it drives me nuts."

"Don't worry," she said. "Trust me. I'm very good at this."

She eased her comb through his hair and fanned it out over his broad shoulders. "I'll trim it to shoulder length. That'll get rid of the split ends. Where's your part?"

He twisted around, puzzled. "My what?"

"The part in your hair," she explained. "It changes the cut."

"Jesus, this is complicated. It's wherever it happens to be at any given moment that I yank my hair back. I never really noticed."

"Oh, you are hopeless," she snapped.

She trimmed his hair with slow, methodical precision. She drew it out as long as she could, so she could linger close to him, but she finally had to straighten up and run her hands through his hair. "All done," she said. "Now for a blow-dry, and you're all set."

He recoiled. "Like hell. That's where I draw the line."

She brandished her blow dryer. "But Connor, it's just a—"

"Get that thing away from me before you electrocute us both!"

"You are such a baby." She gathered up the cut ends, dropped them in the trash basket, and hurried from the bathroom. She shoved her sticky, hair-covered bottles into her toiletries case with none of her usual anxious neatness. She was so angry at herself. All those openings, and she had just let them go by, one after the other. Idiot. Coward.

"Erin."

She turned. He leaned in the bathroom doorway, still naked to the waist. The slicked back hair accentuated the stark, chiseled beauty of his face. She sank down onto the bed. "What?" she quavered.

"This was really nice of you. Really sweet. Thank you."

"You're welcome," she whispered.

Sweet. He thought she was sweet. And nice. There it was, like an evil enchantment. She tried to swallow it, but it wouldn't go down.

People had called her that all her life. Ever since she'd been an unnaturally well-behaved little girl who tried to be perfect, and make the world harmonious for Mommy and Daddy. Since they couldn't be harmonious on their own and needed all the help they could get.

Sweet and nice. Respectful and polite and studious. Straight As, honor society, squeaky clean, pure as the goddamn driven snow.

She couldn't endure it any longer.

"Uh . . . Erin? Did I say something wrong?"

She looked up at him wildly. "No, of course not! I, uh, need the bathroom for a while, if you don't mind."

He nodded. The smile he gave her was so sexy, her toes curled up. She snatched her toiletries case and her nightgown, and hustled into the bathroom while she still had partial control of her face.

She squeezed her eyes shut beneath the pounding spray of the shower. She was going to have to do something dramatic to break this awful spell. Worst case scenario, he would just laugh at her.

No. Connor was brusque and hard-edged, but he wasn't cruel. If he didn't want her, it would be so painful for him to have to reject her. But it wouldn't kill them. They would both live through it.

She turned off the shower. Then again, maybe it would kill her. But even the prospect of death by embarrassment was no excuse for cowardice. She toweled off, and put on her nightgown and panties. She put her hand on the door-knob—and stopped.

She'd bought the nightgown because it was like something out of a Regency romance, gauzy and lace-trimmed and romantic. But it was so virginal. Nowhere near sexy enough to make the statement she needed to make. Neither were her white cotton bra and panties. If she wanted to go past the point of no return, she had to be bold. Once she stepped out that door, she was going to be as mute as a statue anyway. If there was a message to be sent, it had better be a nonverbal one.

She pulled off the nightgown and hung it on the hook. Peeled off the panties, folded them and refolded them. Her cold fingers were clutching the door handle when she remembered her hair. She pulled the bun loose, let it tumble around her shoulders.

She stared into the mirror. Naked, with her hair down, she might almost pass for sexy. Too bad she'd left the makeup case out on the bed. No help from that quarter. She would have to do this *au naturel*.

A better chance to seduce him would never come her way. And she might not be talented, but oh, was she ever motivated. She tried to take a deep, bracing breath, but no air would go into her lungs.

She pushed the door open and walked into the room.

Chapter

8

Connor turned at the sound of the door.

His shocked silence made her feel both terribly alone and terribly exposed, as if she stood naked on a stage in front of a murmuring crowd, and Connor's burning gaze were a spotlight. The silence went on and on. He opened his mouth. Closed it. His Adam's apple bobbed.

"Holy shit," he said hoarsely. "What the hell are you doing?"

Her lips started trembling, then her whole jaw. "I don't know," she whispered. She had no idea what she was doing. But whatever it was, it was obviously the wrong thing.

Well, here it was. Worse case scenario. Times like these were a girl's opportunity to show her true quality. "I'll just, um, put my clothes back on," she mumbled. "Excuse me."

Her eyes filled up as she turned. She launched herself in what she sincerely hoped was the direction of the bathroom door.

He grabbed her from behind, spun her around, and shoved her hard against the wall. "Not so fast. Wait a goddamn minute."

His furious face was inches from hers. His naked chest

grazed her nipples. She opened her mouth, but nothing intelligible came out. "I—"

"Don't you dare come waltzing out of that bathroom buck naked and then just leave me hanging!"

She gasped. "But I—but I thought—"

"What? You thought what? That strutting around naked in front of me would be good sport? Big joke, huh? Dangle bait in front of me and watch me jump."

His inexplicable fury bewildered her. "Connor, I—"

"Don't you dare tease me like that, Erin. *Don't . . . you . . . dare.*"

She finally found her voice. "You got it wrong."

"Wrong how? Say it louder. I can't hear you."

She shoved against his chest, but he would not budge. It was as if he were rooted to the ground. "Do not yell at me!"

"Let's hear it, Erin." His voice was soft, but no less menacing. "How am I wrong?"

She reached to cover her breasts, but his hands flashed out and wrenched hers wide open, pinning them against the wall. He leaned closer. The hard bulge in his jeans pressed hard against her pubic bone. "No way, Erin. This was your idea. Take responsibility for it."

She stared into his eyes. "I just wanted . . ." Her throat closed, and she tried again. "I wanted to—"

"What? What did you want? What crazy game are you playing with me?"

"Don't swear at me! I am not playing games! I wanted you!"

His face went blank. "Huh?"

"I want you!" Anger gave her the strength to wrench her hands loose. "God, Connor! Is it so hard to get? Could I possibly be more obvious? What do I have to do, send you a singing telegram?"

"Me?" he repeated.

She shoved at his hot chest, and this time he stumbled back. "Yes, you! Idiot! I had no idea you would be so ridiculous about it!" She dove for the bathroom. "Let it go. Never mind. I promise, I will never—"

"Fuck, no." He grabbed her shoulders and pulled her around to face him. "We're not letting this go. No way."

She'd been hoping for a smooth segue into a sensual dance, in which Connor would take the lead and she could follow his cues and hide how awkward and inexpert she was. It wasn't going to be like that.

He was so worked up. Trembling in the grip of some intense emotion. A thrill of delicious, primitive terror went through her. "Ease up, please," she whispered. "Your hands are hurting me."

His hands dropped. "Sorry," he said gruffly.

She rubbed the sore spots his fingers had left. "You scared me."

He shook with a short burst of ironic laughter. "Yeah, well, you scared me, too."

"Dad said you had nerves of steel. I wouldn't have thought that just a naked girl could faze you."

He let out a long, ragged sigh. "It depends on the girl. God. Look at you," he said softly. "Your body is gorgeous."

She blushed. How gallant and sweet of him, to carry on about her perfectly ordinary body. "Um, thank you."

He stared as if he were in a trance. A flush was burned into his high cheekbones. She reached up and touched it with her fingertips. The muscles of his face shifted beneath hot, velvety skin.

She explored his neck, his shoulders, and slid her arms around his waist, sighing as their torsos touched. "I like your body, too," she whispered. She brushed her fingers across the ridges of muscle and bone and scar tissue. Her faintest touch made him shudder and gasp.

He placed his hands tentatively on her shoulders. "My hands don't know where to land." His voice shook. "You're so soft and warm. And you're naked. Everywhere."

"So touch me everywhere," she said.

He threaded his fingers into her hair and let them slide down its smooth length. "Am I dreaming? Prove to me that I'm not dreaming."

"OK." She slid her hand down over his back and pinched his muscular butt. "How's that?"

He hid his face against her hair, laughing silently. "I'm convinced," he said." My dream Erin would never do a thing like that."

The implications of those words sank in. "Dream Erin?" she whispered. "You mean you've thought about me before?"

"God, yes. I've wanted you for years." His hands were all over her, bold and eager. Circling her waist, caressing her bottom, her hips.

She hid her hot, smiling face against his chest. "I bet your dream Erin would never pinch a man's butt, huh?" She started to shake with helpless laughter. "I bet she's a picture-perfect porcelain doll with shiny black patent leather shoes and ankle socks who never puts a foot wrong, right?"

He frowned, baffled. "Huh?"

"I bet she's a mealy-mouthed twit with an apple for the teacher. I bet she would never scare a guy half to death by jumping out of the bathroom stark naked. But guess what, Connor? Say good-bye to your dream Erin. She's history. No more Ms. Nice Girl. I quit."

"Look out." He looked fascinated. "Are you going to put on a leather miniskirt and five-inch heels and rob banks?"

"No. I'm going to seduce you," she announced.

A delighted grin lit up his face. "I'm cool with that. But if it makes you feel any better, my dream Erin never wore patent leather shoes. She was always bare naked. Wide open while we made love. All that creamy skin damp and rosy."

"Oh, my," she gasped. "Really?"

He nodded. "Turn around."

She was startled at the abrupt command. "What?"

He cupped the curve of her bottom. "Your ass drives me

crazy. Turn around, right here. In front of the mirror. I want to look at it."

It was ridiculous, after all the bold lengths she'd gone to, but her face still burned. "I . . . but it's, ah, too big. Cindy's always giving me *Buns of Steel* videos for Christmas as a joke, and I—"

"Cindy can weld her scrawny buns into steel if she wants. I like a round, beautiful ass like yours. You're the one who took your clothes off for me, Erin. I've been sneaking guilty peeks at your ass for years. Now's my chance to get a good, long look. So turn around. Now."

She did not miss the command hidden beneath the lazy sensual tone. And he was right. This had been her idea. She turned her back to him.

He clasped her waist, and pushed her forward gently. She swayed and caught herself on the low table. She stared straight into the mirror, back arched, bottom sticking out. Her face was bright pink.

Connor smiled, a hot, predatory smile that made the muscles of her thighs clench. The pose he had put her in was an explicit invitation.

He was testing her. Her arms trembled. She didn't move. She would not chicken out. No way. She'd come this far.

His hands slid lower, worshiping every curve, caressing her inner thighs and brushing boldly over the fuzz of hair that hid her sex. He pulled her up, and back against him, his arm tight around her belly, his erection pressed against her bottom. "You make it so hard to do the right thing," he muttered.

She struggled to concentrate. "The right thing? What is that?"

"To not touch you," he growled. "I bullied you into this whole thing. Seducing you puts me deep into dickhead territory."

"Wait a minute, here. Who is seducing who? Who gets

the credit for this, Mr. Connor Do-The-Right-Thing-At-All-Costs McCloud?"

"That's not the point."

She lifted her chin. "I think it is the point. You're pathetically misguided about what the right thing is, Connor."

His lips quirked. "Is that right?"

"The right thing is for you to satisfy my carnal desires," she said. "That is the only honorable response to this situation."

An appreciative grin spread slowly over his face. "Wow. My dream Erin would never have said a thing like that, either."

"Good-bye, dream Erin. Hello, real Erin. Get used to it."

"Oh, I'm adjusting," he assured her. "You took me by surprise at first, but I'm getting used to the hardcore Erin real quick." He cupped her breasts, rolling her nipples between his fingers. "Just look at these tits," he murmured. "Wet dream material. So? Tell me your carnal desires, sweetheart. I stand ready to serve, in any way."

She hesitated, and decided that pretending she knew what she was doing would be too stressful. "I'm not quite sure where I want to go from here," she admitted. "I was hoping you might have some ideas."

He snorted. "Oh, I know exactly where I want to go from here. Only problem is, I've got no condoms."

Her eyes widened. She had completely forgotten that small but essential detail.

"I wasn't looking to score with you when I drove down here," he said roughly. "I didn't even let myself consider it. I cannot believe that I have a chance to make love to you, and I've blown it."

She hesitated, biting her lip. "Couldn't we just . . . do it anyway?" she asked. "I've heard that if the man stops in time, that—"

"Theoretically, sure."

She rushed on, eager to get the thought out while it was still intact. "My period is as regular as clockwork, and it ended night before last, so I'm probably not— "

"Probably being the key word. Erin, I'm so turned on, I'm lucky if I don't come in my pants right now just looking at you. You can't ask me not to come inside you. Not the first time, anyway, and probably not the second time, either. Because I can't promise it."

Another thought occurred to her. "I'm sorry, I should've said this sooner. If you're thinking about being safe, I can tell you my sexual history in about a minute, and everything I've done has always been with a condom, so—"

"No, Erin. Actually, that was the last thing on my mind," he said gently. "But since we're on the subject, I always made a point of being safe, too. And I tested negative on my last physical, which was before the coma, and all that. And I haven't been with anyone since long before then. So, uh . . . just so you know."

"Thanks," she murmured. "That's a very long time." Not as long as her own spell of celibacy, of course, but she was a special case. "So, we could do, um, other things, couldn't we?"

His smile was slow, sexy, merciless. "Oh yeah? What things?"

"Oh, there are lots of possibilities." She tried to sound casual.

"Name them for me," he said softly. "Tell me your favorites."

Her eyes dropped. "I can't," she whispered.

He pulled her against him. "That's about what I figured."

She hid her face against his chest. He didn't feel like he was losing interest just because she was shy and inexpert, judging by the hot bulge pressed against her belly. That was promising.

He wound his hand into the hair at the nape of her neck

and tilted her head back. "Would you tell me something, Erin?" he asked. "Because it's driving me crazy, not knowing."

She met his searching gaze. "What?"

"The sex you say you've had, was it with Georg Luksch?"

She wrenched out of his arms. "I never let that horrible man touch me! How could you even ask me that?"

"Don't get pissed off," he soothed. "I wouldn't blame you if you had. Nobody would. A guy who looks like that—"

"Like what?" She lunged for her suitcase, rummaging for some clothes with trembling fingers. "He looked like a gigolo! He didn't interest me in the least!" She found some cotton panties and yanked them on inside out.

"Oh, come on. He looked like a goddamn Calvin Klein ad."

"Not after you were done with him, he didn't!"

He winced. "I'm sorry you had to see that. But I'm not sorry I did it."

"Whatever," she snapped. "Think what you want, Connor. I don't care. I was ravished, soiled, dishonored. I did everything there is to do with him. I am absolutely ruined. OK? Now deal with it!"

She wrenched a pair of pants out of her suitcase and sat on the bed to pull them on. Connor yanked them out of her hands, flung them away, and pushed her down onto her back. His hot, half-naked body sprawled heavily over hers. "Bullshit. Look me in the eye, Erin."

She struggled wildly against him. "Get off me!"

"Look me in the eye," he repeated. "That's all I ask."

She glared at him for a moment. "Satisfied?"

He relaxed, and nodded. "Yeah. You never let him touch you."

"Oh yeah? How do you know? Maybe I lied!"

"You can't lie to me," he said calmly. "I can read you."

"Oh! That is so arrogant! You don't know me, Connor!

And you think you can look into my eyes and read my mind?" She swatted at his chest. "I can't even read my own goddamn mind!"

"I do know you," he said stubbornly. "And you never let him touch you."

She turned her face away, her throat quivering. "No," she admitted. "He wasn't my type. And he made me nervous."

He rolled off her and propped his head up on his hand. His other hand splayed possessively over the curve of her hip. "Good," he said.

"I don't see how it changes anything."

"It doesn't," he said. "But it does make me feel better. I had nightmares for months about that bastard touching you."

She sat up, startled. "You did?"

His direct, silent gaze was her answer. His hand stroked, settled into the curve of her waist, pulling her until their bodies touched again.

"So did I," she whispered. "It was bad. For a while."

He pressed tender kisses against her neck and jaw. "We were discussing, what was it? Oh, yeah. Sexual possibilities that don't include intercourse," he mused. "Now there's an interesting topic. I think we should get back to it." He plucked at the elastic of her panties and gave her a wistful look. "I liked it better when you were naked."

"That was before you made me mad," she said.

"I could make you forgive me." He covered her face with soft kisses. "Let's get those panties off you, and I'll show you what I mean."

Cold fear tightened in her belly. *Face the facts, babe. One hurting puppy. Lousy lay.* Bradley's boredom and frustration at how long she took, how difficult she was. She let out a nervous giggle. "Oh, I'd rather concentrate on you first. You're the one who needs to—"

"The rules are real clear," he said. "Ladies first. It's the law."

"But I'm not, ah . . ." She trailed off, miserable.

He gazed searchingly into her face. "I thought this was what you wanted," he said slowly. "You having second thoughts?"

"Good Lord, no! It's just that I . . . it's not that simple, to make me have an orgasm. I'm not . . . very responsive, and I don't want to bore you, and I get so anxious when I'm under pressure, which makes me tense up even more, so I was hoping we could skip that part and try some other things, and that way maybe I'll have a chance to loosen up—"

"Erin. Shhh." He cut off her anxious babbling with a kiss. When he lifted his head, she was dazed and breathless. "No pressure. And I won't get bored. I have a really long attention span. You have no idea."

"But I—"

He covered her mouth with his, and all her doubts and fears melted into a vortex of tender confusion. His lips were velvety, coaxing and insistent. His tongue flicked against hers, and he deepened the kiss, sweet and clinging, like he wanted to draw the soul from her body.

He slid his hand into her panties, his fingertips brushing over her soft thatch of hair. She pressed herself against his hand, and his fingers parted her tenderly.

"Oh, yeah. That's so beautiful," he murmured. "You're already wet and soft. There's nothing wrong with you, sweetheart. You're plenty responsive. Feel this. You're almost there, right now, and all I did was kiss you. I've barely started touching you. You were made for this. You're melting for it, like hot caramel. Feel this, put your hand right here. Feel how this beautiful clit is sticking out, all swollen and tight like it just can't wait for me to suck on it. Feel this?"

He pressed her own fingers against the hot, throbbing glow of pleasure at the top of her cleft while his fingers delved inside her. She hid her face, panting. Her body moved of its own volition. She thrust herself against his hand. Pleasure swelled, unbearably sweet. She trapped his hand between her thighs and pressed her own down on top of it, her muscles clenching and releasing. The feeling grew, cresting.

"Connor. Oh, God. Don't . . . don't . . ."

"I won't leave you," he soothed. "I'm right here. Let go."

Something huge was gathering inside her. She panicked, and fought it. "Connor . . . something strange is happening. I . . . I'm scared."

"Go with it. It's OK, Erin."

She shook her head. "Please. Stop. I can't. I can't—"

"Go with it." His voice was implacable. He slid his tongue into her mouth, thrust his hand deeper, insisting.

It overtook her. The world dissolved into pulsing black heat.

When she finally opened her eyes, she was surprised to find herself in one piece. Her same old, familiar self.

Connor pulled her face around and smoothed damp hair off her forehead. "Are you all right?" he asked.

She gazed at him, speechless.

"That wasn't so bad, was it?"

She let her face drop to the side and nuzzled the hand that was stroking her cheek. "What . . . what was that?" she whispered.

He looked alarmed. "Uh . . . you came, Erin," he said slowly. "You're not telling me that was your first time?"

Her body still thrummed with residual pleasure. She closed her eyes and pressed her thighs together, savoring it. "Ah, no. I mean, yes. I thought that I had, but I've never felt the whole world go away like that. It scared me so much, I think I fainted. I thought I was dying."

She felt his smile against her neck as he nuzzled her. "The little death. The most beautiful thing I've ever seen."

The sweet, rippling shivers slowly gave way to a relaxed glow. She wanted to croon and purr, but when she cuddled closer, she felt the unyielding heat of his erection against her belly, and remembered that there was more to this. "Connor? What about you?" she asked.

His eyebrow quirked. "What about me? I'm in heaven."

She reached down, and stroked the long, thick bulge in his jeans. He let out a sharp gasp, and placed his hand over hers. "Not yet."

"Not yet?" She was baffled. "Then when?"

He hooked his thumbs into the elastic of her panties, tugged them down, and then slid down the bed. He dragged her along with him, until her legs dangled off the foot of the bed in a tangle of bed coverings. "Connor? What are you—"

"One orgasm is good," he said. "Two are better."

She pushed herself up until she was perched on the edge of the bed, legs clamped together in a paroxysm of shyness. He knelt in front of her, a faint smile touching his lips. "Open up for me." He covered her knees with beseeching kisses, his mouth hot and deliciously ticklish. She giggled and pushed his face away. "Please," he pleaded. "Let me in."

His smile and his sweet, silly kisses made her heart go soft. She dashed the tears away with a murmur of embarrassment. It took some concentration, but slowly the muscles in her thighs loosened. He pushed them wide, his face fascinated. He drew his fingertip down the folds of her labia, parting them, and thrust his finger deep inside her.

She gasped, and she was outside herself, observing her own behavior with a cold, horrified eye. Legs spread, completely at his mercy. Crazy and wanton. That shrill, lecturing voice echoed through her mind, reminding her of betrayal, Dad and Novak, Georg and Crystal Mountain, all the reasons why she shouldn't—

"Don't," he said.

She met his sharp gaze, startled. "Don't what?"

"Wherever you were going in your head, don't go there. It's a wrong turn."

The sharpness of his perceptions made her feel transparent. "You can't tell me what thoughts to think," she said.

He slid his finger out of her and licked it, sighing with pleasure. "I can try, can't I?" he asked. "Jesus, you're delicious. All I want you to think about is how it feels when I go down on you. That's it, Erin. No other thoughts are invited. This is a private party."

He swayed forward and put his mouth to her before she could think of a reply, and all thoughts fled. All that remained was the liquid, swirling sensations of his lips and his strong, eager tongue, lapping and laving her, flicking expertly across her most sensitive flesh. She gripped damp, silky handfuls of his hair and pushed herself against his mouth. His growl of satisfaction reverberated through her body.

He shoved her down onto her back and folded her legs up high. She writhed, struggling in his strong grip, but she was struggling toward something, not away. He drove her onward, toward a tantalizing promise that blazed on the horizon of her mind like the fiery glow of sunrise.

That huge, inevitable wave of pleasure that had so terrified her before gathered again. This time she didn't resist it. The explosion throbbed through her entire body, an endless eternity of rippling pleasure. It took a long time to float back. "I'm melting," she whispered.

"Yeah. Like homemade vanilla ice cream scooped over hot Dutch apple pie. Yum." His smile was so sweet, it made her heart hurt. "You want some more? I could do that to you all night long. Easily."

She struggled up onto her knees. "It's your turn, Connor," she said shyly. "Do you want me to, um . . . go down on you?"

He jerked up onto his elbows, opened his mouth to speak, and closed it, looking shy. "Uh . . . that's one of those do-bears-shit-in-the-woods and is-the-Pope-Catholic type questions, Erin."

"I take it that's a yes," she said primly.

He flopped down onto his back and put his hand over his face. "You don't have to if you're not comfortable with it," he mumbled.

She leaned over him. "Connor? Are you blushing?"

"No," he snapped. "I just turned red because I'm excited. So shoot me. God, this is embarrassing."

"Don't be embarrassed. I love it. How sweet."

"Sweet," he muttered. "Huh. Great. I'm glad it works for you."

She put her hands on his chest, and petted the flat, silky golden hair. "So tell me what you want me to—"

"No way." He flung his arms wide. "I am at your mercy. Do with me as you will. If you want to go down on me, fine. I'm all for it."

She unbuttoned his jeans. He wore nothing beneath them. His penis sprang out eagerly into her hands. Long and thick, flushed.

"No underwear?" She covered her nervousness with laughter.

"Hate 'em. Never bothered with them when I was a kid. Never got into the habit as an adult, either. They make my dick feel strangled."

His skin was so much softer than she had expected. Living velvet sliding over the thick stalk as she clasped him, squeezed him. The blunt, heart-shaped tip was as large and swollen as a red plum. It wept one gleaming drop of fluid. She touched it with her fingertip, swirling it around his hot, smooth flesh. He cried out, arching off the bed.

She froze, alarmed. "Please tell me if I do anything wrong."

He clutched handfuls of sheet with white-knuckled fists. "Anything, everything, whatever. It's all good. Don't stop."

His low, shaky tone emboldened her, and she dragged his jeans down over his hips. She pulled them off and got her first look at the surgical scars that furrowed his thigh. Long and jagged and puckered.

She ran her hand over his ravaged flesh. An ache swelled

inside her for his suffering, bound together with tenderness, and anger, and the urge to give him more pleasure than he had ever dreamed possible.

She clambered over him, letting her hair trail over his chest until she was straddling him. He held up his face to a soft rain of kisses like a man dying of thirst. His body trembled with the effort of staying still. "Oh, God, this is so sweet," he murmured.

She played with him, discovering his body with her hands and her lips. He squeezed his eyes shut and shuddered violently when she took him into her mouth.

She could barely manage it, there was so much of him. He was so big and thick. She loved his warm, salty, sexual taste, his musky male smell. His heartbeat pulsed between her hands, against her caressing tongue. His scarred, beautiful body was a heart-wrenching contradiction of power and vulnerability, of strength and yearning.

He gripped fistfuls of her hair. His tone grew more pleading as she experimented with her tongue, with her hands. The bolder she was, the harder he thrashed. She pulled him deeper, swallowing him whole, suckling him hard, swirling her tongue, milking him with her hands.

His hands tightened in her hair. "It's coming down on me. Oh, God." He convulsed, and exploded.

Pulsing jets of hot liquid spurted into her mouth, and she shuddered at the energy that burst against her face. She braced herself, and rode out the long storm. It faded into stillness.

She swallowed, raised her head, wiped her mouth. She kissed his thigh, the dark blond hair at his groin, the sensitive tip of his penis.

His fingers tightened in her hair. "Oh, Erin."

His voice was rough and shaky. He hid his eyes behind his trembling hand. She pressed her cheek against the hard muscles of his belly, and nuzzled him tenderly. "Are you OK?" she asked him.

He opened his eyes, and laughed. "I just had a religious experience."

She pulled herself up onto her knees. "Me, too."

He grinned as he studied her face. "Really? You liked doing that?"

She nodded. His penis was still half-hard, curved across his thigh against its nest of hair. She ran her fingertip slowly along its length, from root to the gleaming tip. He hardened and thickened instantly.

"I loved it," she said. "It made me crazy. Just look at me, Connor. Look at what you've done."

He propped himself up onto his elbows and stared at her. Her fingers curled around his penis and squeezed him. "Whoa," he whispered. "Check you out. You're on fire."

She let her head fall back and trailed her fingertips over her hot face, her lips, her throat. She caressed her breasts, her belly, and slid her hand between her legs, seeking relief from the shimmering tension. "I feel so much, it hurts," she said. "Inside, outside, everywhere. Did you put a spell on me? Did you slip something into my pie when I wasn't looking?"

"Oh, no, sweetheart." He rose up to his knees. "It was all inside you to begin with. The red-hot love goddess. It's what you always were. You shine, Erin. You almost hurt my eyes." He pulled her hard against him, arranging her thighs so that they straddled his. "Oh yeah. Give me some more of that. Right now."

He slanted his mouth over hers in a fierce, devouring kiss. No tenderness or gentleness, just raw, possessive male triumph. She gave herself up to it, quivering with helpless excitement. He thrust his fingers deeply into her slick heat. "Is this what you want?"

But she couldn't reply, she was wailing, convulsing around his hand, and riding a long shuddering wave of ecstasy.

He held her afterwards, murmuring sweet words and rocking her like a child. Her head rested limply on his shoulder. When she could move again, she flung herself backwards, pulling him down on top of her. "Please, Connor," she said. "Make love to me now."

His face was a taut mask of self-control. "Damn, Erin. Have mercy on me. We shouldn't do this, not without latex—"

She pulled him down and clasped her legs around him. "I am a grown-up. I take full responsibility. I promise."

He wrenched her arms from around his neck and pinned them above her head. "Fuck responsibility," he snarled. "It's not that simple, and you know it!"

"Please." She pulled him closer with her thighs, pressing her moist labia against his belly like a hot, pleading kiss. "I need you."

He closed his eyes, panting. "I can't say no to you," he said. "You drive me completely nuts. I'm helpless before you."

"Good," she said. "That's excellent. Helpless works for me."

"I don't know if I can do it without coming inside you, though," he warned. "I've never done it with a red-hot love goddess before."

She rubbed her breasts against his chest. "Then it's time for a challenge. Come on, Connor. Be all that you can be."

He dissolved into silent laughter. "Jesus, that's harsh." He shifted her legs, bending her knees so she was wide open to him.

She struggled up onto her elbows and grabbed for the pillows. "I want to see it," she told him. "I don't want to miss a single thing."

"OK." He tucked the pillows behind her, and poised his body over hers. "I'm so out of my mind, I think I've, uh, forgotten how to do it."

She smiled up at him through her eyelashes. "It'll come back to you," she said. "You certainly had no problem with foreplay."

"You're pretty terrifying in the foreplay department yourself. You practically drove me insane with your hair goop. OK, here goes."

He took himself in hand and pressed the blunt tip of his penis against her. He stroked her, moistening himself. The gentle contact was as sweet as a kiss. His fragrant hair tumbled around her face, and she ran her fingers through it. "Oh, your hair," she whispered.

"What about it? Is it tickling you? Want me to pull it back?"

"No, no," she said. "It's almost dry. It looks beautiful."

He nudged inside, and pressed against her body's resistance. "Oh, God, Erin," he groaned. "You're so tight. You're driving me nuts. This is so dangerous, baby. I'm right on the edge."

"Please, Connor." She would not permit him to leave her with this ache unsatisfied. She grasped his waist, pulled him deeper inside herself, but he was so big and hard and unyielding. "Don't leave me."

"Calm down," he soothed her. "I'm not going anywhere. I just don't want to hurt you. Just a little bit at a time . . . like this. Arch your back. Oh, God, yes. You squeeze me so tight."

He pushed relentlessly deeper. She was afraid to move, scarcely breathing. Connor arched over her, his thick shaft thrust halfway into her. He worked himself deeper with each short, sliding thrust. "Are you all right?" he asked anxiously. "We can still stop if you—"

"Shut up." She smiled to soften the sharp words.

"Move against me," he commanded her. "That'll make it easier."

She moved her hips, and it all slipped into focus. The gliding movement, the angle, the delicious, throbbing fullness of his thick shaft inside her. The wonderful, marvelous point of it all. He pushed deeper.

She gasped. Connor gazed searchingly into her face. "More?"

She reached up, embracing him. "All."

Chapter

9

He took her at her word, and drove inside her.

They both cried out. It was like falling off a cliff, the moment of shocked inevitability when he knew that this was too good, he was too turned on. He was going to completely lose control.

He slid his arm beneath the arch of her back, pulling her tighter. Shocked gasps jerked out of her with each heavy thrust. He was riding her too hard; she was too small and tight for this, but he couldn't slow down, couldn't ease off. He was locked into this hard rhythm. She had teased and tempted him into this, and now he was all thundering blood and pumping muscles, no judgment, no wits. He had prided himself on his self-control, and she had blasted it to hell and it was gone.

Erin's face was cherry red. Her mouth was open, her bosom heaving, and her soft thighs clenched around his, and oh, dear God, there she went again. Crying out, arched like a bow, her tight cunt clenching around his cock in yet another shaking-apart, violent orgasm. The woman was un-fucking-believable, white-hot. Burning him alive. No way could he make this last, not at this level of intensity. The big drum roll was getting louder, his orgasm crashing down on him.

He barely managed to wrench himself out in time. He spent himself across her belly in long, scalding spurts.

He collapsed on top of her with a breathless sob. He'd wanted to fuck this girl for years, but he had no idea that it would feel like this.

She murmured, squashed beneath his body. He lifted himself up. They were practically glued together with his come. He wondered if that would disgust her. Then she put her hand to the sticky mess pooled in the soft indentation of her navel. She swirled her fingertips around, until her belly gleamed.

That answered that.

Unbelievably, his cock jerked up to attention, like a helpless marionette. "Don't, for God's sake," he pleaded. "Give me a break. Let me get myself together. I'm destroyed."

She shook her head. Her eyes were solemn and perilously beautiful. She brought her wet, gleaming finger to her mouth and suckled the pearly liquid off of them, one after the other. Her pink tongue swirled tenderly around each fingertip. She was going to drive him straight out of his fucking mind.

He flung himself facedown and hid his face in the crumpled sheets. "You want me to beg for mercy? I'm begging. Ease off."

"Beg in vain." Her voice was cool. "No mercy for you."

He convulsed in silent laughter, pressing his face harder against the sheets. "You heartless, insatiable bitch."

"Oh, I've only just begun. You have no idea what you're in for, Connor McCloud."

He rolled away and sat on the bed with his back to her, covering his face with his hands. "OK. Do whatever you want, but give me a time-out. Just a few minutes to get myself in hand."

Sheets rustled, the bed shifted. She pressed her hot, silky

body against his back, and wrapped her arms around him. She seized his cock with both small hands. "I've already got you in hand, Connor."

He squeezed his eyes shut in another spasm of silent laughter, or maybe he was weeping dry tears. They felt pretty much the same to him. "Hell and damn. I walked right into that one, didn't I?"

"You walked right into this whole thing." Her voice was clear and quiet. "I didn't ask you to follow me. I didn't ask to be guarded. Don't blame me if you got more than you bargained for."

His laughter died away. He stared down at her small, graceful hands, wet with his come. Stroking his stone-hard, aching cock as if he hadn't just had two explosive orgasms in the past twenty minutes. Three in the past hour, if he counted that violent but relatively superficial release he'd given himself in the shower after dinner.

His last, futile effort at self-control.

Erin's fist curled around the head of his cock in a tight, swirling caress. "Jesus, woman. You are something else."

She nuzzled her face against his neck, nibbling his throat. If she kept this up he was going to come again. He blocked her hands with his own. "Erin. For God's sake. What do you want from me?"

She kissed up and down the taut tendons that stood out at his throat. "I want to know you," she said softly. "In the Biblical sense. Everything you are. Good, bad, everything. And I want you to know me the same way. I want it so bad, Connor. I'm tired of feeling so cold."

"You're not cold," he said. "You're burning me to a crisp."

She waited silently. A warm, soft weight against his back.

He picked through her words, feeling around for the snare that had to be there. "You want that? You think you want to know me?"

"I know that I do," she said. "I've always wanted it."

He twisted to look into her eyes. The sensual glow in their

honey-brown depths fuddled him, made him forget what he had meant to say. He groped for his train of thought, furious at the casual power she wielded over him. So easy. Like it was nothing to her.

"It's dangerous to really know somebody," he told her. "It's dangerous to rip the masks away. How do you know if you'll like what's underneath? We don't even really know what's underneath our own."

She had the regal, intergalactic princess look on her face again. "I'll risk it," she said quietly.

He seized her arm, yanking her around so that her face was inches from his. "I'm trying to do the right thing, and you pull the rug out from under my feet every way I turn. Maybe ripping my masks off isn't such a bright idea, Erin. You keep this up, and maybe you're going to find yourself fucking some guy you don't even recognize."

She pulled herself out of his grip and slid off the bed until she stood in front of him, her spectacular tits bobbing right at eye level. "Too late," she said. "You already ripped my masks away. How was it for you, Connor? You just had sex with a woman you didn't recognize. Did you enjoy it? I sure did. I'll admit it, I'm not ashamed. I loved it. I didn't even recognize myself, and I . . . *loved* it."

"I recognized you," he said. "I've always known you. I've had you in my dreams, a million times."

She gazed down, as serene as a medieval Madonna. She cupped his face in her hands, tipped it up. The exquisitely gentle kiss she pressed against his forehead was like a benediction.

"I show you mine, you show me yours," she said. "It's only fair."

She reached for his hands, placing them at the curve of her waist, and swayed forward until her head was bent over him, her hair swirling around his shoulders, her tits swaying right in his face. He smelled the sharp smell of his come, and the hot, rich scent of her female pleasure mixing with it, a rich, heady sexual spell. His swollen cock bobbed in front of him. At her beck and call.

The invitation was obvious. He pressed his face against her breasts with a ragged sigh of surrender, rubbing her tight, puckered nipples against his cheeks, and then cupped her breasts in both hands and suckled her. He wanted to imprint every detail onto his long-term memory. Every shape and shade and contour, every sigh and shudder, every delicate difference in texture; the translucent gold perfection of her skin, the plump, lush curves and hollows, all of it calculated to drive him to screaming sexual overload.

He lost himself. He could do this forever. He wondered if he could make her come just by sucking her tits. He'd read somewhere that it was possible. Now there was a challenge that he would readily embrace. His mouth moved over her, wallowing in her sweet, generous response, her pleading moans, the nails digging into his shoulders.

She sagged over him, quivering, and embraced his shoulders. Her hair draped across his face, and he pushed the thick, fragrant fall of dark satiny hair out of his eyes, his gaze flicking up to her face.

Tears stood in her shadowy eyes.

A chill shuddered through him. His fingers tightened around her waist until she gasped. This wasn't only to please her and make her hot for him, and she knew it. He saw it in her eyes. The witch was on to him, she'd pulled him so deep into her spell that everything was bared to her. And now she'd ripped away a mask that was so much a part of him, he hadn't even known he was wearing it. Hadn't wanted to know.

Beneath it, he was raw, needy. Famished for her female nurturing. Desperate to assuage a child's ancient grief, a loss so deep and huge, it was part of the landscape of his mind.

Her eyes swam with tears. They spilled over, sliding down her face. He was completely naked to her. Wide open. It was unbearable.

Shame transformed instantly into anger. For a moment, he hated her for witnessing his weakness. He shoved her away from him.

She stumbled back, startled. When he dared to look at her again, her gaze was wide and cautious. She was wiping her eyes, covering her breasts with her hands, backing away. Too late for that. Power welled up inside him, sexual and dangerous. His cock jutted toward her.

He advanced on her. "You want to know me, Erin? I'll show you everything I've got. Let's go into the bathroom and get started."

Her eyes were full of tremulous uncertainty. "Connor? I—"

"I want to wash my come off you. Then I want to fuck you in the shower. And I want to do it now. So *move.*"

Her mouth snapped shut, and she gave him a jerky nod. Her slender back trembled as she preceded him into the bathroom.

He'd scared her. He almost relented, and then he thought of that naked moment at her breast. She had tricked him into this. No masks, no mercy. She showed him hers, he'd show her his.

It wasn't his fault if she didn't like everything she found.

The bathroom was still humid and perfumed from her hair goop. He wrenched aside the shower curtain, set the hot water running, and motioned for her to get into the tub.

She was silent and wide-eyed, hot water pounding down and soaking her curtain of dark hair. He grabbed the shower gel, sudsed up his hands and turned her around, yanking her back against him so his cock was pressed against her ass. He washed his sticky come off her belly, her breasts, touching her with proprietary boldness. She reached down to wash between her legs, but he grabbed her hand.

"No. Don't wash your lube away. It's better than soap or water, and you're really tight and small. You're going to need all of it."

She shivered at his matter-of-fact tone. He covered her soapy hands with his and pressed them against her breasts, glad for any excuse to fondle them. He shoved her legs wider so he could nudge his cock between her thighs and set his teeth against the tender curve between neck and shoulder.

"Still want to know what's under my mask, Erin?" He slid his fingers down to tangle in the curls between her legs. "Still convinced?"

He was taunting her. He couldn't help it. He almost wanted her to chicken out, so they would have to stop. So they wouldn't slide down this slippery slope to God knew what.

She pressed her body back against him, clasping his cock between her clenched thighs, and turned up her wet, flushed face to him. Her eyes glowed with primal female challenge.

"Yes," she said simply.

Water pounded around them. If she had been any less heightened, the look on his face would have terrified her. He pushed her until she tipped forward.

"Brace yourself against the wall." His voice was harsh and breathless. "Spread your legs wider."

"Connor?" She caught herself against the cold, wet tile.

He gripped her hips and bent her over. "You want me to put my mask back on? Just say the word if the real me is too scary for you."

"This does not give you the right to act like a prick!" Her voice choked off when he slid his fingers between her legs.

"Oh, I'm not acting," he said. "I thought that was the whole point."

He nudged the head of his penis between her soft folds, and pushed. He seemed impossibly large from this angle. Her body bore down on him, and he slowed, stroking her hips. "Arch your back," he commanded. "It'll make it easier for you."

"This isn't for me, though," she snapped. "This is all for you."

He shoved himself deeper. "You showed me yours, and I'm showing you mine. I'm just following my instincts. That's all there is under the mask, Erin. Instinct. Appetite. We're all just selfish, hungry animals underneath."

That's not true, she wanted to cry out, but she was too overwhelmed by his body, penetrating and invading her. Her arms trembled with the strain, and her hair hung down like a dripping curtain before her eyes. He thrust into her again, and a blaze of startled heat kindled. She quivered, softened around him.

He made a low, approving sound and gripped her hips, pulsing and pressing himself against that hot spot deep inside, a font of sensation so new, her brain barely knew how to process it. She pushed against him, seeking more, but he controlled the rhythm completely.

"See? It's not just for me," he said. "You get it now?"

She reached down to touch herself, but a single trembling arm wasn't strong or stable enough to brace her weight against the wall. She had to use both. He slid his own hand around her hips immediately, and found her clitoris with his fingertip, teasing it tenderly.

"I've got you," he said. "I'll take care of you, Erin."

Then he let himself go and took her deep and hard. She cried out and stumbled closer to the wall, bracing herself with her folded forearms. She gave in to it. Every deep, gliding thrust stoked that secret glow inside her, every seductive stroke was slicker, more liquid.

But Connor was angry with her, and she didn't know why. She felt the barely restrained violence with which he was using her body, and thought of how her father had betrayed him, abandoned him to die. The searing anger that must have caused. Rage that had no outlet.

Until now, a voice in her head whispered. She'd offered herself up on a silver platter. Here she was, naked and bent over for his pleasure.

He felt the fear and shame that clutched her, and stopped. He was shoved so deep inside her, she felt him pressing against her womb.

"Had enough, Erin? Want the mask back?"

"No, I don't want masks! That's not what I want at all, Connor—"

"Then what the fuck do you want?" he panted.

I want you to love me. She stopped the words just in time. "I want to turn around," she said. "I need to see your face. Your eyes."

He pulled out and spun her around, pushing her back against the wall. He wasted no time in scooping her leg up to dangle it over his arm.

He drove inside her once again. Water pounded, steam billowed. Erin gasped for breath and hung onto his shoulders, just as she hung onto the piercing comprehension that had come to her when she had held his head at her breast. The pang of grief and empathy for a bereft, motherless little boy. The longing she ached to soothe.

That was the shining truth beneath all this push and shove. She was in love with him. She wanted all of him, every face, every side: the furious demon lover, the grieving child, the tender seducer, the gallant protector. She loved them all, and if surrendering could prove that to him, then surrender she would. She had no choice anyway; he ravished her senses, he flooded her body with wild heat. She melted around him in an endless, shivering climax that embraced everything he was: his body, his passion, his pain, his anger. She wanted it all.

He wrenched himself out of her with a shout, seizing her hand and wrapping her fingers around his shaft. He erupted. Jets of hot semen welled up and trickled over their interlocked fingers.

They sagged to their knees together in the ankle-deep water. After three tries, Connor finally managed to raise his arm high enough to push down the faucet knob. Silence, and then the hollow drip of the shower. They clung to each other, trembling.

Connor was the first to raise his head. He tried to smooth back the soaked hair that clung to her face. "Erin—"

"No," she said.

He frowned. "No, what?"

"No, you didn't hurt me, so stop worrying. It was fabulous."

He looked mystified. "How did you know what I was going to say?"

"Must've learned the mind-reading trick from you," she said, nuzzling his throat. "You made me angry, but you didn't hurt me. You couldn't. You don't have it in you. You're too sweet."

He stared down at her, incredulous. "After what just happened here, you still think I'm sweet?"

She kissed the scar on his shoulder. "Oh, yes. You're lots of things, Connor McCloud. And one of them is very, very sweet."

Connor wiped the water off his face and reached for her. "You're nuts, Erin. You trust me more than I trust myself."

"It's scary to lose control," she murmured.

His arms tightened around her. "Tell me about it."

He reached for the shower gel and pulled her up onto her knees, sliding his soapy hand between her legs. She gasped and clutched his shoulders. She wasn't used to being touched at all, let alone this intimately, and his hands made free with her body, laving and rinsing, his fingers sliding tenderly into the folds of her sex. As if to tell her that she was all his, to touch and handle as he pleased.

Two could play that game. She soaped her hand and reached for his penis. He caught her wrist and stopped her.

"No more of your sex goddess tricks," he growled. "I have to chill out now. It's a physiological necessity."

"Don't worry," she assured him. "You're safe, at least for a little while. I need to rest, too."

The haunted look in his eyes gave way to a slow, appreciative smile. The water swirled around them, until the drain swallowed all the water. They were tangled together in an empty tub.

"I don't know if I can move," she confessed. "I'm limp."

He hauled himself up until he sat on the edge of the tub. She barely caught the tightening on his face as he rubbed his scarred leg.

"Does it hurt?" she asked hesitantly.

He shrugged. "It worked better before it got smashed to pieces. I'm just grateful that I can still walk on it."

She brushed her hand down the length of the series of surgical scars. She leaned forward, and tenderly kissed every one of them.

He murmured incoherently, and hid his face against her wet hair.

They stayed that way until Erin started shivering. He helped her to her feet, and they toweled each other off in a shy silence.

The room looked as if a hurricane had struck; blankets on one side of the bed, coverlet on the other, pillows on the floor, sheets torn half off the mattress. Erin's clothes were scattered everywhere. She started making the bed. Connor put his hand on her arm.

"Leave it." He picked up the blankets and pillows and tossed them carelessly onto the ravaged bed. "We'll just sleep on the other one."

It was hard for her to leave it messy, but the nagging, neatnik voice in her mind that usually ruled the roost was muted and faraway. She had bigger things to occupy her mind. An unmade bed was the least of her concerns. Her clothes were another matter, though. She repacked them all, and when she looked up, Connor was stretched out beneath the covers, watching her.

She glanced down at herself. Stark naked in front of him, and she wasn't self-conscious at all. She was transformed.

"You're so beautiful, Erin," he said softly. "You blow my mind."

Self-consciousness rushed back in a big, sweeping whoosh.

She let her tangled hair fall forward over her hot face as she shoved her toiletries case into the space allotted for it. That comment merited a graceful acknowledgment, if her throat would only stop shaking long enough to make one. "Thanks," she whispered.

He turned the covers down on her side of the bed and beckoned to her, baring all the rippling, lean muscles of his gorgeous torso in the process. "Come to bed with me?"

"In a minute. I have to try and get in touch with Cindy. Even though she probably won't talk to me."

"What's with Cindy? She OK?"

"I don't know yet." Erin dug her organizer out of her purse and curled up in the space Connor made for her. She tried the cell phone number first. It rang and rang. Then she tried Cindy's group house. Caitlin, one of Cindy's roommates, picked up. "Hello?"

"Hi, Caitlin, this is Erin, Cindy's sister. Is she there?"

"Uh, no. I haven't seen her in a while. But when she gets back, I'll sure tell her you called, OK?"

"Thanks," Erin said. "Ah, Caitlin, this guy she's seeing, this Billy. Do you know where she met him? Or anything about him at all?"

There was an awkward pause. "Uh . . . I'm afraid I don't. I've only met him a couple times," Caitlin said. "But he seems real nice to me."

"OK. Thanks. 'Bye, Caitlin." She hung up. The cold lump of anxiety in her belly was back.

"What's up with Cindy, Erin?" Connor's voice had taken on a hard, steely note that she had come to recognize.

She started working the comb through her tangled hair, and the task calmed down her trembling fingers. "She's left college during exam week. She's lost her scholarship. And now she's staying down in the city, God knows where, with a guy named Billy who drives a Jaguar and gives her expensive gifts. I called her new cell phone number yesterday. She told me that college was a stupid waste of time, and that her financial problems were over. She'd found new ways to make money."

He sat up, scowling. "Ouch."

"My sentiments exactly," Erin said fervently.

"Did she sound like she was high?"

She gulped. "Couldn't say. I don't have much experience with that. She sounded giggly and euphoric, but Cindy's always been giggly. And I think she's in love. That could account for the euphoria."

"We need to find out more about this guy Billy."

His casual use of the word "we" made her chest ache with gratitude. Not that anyone could help, but at least he cared. She scooted behind him and started combing his hair. "There's nothing we can do until she answers her phone and tells me more," she said.

Connor winced when she hit a tangle. "Erin, isn't once a night enough for this combing business? You'll comb me bald."

"You can't go to sleep with your hair tangled like that," she fussed. She worked through it till every lock was slicked back from his face. "Her roommates probably think they're protecting Romeo and Juliet by not telling me anything," she said. "Fluff-brained idiots."

He turned around, grinning. "There's more than one way to get information," he said. "I've got an idea."

Connor groped in the pocket of his coat for his cell phone and dialed Sean's number as he slid back into bed, into close contact with Erin's slender, curvy body. Good thing Sean's latest bed toy had mutated into a gigantic bloodsucking insect. Otherwise the chances of getting Sean at this hour would have been next to zilch. Sean's evenings almost always ended up in some woman's bed or other.

"What is it?" Sean's voice sounded breathless and annoyed.

"Jesus, Sean, have you already found a new girlfriend?"

"None of your goddamn business, but if you must know, I'm at the dojo. I just finished teaching my kickboxing class for Davy. What's up? You in trouble yet?"

"Not yet, but I've got a job for you. Urgent. Detective type stuff."

Sean groaned. "Oh, God. You're not unloading one of Davy's duller 'n dirt watching-the-paint-peel stakeout gigs on me, are you?"

"Nah. I know the exact limits of your attention span. This one's right up your alley. It involves visiting a house full of fresh, juicy, college chicks and prying information out of them."

There was a thoughtful pause. "I'm listening," Sean said.

"I thought that might grab you." Connor related the facts to Sean with blunt concision. "We need to know who this fuckhead with the Jaguar is, and where he's been. And we need to know it now."

"Got it. One thing. The chicks. Are they genuinely cute? Or are you shitting me?"

Connor looked at Erin. "Cindy's roommates. Are they cute? Sean wants to know."

Erin opened and closed her mouth, bewildered. "Uh, I . . . well, I never thought to . . . uh—"

"Drop-dead gorgeous, every last one of them," Connor said into the phone. "There's a platinum blonde, and a redhead, and a black chick, and an Asian—"

"Oh, piss off," Sean muttered. "What's the address?"

"Address?" Connor gestured for her organizer, and Erin passed it to him. He read off the address to his brother. "Get on it quick, Sean. I've got a bad feeling about this."

"You've got bad feelings about everything," Sean grumbled. "I'm on it, don't worry. First thing tomorrow."

Connor hung up. "If anybody can charm information out of a houseful of females, Sean can," he told her. "He's a goddamn Adonis. It's cruel to sic him on them during finals weeks, but hey, this is war."

"Doesn't your brother have a job? How is he free on a Monday?"

"Sean's a free agent. Both of my brothers work for themselves. Our upbringing wasn't conducive to fitting easily into hierarchies."

"You fit in, didn't you?" she asked.

"I thought I did." Her question made him feel bleak. "I guess I wasn't cut out for a real job any more than my brothers are."

"One more thing," she said, frowning. "You say your brother Sean is so cute. Is he as good-looking as you?"

He laughed at her. "Hah. Even at my best, Sean leaves me in the dust. And Davy, too, in a different way. Davy's got forty pounds of solid muscle on me. But Sean's the pinup loverboy of the three of us."

She shook her head. "I cannot believe that," she said. "He cannot be cuter than you. It's physically impossible."

Damn. He was going to blush again. The soft look in her eyes made him want to roll around on the bed, as blissed out as a dog whose belly was being rubbed. "Come back to bed," he pleaded.

She crawled under the blankets he held up and nestled close to him. "Thank you for calling your brother," she said gravely. "I feel better already. Just because somebody's doing something."

He fitted her tightly against him. "It's nothing."

"Not to me." She kissed his chest. "My hero."

He stiffened against her. "Oh, God. Not you, too."

She pulled away from him. "What do you mean, not me, too?"

"My brothers, the Cave. And now you. I can't outrun it."

She sat up, and shook her head, bewildered. "Outrun what?"

"The hero crack," he snapped.

Her eyes were large and hurt. "It wasn't a crack. I didn't mean to offend you. I actually meant it as a compliment."

He rolled over onto his back and stared at the ceiling, ashamed of himself. "Sorry," he muttered. "I'm not offended. Just self-conscious."

She kissed his chest. Her soft lips against his skin, her delicious warm weight made his body stir . . . and then throb.

"Well, whatever," she said briskly. "In any case, thank you. You're a sweetheart, and I appreciate your concern for my little sister."

"I care about Cindy, too," he said. "She's always been my pal."

"I know," she said. "I used to be so jealous that you joked around with her, but never with me."

He gaped at her. "Give me a break. Cindy was just a scrawny kid. But you? The teen dream with the sexy, pinup-girl body? Like I was going to tickle you or arm-wrestle you or so much as touch you with a ten-foot pole in front of your dad. I don't have a goddamn death wish."

"Oh, please," she murmured. "Don't exaggerate."

"Exaggerate, my ass," he muttered. "Besides, your mom was on to me from the start."

"What do you mean? On to what?"

"On to the fact that I liked you," he said. "She always hated my guts, and I'm pretty sure that's why."

"Mom did not hate you!" Erin protested. "That's ridiculous!"

"Sure. I was the only one of your dad's colleagues who called her Mrs. Riggs. In nine years, she never invited me to call her Barbara."

"Oh. Well. Mom's kind of . . . formal sometimes," Erin faltered.

Connor shot her a dubious glance. "Jesse called her Barb."

"Jesse was different," she said lamely.

"Yeah. Jesse never got busted staring at your tits." Connor pulled her closer and cupped her breast tenderly. Her nipple tightened. "I didn't blame her one bit. I'd feel the exact same way if I caught a man looking at my innocent young daughter the way I was looking at you."

"How . . . how were you looking at me?" she asked breathlessly.

He reached across her and flipped off the bedside lamp. "Like I wanted to throw you down onto the nearest bed and do . . . this."

He rolled on top of her and kissed her.

This was no good-night kiss. Connor's tongue deep thrust into her mouth. He nudged her legs apart and settled himself between them. Their dynamic had shifted since that wild scene in the shower. They had crossed over an invisible line, and there was no going back.

He reached between her thighs, bathing his fingers in the liquid pooled in her secret depths with a murmur of discovery. "Jesus," he muttered. "You're red-hot, Erin. You're ready for me right now." He guided his thick shaft to her tender opening.

She flinched as he nudged and prodded his way in and gripped his arms for ballast. "I thought you had to rest," she said breathlessly. "I thought it was a physiological necessity."

"It was," he said. "I rested."

He loomed over her in the darkness, overwhelming her. He'd used her body so hard, but with such terrifying skill. She would never have dreamed that anything so rough could give her pleasure. She was the one who had seduced him, she reminded herself. She had torn their barriers down, and there was no restoring them now.

"Is that all the rest you need?" she whispered.

"I want more of you, Erin. I want to be inside you. I'm not going to come this time, though."

She was startled. "You don't have to? I thought—"

"Nah." He grazed her throat delicately with his teeth. "Not this time. I can make it back off if I stop and concentrate. The next time I come, I want to be shoved inside you as deep as I can get. For that, we need a condom." He withdrew, and thrust heavily back in.

"Oh," she gasped.

"But you're a girl. You don't have to economize on your orgasms," he said. "No spending limits. An invitation to excess." His hips pulsed against her, pressing and circling against her every sensitive point.

"Ah . . ." Her fingernails dug into the hard muscles of his shoulders. "I . . . um . . ."

"I want to feel you come again. I love it when you clench up around me and explode. I want to feast on your pleasure. Will you give me that?" He did something wickedly marvelous, a licking caress up and down her labia with the head of his penis. "Pretty please."

Her moan became a gasp when he thrust again. "But you—"

"One thing to consider, though. If I don't come, that means there's no built-in stopping point. I could fuck you all night long. Literally." He slid inside her a couple of teasing inches, then out, swirling around her clitoris. "So it's up to you to say when you've had enough. Because I'm never going to want to stop. Get that? My job, to make you come. Your job, to tell me when we're done. And don't worry about hurting my feelings. I'm tough. That clear?"

He waited for her signal. She hesitated, sensing yet another point of no return. One out of so many. She hardly noticed them anymore.

She arched back with a sigh, offering herself to him.

He seduced her with a lazy erotic dance, feeling his way

into her inner self like a cat burglar stealing into a treasure trove. Once inside, he plundered her, conquered her with pleasure. They surged and writhed together until she was shimmering, liquid, mindless. A lake full of mist and moonlight. She had no borders left at all.

Another wave was building, bigger than any that had come before. She fought it. It was too far, too much. She couldn't control her body, it moved on its own, jerking up to meet him. He was driving her into chaotic madness, his hot mouth fastened on her breasts, his strong hands caressing her, his voice muttering rough encouragement. There was no end to how far he could push her. There were no limits at all.

It frightened her. To tell him to stop would be to admit defeat, but he wasn't tired at all. He was insatiable, triumphant. She lifted her hand and cradled his hot face. "Please," she whispered.

"Please, what? Please, more? Or please, enough?"

She could barely move her lips. "Please, enough."

He reached over and flipped on the light. "Why?"

She blinked in the sudden glare, and shook her head.

"Why, enough?" he demanded. "You were right there, on the edge of a big one. I could feel it coming on. Why stop? You still scared?"

"No," she lied.

He slid his arms beneath her, gathering her tightly against him. "Then give it to me," he urged. "Just one more."

"Connor, you promised you would stop if I—"

"Give it to me, Erin," he commanded. "I want it."

His voice rang with all the force of his will. It was not just her body he wanted to conquer. He was grasping for a bigger prize.

He drove her ruthlessly onward, and took what he wanted with a shout of triumph. She shattered, and flew to pieces.

She was weeping softly when she finally remembered who she was, and too exhausted even to be embarrassed. Connor turned out the light and pulled her against his chest. She lay in his arms, feeling the deep drum of his heart gradually slow.

Her eyes stung. What an idiot, to think she could control this, or him. Use him for sex, hah. She had thrown herself at him, and now she was all his. He could use her any way he pleased, and he knew it.

She was his, but she had no idea if he was hers.

Chapter

10

Connor jerked awake when the phone rang. He reached for it, but Erin was closer, and she grabbed it first.

"Hello?" She waited. "Hello? Hello!" She rattled the lever, hung up, and fell back onto the bed. "Must be a glitch in their wake-up call system," she said sleepily. "Did you ask for a wake-up call?"

"At three-seventeen in the morning? Like hell."

Every moment that passed, his eyes picked more details out of the gloom: the curves and contours and lovely shadows of her face. He pulled her close to his body, which sprang to throbbing attention at the contact with her silky, flower-petal heat. He was contemplating whether seducing her again would be overdoing it when she let out a soft snore.

There was his answer. He nuzzled his nose into her hair, and concentrated on the yogic breathing exercises Davy had inflicted on him when he was wrestling with pain management and weaning himself off Percocet. Fill the abdomen, then the chest. Hold it in, one . . . two . . . three, then slowly release. Each breath relaxing more deeply, letting the tension melt away, the heart rate slow, each muscle let go—

The phone shrilled again. He sprang for it, and Erin

jerked into shocked wakefulness. "Who the fuck is this?" he snarled.

There was a pause, not dead air, but a live line in which he knew someone was listening. Then the person on the other end started to laugh. A low, rasping chuckle. "Hello, McCloud. I understand you are enjoying yourself. Very wise. Who knows what tomorrow may bring?"

"Who is this?" he demanded.

"You know who I am," the man said. "You know my voice, no?"

Erin turned on the light before he could stop her. He turned his face away. He didn't want her to see how scared he was. "What do you want?"

That hideous, theatrical laugh again. "You know what I want, McCloud. You took something from me. I want it back."

"Where are you?" he asked, just for the hell of it.

Click. The phone went dead.

He let the phone drop to the bed. Erin touched his shoulder, and he jerked as if her hand were a live wire.

"Who was that?" she asked.

"Novak," he said.

Her hand dropped. "That's not possible."

"I know," he snarled. "But it was him. I know his voice."

"But how . . . who knew that we were coming here?"

"No one," he said. "Not even my brothers."

He hung up, and called the front desk. It rang six times before a sleepy, youthful male voice answered. "Uh . . . uh, good evening, Crow's Nest Inn, can I help—"

"Did you just put through a call to Room 404?"

The kid yawned. "Uh . . . actually, I was asleep, so no. There haven't been any calls since before midnight."

"Could the call have gone to an automated voice mail system?"

"No, sir, we don't have one of those." The kid was waking up, his voice getting strident and defensive. "If somebody called you, it woulda had to have been from inside the hotel. Room to room."

That would have made his blood run cold, if it had not already been subzero. "Did you give our room number to any other guests?"

"No way!" The kid's voice was shrill with outrage. "That's not allowed! We'll put a call through, but we never give out room numbers!"

He was stupid to alienate the guy, but too freaked out to care. "Then I need a list of all the guests in the hotel. Right now."

"I'm gonna have to talk to the manager about that. I'm not authorized to do that."

"Get him," Connor ordered. "Now."

"I can't." The kid's voice was triumphant. "He won't be in till nine o'clock tomorrow morning, and besides—"

Connor slammed the phone down. Only Erin's big, worried eyes kept him from hurling the fucking thing against the wall.

He was losing it, and Erin was staring at him, clutching the sheet to her chest. Afraid for him. Or worse, *of* him. He dropped his face into his hands, and groped for a plan. He was tempted to call Nick, but he knew how that would play. Even if Nick believed him, which was doubtful, and even if Nick could get someone out here relatively quickly with a warrant to scour the hotel, Novak would never make it so easy. Connor would end up looking like a bozo with his head up his ass, and matters would be worse. And Erin would end up going to meet this Mueller asshole. Alone.

You have something that I want. He shuddered.

Erin scrambled across the bed and draped her soft, comforting warmth against his shaking shoulders. "There's no way that Novak could know that we're here."

"I heard him, Erin," he said grimly. "I know that guy's voice."

"Voices can be deceiving, particularly on the telephone,"

she said. "Did he say who he was? Did he actually say the name Kurt Novak?"

He ran the brief conversation through his mind. "No," he admitted reluctantly. "But he called me by name."

"Hmm," she murmured. "And what else did he say?"

"He said, 'You know who I am.' And he said I took something from him, and he wanted it back. I assume he was referring to you. Then he hung up."

"But he did not say who he was," she repeated.

"Erin, goddamn it—"

"Is there any way at all that you might have dreamed some of it? Projected Novak's voice onto some silly prank call?"

"You saw me talk to him," he snapped. "Did I look like I was dreaming? What are the odds that we would get a call like that tonight?"

She laid her hot cheek against his back. "I'm a deep sleeper," she said. "I've seen and heard strange things while coming out of a dream. You're so worried and stressed, it would be understandable if you—"

"I am not losing it." He bit the words out viciously.

She went very still. "I never said that you were." Her voice was crisp. "Don't you dare get huffy on me, Connor McCloud."

He groped for her hand, which was still resting on her shoulder, and pressed it to his lips. As much of an apology as he could manage.

It seemed to satisfy her. Her hands began to move again, sliding over his chest. "OK. Let's try this from another angle," she said. "Could he have found us by following the trail of your credit card?"

He could tell from her tone that she was just humoring him, but he appreciated the effort. Almost as much as he appreciated her sweet, stroking hands. He shook his head. "I used a fake ID. Complete with Social Security number, credit history, driver's license."

Her hands stopped moving. "Isn't that, um . . . against the law?"

"Sure it is. My buddy Seth set it up for me. For my birthday present, believe it or not. Trust Seth, to come up with the perfect gift."

"Oh." Her voice was small and thoughtful.

"I gave him all kinds of moralistic shit about it at the time. He just laughed and said, 'Happy birthday, tight-ass. Your day will come.'"

Her soft lips moved against his neck. He wanted to tell her that he didn't need to be gentled like a skittish horse, but it would be a lie. She scooted around until she was facing him, and put her arms around him. Hugged him, her lush tits pressed against his chest.

His physical reaction was immediate, and predictable. He struggled to focus on his problem through the rising haze of lust. "Maybe . . . maybe they, uh, tagged my car," he mumbled.

She made a dismissive gesture with her hand. "That's enough of that," she said. "It's three-thirty in the morning, and you need to get some rest, no matter who was on the other end of that phone."

He settled his hands in the curve of her slender waist. "Erin—"

"You've got alarms on the doors and windows. You've got your gun right at your elbow. If you can't relax now, then when can you?"

"Never," he said. "How am I supposed to sleep? I'm as pumped up as a racehorse at the starting gate."

She curled her fingers around his stiff cock, and squeezed him with seductive tenderness. Her siren's smile made his brain melt down to molten lava. "Could you if we, ah . . ."

"Don't tempt me," he growled. "We've been at it for hours. I don't want to hurt you."

She laughed softly. "That is so sweet of you," she whispered against his mouth. "And so misguided. You are so cute, Connor."

She kissed him. Her lips were so delicate and soft, her tongue flicking against his with shy insistence. She cut through his resistance with no effort at all. He dragged her closer and kissed her back. Frantically, like someone was trying to take her from him.

Someone is, a laconic voice in his mind observed.

He shoved the voice away. This moment was his, and he would allow nothing to diminish it. She flung her thigh over his lap, and her wiggling and writhing almost got him off then and there. He fought the excitement down to a dull, pounding roar in his ears.

Then she seized his cock and attempted to push him inside her. He flung his head back with a startled gasp, and hung on to his self-control. She was too tight to take in much of him in this position, but it was amazing. A hot, suckling kiss, just the head of his cock gripped tightly inside her. She moved against him, tentative and awkward, and his heart practically exploded with tenderness. She was so generous and sexy and gorgeous. All he wanted was to sprawl over backwards on the bed and let her have her wicked way with him, but he didn't dare, not without a condom. He had to be on top, to control the timing and the angle. He was on the brink of exploding inside her right now.

He was still shaking with adrenaline, but Erin had shoved that hellish phone call into another room in his mind and slammed the door on it. It waited for him, grim and patient. It wasn't going anywhere.

Let it wait. He cupped the curves of her ass cheeks, and stood, lifting her with him. Still joined just a couple of wet, tantalizing inches. He turned around and laid her down on the rumpled bed, never once breaking that hot, clinging contact. He stayed on his feet as he sank his full length into her welcoming body.

Maybe it was the adrenaline, maybe just the sight of her smiling, holding out her arms to him, but the whole thing flew right out of control. Out of nowhere, he found himself panting and heaving and pumping against her; she was making those soft, sobbing sounds, and the bed was rattling and shaking. He knew he should slow down and make her come first, but it was beyond him. He would make it up to her later a thousand times over. This time was all for him. He craved the oblivion of this hot, slick, mindless thrusting, the deafening crash and roar as his orgasm blasted through him, obliterating thought.

Every instinct screamed to just let go, fill her with his come.

He wrenched out at the last possible instant and spurted across her damp, trembling body.

God, that had been close. More intense every goddamn time.

He sank down to trembling knees and pressed his face against the amazingly soft skin of her inner thigh. The warm, rich sea smell of her sex was intoxicating. He trailed his fingers over her cleft, caressing the soft fuzz of damp ringlets. She was still shaking. Her fingers were tangled in his hair, stroking him. He could lose himself exploring her body, and never get tired of it. He could eat her again right now. Just bury his face in her beautiful, juicy cunt and worship it.

Then it hit him, what was waiting for him, behind that door in his mind. The phone call. He'd been better off in the drugged haze of sex.

He stood up. She started to follow, and he pushed her back down onto the bed. "Stay there," he said.

"But I have to—"

"I'll wash you," he told her. "I just need a minute alone. Please."

He stumbled into the bathroom and winced at the mirror. His eyes looked crazed. He looked like a guy who heard impossible voices in the night, who mixed up dreams with reality. A guy who would kidnap a vulnerable girl, drag her off to a secluded hotel room and fuck her all night long. How many times—nah, no point in counting. One just blended into the next. It was one long fuck session, interrupted by conversation and the odd nap. And the occasional death threat from a homicidal maniac, of course. Just to liven things up.

He choked on his own bitter laughter, and hunched over the sink. He washed his cock and splashed water on his face, then took a deep breath, and put his hand on the doorknob.

He stopped, running over that goddamn phone call in his mind. It was improbable, ridiculous, to think that Novak could have found them here. No one had known. He had only decided himself at the last moment. But the alternative was even scarier—at least to him. That what he'd heard wasn't real. He turned on the water and splashed his face again. He was afraid to go out and face her. Ashamed that she might think that he was . . .

No. He turned his back on the unthinkable. He couldn't afford to doubt himself. He shook it off, a fierce, angry shudder of refusal.

He had promised to wash her. He ran hot water over one of the washcloths hanging on the rack, and shoved the door open.

Erin was perched on the bed, knees drawn up to her chest. He knelt in front of her and sponged every trace of his come off her belly, her breasts. She stretched and smiled, opening to his touch. He wanted to sponge her between her legs, too, but the washcloth was sticky. He flung it aside. His tongue was warm and wet, and would do just as well.

She gasped as he pushed her legs open and put his mouth to her again. "Connor! For God's sake—"

"Let me." God, she was juicy and sweet.

Erin sagged back onto the bed. She was tugging at his hair, saying something urgent, pleading, but it degenerated into shocked gasps of pleasure soon enough. He owed her an orgasm after his latest caveman performance. It was a matter of pride.

He laved her with his mouth, every precious pink fold, every delicate detail. He fastened his lips and tongue around her clit, and the taut, swollen nub thrummed against his mouth. He suckled and nibbled and insisted until she came, right against his face.

He slid up into her arms and hid his face against her breasts. She pulled the blankets over them, murmuring sweet words that almost untangled the knot of fear in his chest.

The world was getting weirder by the minute, but this, at least, was amazing and sweet. He would take all the comfort he could from it.

He waited until she was fast asleep, and gently untangled himself from her slender limbs. He propped his back against the headboard and stared with hot, suspicious eyes into the ominous shadows. Sleep was a million miles away. His gun was inches from his hand. He monitored the soft rise and fall of her breath with his other hand.

He had come down here to guard her, so by God, he would do it.

Tamara stretched her perfect body, well aware of the effect she made in the rumpled sheets. She smiled through her lashes at the man lying beside her. He was playing with a strand of her fiery hair, his face relaxed and calm, but that could change in an instant. A raised eyebrow, a smile that struck him as false, and the world could explode.

She was well used to living in several different realities at once, but this was the finest line she had ever walked.

She channeled the emotional energy of that rush of fear into a sensual wiggle and a satisfied smile, and struggled to remember why she had decided to do this, why it had seemed so incredibly important at the time. Usually she loved risk, even craved it. But as the days with Novak crawled by, she was loving it less and less.

Stultifying tedium looked very attractive to her right now.

"You were inspired tonight," she murmured. Her voice was throaty and relaxed. Whore's talk had always come easily to her.

"Perhaps Nigel's report inspired me." His lips curved in a dimpled, deceptively sweet smile. "He could hear McCloud halfway down the corridor. Like a wild boar in rut. Poor Erin."

She chuckled. "Surprising. I would have thought that your phone call would put a damper on things."

"Not at all. He reacted just as I would have expected. Fear and anger leads directly to the desire to conquer and punish and control." He wrapped the lock of hair around his finger and tugged it. She winced, and cried out. She had learned, to her cost, that hiding pain was a big mistake. "I studied him, you know," he went on. "I profiled him, just as he has profiled me. We have a great deal in common."

"Really? What?"

He let go of her hair, to her relief, and stared up at the ceiling. "Unusual childhoods, for one thing. We both suffered the traumatic loss of our mothers at an early age, for instance."

She made a soft, distressed sound, but he was not trolling for sympathy. His eyes were remote. "We both had mentally imbalanced fathers. We both have physical defects. His were inflicted by me, and mine, indirectly, by him." He held up his maimed hand, and passed it over the puckered bullet scar that marred his pale thigh.

"Fascinating," she murmured. "I never thought of the symmetry. The matching injuries. Hand and thigh." She leaned over, ran her hand over the scar on his thigh, and took a calculated risk. She drew his hand to her lips and kissed each scarred stump.

He smiled his appreciation of the gesture, and she shuddered with her relief. "What else?" she urged.

"Intensity," he mused. "Inability to compromise. He is a good enemy. I will be sorry to lose him. It will be almost like losing a friend."

Like he knew what it meant to have a friend.

The dangerous thought flitted through her mind before she could suppress it, and fear followed in its wake. She could not afford to let such things float to the surface of her conscious mind. He was supernaturally acute, sniffing out every slightest scent of treachery.

His eyes focused on her with unnerving intensity. "I have always been good at sensing fault lines, exploiting them," he said. "So was Victor. He actually had the gall to try it on me. Remember?"

"Yes," she said quietly. "That was why you killed him."

"I found his weak point, and then tap, tap, crack, and he came apart. That is how I will destroy them all. Tap, tap, Tamara. That's all it takes, and they will fall over their own feet to destroy themselves."

She hoped her smile was not shaking. "Brilliant," she said.

"Erin will be the hardest, but I think I have the key to her now."

"Her weakness is Connor McCloud, obviously," Tamara said.

"Look deeper than the obvious," he snapped. "Erin likes order. Chaos makes her frantic. Her father's disgrace, what happened at Crystal Mountain, it shook her to her foundations. When the rest of her world falls to pieces, we will see what she is really made of."

"Brilliant." Her voice sounded mechanical to her own ears.

"This is moving fast," he said. "We must accelerate things, to keep up with McCloud's and Erin's immoderate lust."

"I spoke to our operative in Marseilles earlier, right before you came to me," she told him.

He seized a lock of her hair and tugged it again, cruelly hard. "You should have told me immediately."

She forced herself to whimper and cringe. Her own nature would have dictated stoic silence, but she did not want to challenge him. Oh, no, no, no. Even she knew when to bend. "I'm sorry," she said. "You were so passionate . . . it drove it right out of my mind. Please . . ."

He let go of her hair and backhanded her across the face. "What did he say?"

She touched her throbbing cheek. Another bruise. She was brilliant with paints and powders, but there were limits even to her genius. "Martin Olivier is ready to play his part," she said. "They've coached him carefully. He will be captured by the police, and confess to seeing you and Georg at the rendezvous point outside Marseilles. Whenever you want him to."

"Call them," he said slowly. "It must happen the day after tomorrow. That gives Ingrid and Matthieu time to arrange poor Claude's transport to Marseilles."

"Isn't it dangerous to move a man in a coma?" she asked timidly.

Novak shrugged. "Claude has never disobliged me in his life. He would not dare to die before it is convenient for me. Yes, Tuesday morning would be best. That will also give Erin and McCloud time to generate some titillating X-rated video footage for us when they get back to Seattle. I need it for the grand finale. Speaking of which, Rolf Hauer is in place to take care of Claude? That has to happen shortly after Martin's confession. Preferably the same day."

"He is in Marseilles, awaiting orders," she assured him. "All the pieces are in place. Your choreography is absolutely brilliant."

He stared at her for a long, uncomfortable moment. "You flatter me, Tamara," he said slowly. "I hope very much that you don't ever presume to manipulate me with flattery. I dislike that."

The white-hot glow in his eyes terrified her. "God, no. Really, I—"

"You know, of course, that your knowledge of all these details binds you to me for life. And beyond."

She forced herself to relax against him and smile up into

his eyes through her lashes. "Yes," she said softly. "I am honored by your trust."

He parted her legs and thrust his hand inside her. She reminded herself, as she moved sinuously against him, that this couldn't last much longer. And he would pay for every insult to her body, in blood.

He lost interest in touching her very quickly, thank God, and flopped onto his back. "I wish I could have watched them tonight."

"You'll have your chance," she said. "This is just the beginning."

"I've developed quite a taste for video voyeurism. I imagine you did, too, during your time with Victor, hmm? It was his passion."

She covered up her shiver at the mention of Victor's name with a rippling laugh. "Oh, I humored him."

"Did you, my beautiful whore? How? Tell me everything."

She gathered her ragged acting skills together. She'd never felt so alive as during that brief time she had spent in Victor Lazar's bed. He had seen past all her tricks and accepted her for what she was.

And he had wanted her, too, with a searing passion that had shocked emotions to life inside her that she had thought were safely dead. One of the few things she absolutely could not bear would be for her current employer to paw through her memories of Victor.

But then again—her anger and her fear reminded her of why she was doing this in the first place. That was very good. That helped.

"There's not much to tell," she said lightly. "He was more dull and straightforward in bed than one would have thought, to know him. Far less fascinating and challenging than you, for instance."

He kissed her, his long tongue thrusting like a snake into her mouth, and sank his sharp teeth into her lower lip, holding it fast. They sank deeper, almost breaking skin. She went rigid with terror.

He laughed, and released her. "I think you are lying to me."

She rolled onto her back and shook her head. Smiling, smiling, smiling. Like a dog who showed its throat to the head of the pack in hopes of not being ripped to shreds. "I wish that I were," she said. "You know how I hate to be bored. I would make up some kinky stories for you if I didn't know that you prefer the truth, boss. Even if it's less interesting than a juicy lie."

She looked directly into his eyes, projecting with all her considerable strength. Warm, glowing. Oh, so disarmingly sincere.

He stroked her cheek, nodded and smiled. He bought it.

She was so relieved, she had to do something with the rush of emotion, so she rolled up onto her elbow and kissed him, trailing her fingers down the front of his wiry, cruelly strong body. She found him already hard. Good. It was easier for her to cover while fucking than while talking. Men were so much more stupid when they were fucking. Her hand tightened, moving in a swirling, expert caress.

He murmured with pleasure. "What a mysterious creature you are, Tamara," he said. "Intriguing. Full of secrets."

"Not to you," she assured him.

"So strong and fearless. A person's greatest strengths and her greatest weaknesses are one and the same, did you know that?"

"Are they really?" She shimmied down his body and replaced her hand with her skillful mouth.

"Yes. I will exploit both your strength and your weakness."

He was quiet for a few minutes, his fingernails digging painfully into her scalp as she did her best to distract him from this dangerous train of thought. She was skillful enough to do it on total autopilot, and lucky for her, because she couldn't control her thoughts. Her thoughts were thinking her. Crazy thoughts, out of place in this room, with this deadly man. Thoughts of love, of all things. She wondered, inside that barricaded part of herself, if what she had felt for Victor was love. She would kill to avenge him. If that wasn't love, what was?

It didn't matter. It was closer to love than she had ever hoped or wished to come. It had been scary. It had hurt. It had made her feel weak and vulnerable, and then he had died, at Novak's hand. She had been so angry, she'd wanted to lob a nuclear bomb at someone.

A woman like her could not afford to have a heart. It could get her killed, and she still wanted to live. She was not yet that far gone.

All too soon he tired of her efforts. He wrenched her head away from his groin. His eyes were lit up with a phosphorescent glow, a look that always portended danger. "I miss him from time to time, you know."

She wiped her mouth, blinked innocently. "Who?"

"Victor. It's sad, to lose a friend. I have so few, the world being what it is. But he crossed the line, Tamara. He crossed me."

She smiled demurely, still pumping his stiff penis with her hands. "And when have I ever crossed you, boss?"

He stroked her cheek with the stubs of his fingers. A surreal parody of tenderness. "Never, I hope."

He wrenched her up by the hair and flung her facedown onto the bed. He shoved her legs open and drove inside her, so hard and so suddenly that she slid up the bed and hit her head against the headboard before she had a chance to brace herself. She saw stars, put her hand out to cushion her head, and thought about killing him.

Usually, it helped. This time it only maddened her. His defenses were so smooth and impenetrable. She was seldom alone with him, only when she was naked in bed, and he was far more physically powerful than she. He always had whoever served him sip his drinks and taste his food before eating. He was always armed. He never slept. Never, as if he had a supernatural font of energy. Like a perpetual coke high, but he never touched drugs. Which was too bad. She was good with drugs. It would have been so much easier to kill him that way.

His arm snaked around in front of her neck, arching it back and cutting off her air. She gasped, hovering on the brink of fainting.

"So fearless," he crooned, his body pounding into hers. "Never cross me, Tamara. I would be so hurt."

"Never," she choked out. "Never."

Chapter

11

Erin's dream was a snarl of erotic images, a volatile mix of pleasure and danger and painful longing. Male voices merged with it, and the click of the door closing pulled her to wakefulness.

A deep, sensual ache permeated her body. Her skin was strangely sensitized. The brush of the sheet against her body made her want to writhe and stretch. She opened her eyes a tiny crack and peeked.

Sure enough. It was the hotel room. Oh, God. It hadn't been a dream. It was real, all of it. Hours of it. A delicious shiver rippled through her. She took a deep breath and rolled over to face him.

Connor stood by the bed, looking down at her. He wore only his jeans, his hair waving loose over his shoulders. His eyes looked somber and shadowed. "Good morning," he said.

"Good morning," she echoed. "Did you sleep well?"

He shook his head. She thought of last night's strange, inexplicable phone call, and how badly it had upset him. Of course he hadn't slept, poor baby, but it was probably better to avoid the subject entirely. He was sure to be twitchy and defensive about it.

She sat up, pulling the sheet up to cover her breasts. "Was someone just here? I thought I heard voices."

He held up his hand. It was full of condoms. "Turns out there's a vending machine in the men's bathroom in the lobby. I was too crazed to think of it last night. The desk clerk brought them up for me."

He was so casual about it, like it was a given that they were going to make love again, again and again. Heated images from the night before raced through her mind, and liquid heat rushed and throbbed between her legs. She blushed and shrank back against the headboard.

His face hardened. He dropped the condoms onto the bedside table. "Don't give me that scared rabbit look. You don't have to be afraid of me. I would never force you."

Oh, good Lord, he was so proud and high-strung, and now she'd hurt his tender feelings. She grabbed his hand as he turned away and tugged at it. "Connor, don't. I'm just shy, and tired, and kind of overwhelmed. It would be too much, to make love again. That's all."

A slow, cautious smile curved his mouth. "That's cool with me," he said. He lifted her hand to his lips and kissed it. "They'll keep."

She stared at him, dazzled at how gorgeous he was. She finally managed to drag her eyes away, and focused on the heap of condoms. "Good heavens," she said blankly. "How many did you ask for?"

"I figured twelve would hold us until we have a chance to get to a drugstore," he said. "Based on how things went last night."

Her eyes widened. "Twelve? Connor, I have to walk past that guy when we check out of here! *Twelve?*"

"Sorry." He blinked innocently. "Don't worry, Erin. We don't have to use them all this morning. I was just being, you know—prepared."

She drew her knees up to her chest and hid her face against them. "This is a big deal for me," she said. "I don't know how to be cool and casual about it. I'm not quite sure how I'm supposed to act."

He sank down on his knees next to the bed. "Don't act," he urged. "Just be. No masks, right? Didn't we establish that last night? I go for that, Erin. It turns me on. And this is a big deal for me, too. Believe me. Now give me a good-morning kiss."

His warm, teasing smile was magnetic. She swayed toward him, and their lips met. Soft and tentative, for the first nanosecond, anyway.

A blast of sexual energy roared through them. She found herself writhing beneath him, the sheet torn away from her naked body, both her hands buried in his thick hair. His mouth moved over hers in a savage, sensual kiss calculated to lead them straight into another bout of wild sex. He could manipulate her so effortlessly.

It took a huge effort of will to turn her face away. "That's enough," she pleaded. "I have to get ready. I have to concentrate. Don't do this to me, Connor. Please."

He rocked back on his heels. "So concentrate. Be my guest."

"You're distracting me," she snapped. She scrambled out of the other side of the bed. Her nightdress was the quickest way to cover herself. She tugged it out of her suitcase with desperate haste.

"Gee, sorry." His eyes roamed over her body.

She yanked it over her head and let it drift into place. "I have to take a shower, and iron my suit. And I have to do something about your clothes, too. They're in a terrible state."

He looked suspicious. "What's wrong with my clothes?"

She pulled out her travel iron and plugged it in. "The clothes you wore yesterday are all right for the meeting, if I iron them, but you won't be going to the restaurant anyway, so it doesn't matter if—"

"Hold on." His eyes narrowed. "Back up a step. What's this about me not going to the restaurant?"

She heaved her suitcase up onto the bed and braced herself for a struggle. No way could she contemplate having a business lunch with her most valued client while Connor hovered over her, being intense and difficult. "I looked up the restaurant on the Internet before I came," she said. "It has a formal dress code. I don't see a garment bag lying around here, so I assume you didn't bring a jacket and tie."

"You're not going anywhere that I don't go, Erin." His tone was cold and flinty-hard. "I thought we had an understanding."

"Don't be silly." She laid a fresh towel against the desk for an ironing board. "I arranged this lunch with Mueller before you entered the picture. Nothing can happen to me in a crowded four-star restaurant. And you promised that you wouldn't disrupt—"

"Wait a minute. Hello. Earth to Erin. Let's just set aside the fact that I'm currently your bodyguard. Let's ignore that phone call we got last night. Let's assume that trifling detail wasn't even an issue. After what has just happened between us, you are still planning to have lunch with your goddamn millionaire while I wait out in the lobby like an asshole?"

She gaped at him, appalled. "Connor, be reasonable. I've never even met the man. There's no reason to be jealous. This is about my work. It isn't about you, or Mueller, or—"

"Like hell it isn't. You played your cards wrong, sweetheart. After a night in bed with me, you can forget the romantic, private gourmet lunch with another man. Just . . . fucking . . . forget it."

The possessive fury that emanated from him was like a blast of wind in her face. He advanced on her. She backed up. The wall bumped into her back. "Stop, Connor," she said. "You're making me nervous."

"Good. Be nervous. That'll make two of us, and I wouldn't mind some company."

"Connor, I—"

"I'm not letting you out of my sight. If you so much as

have to pee, I am following you into the ladies' room. That is how serious I am about this. You reading me? Are we finally communicating?"

He pinned her to the wall, crushing her breasts against his chest. She lifted her chin. "You're acting like a caveman," she informed him.

"I'm not acting," he said. "No masks, remember?"

"That's not fair!" she snapped. "I will not be bullied! Just because we spent the night together does not give you the right to—"

"I'm not bullying you, Erin. I'm just telling you how it is."

He cut off her reply with a hard, marauding kiss. She struggled, but he just swallowed her muffled protests and moved his strong hands over her body. Oh, please. How ridiculous. Trying to stake his claim by brute physical force, the rude, arrogant . . .

And all at once, her anger betrayed her, lending all its furious heat to the hunger that flared inside her. She shuddered in his arms.

He wrenched the wide, scooped neckline of her nightdress down over her shoulders, exposing her breasts, and trapped her arms behind her in a tight swathe of white cotton and lace. He spun her around, pinned against his chest. A brief moment of fruitless struggle, legs pumping in empty space, and he sank down onto the bed with her on his lap, facing the mirror. He yanked the nightgown up over her waist.

Their eyes locked in the mirror. She went very still in his arms. She should be spitting mad. She should tell him straight out that this display of macho, he-man garbage did not impress her in the least. But the words weren't coming. She was speechless, her thighs clamped tight around an embarrassing secret. She was turned on.

No, worse than that. She was extremely turned on. She

vibrated in his arms. Her face was red, her breath shallow and labored, her eyes dilated. She couldn't hide it from him. He knew it. She saw it in the triumphant glow in his eyes, the proprietary way he nuzzled her neck. So confident of his power over her.

Dear God, this was awful. She'd been kidnapped by a repressed part of her subconscious, her body taken over by a wanton nympho with no dignity who was sexually aroused by bad behavior.

She shut her eyes to block him out. "Why are you doing this to me?" she demanded. "Why are you torturing me like this?"

"There's torture and there's torture." He shoved the hair away from her neck, and ran his lips over an exquisitely sensitive spot. She jerked and quivered. "And you're torturing me, too, Erin. The virgin bride nightgown is a calculated cocktease, did you know that? I take one look at the thing and in my mind I'm ripping it down the front and throwing you onto a Victorian four-poster." He stroked the tops of her clenched thighs. She thrashed uselessly in the unrelenting circle of his arms. "Open up," he urged. "Let me in."

She bit her lip. "Oh, God. Please, Connor."

"I never know exactly what you're begging me for," he murmured. He kissed his way up her neck, tugged her earlobe between his teeth, and suckled it. "I'm always off balance with you. Always guessing."

"Hah!" She shook with breathless, almost hysterical laughter. "You, off balance? Give me a break. I'm the one who can't move. I'm the one who's being yelled at and pushed around and manhandled!"

His grin flashed. "Open up for me," he pleaded. "Then look in the mirror and watch what I do to you. I promise, it'll be good."

She glared at him in the mirror. "Why are you even asking?" she snapped. "Wouldn't it be more Neanderthal to just make me do it? Shove my legs open, Connor. Go ahead. Doesn't that fit your script better? You'll do whatever you damn well please with me anyway."

His warm, callused hand stroked over her hip with exquisite tenderness. "Nah. It's more satisfying to coax you into opening those beautiful thighs of your own accord." His voice was low and silky. "The conquest is deeper that way. It's a bigger rush. Way bigger."

She wiggled madly. "Conquest, my butt. This is nothing but a stupid power trip, and I'm not falling for it."

He kissed her neck again, the seductive bastard. "All I want is to make you melt," he crooned. "Go with it, Erin. If giving in to me makes you hot, that's great. I don't think any less of you for it."

"It's bad for your big fat ego!" she flared.

He shook with laughter. "We'll worry about my big fat ego another time. Like, after I make you come. Then you can tell me what a controlling bastard I am. All you want."

She flung her head back against his shoulder. She shook with confusion. "This is not OK with me," she said. "I am not a submissive person."

"Of course you're not," he soothed. "And thank God for it. You're a beautiful, regal intergalactic princess, and you drive me fucking nuts. Now open up, baby. Let me pay tribute to your surpassing beauty."

In your dreams, buddy, she thought. Meanwhile the wanton nympho who had taken over her body obeyed him, spreading her thighs wide. The glistening, flushed folds of her labia pouted out of her thatch of pubic hair, splayed wide for him to see, and touch, and toy with.

She stared into the mirror, astonished. For so long, her sexual life had been limited to solitary experimentation in the safety of her own narrow bed, tinged with shame and loneliness and wistful longing. It was there that she had spun all her romantic dreams of Connor—and tried not to think about Bradley. Whenever Bradley came into her mind, any tension or heat she'd managed to generate drained away, leaving her more depressed and lonely than before.

The woman she saw in the mirror was another person entirely.

Her pose was aggressively sexual. Pornographic, even. Arms pinned back, face flushed, breasts jutting out. Connor's muscular arm was clamped around her belly. His other hand fondled her, spreading her nether lips gently, murmuring with pleasure at how slick and wet she was. He spread the moisture everywhere while his thumb circled her clitoris, pushing and coaxing her into moaning, shivering madness.

Her real-life Connor was so much harder and rougher and more problematic than her fantasies. Aggressive and demanding, and yet so tender, so ruthlessly skillful. And his appetite for her was voracious. She had never imagined anything like it. She still couldn't.

He slid his longest two fingers deep inside her, hooking them under her pubic bone, and pressed against that sweet hot spot inside her sheath as he pressed his palm down against her mound. He squeezed and circled, his strong hand sliding in her swollen, quivering flesh. She clenched around him, writhing against his pumping hand. The power grew and swelled within her until it became a heavenly torture. She screamed when the tension finally broke.

It throbbed violently through her, charging her with shimmering warmth. When she opened her eyes, she was still sprawled on his lap. He held her limp body securely in place while he petted and stroked her lazily between her legs. Like he was petting a kitten.

She turned her face up to him. He gave her a long, clinging kiss and smiled into her eyes. So smug and satisfied with himself.

She clambered off him, extricating her arms from the nightdress and shimmying out of it. Her desire to cover herself was completely gone. She looked the nightdress over. "You ripped it," she observed.

"I'm sorry," he said. "Can you fix it?"

"I think so. It's on the seam. No biggie." She flung the garment in the general direction of her suitcase and looked down at him. She'd left big wet marks on his jeans, and she was not the least bit embarrassed about it. Her inner thighs and bottom were slick and wet. She was thrumming with readiness, and the thick length of his erection was clearly visible against his jeans. She reached for his hand, the one that had pleasured her, and pulled it up to her face. His fingers were still glistening with her juice. She suckled them. Tasted herself.

His eyes widened. "Whoa. Jesus, Erin. I thought you said you were tired. You said you didn't want to."

The feverish heat was burned into her face. "I'm OK."

"OK's not good enough. Do you want me to fuck you?" he demanded. "Don't dance around it. Don't play games with me."

She laughed in his face. "Oh, you're a fine one to talk about games."

"Just say it," he snarled. "I want to hear the words."

She seized a condom from the bedstand and ripped it open with her teeth. "Take off your pants, Connor. Is that clear enough?"

He nodded, and stood up, unbuckling his belt. "You got it."

He stepped out of his pants and stood in front of her, his cock bobbing in front of him. He should be feeling guilty as hell. He had maneuvered her into this. She had to be sore, because he was. But he couldn't resist. She had that wild, sex goddess glow of arousal in her eyes that brought him right to his knees.

She plucked the condom from the foil package, and attempted to smooth it on him. He reached down and covered her fumbling hands.

"That's backwards, sweetheart," he said gently. "Turn it around."

She made a huffy noise and leaned her hot forehead against his chest. She was so cute when she tried to act nonchalant. Her efforts to roll the latex over his cock were driving him nuts.

Ah, mission finally accomplished. She stepped back, gripping him with an authoritative hand. "Just one thing," she said. "Don't drive me to the edge and leave me all alone there. Don't do that to me again."

She punctuated her statement with a tight squeeze of her hand, milking him from root to head. He struggled to remember what she'd said. "What the hell are you talking about, Erin?"

She stabbed at his chest with her finger. "Don't play dumb. You know exactly what I'm talking about. If you make me lose control, you've got to come with me. All the way. I can't take any more of your dominating, calculated power trips. At least not today."

He tossed her onto the bed, landed promptly on top of her soft, hot, squirming body. "It's not that simple," he growled. "You can afford to lose control. I can't."

She shoved at his chest. "Why not?"

"Because I'm bigger and stronger, that's why. I don't know what you're complaining about. You trick me into losing control almost every time we do it. It freaks me out. I'm supposed to protect you."

She heaved furiously beneath him. "I'm not made out of glass!"

"Thank God." He shoved her into position: flat on her back, legs folded up high, open and drenched and ready for him. "Are you sore?"

"I'm all right," she snapped.

"I didn't ask if you were all right." He enunciated each word with exaggerated clarity. "I asked if you were sore."

"Yes, I am, but I don't care! So don't stop, or I'll have to kill you!"

He couldn't help but grin. "I'll be gentle," he said. He guided his cock to her and slid it over her labia. "Tell me if I hurt you."

"What if I don't want gentle?" she demanded. "Stop being so goddamned anxious! You're driving me nuts!"

That made him laugh out loud. "Oh, God, I love it when you're a heartless, insatiable bitch."

He thrust inside her, hard as he dared. She was wet and hot for him, but she was delicate and small, and he was a big man. She could snap at him all she wanted, but he wasn't going to risk hurting her.

This tart-sweet furious sex kitten persona of hers made him burn with lust. He kept veering back and forth between the screaming berserker who wanted to fuck her brains out, and a shaking tenderness that made him want to cry.

God forbid. That would be all he needed.

He pulled out, gasping as her sheath clutched and hugged him, and thrust even deeper, seeking a gentle, surging rhythm. It was so good. He could do this all day, all night. For the rest of his life.

Erin smiled her fey, mysterious smile and brushing her tingling hot magic fingers over the surface of his throat, his chest, his shoulders. "Let go, Connor," she pleaded. "I love it when you go wild."

She could make him do anything when she looked at him like that. Her eyes glowed like the sun shone behind them and lit them up like stained glass: glowing amber, honey-streaked sunset warmth. Her plump breasts were crushed against his chest, her quivering thighs were clenched around him. She gasped with pleasure with each heavy, gliding stroke. She was working up to another explosion. He could feel it build, and he knew just how to give her what she was whimpering for. He knew it in his bones, in his blood.

It came to him, out of nowhere. He pulled back, held himself motionless above her. "I'm not leaving you alone with Mueller," he said.

She started to protest, but he trapped her face between his two hands and kissed her deeply. "That's the deal. I give you what you want, you stop fighting me. Nod if we understand each other."

She shook her head. "This isn't fair. You can't manipulate—"

"Oh, yes, I can. And I will," he promised. "I will."

She glared up into his eyes, clutching at him in helpless frustration. He rocked against her with soft, licking, maddening thrusts with just the head of his cock when he knew damn well she wanted it deep and hard. His thumb barely tickled over the slick, quivering bud of her clit. Teasing and tantalizing. No mercy.

She threw her head back and cried out through clenched teeth, clawing at his shoulders. "Goddamn it, Connor—"

"Do we have a deal?"

"Yes, just do it! Now!"

He let go, and sealed the bargain with his body. He gave her everything he had, everything he was. It went further than he had planned, further than he'd ever dreamed. It carried them away.

Passion fused them together. All the truths of their hearts were known to each other. Nothing could be hidden, nothing held back. No boundaries, no borders. One being.

They writhed together in the heart of a burning star.

Sometime later, he rolled off her and flopped onto his back. He was chilled by the sweat cooling on his skin. That had been way out there. He was almost afraid to meet her eyes.

"Wow," she whispered. "You don't do things halfway, do you?"

"Never. In my whole life," he said. "Better get used to it."

They subsided into shy silence. Not a word about Mueller. Not a word about that weird, coercive bargain he had struck with her. And certainly no discussion of . . . of that. Whatever the hell it had been. Souls touching. Yikes. Sounded like New

Age bullshit. Better not to even touch it with words. It was made out of emotion and energy. Only the wisdom of their joined bodies could comprehend it.

Erin climbed out of bed. She kept her face turned from him. "I have to get ready," she said hesitantly. "I'll just jump into the shower."

They both needed a time-out, so he waited his turn, and showered after she was done. When he came out, Erin was busy making the second bed. The first one was mathematically smooth and perfect.

He stared at her, bemused. "Why are you doing that?"

"I can't think straight if the bed's not made." Her voice was snippy and defensive. "And I need the space to organize myself. Here, use my comb, and be nice to your hair, please. No ripping or tearing."

He pulled on his chinos and sat down to watch the floor show. Erin was a sight to behold bustling around in her bra and panties. She ignored him as she ironed her things, and then laid her suit out on the bed and held up an imperious hand. "Your shirt, please."

He fished around on the floor until he found it, and handed it to her. "You're sexy when you iron," he told her.

She sniffed. "If you value your life, you will never say anything so stupid to me ever again. Did you know there's a button loose on this?"

"Nope," he told her. "Never noticed. Never would have."

She set aside her iron and dug into her suitcase again, this time producing a big sewing kit. She pulled out spools of thread and held them against his shirt with a worried frown. "I've got taupe, and I've got white, but this shirt is really closer to oatmeal," she fretted. "What I really need is beige, and I thought I had some in here." She upended the whole thing onto the bed and began sifting through the heap.

He gaped at the spectacle. "I had no idea you were like this."

Her eyes narrowed. "Like what?"

"The type that quibbles over taupe or beige. I never would have dreamed that you were so, uh . . ."

She brandished her needle. "If you say anal retentive, I will stick this needle into your arm a half an inch deep."

He took a cautious step back. "How about obsessive-compulsive?"

"I prefer to think of myself as detail oriented," she said primly. "Take off your pants, please. I want to stitch up that rip in the back, and then they need to be ironed. Badly."

"Detail oriented, huh?" he said, shucking his pants. "Check me out, Erin. I've got a few details I'd like to orient you toward."

She looked, all innocence, and squeaked. His erection bobbed right in front of her, practically at eye level. "Connor, please! You've had your way with me twice this morning! Don't you ever get enough?"

"Once," he said. "It was twice for you. Only once for me."

"Now who's quibbling over details?" she said tartly. "You had your way with me all night long."

"It's not enough," he said. "I'm never going to get enough of you."

The air was suddenly too hot and thick to breathe. His cock stuck straight out, begging for her attention. Damn thing had no dignity at all.

Her lips tightened. "I'm on to you, Connor. You would love it if I was late to this meeting, wouldn't you? Or if I missed it completely. That would suit you right down to the ground."

"I could care less about your meeting, sweetheart."

She turned her head resolutely away. "That's enough of your tricks. I'm in work mode now, and if you value those precious body parts that you are waving around at me, you will wrap a towel around them and hand me those pants. Right now."

He winced. "Ouch. How long does this work mode of yours last?"

"As long as it takes to get the job done," she said briskly. "Right now, my job is to make you presentable. When we get to the resort, I become an expert on ancient Celtic artifacts." She jabbed her finger toward his chest, and he darted back, wary of her needle. "Your job is to be polite and unobtrusive, and not say anything that will reflect badly on me while I do my job. Is that understood?"

His jaw tightened. "My job is to guard you, Erin."

She snatched the pants away from him. "Then guard me politely and unobtrusively, please."

"This work mode of yours is a bitch," he grumbled. "I liked you better when you were in red-hot sex kitten mode."

She harrumphed, and stitched up the rip in his pants with quick, expert skill. "Isn't that just too bad. No masks, Connor. This is the real me, so deal with it. Put a towel over yourself, please."

"What's the matter, Erin?" he taunted. "Is my cock distracting you?"

She snatched up the scissors, and he jerked away. She smiled sweetly, and snipped the thread. "Relax. And don't think I'm fixing up your clothes because I'm playing out some sick domestic fantasy. It is in my own best interests for you to look decent. Is that understood?"

"Yes, ma'am," he said meekly.

She glared at him. "Are you making fun of me?"

"Hell, no. Not while you're holding those scissors."

Erin muttered to herself as she rummaged through the sewing stuff. She held up a spool, her face bright with triumph. "Beige!"

He tried not to laugh. "I'm happy for you, babe."

He was ready as soon as he put on the clothes she handed to him, but Erin's complicated toilette had barely begun. He followed her into the bathroom against her protests to watch. It was so sexy and feminine and fascinating, the way she dabbed at her face with all those tiny tubes and pots and brushes. Best of all was the hair. She brushed it until it was smooth and glossy and swept it up, twisting until it fell into place. Then she anchored the gleaming coils with hairpins. The finished result was a goddamn miracle of engineering.

They were finally ready to go. Connor dismantled the squealers and tossed them into his grip. He stepped out into the hall, looked both ways, and gestured for her to follow. She reached up to stroke back a stray lock of his hair and straighten his collar.

He stiffened. "What? Do I not look OK?"

She touched his jaw and petted the frown line between his brows with her fingertip. "You look very handsome," she said softly.

He stared down at her, at a total loss for words.

When finally he shook off the spell, he gestured for her to precede him down the hall. She glanced at his leg as he fell into step beside her. "You're limping more than before. Are you all right?"

He stabbed the elevator button. "My bum leg's not used to wild crazy sex in the shower."

"Oh," she whispered. "Sorry."

"It was worth it," he said, as the door opened. "Believe me."

She stared, aghast, at how much he ate. A stack of blueberry pancakes, a four-egg omelet, home fries, English muffins, spicy sausage patties. He polished it all off with unflagging zeal.

"Dear God," she breathed. "Where do you put it all?"

"I don't know." He grinned. "Everything just tastes so great." He signaled the waitress. "Could you bring me a Belgian waffle, please?"

Erin hid behind him, blushing and cringing while he took care of business at the checkout desk, and they headed out to the car.

"How far are we from the Silver Fork Resort?" she asked.

He braced himself for trouble. "About forty minutes."

"Good God!" She looked at her watch. "We're going to

be late! I had no idea we were so far! Why didn't you tell me?"

"What for?" He opened the car door for her. "They'll live if you're a few minutes late, Erin."

"You really are trying to sabotage me, aren't you?"

The chill that awaited him when he got into the car was his own damn fault, and he knew it, but it was still a big drag. He'd destroyed the equilibrium they had found, and he missed it. Forty minutes of frigid silence as he negotiated the curves of the coastal highway was plenty of time to examine his motives, but when they arrived at the pretentious wrought iron gates of the resort, he still hadn't decided if he'd made her late on purpose or not. Oh well. Big fucking deal. They were only seventeen minutes late.

Erin jumped out of the car as soon as it stopped moving. Connor got out and hurried after her, seizing her arm. "Hey. Not so fast."

"I am furious with you," she hissed. "Don't touch me."

"You're my adoring fiancée now, remember. Don't fight me, Erin, because I don't give a shit what these folks think of me. And I will not hesitate to embarrass you if it suits my purposes."

"You overbearing lout." She wrenched her arm away.

He wrapped his arm around her shoulders, tilting her face up to his. "If you want to argue, let's just get back into the car," he suggested. "I don't care how late you are. We can park on the other side of those dunes and get into the back seat and discuss it. I really enjoy the way we resolve our differences. I'm more than ready for another argument."

"Don't you dare try to intimidate me with sex," she hissed. "That is a dirty, nasty trick!"

He held her perfectly still, and smiled. She went up onto her tiptoes and glared like she was facing down a panther. He was getting hard again, for God's sake. "God, you're so beautiful when you're mad."

"Go to hell. You really do have a death wish, don't you?"

"I wasn't saying that to piss you off," he said. "I'm just stating a fact. You're ten feet tall like this. You're an Amazon. A lesser man would be facedown on the ground gibbering by now."

Erin's lips twitched in spite of herself. "Gibbering?"

"At the very least," he assured her.

She tossed her head and started up the steps. "I will not be won over by cheap flattery," she informed him.

He hurried after her. "What would win you over, Erin? How about four hours of nonstop oral sex?"

"Pig," she whispered back.

He got there just in time to open the door for her. "Oink, oink."

A man and a woman rose to their feet when Connor and Erin walked into the lobby. One was a dried-up, shriveled guy in his fifties with an expensive gray suit. Gray hair, gray eyes, grayish skin. He gave Connor the creeps. The gray guy gave Erin a brief, tight smile of welcome. His eyes flicked coldly over Connor as he shook Erin's hand. "Ms. Riggs. Thank goodness. We were beginning to worry."

The woman, a stunning redhead, stepped forward with a dazzling smile. She had brilliant emerald eyes, flawless skin, a voluptuous body. She was dressed in a snug, costly look-ing, ice-blue suit.

Erin shook the redhead's hand. "I'm so sorry if I kept you waiting." She nodded toward Connor. "This is my . . . ah, this is Connor McCloud. Connor, this is Nigel Dobbs, and this is Tamara Julian."

Connor nodded and held out his hand.

Dobbs took it gingerly. "Er, how do you do?" He sounded as if he would really rather not know.

"Doing great, thanks," Connor said.

"Hello, Connor McCloud," Tamara said, in a throaty voice.

Tamara Julian clung to his hand when he tried to pull it back. Her bright emerald eyes swept over him with frank feminine appraisal.

Here was trouble that he did not need. He gave his hand another tug. This time he managed to retrieve it. He looked at Erin. "So? Better get cracking on those artifacts, babe. It's a long drive back to Seattle."

She slanted him a warning look. "It'll take as long as it takes, Connor, as you well know. Did Mr. Mueller arrive safely last night?"

"When I informed him that you would be unable to dine with him, he changed his plans," Dobbs said. "He will meet with you later this week when he passes through Seattle. Had he stayed, he would have been uncomfortably rushed to make his plane to Hong Kong."

Connor let out a breath he hadn't known he was holding.

"Oh. I see." Erin's voice was subdued. "I suppose that makes sense, although I'm sorry that I won't be meeting him today."

"Damn shame," Connor said. "Ain't that just too bad."

Nigel Dobbs gave him a freezing look. "Indeed it was."

"You two should have stayed here last night," Tamara said. "It would have been a pleasure to have you both at dinner."

"We wanted to stay in our usual love nest," Connor said. "I can't bear to leave this gorgeous woman unaccompanied." He wrapped his arm around Erin and gave her a squeeze. "I'd pine away without her."

Tamara raised her dark, perfectly shaped brows. "How very sweet," she said. "A model fiancé."

"I try," Connor said.

"Keep trying," Tamara said.

"Ahem. Shall we?" Dobbs said icily. "Follow me, please."

Erin tugged at his arm, but Connor was frozen in place, staring at Tamara. "Have we met?" he asked.

Her smile widened, dazzled. "If you have to ask, then the answer is no," she purred. She placed her hand on his chest, and pressed. "Believe me, Mr. McCloud. If we had met, you would remember."

Connor followed them all down the corridor. Erin was freshly pissed off at him again for some reason, but hell, she so often was. He'd better get used to it and not let it block his concentration. Something was nagging him about the redhead.

He'd seen her somewhere. That prickling feeling on the back of his neck was a sure sign. But what Tamara had said was literally true: aside from his weird freak memory, he was a relatively normal flesh and blood guy. No way was he capable of forgetting that face or that body.

So what? So where? How? *Damn.*

He stared at Tamara's back as she marched ahead of them, heels clicking against the pavement. He deliberately unfocused his eyes and brain and threw out the net in his head, to reel in vague, half-formed connections, memories. They flashed by like silver fish, at the blinding speed of thought. The color of her suit jacket melted, blended like ocean foam. A vague pattern began to form. He was reaching for it, grasping—

The vicious elbow jab to his ribs took him by surprise. "Oof!" he grunted. "What the fuck was that about?"

Erin's face was pink, her lush mouth compressed into a furious line. "Could you be slightly less obvious in your ogling, please?"

Then it sank in. Ogling. Tamara. His vacuous gaze while he fished in his mind, probably focused on Tamara's ass.

Whoa. This was beautiful. Erin was jealous.

His mood soared. He rubbed the sore spot on his ribs, grinning. "Sorry, sweetheart."

"You are vulgar and crass, and I am going to make you pay."

He swooped down and landed a smacking kiss close to her mouth before she had a chance to jerk away. "I can hardly wait, babe."

If Tamara Julian and Nigel Dobbs overheard their whispered conversation, they made no sign. Connor groped around in his mind for the ephemeral, half-formed pattern, just for the hell of it, but it was long gone, and the space in his mind that it had risen up from was now shut up as tight as a clam. Damn. Nothing to be gained by pounding around for it and wrecking his focus now. He'd have better luck just letting go of it, waiting for it to pop up later in some distracted moment while merging on the freeway, or taking a shower.

It was maddening to have lost it, but almost worth it just to know that he was capable of making Erin Riggs jealous. What an ego rush.

Dobbs and Tamara stopped at a handsome carved door. Dobbs unlocked it and waved them in. They entered a room with a long gleaming wooden table upon which were arranged several swatches of black velvet. Each had an object lying on top of it.

"Ms. Julian laid out the folders with the provenance information for you already," Dobbs said.

Connor felt the change in the quality of Erin's attention as he would have felt a dramatic shift of temperature. She pulled a tape recorder out of her purse, and walked the length of the table. In one swift, photographic glance, he took in a jewel-studded bronze shield, a big silver cauldron covered with relief panels, a bronze helm with a weird, stylistic bird perched on top of it, a bunch of shiny golden collars, bracelets, and brooches. "Testing," Erin said absently. "Testing," her sweet, low, recorded voice said back to her.

He was all alone in that room, with Dobbs and Tamara. Erin was elsewhere, all her energy focused down to a fine, cutting point.

He didn't like it. She'd forgotten that he existed. She was a thousand miles away, thousands of years away. Her eyes glowed with highly organized mental activity that he could not fathom. If he grabbed the redhead and French-kissed her, Erin would never even notice.

Detail oriented did not even begin to describe it.

Erin sank down onto a rolling chair and pulled herself close to the first object, the bronze shield. She flipped through the papers in the folder, and began to speak softly into the tape recorder. ". . . oblong bronze shield, first century B.C.E., decorated with red enamel, garnets and amethysts . . . vegetal style . . . British insular . . . arabesque motifs . . ."

He'd gotten accustomed to her full, undivided attention. Now he was the one who was jealous. Of a bunch of old artifacts. How pathetic.

The three of them watched her for a while. Dobbs shot him a sly look. "She's quite something, no? Such amazing focus. The rest of the world just doesn't even exist for her. It's like a trance."

He gritted his teeth at the smug, proprietary tone of the guy's voice. So happy for himself, just because he had a handle on some part of Erin that Connor did not know. "Impressive," he grunted.

"Mr. Mueller was so looking forward to seeing her in action."

"Poor bastard," Connor said. "Unlucky."

Dobbs's eyes narrowed to pale, pinkish slits. "I gather you've never had the opportunity to watch Ms. Riggs ply her trade."

Connor gave him a toothy grin. "First time for me. Big thrill."

"A remarkable young woman. As you will discover." *If you get the chance before a high-class woman like that dumps you back into the gutter where she found you* was the screamingly obvious subtext.

"Looking forward to a lifetime of it," Connor said, teeth clenched.

"Indeed." Dobbs sounded amused. "I wish you luck."

"It's fortunate that she can surprise you." Tamara's voice was seductively husky. "Or don't you like surprises, Mr. McCloud?"

"That depends on the surprise," he told her.

"Surprise is the element that keeps passion fresh. Are you

capable of surprising her, Mr. McCloud? Have you even attempted it?"

Nigel Dobbs made a shocked noise. "Ms. Julian, if you please! Don't embarrass our guest with inappropriate personal comments!"

Tamara let out a throaty laugh. "Something tells me that Mr. McCloud doesn't embarrass easily."

He looked the taunting bitch straight in her tilted emerald eyes, and noticed two things. The first was that she didn't flinch, which was to her credit, and very unusual. Most people looked away very quickly, when he gave them the death-ray look.

Then they backed away.

The second thing was that her eye color was fake. He would give a great deal to know the original color. Something pale, like blue or gray, or the green wouldn't glow so bright and pure.

Silver fish, flashing by in the azure depths at the blinding speed of thought. Too swift to grasp and hold.

He thought of Erin's shock when he grabbed her in the airport. Of his own, when she jumped out of the bathroom at him buck naked.

Yeah, they knew how to surprise each other. No problems there.

"I don't embarrass easily," he told her. "But the way I surprise my girlfriend is nobody's goddamn business but mine."

Her eyes widened, and then dropped. There was an awkward silence. "I, ah . . . beg your pardon," she murmured.

"It's OK." He gave her his hard, impenetrable cop smile.

Her lashes fluttered winsomely. "I didn't mean to offend you."

"No offense," he said. "No embarrassment. Just the facts."

She crossed her arms over her impressively stacked bosom, her composure firmly in place again. "Such directness is startling."

"I thought you liked surprises."

Her mouth curved in an appreciative smile. "Touché."

Dobbs cleared his throat aggressively. "Ms. Julian. If you please. Could you entertain Mr. McCloud while Ms. Riggs is occupied here?" Dobbs asked. "Get him an espresso at the bar, or show him the view from the veranda. We don't want him to be bored and restless."

"That sounds like an excellent idea," Tamara said warmly. "Ms. Riggs always takes quite some time to conduct her—"

"By all means, Connor," Erin cut in.

They turned, startled. It was her ringing, intergalactic princess voice, the one that always sent a surge of raw heat to his groin. "Go right ahead. I would hate to bore you with Iron Age Celtic grave goods. Let Ms. Julian get you an espresso. It's a perfect opportunity for the two of you to discuss all the places where you might have met."

Erin's agate-brown eyes blazed. She wanted to rip his head off. Even in high-octane work mode, she was tracking him, recording everything he said. Which was a twisted compliment in and of itself.

A stupid grin was spreading all over his face. Everybody was looking at him, waiting for the next line in the vaudeville routine. He planted his ass in a chair and folded his arms over his chest. "I can't imagine anything more fascinating than Iron Age Celtic grave goods, sweetheart," he said. "I'm not missing this show for any money."

Chapter

12

The pieces were breathtaking, every single one of them. The most famous museums in the world would've fought to the death to acquire them, not only for their historical significance, but for their sheer beauty. There was a bronze shield in an exquisite state of preservation, studded with gems and decorated in the swirling, sensual style that characterized the La Tene period, 500 B.C.E. to 200 C.E.

There was a silver cauldron that had been fished out of a peat bog in Denmark, embossed with hammered picture panels that writhed with ram-headed serpents, dragons, griffins, and Celtic deities. There was a battle helmet that would make the curator at the Huppert weep with envy, with a menacing bronze raven perched on top, complete with flapping mechanical wings. There was a hoard of golden torques, the twisted ropes of gold that were worn around the neck as collars, with richly decorated, gem-studded finials. A dazzling wealth of armbands, brooches, and cloak pins. She could write a book on every single exquisite piece. Her mouth was practically watering.

Were it not for her intense awareness of Connor's presence

and the bizarre turns her life was taking lately, she would've been in heaven. But even while she was busy crunching data, she felt him behind her, watching her with the same quiet, potent intensity with which he did absolutely everything. He was a huge, warm, distracting presence.

Her ex-boss Lydia would have cheerfully killed to acquire any of these pieces for the Huppert, but something was odd about two of the torques. They were strangely similar to a style she'd studied in Scotland. She'd been lucky enough to work on an Iron Age cemetery in Wrothburn, Scotland, which had been unearthed during the construction of a shopping mall parking lot only two years before.

It had been the biggest discovery of Iron Age grave goods since the 1970s, and a very distinctive style of torque had been uncovered, characterized by bearded dragon-headed finials, the writhing symmetrical dragons' tails hiding the gap in front of the torque. She'd never heard of that style being found elsewhere. She'd even written an article speculating on the possible ritual and magical significance of the bearded dragons.

And yet, the provenance stated that they'd been discovered in Switzerland in the 1950s. Very odd. She clicked off the recorder.

"I need to do some research before I can write my final report," she told Nigel Dobbs.

"But they are authentic, of course?" He twisted his hands.

"Oh, good heavens, yes. They're stunning. Some of the most beautiful examples of early La Tene art that I've ever seen. Museum quality, each one of them. Mr. Mueller's taste is impeccable."

"Exquisite," Connor muttered. "Remarkable. Truly stupendous."

She ignored him stonily. "May I keep the copies of the provenance papers, and return them to you later on this week?"

"Of course, of course," Dobbs said. "Keep them, by all means."

The door swung open. Tamara Julian appeared, bearing a silver tray with four steaming demitasse cups and a plateful of petit fours. She bestowed a dazzling smile upon Connor. "If I can't tempt you out to the bar for coffee, then I'm forced to bring it in to you," she said.

Erin saw herself knocking the tray up into Tamara's face, sending espresso splashing all over the fawning bitch's perfect designer suit. She clamped down on the childish impulse and snagged a cup off the tray. "Thank you so much," she said. "I was fainting for some caffeine."

"Refresh yourself, by all means," Dobbs said, rubbing his skinny hands together. "I trust you and Mr. McCloud will stay to lunch?"

Erin's eyes slid to Connor. He looked back at her, impassive.

"Ah, thank you, but I have some pressing business at home," she said. "I would prefer to get back to Seattle as soon as possible."

To say nothing of the fact that watching Tamara drool all over Connor would do absolutely nothing for her appetite. She'd thought that she actually liked the woman on the three other occasions that they had met. She'd even been impressed by Tamara's intelligence and wit.

She was liking Tamara a whole hell of a lot less right now.

Tamara pouted. "Oh, must you? The chef here prepares a stunning bouillabaise, and the lobster pastry is absolutely divine."

"Not this time," Connor said. "We'll grab something quick on the road. Are we done here, sweetheart?"

"Not quite." Dobbs opened a briefcase on the table and pulled out a folder. "Mr. Mueller had intended to make this proposal to you at dinner last night. In fact, that was the reason he made this long journey in one single push. He suffers from rather delicate health, you see, and it was quite a sacrifice for him to—"

"I'm so sorry, Mr. Dobbs," she said hastily. "I didn't mean—"

"I'm not reproving you, Ms. Riggs. I am simply telling you the facts as they are so that your future decisions can be more informed. Mr. Mueller has authorized me to make this proposal on his behalf. We are aware that you worked at the Huppert. Is this correct?"

"Yes," she said. "I was there for two years."

"Mr. Mueller was intrigued by your organization of the Bronze and Iron Age Celtic exhibit last year at the Huppert. He thought it inspired, even brilliant. You have an innovative spirit to go along with your formidable technical skills, Ms. Riggs."

"Ah . . . thank you." She was flustered and confused.

"Mr. Mueller has been considering a grant to the Huppert for a new wing. Devoted principally to Bronze Age, Iron Age, and Romano-Celtic artifacts. His Celtic collection will be donated, as well."

"Oh. That would be, ah, amazingly generous of him," she said. Lydia was going to have kittens for joy. Hurray for Lydia.

"Yes, Mr. Mueller is very altruistic," Dobbs said. "He believes that the beauty of the past is for everyone's enrichment."

"How incredibly admirable of him," Connor said.

Erin cringed, and Tamara's lips quirked, but Dobbs just nodded as if he didn't hear Connor's sarcasm.

"Indeed it is," Dobbs agreed. "Mr. Mueller is not interested in the circumstances behind your dismissal from the Huppert, but it was a terrible error in judgment on the part of the museum administration."

"I, uh, rather thought so myself," Erin said desperately.

"To put matters simply, Mr. Mueller would be disposed to

donate these funds only if he could be assured that you and you alone would be the curator of the Celtic collection."

Her jaw dropped. "Me? But . . . but I—"

"You may be reticent because of your personal differences with the museum administration. We invite you to think it over. Mr. Mueller will understand entirely if you do not wish to benefit the Huppert with your expertise. They were fools to lose you."

"But if I should, ah . . . if I should decide not to—"

"Then Mr. Mueller will simply donate the funds elsewhere." Dobbs smiled thinly. "There is no lack of worthy beneficiaries. A thousand places to put every penny, believe me."

Erin struggled for something to say. "I am, uh, overwhelmed."

Nigel Dobbs chuckled. "Of course you are. Think it over."

"Ah, yes. I will. Of course."

"And we do hope you will be able to carve out a moment in your busy schedule to meet with Mr. Mueller when he comes to Seattle."

"Goodness, yes," she said weakly. "Of course. Whenever it's convenient. Any time at all."

"Don't forget our engagement party, honey." Connor's voice had a sharp, warning tone. "It'll be a crazy week. Think before you speak."

Erin glared at him, horrified. "My priorities are very clear when it comes to my work, Connor! You'll have to get used to sharing me."

He slouched in his chair, eyes narrowed. "I don't share, baby."

She turned her back on him. "I will be delighted to meet with Mr. Mueller at any time," she said firmly.

"Very well. We will be in touch with you as Mr. Mueller's plans develop." Dobbs's voice was markedly cooler. "And Ms. Riggs . . . think long and hard about your priorities. Mr. Mueller's offer represents an enormous commitment of time and effort. If your other interests are too, er, *compelling*, do be honest. We are talking about a minimum of fifteen million dollars for the new wing. To say nothing of the value of the collection itself. It is an enormous, I repeat, enormous responsibility."

"I understand," she said tightly.

Connor rose to his feet and stretched, popping his knuckles. "Great, then. We're done here, huh? Pleasure to meet you, Mr. Dobbs, Ms. Julian. Come on, babe. Your chariot awaits."

Erin smiled over her gritted teeth as she shook hands with Dobbs. "Thank you again, and thank Mr. Mueller for me, too," she said. "I am so gratified by his faith in me. It means a lot to—"

"Et cetera, et cetera, blah, blah, blah," Connor cut in. "Dobbs can make up the rest. It's all filler, anyhow. Come on, babe."

That was it. The final indignity. She whirled on him. "Don't you *dare* speak to me like that, Connor McCloud!"

The appalled silence was finally broken by a slow, deliberate clapping sound. "Excellent," Tamara said, still applauding. "Much better. Your man needs a very strong hand, Ms. Riggs. Don't let him get the better of you for a second, or you are finished."

Erin opened her mouth to throw the woman's unsolicited advice right back in her face. The look in Tamara's eyes stopped her. Wide and bright and full of false innocence, waiting for Erin's reaction with predatory eagerness. She was taunting them deliberately.

She would not play this sick game. "Thank you so much for your generous advice, Ms. Julian, but I think I can handle him."

"Oh, yeah. Handle me, baby," Connor said softly. "I just can't wait to feel that strong hand of yours wrapped around me."

She gave him a sweet smile that promised instant death. "We will discuss it in the car, honey." She faced Dobbs and Tamara. "I'm so sorry. Connor's acting out. He must be feeling threatened. I'd better get him safely away. Please excuse us, and have a lovely day. I'll be in touch with you. Come on, Connor, let's go. Right now."

He trailed after her. "See you folks later. Have a good one."

Tamara's laughter followed them all the way down the corridor.

Connor fell into step beside her, his long legs making one leisurely stride for her every two steps. "Erin—"

"In the car."

"Hey. I just want to—"

"Not one word, if you value your life. We will discuss it in the car."

He subsided. They paced silently out to the Cadillac. Connor unlocked her door, opened it. She got in and covered her hot face with her hands. She was literally shaking with rage. She had never been so angry in her life. Not even after Lydia had fired her.

Connor got in. He glanced at her, and looked swiftly away.

"Connor." Her throat vibrated. She swallowed, trying to steady it. "Did you see Kurt Novak lurking behind any columns?"

"No. But I—"

"And did Nigel Dobbs or Tamara Julian do or say anything that would lead you to believe that they intended to do me bodily harm?"

"Not directly, but I—"

"Then what in holy hell possessed you to be such an idiot? You deliberately embarrassed me! Why? What did I do to deserve that? What was the purpose of it? *What?*"

He winced at her shrill tone. "I didn't like them," he said defensively. "I didn't like that calculating redheaded bitch—"

"Well, she certainly liked you!" Erin cut in, with vicious emphasis.

"—and I didn't like Poker-up-the-Ass Dobbs, either. And just because this Mueller character gets off on playing God with his fucking fifteen million dollars is no reason to kiss his ass. You—"

"Kiss his ass? Is that what you think I was doing? You bastard!" She launched herself at him in a scratching, flailing, yelling fit, lost to all reason. He caught her wrists and wrestled her down until she was pinned to his lap in a breathlessly tight, furious embrace.

"Let me just say, in my own defense, that I was exactly as polite to them as they were to me," he said. Each word was like a chip of ice.

She heaved and struggled against him. "You're imagining things!"

"Bullshit, I am. They were fucking with me, and when people fuck with me, I do not smile and nod and take it, Erin. Ever. No matter how big a pile of money they're squatting on. Is that clear?"

She wrenched at her trapped wrists. "I heard that interchange, and I did not hear any rudeness!"

"Then you weren't listening closely enough," he said flatly.

Erin panted, staring at the tight, unrelenting grip he had on her wrists. She carefully organized her thoughts. "Uh, Connor?"

"Yeah? What?" He sounded apprehensive.

"For the record. If you really had been my fiancé, hypothetically speaking . . ."

He jerked his chin impatiently. "Yes?"

"Just be aware that after a scene like that, you would no longer be my fiancé. It would be over."

"Oh yeah?"

She focused on the button she had sewed onto his shirt this morning. "If that scene had been for real, it would have demonstrated that you had no respect for my intelligence. Or any respect for me at all. It would prove that you didn't trust my judgment, or have any regard for my professional dignity. And that would be unforgivable."

He went very still for a long moment. "Well, then," he murmured. "It's a damn good thing it was all theater, then, huh?"

"Theater?" She wrenched at her wrists, in vain. "Hah! It was a crazy melodrama! Your jealous boyfriend act was ridiculous, Connor! And you made me look ridiculous, too!"

A muscle pulsed in his jaw. His eyes shifted away from hers. "Now I'm screwed," he said sourly. "You're giving me the look."

"What look is that?" she demanded.

"The intergalactic princess look. Don't. I already feel like a jerk."

"Good," she said.

He sighed. "I won't apologize for being rude to Mueller's lackeys, because they deserved it. But I'm sorry if I was rude to you."

She stopped wiggling, startled. "Uh . . . thank you."

"But look at it from my end. I was trying to communicate with you, and you were blocking me. You can't come running when that guy crooks his finger. We've got to pick our times and places carefully."

"No!" She convulsed, almost breaking out of his iron grip. "Not we! No more meetings with you in tow. No way. Never again. I will not allow you to ruin this for me! It's too important!"

"Jesus! I cannot get through to you, Erin! I am not reassured by the fact that Mueller didn't show. I was not impressed by Dobbs or Julian. And I was disgusted by the way they were jerking you around."

"Oh, God. Is that what you think of Mueller's offer?"

"Yeah. It is." The look on his face was a grim challenge.

She forced herself to stop struggling. "Please let me go, Connor," she said quietly. He let go, and she clambered off his lap and slid to the other end of the seat. "I would love to get jerked around like that more often," she said, straightening her clothing. "The chance to curate a collection like

Mueller's, to bring in a donation of that size, to be responsible for a new wing. For where I am in my career, it would be an unbelievable coup."

"Yeah, exactly," he said. "Unbelievable."

His tone sent a chill through her. "You can't possibly still be thinking that he's Novak."

He shrugged. "It bugs me that he didn't show his face once he found out I was with you. Until I meet the guy in person, I'll continue to assume the worst."

She sagged down onto the seat, deflated. Her anger was draining away and her energy with it, as if a vortex had opened up beneath her, sucking it up. It felt horribly familiar. It was the same vortex that had been sucking everyone she cared about into its big black maw.

This was such an old struggle. In that moment, she had a dim, aching flash of just how old it was. She'd been fighting this vortex ever since she was a tiny child. By trying to be good, orderly, disciplined. Trying to make sense of the world. All her life. With all her strength.

It wasn't enough. It was taking her down, like it had taken Dad. Like it seemed to be taking Mom. Maybe Cindy, too, for all she knew. Nothing could stop it. Certainly not her feeble efforts.

She squeezed her eyes shut. "So it's all a vicious conspiracy? Everything I do, everything I try to build, it's all an ugly joke, and I'm the butt of it. I'm never going to crawl out of this godawful stinking hole, am I, Connor? Monsters are waiting around every corner."

"Erin, please—"

"It's like quicksand," she quavered. "The harder I try to climb out, the deeper I sink."

"Erin, please," Connor pleaded. "Don't freak out on me. I could be wrong. Hell, I probably am wrong. Maybe I'm a paranoid idiot, and if so, I give you permission to kick my ass, OK? Please, don't cry. Come here."

"No." She shrank against the door. "Please, just shut up and leave me alone."

He knocked his head against the steering wheel with a snarl of raw frustration. "Oh, Christ. What a mess," he muttered, starting up the car with a roar. "Put your seat belt on."

The car was ominously silent for the next couple of hours. Erin kept her face averted. Connor finally pulled over at a roadside restaurant and parked. "Let's get some food," he said.

"I'm not hungry," she told him. "But go right ahead."

He marched around the car, wrenched the door open, and yanked her out. "You need to eat."

She was too tired to fight. "Don't, Connor," she said. "I'm coming. Please calm down."

"Hah," he muttered.

She ordered a bowl of chicken soup rather than argue over food, and made a show of eating it while he devoured his cheeseburger. She stopped at the bank of pay phones in the restaurant lobby on their way out, and plugged all her change into one of the phones. Her last quarter slipped from her fingers, and the damned thing rolled everywhere, deliberately eluding her. Connor finally subdued it by stomping it under his boot. He plugged it into the slot for her.

She dialed. A recorded voice said that the money she'd deposited was insufficient for that call, and would she please deposit another—

"Goddamn this worthless piece of garbage!" she shrieked.

She started pounding on it. Connor grabbed her fists and held her fast. "Hey. Cool it before they call the cops on us, babe," he soothed. "The screaming is making the hostess nervous. What's the problem?"

"Do you have any goddamn quarters?" she demanded.

"Shhh. I've got better than that." He wrapped his arms around her tightly from behind, surrounding her with his warmth. "I've got a cell phone, and it's still charged up.

Come on out to the car. You can make your call there, where it's private and quiet."

He flipped open the phone and handed it to her as soon as they got to the car. She dialed the cell phone number for Cindy. Nothing.

She dialed Mom's number, crossing her fingers. It was Monday evening. Mom should have gotten the phone turned back on by now.

It was still disconnected.

She snapped the phone shut, handed it back to him, and twisted her hands in her lap.

"Dead end?" he asked.

She nodded.

"Who were you trying to reach? Cindy?"

"And my mom," she whispered.

"What about your mom?" he prompted. "Is she OK?"

She let out a tight, hitching breath and shook her head.

"Tell me, Erin." There was no harsh note of command in his quiet voice this time.

She looked into her lap. "Mom's losing it," she said. "Most days she won't even get out of bed. She won't pay her bills. She didn't get her phone turned back on. She's going to lose the house. There's no money left to pay the mortgage. And now she's seeing things. In the TV. Impossible things. The videos that Victor Lazar used to blackmail Dad. Of him, with his mistress. In bed." Her voice trailed off.

Connor made no comment. She looked up. His eyes were full of quiet comprehension. "I watched my dad fall apart," he said. "I know how it feels."

Her throat shook. "It's horrible. It's . . . it's like—"

"Like the earth opening up beneath your feet," he finished.

She started to cry, deep and wrenching sobs. He pulled her onto his lap, tucked her head beneath his chin, and rocked her tenderly. She let the storm rage through her, leaving her limp and exhausted, and so relaxed in the warm circle of his arms that she fell asleep.

The better part of an hour and a half went by. His bad leg was stiff and cramped beneath her warm weight, and they should have gotten right back on the road, but it was worth it, to hold such a fragrant, beautiful creature in his arms. He sneaked all the pins out of her hair and hid them in his jacket pocket, and her glossy bun had uncoiled and wrapped itself around his hand like a live thing before it lay quiet against her slender, graceful back. He pressed his cheek against her hair. So smooth and soft. Like nothing else on earth.

A car horn blared. She woke with a start. "What? Where are we?"

He stroked her back gently. "Same place we were before."

"But it's getting dark." She consulted her watch. "Good God, it's been over an hour. Why didn't you wake me?"

"I didn't want to disturb you," he said simply.

She scrambled off his lap. "We'd better get going," she murmured. "What happened to my hairpins?"

"Guess they fell out," he said, with a perfectly straight face.

He never would have thought he could be grateful for a woman's crying jag, but he was grateful for this one. It had drained away all their bitter tension. Erin yawned as he started up the car, and he reached out and touched the curve of her cheek. "Why don't you try and sleep some more?" he suggested. "It's been a hell of a day."

He waited until Erin's head was lolling against the seat, her rosy mouth slightly open, hair waving across her face like a feathery dark veil. He pulled out the phone and pushed the scrambler code for Sean.

"Hey," Sean said.

"So?"

"I can hardly hear you, dude," Sean complained. "Speak up."

"I'm on the road. Erin's sleeping, and I don't want to wake her. Tell me what you've got."

Sean grunted. "Well, I checked out the babe lair, and you know what? Most of them actually were pretty damn cute. They couldn't tell me much about Billy the Fuckhead, though, except how loaded and hunkadelic he is, and that Jag just makes them all come. No surname, place of origin, occupation, or details of any kind. But I've spent the afternoon tracking down the Vicious Rumors, and—"

"The what?"

"Cindy's band," Sean explained. "She plays sax in an R&B bar band. She's a music major, you know. They tell me she's not half bad, either. Anyhow, I bought a pitcher of beer and a platter of wings for the lead guitarist and the drummer. They told me that this guy Billy got them some gigs in various roadhouses over the past couple of months. He's some kind of agent, or so he told them. He strung them along with big talk about record deals, national tours, and shit like that, but nothing ever came of it but a few sleazy gigs for thirty bucks a head in some roadhouse dives. Then he lost interest in them and sort of sucked Cindy up into his wake. She hasn't rehearsed with the Rumors for over a month. They're worried about her, too. They don't like the Fuckhead. And they want Cindy back."

"Surname? License number? Anything? If they worked for him they must have paperwork, right?"

"Nah. It was all cash under the table, and the cell phone number they had for him no longer works. He called himself Billy Vega, but Davy hasn't uncovered anything under that name yet. It's an alias."

"Shit," he muttered.

"But don't despair. They told me that the Vicious Rumors soundman had a big, sloppy crush on Cindy. Ever since she ran off, he's been hiding out in his parents' basement, nursing his broken heart watching his *X-Files* videos and drinking Jolt."

"Ouch." Connor winced. "That's bad."

"Yeah, love hurts. I'm on my way right now to roust the sound man out of his basement. We'll see if jealousy made him notice anything special about this guy. And I've got a list of all the roadhouses where Billy got gigs for the Rumors. That's my plan for the evening. Country music, cheap beer, and secondhand smoke. What a glittering life I lead."

"Great. Carry on. And thanks. I owe you one, Sean."

"You're gonna pay up, too. When we get this business straightened out, you're gonna make me some of your special chili, like you used to. Maybe not just once. This counts for three times."

Connor hesitated. "Uh, it's been two years. I don't even know if I remember how."

"Tough shit. Start practicing, because that's my fee. You do the chili, I bring the beer, the chips, and the pepper jack cheese."

Connor grinned into the dark. "Deal. I'll dig out my chili recipe. And Sean? You know what? You're a good guy."

Sean snorted. "Tell that to some of my ex-girlfriends. Oh, and speaking of which. Did you get laid last night?"

Connor let several seconds tick by. "You cannot even imagine how off-limits that is as a conversational topic," he said softly.

Sean gasped. "Really? Hot damn! So this is serious, huh?"

"Serious as death," Connor replied. "Don't touch it."

"Oh boy. I've got the shivers," Sean moaned. "What did she do to you, man? Did she—"

"I'll call you tomorrow, Sean."

He clicked the phone shut, dropped it into his pocket, and glanced over to make sure Erin was still asleep. Her eyelashes were dark fans against her cheek. Twilight had leached all the color out of the car, but he had already memorized her colors, the soft golden tints and faint blushes and glossy deep hues of eyes and hair. Her blouse had come untucked. Buttons gaped over her sweet, sexy tits, showing a tantalizing glimpse of the white cotton bra. He wanted to buy her expensive lingerie made out of sheer, fluttering silks and laces. Things that hung together with delicate straps and hooks and snaps. He wanted to watch her put them all on, scrap by diaphanous scrap.

Then he wanted to immediately rip them off her again.

A shiny black Ford Explorer passed him, not for the first time. A cold, tingling thrill of recognition raced through him. That Explorer had been one of the cars he had taken note of when they'd pulled into the restaurant parking lot, but he'd been so focused on Erin when they came out that he had forgotten to monitor the cars again.

They'd been in that restaurant for a half an hour. They'd sat in the parking lot for an hour and twenty minutes more. Any car that had been there when they arrived should have damn well moved on long before they left. His gut was cold, and his neck was prickling. He stepped on the gas, pulled up closer to the Explorer, and checked the plate.

Sure enough, it was the very one. Brand new, black and shiny as if it had just been licked clean. Just the driver, no passengers. He eased off the gas, let it pull ahead. There was an exit in a couple of miles. He put on his turn signal and got into the exit lane, to see how it behaved.

The Explorer swerved abruptly into the exit lane ahead of him. It slowed down until he was riding its bumper, then slowed down even more. Fifty-five . . . fifty . . . forty-five . . . thirty-eight . . . Jesus.

The Explorer swerved suddenly back to the other lane. Connor pulled up alongside, and glanced at it.

Georg Luksh was grinning in the passenger seat, like some death's-head jack-in-the-box. His long hair was cut off, but it was definitely him, still missing the four teeth that Connor had knocked out of his head last November. The window rolled down. He leveled a rifle at Connor, and fluttered his fingers in an effeminate wave.

The Cadillac shuddered as Connor jammed on the brakes. The Explorer surged ahead, picking up speed.

Erin jolted awake. "What? What happened? Connor?"

"I thought I saw—" He stopped when he heard the panic in his own voice. He could've sworn he had seen no one in that passenger seat at first.

"I can't believe it," he muttered.

"What can't you believe?"

His mind was too busy churning out possible explanations to answer her. Georg could have been crouched down, waiting for a chance to pop up and scare the shit out of him. But it sounded so improbable. So . . . paranoid.

"What? Please, Connor, what did you see?" Erin pleaded.

He pulled up closer to the Explorer. The passenger seat was empty. His stomach sank down to cold, new depths.

He took a deep breath. "I thought I saw Georg," he admitted.

Erin put her hand over her mouth. "Where?"

"In that black SUV ahead of us."

She studied the SUV. "That's not Georg driving. That guy's too tall, and his head is too narrow."

"Not driving," he said. He already knew just how this was going to look and sound to her. His stomach was already clenching. A vague, sick feeling, like shame.

Erin stared at the SUV. "There's nobody in that passenger seat."

"I see that," he said tightly. "Believe me. I noticed that weird, wacky detail already with no help from you."

"Connor?" Her voice was timid and small. "Maybe it's just . . . are you tired? I'd be happy to drive, if you need to rest, and I could—"

"No," he snarled. "I'm *fine*."

She turned her face away, so that all he could see was the graceful sweep of her hair.

"Shit," he muttered. "I'm sorry."

"It's OK," she whispered.

Oh Christ, the exit. He swerved at the last moment and pulled off the highway. He did not want to share that dark, empty road with a phantom nightmare SUV. Not unless he could go after the bastards full out, run them to the ground, and grind them into paste.

Which was not an option tonight. Not with Erin in the car. He pulled out his cell phone and dialed Davy on the scrambled line.

Davy picked up instantly. "What's up? You in trouble?"

Davy could always smell the trouble his little brothers got into, even when he was oceans away. "You talked to Sean?" Connor asked.

"Yeah. He told me all about the quest to rescue Erin's little sister from the evil fuckhead. I'm working on it, too. You need something?"

"Run me a license plate number, please." He rattled it off.

"Got it. What's wrong, Con? What's special about the car?"

His stomach rolled. "Don't ask," he said. "I'll tell you later."

Davy waited, hoping for more, and grunted in annoyance when no more was forthcoming. "Take it easy," he said. The connection broke.

"Um, Connor? Where are we going?" Erin asked.

He hated her low, guarded tone. He'd used it himself while trying to reason with crazy people. "We're finding another road," he said. "I don't want to share the highway with that thing."

"It'll take us all night to get back to Seattle if we don't use I-5."

"Get the map out of the glove box," he ordered.

He'd forgotten shoving all the Mueller printouts into the glove box at the airport. They exploded out over her feet, a blizzard of paper. She gathered them up and peered at them in the dim dashboard light. "Are these the results of the check your brother ran on Mueller?"

"Yeah." He felt almost guilty, as if she'd discovered a dirty secret. "Get out the map."

She sounded as if she were going to say something else, but then thought better of it. Probably didn't want to push an unpredictable head case like him over the edge. Poor Erin, stuck in the middle of nowhere in the dark with a guy who saw things that weren't there.

His misery deepened and spread. Like a pool of blood, widening inexorably on cold concrete. She studied the map. It was terribly quiet.

His cell phone rang. He snatched it up. Davy. "Yeah?"

"That license plate is a 2002 Ford Explorer, color black, which belongs to a guy named Roy Fitz. A sixty-two-year-old divorced used car salesman in Coos Bay, Oregon. He has bad credit. Does that help?"

Connor let out a long, silent sigh of misery. "Uh, no. Not really. But I appreciate the help. Later, Davy."

"Goddammit, Con, what the hell is—"

"I can't talk about it right now," he snarled. "I'm sorry. Good-bye."

Great. Now he could feel bad about being rude to his brother, too.

Erin tidied the Mueller papers into a neat sheaf, folded them, and tucked them carefully into the glove box. The map rustled as she opened it up. She switched on the interior light and peered at it for a couple of minutes. "We can take this road up to Redstone Creek, and then connect with the Paulson Highway north until we reach Bonney. Then we'll make our decisions as we go. Sound good to you?"

Her voice was gentle and matter-of-fact. He was so grateful to her for that, he could've burst into tears and kissed her feet. "Sounds fine."

She flipped off the light. "Shall we listen to some music?"

"Anything you want."

She spun the dial until she found some classic blues. Probably she remembered that he'd settled on blues the day before. She was trying to chill him out with his favorite music. Detail oriented.

"Thanks," he muttered.

She reached out, stroked his cheek with her fingertip. Smoothed a hank of his hair back behind his ear.

The sweet, soft caress unknotted the tension that clenched his body. Air finally started to go back into his lungs.

He just might make it back to Seattle with his sanity intact.

Chapter

13

Chuck Whitehead pulled to a stop at the wide spot in the deserted road, not far from the Childress Ridge Lookout. He kept focusing on irrelevant things, like the colored plastic ribbons that the Forest Service tied around the trees. His hands were clammy. He felt the constant urge to pee. The last ten hours kept running through his mind like an endless video loop, ever since he'd gotten home from his job at the DNA lab. He'd said good-bye to the hospice home health aide who looked after his wife Mariah while he was at work, headed upstairs to check on her—and found a gun shoved up beneath his chin.

The man who held the gun had told him what to do, and he had done it. Every last detail. He had the proof inside his jacket. He could show them. He was cooperating.

He flipped off the headlights so as not to run down the battery, and was horrified by the near-absolute darkness. The hills hunched over him were black, the sky barely lighter. It was overcast tonight.

The man had told him that this was where they would give Mariah back to him, but how could they have transported someone as fragile as Mariah to such a deserted place? She'd been on oxygen support with a morphine drip for over two weeks now.

But the man had told him to come here, so here he was.

No police, the man had said. One word to the police, and Mariah would die.

Time crawled by, marked by his thudding heart, by his labored breathing, by the digital clock blinking on the dash. Someone knocked on the back window. He jumped and screamed.

He had done what was asked of him, he reminded himself. No one could fault him. He opened the door, forced himself to stand. The dim light shed by the interior car light blinded him and revealed nothing.

"Shut the door, please," said a soft, cultured voice. An older man. Upper crust, Englishy-sounding foreign accent. It was the same guy who had come to his house. South African, maybe. He shut the door. He had dated a South African girl once, his brain offered, hysterically irrelevant. Her name had been Angela. Same accent. Nice girl. His life was flashing before his eyes. Not a good sign.

His eyes were beginning to adjust. He made out a tall, thin figure in black. He appeared to be wearing a device that covered his eyes.

"Are you South African?" The words popped out, and he cursed himself. He might have just killed them both, asking useless questions.

The man was silent. "No, Mr. Whitehead," he said finally. "I am not. Because I do not exist. Do you understand?"

"Yes," he said quickly. "Of course."

The man came closer, reached for him. Chuck flinched, and then realized he was being patted down for weapons. What a ludicrous idea. Him, and weapons. The man satisfied himself as to Chuck's unarmed state, and headed off into the darkness. "Come with me," he said.

"Is Mariah here?"

The man did not answer. The gate creaked as he pushed it

open. His feet crunched in the gravel. Chuck stumbled after him. If he lost the sound of those footsteps, he would lose Mariah forever. He was losing her anyway, but not so horribly, so inconclusively. Not like this.

"Excuse me? Uh, sir? Please wait up. I can't see anything. Excuse me! Sir? I don't know your name—" Chuck tripped and fell, scraped his hands bloody, and got up. The steady, crunching footsteps were getting further away. He forced himself to a lurching run.

"You may call me Mr. Dobbs," the voice said gently.

Chuck followed the voice through the dark, ahead and to the right. Mr. Dobbs. His nightmare had a name. The lookout tower loomed above him. The trees made the darkness even denser. He stumbled into a pole, bashed his face, and whimpered. He would never find the road out again without help.

"Mr. Whitehead?"

The voice came from ahead of him, to his left. Dobbs must have night vision goggles to negotiate this pitch darkness.

"Hold out your left hand. You will find a wooden plank. Follow it toward my voice."

Dobbs's voice was helpful, encouraging. He caught himself feeling grateful, like a whipped dog that licked its tormentor's foot. He groped around, knocked his knuckles against a plank, and stumbled forward.

An eternity of splinters and shuffling.

"Stop, now. Put your hands in front of you," Dobbs commanded. "You will feel the rungs of a ladder. Climb it."

Panic weakened his knees. He was getting further, not closer, to any sort of place that his wife might conceivably be. "Is Mariah here?" He felt like a sheep, bleating out his plaintive, repetitive question.

"Climb, Mr. Whitehead." Dobbs's voice was gentle and pitiless.

He climbed, straining toward darkness, with darkness pulling him from below. His aching muscles struggled against it.

He hated himself for how easily he had been unmanned, almost more than he hated Dobbs for doing this to him. Higher, impossibly high. The air felt thinner. It moved around him, cold against his neck.

"You have reached a platform. Put your foot out, at two o'clock from your body."

Dobbs was below him, on the ladder. If he let go, he might knock him off and kill him. And himself, too, not that it mattered.

And then he would never know what had happened to Mariah.

He groped with his foot, found the platform, and flung himself onto what he hoped was a surface that could take his weight. He landed like a sack of rocks and huddled there, weeping silently.

Dobbs climbed the rest of the ladder. "Do you have the documentation for the work you were requested to do, Mr. Whitehead?"

Requested. What a way to put it. Chuck struggled to his feet and rummaged in his jacket. "I did the extraction from the blood sample," he said. "Just like you told me. I ran the probes, and it looked fine, the DNA wasn't degraded. I switched the cell pellets in the freezer. Just like you said. I've got the old cell pellet here for you."

"Put the cell pellet and the documentation down on the platform," Dobbs said. "Then walk ten paces straight ahead."

He paced. Wind whistled by his ears. He felt a sense of huge, empty space before him. "I printed out the test run results," he said desperately. "I modified all the computer records for Kurt Novak's ID file. I can show you how I—"

"Never say that name out loud again. Did anyone see you?"

"There's always a couple of grad students in the lab at

night doing rush specimens, but they pretty much leave me alone," he babbled. "Everybody does, these days. I'm kind of a downer lately, what with—"

"Shut up, Mr. Whitehead."

He had to ask, one more time. "Is Mariah here?"

Dobbs clucked his tongue. "Do you think I am completely heartless, to bring such an ill woman to a place like this? Poor Mariah can barely speak, let alone climb a vertical ladder. Use your head."

"But I . . . but you said—"

"Shut up. I wish to examine these. Keep your back turned."

He waited. An owl hooted. Mariah had loved owls. She had big, round, owl-like eyes. Now huge in her wasted face.

"Very good, Mr. Whitehead," the man said approvingly. Papers rustled. "This is exactly what we needed. You've done well. Thank you."

"You're welcome," he said automatically. "And . . . Mariah?" Hope was stone dead, but the cold zombie of curiosity still shambled on.

"Ah. Mariah. Well, she is back in her bed, in your house. I deposited her there immediately after your car left the lab. I replaced her morphine drip, much to her relief. And then I took pity on her, and gave her what you were too weak to bestow."

The dark was scarcely darker with his burning eyes squeezed shut. He shook his head. "No," he whispered.

"Mercy," the voice continued. "The morphine, turned up while she watched. Her breathing getting slower. And finally, peace."

"No." He trembled under the lash of irrational guilt. "She didn't want that. She told me. She told me she would never ask that of me."

"Who cares what she wanted? None of us get to choose."

Hope had gone, and fear had gone with it. Chuck only listened now because he could not stop his ears.

"It will be clear to everyone what happened," the man said gently. "The message on the computer, a brief note stating your intention of joining your beloved wife in death, farewell, cruel world, et cetera. And now I offer you the luxury of choice, Mr. Whitehead. If you wish to die quickly, take two paces straight ahead. But if you would prefer to die slowly and painfully, that can be arranged. Easily."

Chuck laughed out loud. Dobbs had no idea what it meant to die slowly and painfully. He stared into the void beyond the edge.

He felt as light as air. An empty husk. If he took the two paces, he would drift away like a dandelion seed.

Perhaps if he were braver, luckier, smarter, he would have seen some way out of this trap. Apparently everything hung on his carefully arranged suicide. Nothing would hold up if he were found tortured and murdered, after all.

There was no coin left to bargain with this devil. His resources were tapped out. All his bravery, all his luck, all his wits he had given up to these last few months of tending Mariah.

Dobbs had probably figured that into the calculations when he'd handpicked him out of all the DNA lab personnel. Smart of him to choose the man with nothing left to lose.

In his mind, he was already falling, toward a huge dark owl's eye. It regarded him with calm, merciful detachment.

He took the two paces. The world tipped, air rushed past his face. He fell into the owl's eye, and hurtled toward Mariah's waiting arms.

Connor shot Erin a wary glance when they passed the sign for her exit. "I'd rather take you to my house than your apartment," he said. "The doors are better, the locks are better. The bed is bigger."

"I have to go home," she said.

He sighed. "Erin, I—"

"No, Connor." She gathered all her energy and made her voice resolute. "Cindy could call me there. My mom could call me there. My friend Tonia is bringing my cat back there. The clothes I need for work tomorrow are there. My employee ID, my bus pass, everything. Just take me home. Now. No arguments, please."

He flipped on the turn signal. She let out a silent sigh of relief. He drove aimlessly around, passing up several good parking spaces.

"Looking for a black SUV?" she asked.

He braked so sharply that she jerked forward against the seat belt. He parked the car without saying a word.

Connor rattled the broken lock on the front door of the building with a grunt of disgust. "Someone should sue the landlord."

"He turns off your hot water if you give him any trouble," she said. "I've learned to leave him alone."

The elevator was still broken. She was grateful for his company as they ascended through the echoing stairwell. The decaying building was depressing at the best of times, but at this time of night, with her life the way it currently was, it would be unbearably creepy alone.

She dug the keys out of her purse. Connor took them from her, pushed her gently back against the wall and pulled out his gun.

She sighed. Cops tended to be paranoid. She should know, having been raised by one. They had reason to be, and Connor more than most. She waited patiently while he unlocked the door, flipped on the light, stepped in. A moment later he gestured her in. "All clear."

"Thank goodness," she murmured.

His face hardened at the faint sarcasm in her voice, but she was too tired and wired to care. Let him be huffy if he pleased. She felt restless and tingling and strange tonight. She didn't feel like placating anyone.

Connor locked and bolted the door. "Erin," he said.

She slid her suit jacket off and flung it over a chair. "Yes?"

"I can't leave you here alone. I just can't do it."

She stretched her arms over her head, rolling her stiff neck. Connor's eyes wandered down and fastened on her breasts. She rolled her shoulders, arched her back. "You can't?" she said.

His eyes followed her every move with grim fascination. "No," he said. "Not after what I saw on the highway. Not with that worthless lock and piece of shit door. Not even if your locks were good."

She ran her fingers slowly through her hair, and tossed it. "Not even if I lived in a bank vault? Guarded by a platoon of Marines?"

"You're starting to get the picture."

She kicked her shoes off. One bounced off the wall and skittered to the middle of the floor, the other landed on top of a pile of archeology magazines. "So don't leave," she said.

His eyes narrowed. "I thought you hated my guts."

The uncertainty in his voice gave her an exhilarating rush of feminine power. He was vulnerable to her, too. She glanced at her watch, and unclasped it, tossing it on top of the dresser. "It's three in the morning, Connor," she said. "I'm too tired to hate your guts."

She went into the bathroom and let him puzzle over that while she washed her face and brushed her teeth.

When she came out, he was still rooted to the same spot, wary incredulity stamped all over his face. "You're sure?"

She laughed as she hooked her thumbs into her panty hose and shimmied them down. "Didn't you just tell me that I had absolutely no choice in the matter?" she complained. "I can't keep this straight anymore! Who is the boss around here, anyway?"

"Stop jerking me around," he said. "You know that if I stay here, we're going to have sex again."

Her eyes widened. "Oh, my. Don't be shy, Connor. Tell it like it is." She stepped out of the skirt, clipped it to the hanger, and hung it in the tiny closet, stretching up so that the blouse would ride up over her bottom. "The bed really is incredibly small," she said. "If you'd rather go home and get a good night's sleep, please feel free to—"

"Don't tease me. I'm not in the mood."

The harshness of his tone froze her into place for a second. She exhaled, and resumed unbuttoning her blouse. She tried to act nonchalant as she shrugged off the blouse, hung it up.

"Your energy is strange tonight," he said. "I can't tell whether you want to jump my bones or rip my head off. It's got me off balance."

She reached behind herself and unhooked the bra. She tossed it away and shook her hair back. "If you're so off balance, Connor, maybe you'd be better off lying down."

He stared at her bare breasts, bright streaks of color in his cheeks. "You're pissed at me, and you're coming onto me at the same time. What's that all about, Erin? What's the catch?"

She smiled at him, merciless. "It's a mystery," she said. "You've got to take your chances." She shucked her panties and walked naked in the burning spotlight of his gaze to the bed. She slid between the sheets. Looked at him. Lifted a questioning eyebrow.

He shook his head. "I don't know what to do next," he said. "I can't figure you out."

"So why don't you stop trying, and get your clothes off?"

His shoulders jerked in silent laughter. He opened up his duffel, which she had not even noticed him bring in with him. He pulled out one of his squealers and mounted it swiftly onto the door.

He sauntered over to the bed. He stared at her as he placed his gun on the bedside table and started yanking off his clothes. Seconds later he stood before her naked, smoothing a condom over his jutting erection. She scooted over to make room for him.

He shook his head. "This thing is even narrower than a twin bed. Do you want to be on top, or on the bottom?"

He loomed over her. She stared at the shadows that limned every curve and cut of his muscular, powerful body. He emanated a blast of fierce, macho energy that infuriated and excited her at the same time.

"Oh, go ahead. You be on top, Connor. Why fool ourselves?"

He wrenched the quilt down and shoved her flat on her back. "Where the hell did that crack come from?" he demanded.

Oops. Very smooth move. Now he was furious again. She placed her hands against his scorching chest, her breath quickening. "I don't know. It just comes to me. I can't help it."

He put his thigh between her legs and shoved them open. She was already wet, and he hadn't even touched her. She had transformed in the last thirty-six hours, and Connor was the catalyst. He was so volatile and bossy and sexually insatiable. He didn't politely disappear when she climaxed, like her fantasy Connor had. He stayed with her, his arms jealously tight. Taking up space, demanding attention.

She almost wanted him to shove himself inside her with crude force so her restless, prickly anger could be justified. She was hungry for his strength, his heat. Breathless with anticipation. Maddened.

"What?" she snapped. "Come on, Connor. Aren't you going to show me who's lord and master?"

He cupped her face in his hands. "Is that what you want?"

She wiggled against him. "Since when has what I wanted mattered to you?"

"That's not fair. I may have pushed you around about your millionaire, but I never forced you in bed. You came to me, remember?"

Did she ever. It was maddening, how much she wanted

him, and how much power he wielded over her because of it. "What are you waiting for, Connor? Now who's being the tease?" she demanded.

"You're too angry," he said calmly. "You're setting me up."

She thrashed beneath him. "Oh, please. For God's sake," she flared. "I'm not that treacherous!"

"You don't even know how treacherous you are. This is wilderness territory. For both of us."

"Connor—"

"Tell me exactly what you want, Erin," he said. "Don't set me up to be the asshole, because it's not fair. If you want me to be rough, I'll be rough."

That did it. His arrogant, self-righteous tone infuriated her. She shoved at him. "Oh, don't do me any goddamn favors!"

He seized her wrists and wrenched them up over her head. "OK. I think I've nailed the vibe you want tonight, sweetheart. No favors. That can be arranged." He let out his breath in a sharp sigh when he slid his fingers between her legs and found her wet. "God, look at you. You are such a wild thing, Erin Riggs. You just can't wait, can you?"

"No!" she snapped. "So hurry."

He was still laughing when he kissed her, his tongue thrusting deep into her mouth. She could barely move. She was stretched out, every muscle straining beneath his weight, arms yanked up high.

He took himself in hand, pressed himself against her, and slid just the tip of himself inside her. He teased her with tiny, teasing thrusts, bathing himself with her slick moisture, and then drove inside her. She clenched around him with a muffled cry. He let her move just enough to find her body's answer to his sensual invasion, the tight, clinging demands of her secret flesh upon his thick shaft.

Finally he gave her what she wanted, grinding his hips against her. Each deep, heavy thrust pushed her closer to the resolution of the enigma burning in her mind. She needed all his strength for ballast to drive her toward the answer to all this aching, screaming tension. She struggled closer, straining up, almost there—

"No."

Her eyes popped open. He shifted, and lifted the pressure away from where she so desperately needed it. She clenched her legs around him to draw him deeper. "Connor, I need this! What—"

"No favors."

She almost screamed with rage. "Are you punishing me?"

"No favors, Erin. You'll come when I let you come. Not before."

"Why are you doing this?" She thrashed wildly beneath him.

He subdued her effortlessly. "Because I can."

"I hate you," she hissed. "You evil, controlling bastard. This isn't fair. I give you an inch and you take a mile. Every damn time."

He shook his head. "No. Give me an inch, and I take everything."

There was absolutely nothing she could do. She was spread so helplessly open beneath him that there was no way to clench herself around him and work herself to climax of her own volition. She was at his mercy.

Three more times, he brought her to the brink and then drew back. When he began again the fourth time, she was too exhausted to thrash and writhe. She just squeezed her eyes shut and trembled. He leaned down and kissed her. "Beg me," he said.

"Forget it," she murmured. "Bastard. I'd rather die."

"Just beg me, and I'll give it to you," he coaxed. "It's worth it."

She opened her eyes, stared into the pure, hypnotic green depths of his eyes, and he pulled her in. "Please," she whispered.

He released her arms and surged against her so deep and

strong it almost hurt. But the pain was just a glowing delineation around a deeper, hotter pleasure that grew and swelled until it broke, sending all the tension he had wrought with such cruel skill crashing down on her.

Violent spasms of pleasure jerked and shuddered through her.

She didn't open her eyes for a long time afterwards. It was the only privacy she could maintain, with her body so penetrated, his eyes so intent upon her face. He waited patiently, curved over her body.

The ripples widened, spread, softened to her chest, her throat, her eyes, and suddenly she was weeping, a soothing rush like a summer rainstorm. The enigma had been solved, but the solving of it had uncovered an even bigger mystery, one that mere love games could not resolve. She draped her arms around his neck, pulling his face to hers. "That's enough of that," she whispered. "Be gentle with me now."

He stiffened, and hid his face against her neck. "Oh, no," he muttered. "Erin, I thought this was what you wanted. I thought—"

"I did. I did want it," she reassured him. She grabbed a hank of his hair and pulled him up so she could pet the anxious furrow between his brows with her fingertip. "And you gave it to me. And now I want something different, that's all. No big deal. Just ease off."

"Did I hurt you? Do you want me to stop?"

She kissed him. "Would you relax? There is no hidden message here. No code to decipher. I do not want to stop. Read my lips, OK?"

He jerked his head away, but she wound the hair around her fingers, trapping him. "You are so fucking complicated," he snapped.

She sighed. "Just keep making love to me. Gently. And stop being ridiculous and anxious. What's complicated about that?"

He pried her fingers out of his hair and pressed his face

against her neck, burrowing closer. "I just want to please you."

She was moved by the ragged tremor in his voice. "Oh, but you do," she soothed him. "Didn't you feel what happened? What you did to me? It was intense, but it worked. Just like you knew that it would."

"I thought I went too far," he admitted. "With that stupid lord and master crap. I thought I'd screwed up."

"No. You didn't. I trust you, Connor." Her words softened to a senseless croon as she covered his hot face with kisses. She moved beneath him, caressing his shaft with every delicate, clinging muscle inside her sheath. It was a lazy, licking, tender kiss between their sexes. Their lips joined to match it, hungry for sweet reassurance.

Their power games had transformed into something infinitely more beautiful and treacherous. His dominating energy was rendered down to desperate, shaking need. Now she was the strong one who clasped and held, with the power to give or to withhold. But there was no question of withholding. He was inside her mind, he was everywhere. Her heart glowed for him. Every part of her was liquid and soft, merging with him, surging and heaving like the sea.

Much later, he murmured and lifted himself off her body, and stumbled away into the dark to dispose of the condom. She didn't have the strength to turn her head and tell him where she kept the trash basket. He lifted the quilt, slid into bed again, rolling her on top of him.

"I'll squish you," she protested, without much force.

"Nah. This is another one of my classic Erin fantasies. Sleeping with your naked body on top of me. Your hair draped all over me, your hand against my chest, your breath mixing with mine. Your skin . . ."

The rest of his whispered words blended into her dreams like a swirl of melting honey.

* * *

Kurt Novak and Georg Luksch were not worth this pain and humiliation. They had used him, and thrown him away. He could feel it.

The police flung Martin into the holding cell, and the gate clanged shut. He fell heavily to his knees, retching.

Just his luck, that he should get rough, brutal types for his interrogation, but he had been prepared. He had been very strong. He had told the police exactly what his employers had ordered him to say. He had made the police torture it out of him, as instructed. He had held back as long as he could before finally gasping out where he had last seen Novak and Luksch, and when. He had been desperate, very convincing.

Then he had repeated the same story, no matter how hard they hit him. He had been strong, but there was no one to bear witness to his loyalty. Novak and Luksch would never know or care how brave he had been for them. No one would ever know. He was sure of this.

He was disposable, and they had thrown him away.

His bosses had told him that if he did this for them, that his parents and his uncle would be spared, and that two million euro would be transferred to a private numbered account for him in a bank in Zurich upon his release. His very rapid release. We own the judges, they had told him. It will be arranged quickly, more quickly than the last time. We need you, Martin. That was why we arranged your escape with Luksch and Novak in America. Only you are strong enough for this task. Do not fear. Be strong, Martin. You will be rewarded.

Rewarded. He laughed, but the pain of his cracked ribs stopped him. He huddled in the fetal position on the frigid concrete and wiggled his teeth, one by one. He would lose some of them. The left front, and the incisor. His mouth was full of blood. His tongue ran over the smooth capsule they had soldered to a filling in his back molar.

A microchip, they had told him. So that we can always

find you, always rescue you. Just a precaution. It will do you no harm. It is for your protection, Martin. Trust us.

He suppressed another laugh, wiggling the loose molar with his tongue. Two million euro could replace lost teeth, he told himself. Two million euro could make up for a great many things.

But not all, something whispered. Six months in an American prison, and now this. He was shrinking, curled up on a floor that smelled of urine and vomit. Smaller and smaller until he was the size of a child's doll, with tiny balls like shriveled raisins.

Too small to be seen by the bank personnel in Zurich.

He pressed his tongue against the smooth capsule and wondered if they could listen to him through it, if there could be a microphone so small. He started, hysterically, to laugh again, even though every jolt of his diaphragm hurt like knives stabbing.

"Fuck you," he muttered, just in case they could hear him. And then, for good measure. "Fuck you both. Fuck Kurt Novak. Fuck Georg Luksch. Fuck your mothers, your grand-mothers. Fuck you all."

It happened immediately, as if in answer to his words. A *pop* inside his mouth, a burning. A sharp, bitter taste, and his heart froze in his chest. Arrested, in midbeat.

The pain was huge, but he felt no surprise. He understood a million things in that timeless moment that his heart ceased to beat. The choices that had led him to this stinking con-crete floor. The boredom and greed and restless anger that had gotten him mixed up with that murderous scum. The many cruel things that he had done with them, for them. It raced through his mind, together with all the choices that he could have made, and had not.

He could have married Sophie, joined his uncle's wine business. Sunday mornings strolling in the village square, he with their young son on his shoulders, she with the baby carriage, their infant daughter asleep beneath her pink blanket. A splendid lunch, and then lazy afternoon sex with his wife while the children napped. A game of cards at the club, a beer with the friends watching soccer on TV. Weddings, baptisms, funerals.

The ordinary seasons of a blameless life.

He watched it spin by, until real time caught up with him. The iron fist closed, and crushed his heart out of existence, and what could have been and what truly was were both extinguished.

Chapter

14

She was still on top of him when she woke up. Dawn had lightened the dingy brick wall outside the window, turning it a charcoal gray. She glanced up at Connor's face. He was gazing at her with his usual intensity, but it no longer flustered her. She liked it now.

She shifted on top of him, murmuring with pleasure. He was so solid and warm. Her thigh was flung across his, and his erect penis pressed against her, as hot as a brand. She poised herself over him so that her hair fell around them in a shadowy curtain, and touched his lips with hers. His mouth opened at her urging. Their tongues touched, a delicate, questing flick that melded into a deliciously sensuous kiss. It brought her body to tingling wakefulness.

She expected him to spring to action, but he just lay beneath her, rigid and trembling. She lifted her head. "Connor. Don't you want to . . . ?"

He rolled his eyes. "Like you have to ask."

She dropped a kiss on his jaw. "Then why don't you?"

"You gave me a hard time last night. About pushing you around."

She was indignant. "I never said—"

"I'm sick of it. I'm just going to lie here and see what happens. If you want something, take it. If you need something from me, ask for it."

He folded his arms back behind his head, and waited.

She was disconcerted, but not for long. She didn't need instructions. She had ideas coming at her by the truckload. If he wanted to be a love slave, he'd come to the right place.

She flung back the quilt and rose up onto her knees. This was going to be fun. She leaned over and kissed him, thrusting her tongue aggressively into his mouth, the way he so often did to her. He murmured in surprise, and his body shook.

"Give me your hands." The ring of command in her voice was so unfamiliar, she barely recognized it as her own.

He unfolded his arms. She seized his hands and pressed them against her breasts. "Touch me," she said huskily. "Lightly. With your fingertips. Like butterfly wings."

He obeyed her. His eyes were bright with fascination, and his gentle fingers traced lines over the curves of her breasts. She flung her head back and danced above him, letting pleasure lead her. His breath got harsher, his erection harder. She leaned over so that her breasts dangled in his face. "Suck on my nipples," she commanded.

He writhed beneath her and gripped her waist, murmuring in a pleading voice. He covered her breasts with his hot mouth. She shook with excitement. The tremors were shaking her apart.

She pulled away, panting and flushed. They stared at each other, their eyes bright with discovery.

"Wow," he whispered. "Oh, my queen. What is your royal will?"

She shimmied down his body until she straddled his thighs, and tormented him with her fingertips, exploring every line and curve. He squeezed his eyes shut and moaned when she took his penis in her hands. She swirled her hand around the head, so smooth and bursting with pent-up need. She poised herself above him, and slid the blunt tip of him up and down her vulva. She wiggled, shifted, seeking the right angle, and forced herself down, enveloping him with a shuddering sigh. He was so amazingly thick, as hard as a hot club throbbing inside her.

"God," he muttered. "Please. Erin."

She rose up again, sank deeper. The small, quivering muscles inside her sheath clenched him with loving, jealous tightness, caressing the whole, delicious length of him.

"I'm not wearing a condom," he told her. "If you haven't noticed."

She smiled. "So don't come inside me. You have such excellent self-control. I've seen it in action, so you can't pretend you don't. So use it, Connor. Use it . . . in my service."

She rose up, and took him in again, a hot, slow glide of pleasure.

He panted beneath her. "You know this is stupid," he said. "We've got them, so there's no goddamn excuse for not using them."

She kissed his chest. "Something about you makes me want to play with fire. What an awful bitch I am. Torturing you like this."

He made a sharp, angry sound. "You've been acting strange ever since we got back to town. I'm not saying it doesn't turn me on, but it's starting to really piss me off."

"Oh, no. I'm just terrified." She rocked against him, rising up and sinking slowly back down with a sigh of bliss. "I'm tired of doing the smart thing and being agreeable and sensible and proper. I've been a good girl all my life, and I've only just realized that it doesn't do a damn bit of good. You just get slammed anyway. So why bother? What is the point of all that stupid effort? You just end up feeling like a fool."

He shook his head and opened his mouth. She pressed her finger against his lips. "Ever since I seduced you, I don't want to be a good girl anymore. I want to do naughty things. Get a tattoo. Show my cleavage. Pay my rent late. Drink tequila shots, dance on the tabletops. Blow my paycheck on pretty shoes. Rob a bank wearing a leather mini-skirt."

"Oh, God, Erin—"

"I want to become a cautionary tale for young women. Don't do what Erin did, girls! It's the path to doom! And you know what else I want? I want this. With you. Right now. Give me your hands again."

He offered them, a gesture of surrender, and she placed them gently at the curve of her hips. "Hold me," she said. "Move under me, Connor. Make me come."

His fingers bit into her waist, and his hips bucked as he seized control of the rhythm. All she could do was gasp and hang on for the ride, sometimes deep and pounding, sometimes a sensual dance that slid over and over that glowing ache of need inside her that was wired to everything that mattered, her eyes and throat, her spine, her nipples, her heart, until ripples of bliss overflowed and unraveled her.

He withdrew, panting, and she lost her balance and slid off the bed. He caught her arms, but her legs tumbled off until her knees hit Aunt Millie's braided rag rug. He sat up and pulled her onto her knees.

She knelt between his spread thighs, his penis jutting in her face, hot with the scent of her own pleasure. He wound his hands into her hair, staring into her eyes. "Make me come, Erin," he said.

She took him deep into her mouth without hesitation, gripping him eagerly with both hands and mouth. She followed the cues his body gave her: his sobbing pants, his fingers tightening in her hair, the slick, bursting heat of his penis in her mouth, the salty drops against her tongue. She drew him in as deep as she could, sliding and suckling.

He was primed to explode. In just a few long, luxurious strokes he erupted into her mouth in hot, pulsing spasms.

She hid her face against his scarred thigh. He sagged over her, trembling, and slowly slid off the bed to join her on the floor. He pulled her into his arms and rested his head on her shoulder.

Connor lifted his head a few minutes later. "You feeling any mellower?" he asked. "You work out any of those bad girl demons?"

"Not really," she murmured. "I still feel pretty naughty."

"Oh, God. I'm a dead man."

His tone was light, but dread still chilled her at his careless words. "Don't say that!"

His eyes were puzzled. "Huh?"

"It's bad luck. Don't ever say that again. Please. Ever."

He started to speak, stopped himself, and gave her a brief, crooked smile. He pulled her into his arms again. "OK," he said gently. "Sorry."

She squeezed him tightly, until her arms shook with the strain.

"Let's get one thing clear," he said, stroking her back tenderly. "When you go to drink your tequila shots and dance on tabletops in your leather mini-skirt, I get to come along. With my gun."

She giggled against his chest. "Oh, please."

"I mean it," he said sternly. "No banks, though. There I draw the line. I'm sworn to uphold law and order and all that garbage."

"Don't worry," she said. "One jailbird in the family is enough."

Connor went rigid in her arms. The air in the room was suddenly chilly against her damp skin.

Connor dropped his arms. Erin scrambled to her feet. "I'll, um, just jump in the shower," she babbled. "I'll be right out."

She scurried into the bathroom. The door slammed.

Connor wandered around the room, trying to breathe

away the tension in his gut. He stared at the corkboard over her desk. Photos and postcards were push-pinned all over it. Erin and Ed on a ski trip, squinting and sunburned. His arm was flung over her shoulder. They were laughing.

He realized that he was rubbing his scarred thigh, gritting his teeth so hard his jaw throbbed.

The phone rang. He decided not to touch it. She had a machine. If it was Cindy, he would pick up. Otherwise, it would be suicide to touch the thing.

The shower stopped running just as the machine clicked on. The bathroom door burst open as a woman's bouncy, fake cheerful voice began to speak.

"Hi, Erin, this is Kelly, from Keystroke Temps. I'm afraid I've got some bad news for you—"

Erin burst out in a cloud of steam, naked, her hair dripping.

"—had some complaints about you from Winger, Drexler & Lowe, about your attitude, and your decision to be unavailable for work this morning was just the last straw for them. So the office manager told me to tell you just not to come in tomorrow. And, uh . . . Keystroke Temps is making the same decision. I'm really sorry, Erin, but the decision is definitive and final, and if you mail in your timesheet, we'll mail your last check to you, so there'll be no need for you to come in and—"

Erin lunged for the phone. "Kelly? It's me—yes, I know, but I came back early—but that's ridiculous! I was a perfect employee! My attitude was excellent! I came in early, I worked late, I did ten times as much work as—that's crazy! They can't possibly—"

She listened for another moment, and laughed bitterly. "Kelly, you know, I don't envy you having to tell me this. But let me give you a tip for the future. Don't tell someone to have a nice day after giving them news like that. Trust me, it's the wrong thing to say."

She slammed the phone down and whirled on him, naked and dripping and stupendously beautiful in her towering rage.

"That stupid cow," she snarled. "Have a nice day! As if!"

He backed away. "Uh, Erin?"

She advanced on him. "What could they possibly have complained about? I reorganized their database! I worked out all the bugs in their financial program! I rewrote every single document those idiots ever dictated and turned it into real English! I even got coffee for those bastards, and all for thirteen lousy dollars an hour!"

"I'm sure you did," he said meekly.

"It's not in my nature to make people complain about me! Except for when I work too hard and make everybody else look bad, but I didn't do that this time, I was really, really careful not to, I swear!"

She had him backed up against the wall. He was fascinated by the wild energy blazing out of her. "Of course you were," he soothed.

"I never give anybody any trouble! Ever! It's like a sickness!"

"Only to me," Connor said. "You give me no end of trouble."

She put her hands on her hips. "You, Connor McCloud, are a special case."

"I'll say," he muttered. "Just lucky, huh?"

She cocked her head to the side. Water trickled seductively over her tits. "You do bring out elements of my personality that I didn't know I had," she admitted. "But I never showed those sides of my personality at Winger, Drexler & Lowe, and I certainly—"

"You damn well better not be showing them to anybody else." The words surprised him as much as they did her. "Nobody but me. Got it?"

She blinked. "Connor. I, ah, wasn't talking about sex."

"Well, I am," he said. "I just thought I'd take this opportunity to make that point crystal clear. Since we haven't discussed it yet."

Erin glanced down, seeming to realize that she was naked and sopping wet. "Uh, what exactly do you mean by that?" she asked warily.

He crossed his arms over his chest. "What do you think I mean?"

Her mouth tightened. "Don't play games with me, Connor."

"I'm not playing games. It's a valid question. I want to know how you interpret that remark."

Her eyes slid away from his. "Why does it always have to be me who goes out on the limb? It's not fair to—"

"Just answer me, goddamnit."

She studied his face for a moment. "OK. Here goes," she said carefully. "I think maybe, ah, that this might be your bossy, oafish way of asking me if I'm interested in being exclusively involved with you."

He felt his face go red.

"Did I get it right?" she demanded. "Do I win the prize?"

"That's the gist of it. I would have phrased it differently."

"Oh?" Her eyebrows climbed. "And how would you phrase it?"

He thought about it. "Never mind," he muttered. "Let's stick with the way you said it. It sounds better."

"No, Connor. Your turn. Tell me exactly what you were thinking."

What an idiot. He'd boxed himself into a trap. "We already are exclusively involved, Erin. We have been since you decided to go to bed with me. It's a done deal. I know it, and you know it."

Her eyes went very big and thoughtful. "Hmm. So the key point here is that you're not asking me. You're telling me. Right?"

He shrugged. "Guess so," he mumbled.

"I see," she murmured.

Her cool tone maddened him. "I sure hope so," he snapped.

She wrung her dripping hair out over the sink. "If I have a problem with you, Connor, that's it," she said. "You don't ask me. You just tell me. But you know what? The world doesn't work like that. And more to the point, I don't work like that. I will not take orders from you."

"Goddamn it, Erin—"

"If you would just stop trying so hard to control me, then maybe you'd discover that all that effort really isn't necessary."

She shook her wet mane back over her shoulders. His proud, gorgeous, wet, naked, intergalactic princess. She turned to face him.

"You do not own me," she said quietly.

He didn't remember deciding to move. He just found himself all over her, his hands moving over her damp, shivering skin. Pinning her against the wall. He cupped her face in his hands, opened his mouth, and the dangerous truth just fell right out of him, no holding it back.

"That's true. I don't own you. But I want you so bad. I've had a hard-on for you ever since you were jailbait. I want to know everything you do, every thought you think. I want to have sex with you in every way possible. I'm obsessed with you, Erin Riggs, and I cannot stand the thought of you with another man. It makes me feel—"

. . . crazy

He swallowed the word back, his chest squeezing painfully. "I just want you all for myself." He closed his eyes. "Please."

Erin shivered, and dropped a soothing kiss on his bare shoulder. "Try to calm down, Connor," she murmured. "You're so intense."

"Oh, God, you have no idea." He pressed his face against her wet hair and tried to keep his mouth shut. Anything he said could be used to incriminate him. He had never felt so desperate and out of control. At least not as an adult.

The silence was driving him nuts. "How's that for going

out on a limb?" His voice came out harsh and taunting in spite of his best efforts. "Did I make myself vulnerable enough to suit you?"

Her mouth tightened. She lifted her chin. "Don't mock me."

Enough talk. He would be smarter to use his tongue for something more constructive than digging holes for himself to fall into. She was so fragrant and soft and naked. He pushed her against the wall and sank to his knees. She tried to push his face away, but the element of surprise worked in his favor.

He slid his hand up the creamy skin between her quivering thighs, and forced them apart. She was saying something to him, but once he had slid his tongue into that thatch of silky wet fur, once he'd sought out the enticing secret slit of her vulva, he was long beyond the reach of language. He savored the liquid rush of her pleasure against his mouth, dizzy with relief. At least he had this card to play, and he would make the most of it. He thrust his tongue deep into that hidden pool of delicious liquid bliss and suckled his way slowly, lovingly up her delicate folds, lapping and licking until he held her swollen clit between his teeth. He could wallow with his face between her beautiful thighs forever. In a state of perfect grace.

He shifted his hand and slid two of his fingers inside her, seeking the other hot spot he had found inside her clinging sheath. He pressed it while he fluttered his tongue across her clit, feeling, sensing, listening with his whole self, casting out that wide, soft net in his head that encompassed her every reaction, her every breath and shiver and moan, until he sensed how and where to give her what she needed. Just that extra, insistent push of sensual pressure, and ah. Yes.

Jesus, *yes*.

He held her up while it tore though her, a throbbing earthquake. He drank it all in, with his mouth and his tongue and his hands, loving every pulsing second of it. Her knees buckled. He gently controlled her descent as she slid down against the paneling until her bottom hit the floor, his fingers still thrust deep. Eyes closed, face rosy pink, legs splayed wide, his hand still shoved deep inside her cunt.

She shivered, her eyes fluttering open. She looked down at his hand, up into his eyes. He covered her mouth with coaxing kisses. "You still haven't given me an answer," he said. "About being exclusive."

Her pink tongue flicked across her lips. She whimpered and squirmed as his fingers thrust inside her. "Not fair," she whispered.

"Whatever it takes." He kissed her again, caressing her quivering sex. "So? Are you my woman, or not?"

She seized his wrist and pulled his hand out of her body, clasping it tightly in hers. "Do not manipulate me," she said. "Just *ask* me."

"OK." He braced himself. "I'm asking."

She looked straight into his eyes. "I don't want anyone but you," she said. "I never have."

He was afraid to breathe. Their fingers were a damp, tight, clutching knot, like his heart. "That's good to know, sweetheart," he said cautiously. "Uh, does that mean we're exclusive?"

Her lips twitched at his insistence. "Yes."

"You're sure?" he demanded.

Her sweet smile widened. "What do I have to do to convince you?"

He felt ridiculous for needing so much reassurance. "Send me a singing telegram," he suggested.

He was rewarded by a helpless snort of laughter that was so cute, it made his heart twist. "You certainly know how to press your point."

"I thought it was your points I was pressing," he offered.

That touched off another peal of giggles. "Oh, no. Oh, dear. Connor, please. That was really bad."

"But you handed it right to me," he protested. "What could I do?"

He pulled her closer. He felt so nervous and scared. This was how he wanted her, happy and laughing. Soft and trusting in his arms. He wasn't going to achieve that by throwing his weight around, spewing ironclad orders and ultimatums right and left, but whenever he felt threatened, that's what he did. Every goddamn time.

He pulled her tighter, so her soft laughter would vibrate through his body and push the aching cold away.

Chapter

15

Connor scooped her up off the ground and deposited her on the rumpled cot. She lay there, still giggling, until she saw him rip open a foil packet, and smooth a condom over his erect penis.

She sat bolt upright. "Good God, Connor! This is getting ridiculous. What do you think you're doing?"

"Sealing our bargain," he told her.

He made her heart race when he looked at her like that, his beautiful body naked, his tawny mane long and loose around his shoulders, his hungry eyes. And that hot, sexy, ruthless smile.

He scooped up her dangling legs and draped them over his elbows, nudging the tip of himself gently between her slick folds. He forced his way inside her with one long, relentless push. "I've never had sex with a woman whom I've promised to be faithful to," he said. "Never, in my whole life. It's a big deal."

She dug her fingers into his shoulders and tried to puzzle out the significance of his words. He rocked against her, lazy and slow, angling himself expertly to please her.

"I needed to see how it felt," he added.

"Oh," she murmured. "And how does it feel?"

"Fucking awesome," he said. "To be inside you, and look into your face and think, this is my woman. And oh, God. She is so beautiful."

She wanted to tell him that she loved him, that her heart was all his, forever. Something squeezed her throat shut.

Her father's face floated in her mind, the last time she had seen it, hard with grief and guilt. Connor, leaning on his blood-spattered cane. Vengeance and violence. She couldn't shake free of them, but Connor was prying her heart open by sheer brute force. She couldn't resist him.

She had to hold something back, just some tiny crumb of herself. A corner that was locked up tight and secret and all hers.

He stopped, and held himself motionless above her. "What is it? What are you thinking?"

It took all her nerve to meet his eyes. "I . . . um, nothing."

"Bullshit. Tell me."

She closed her eyes. There was no point in lying to him, but at least she could tell him a different truth. "I was just thinking . . ."

"Yeah?" His eyes were keen and sharp on her face. "And?"

"Of how it feels," she said. "To have you inside me, all over me, and know that you're mine. My man."

"And how does it feel?"

She told him the naked truth. "It feels fucking awesome."

Her own words were the magic key that released her. She came apart around him in a shuddering wave of complete surrender. She could hold nothing back. He held her against him so tightly, his arms shook. "No going back, Erin," he said hoarsely.

She shook her head. "No."

She drifted into a doze. He extricated himself, covered her with the quilt, and went padding about her apartment. When she opened her eyes, he had showered and shaved and pulled on his jeans. He was bent over her tiny refrigerator. He looked dismayed.

He smiled to find her awake. "You've got nothing to eat in this place," he said. "I can't keep up this level of sustained sexual activity without regular feeding."

She giggled. "Sorry."

He sauntered over to the bed and lifted a hank of his wet hair. "I used some of your conditioner," he said. "Smells nice."

"Good for you, Connor. You're making progress," she said. "Where did you get all this energy?"

"I'm totally high. Think of it. I got Erin, the quintessential good girl, to say the f-word, and it isn't even ten o'clock in the morning yet. Who knows what I might get her to do by nightfall?"

She waggled her finger at him. "Don't get any more ideas, you sex-crazed stud. I'm done for awhile."

"Oh, come on," he wheedled. "You're a bad girl now, remember? You've got to get used to excess, and I'm just the guy to help you do it."

She batted his roving hand away and sat up. "Enough."

"And speaking of enough," he said. "Now that we're exclusive, and seeing as how you seem to have something against condoms, you'd better go see your doctor and come up with something you like better. Because I'm tired of walking a tightrope every time we have sex."

Her eyes widened. "But Connor. You're so good at it. And it's so much fun to watch. All that concentration."

"I'm not a goddamn dancing bear," he said sourly. "It would be nice to just relax and have some fun. From here on out, it's condoms until you come up with a better solution on your own. And that's final."

She hugged herself with a shiver of mock rapture. "Oh, I love it when you're stern and masterful. It's such a turn-on. Do it again, Connor. Give me another ultimatum, quick."

"Stop it," he growled. His eyes dragged over the length of

her body, and his gaze became thoughtful. "Unless, of course, you want to have my baby," he said. "Just for the record, that would be fine with me, Erin. More than fine. The timing would be kind of weird, but—"

"I'll go to the doctor. I'll take care of it. I promise." She shivered with a blend of panic and heady, toe-curling excitement. "Let's not rush ahead of ourselves, OK?"

He smiled. "I'm not ahead of myself at all."

"It's better to stay focused," she babbled. "I, uh, have too many things to do today to even think about—"

"Whatever you say, babe. What things do you have to do?"

She took one look at the uncompromising set of his jaw, and sighed. "Oh, dear. You're going to insist on escorting me everywhere?"

"Get used to it," he said. "Tell me what we need to do today."

She flopped back down onto the bed and thought about it. "Well, I have to get my cat back from my friend Tonia, and she'll be furious with me—the cat, not Tonia—so that'll involve lap time and kitty treats. I need to do some research for the Mueller report. Oh, and I need to sign up at some more temp agencies, too. But mostly, I need to track down my sister and check on Mom."

He nodded. "I'll call Sean for a progress report on the Cindy situation, but I can't handle Sean on an empty stomach. OK . . . cat, sister, mom. What else is on our agenda?"

He was so willing to take it all onto his shoulders. His generosity made her heart go all gooey. "Connor, you're a sweetheart, but these are my problems, not yours, and they're not pretty," she said gently. "Please don't think that just because we're involved—"

"Hey." He held up his hand. "Hello! Earth to Erin! You're my girlfriend now. Your problems are now my problems. No question."

She looked down at her hands, letting her damp, tangled hair hide her face. "We've only been together for two days."

"It doesn't matter if it's two days. It wouldn't matter if it were five minutes. And it's not a question of having to, or wanting to. It's just the way it is. So don't fight me. Because you'll lose. OK?"

She gave him a teasing smile. "Oh, my hero."

He rolled his eyes. "Please. Spare me. Cat, sister, mother, any other relatives to take care of? Grandmas, aunts, cousins?"

She shook her head. "None of them will have anything to do with us since the trial. It's like we have the plague."

Connor's hand crept higher, his fingertips brushing her nipple. She grabbed his hand, sliding it back to her belly and holding it firmly there. He let out a wistful sigh. "OK. The asshole relatives can go fuck themselves. It's just as well. There's only so many hours in the day."

She flopped onto her back, giggling. All the things that had so much power to hurt and sadden her before now just seemed ridiculous, with Connor's energy and humor to buoy her up. She slid out from under the quilt, slapping his hands away. "I have to take another shower," she said. "You stop that right now, Connor. Be good."

"I'm always good, baby. Want to see?"

She eluded him, still laughing as she fled to the bathroom.

Connor was fully dressed and waiting by the door when she came out. "I saw a grocery store down the block," he said. "Let's run down and grab some makings for breakfast. I'm starving."

She smiled at him as she toweled herself off, resisting the urge to cover herself. He was her lover. He could look at her body all he wanted. He'd seen it all, from every angle, and he'd loved it. The heated, appreciative glow in his eyes made her almost forget what he'd said.

"You run on down while I get dressed," she said. "The keys are on the shelf by the door. I'll stay. Cindy might call, or my mom."

He dropped the keys into his pocket. He looked troubled. "Do you know how to use a gun?"

"Dad showed us," she admitted. "He took us to the gun range a few times. I never liked them, but I can use one."

He crouched down and took a small, snub-nosed revolver out of an ankle holster. He held it out to her. "Keep this with you."

She backed away, shaking her head. "Connor, no. I'd—"

"Take it, Erin."

She knew that stony tone of his voice. She sighed, and took the gun. Whatever made him feel better.

He dismantled the squealer and unbolted the door. "Don't open up to anybody but me. Anything special you want from the store?"

"Some milk for my tea, please."

"You got it." His grin flashed. The door clicked closed.

She sank to her knees, boneless. The gun dropped to the rug.

Connor's absence changed the energy of the room so completely, it was like a pillar had been pulled from the roof. The need to stand up to him, to be strong and dignified, was gone. She huddled on the rug, half laughing, half crying. She couldn't breathe. Her heart had blown up to the size of a beach ball, and left no room for her lungs to expand. Her wildest dreams had come true. Connor McCloud was her lover, and what a lover. God. No amount of erotic fantasizing could have prepared her for a man like him. For sex like that.

The gun caught her eye. She picked it up with two fingers and placed it on the dresser. Time to get dressed and face the day, to be strong and tough and adult. She couldn't afford to be overwhelmed.

A phone rang while she was pulling on her jeans. Not her phone. She looked around, and realized that it came from the pocket of Connor's canvas coat, still flung over one of the kitchen chairs.

It could be Sean, calling with news of Cindy. She lunged for the phone. Several condoms and a bunch of her lost hairpins came out with it and scattered across the floor. She stared at the display. She had no way of knowing if the number displayed was Sean's, but she couldn't risk missing his call. She flipped open the mouthpiece. "Hello?"

"Who's this?" a deep, puzzled male voice asked.

"This is Erin," she said. "Who is this?"

There was a long, astonished pause. "Erin Riggs?"

"Is this one of Connor's brothers?" she asked.

"No. This is Nick Ward."

Oh, God, no. Nick, one of her dad's colleagues from the Cave. Nick, the tall, black-haired guy with melting dark eyes and dimples. Answering the phone had been a disaster. "Um, hi, Nick. How are you?"

"Where are you, Erin?" There was an edge to Nick's voice.

"I'm at home," she told him. "In my apartment."

"Where's Connor? What are you doing answering his phone?"

"He ran down to the store on the corner to get some breakfast stuff." She was blushing like a tomato, even though no one could see her. "I thought this call might be from one of his brothers, so I . . ."

"Huh." He was ominously silent. "So, what's up, then? Are you two together?"

Images of their intense lovemaking over the past thirty-six hours swirled through her head. "I guess so," she said.

She hated the quaver in her voice. It proved she was still afraid, beneath all the giddy euphoria.

Nick cleared his throat. "Hey, Erin. I don't want to stick my nose in, but Connor . . . he's had a hard time of it in the past year or so, what with everything that's happened—"

"I know," she said.

"Uh, he's got one bitch of a score to settle with your dad. Oh, hell. I don't know what to say. You're a nice kid. Try to keep a little distance, OK? I don't want to see you get hurt."

Erin swallowed hard. "I'm not a kid anymore, Nick."

The key rattled in the lock, and the door swung open. Connor saw the phone in her hand, and froze in place.

"Connor's back," she said tonelessly. She walked over to Connor and held out the phone to him. "It's Nick."

He let the groceries drop to the floor and took it. Erin closed the door and carried the bags to the table.

She wished the apartment had another room to escape into.

The pinched look on Erin's face alarmed him. Connor lifted his phone to his ear. "Yeah?"

"What the fuck are you doing with Erin Riggs?" Nick snarled.

Connor waited several beats before he let himself respond. "We'll have this conversation another time," he said. "In person, so I can express myself fully. Until then, it's none of your goddamn business."

"Is this some kinky revenge on Ed? Seduce his baby princess, and thumb your nose at him? Try and stop me from behind bars, asshole, nyah nyah nyah? She's just a kid!"

"She's almost twenty-seven. Have you got anything relevant to tell me, Nick? Because otherwise, this conversation is over."

"I bet you told yourself she needed protection 'round the clock. What a great opportunity. And now you're nailing her, you self-serving asshole. That kind of protection she don't need."

"Fuck off, Nick. I'm hanging up now."

"Wait a second. I'm going to pass this info on, not to help you, and not as a favor, but just to make you feel like the opportunistic prick that you are. We got word from Interpol. One of the guys that broke out with Novak got nabbed in Marseilles yesterday. Martin Olivier. He confessed that Novak and Luksch were both in France, but he was found dead in his cell before he had a chance to say exactly where. Poison of some kind, they think, pending the autopsy. So it looks like the only person that Erin Riggs needs protection from is you."

Connor pushed his anger aside. His brain was too busy shifting into net-and-fish mode, taking in information, comparing, associating.

"It's a decoy," he said. "Can't you feel it? He's not in France. It's all theater. He's got business to take care of here."

"I might have known you wouldn't be interested in any information that doesn't fit your fantasy, you—"

Connor flipped the phone shut.

Erin was putting on the teakettle. She was pretending nothing had happened. The room was dreadfully silent, apart from the small clinking and rustling sounds she made in the kitchen. She grabbed a bowl and fork and opened the carton of eggs.

"I'll cook breakfast," he offered. "I'm good at it."

The smile she tossed over her shoulder was unconvincing.

Connor slid his arms around her waist, pulling her off balance so that she had to fall back against him. He removed the fork from one small, chilly hand, the egg from the other, and placed them in the bowl.

He covered her hands with both of his, warming them. He pressed his face into the damp satin of her hair. "It looks weird, from the outside," he said. "You and me, together. At least to Nick. Because of all the bad things that have come down."

She nodded.

"But from the inside, from where we're standing, it makes perfect sense," he said, with quiet force. "And it's beautiful."

He waited for a response, but she was mute. He lifted her hair, exposing the delicate curve of her cheek. He kissed it. So soft.

The thought rose up from the depths of his mind, from that part of him with which there was no arguing, no negotiating.

Nobody, but nobody was taking this from him. Just let them try.

He nuzzled her throat. "You with me, Erin?"

"Yes," she whispered.

"This thing we've got, it's amazing. It makes up for a lot."

She shivered, and he felt the exact moment that she softened and leaned back against him. Trusting his support. He was so relieved, he had to hide his stinging eyes in the cool, soothing dampness of her hair.

They stayed that way, suspended in a bubble of speechless intimacy until the teakettle started to squall. Erin took it off the hot plate, and Connor smoothly took over the breakfast preparations.

He was good at it, too. Shortly afterwards, they were feasting on omelets stuffed with peppers, onions, ham, and cheddar cheese. Connor kept sticking toast into her toaster, buttering and consuming it until the loaf was nearly gone. They were very quiet and subdued. Nick's call had wiped out all her goofy euphoria, but Connor's reassurances and his embrace had calmed her back down to almost normal.

Well, relatively speaking. As if she were qualified to define normal.

A key turned in the door lock. Connor sprang to his feet. A gun appeared in his hand as if it had materialized there, leveled at the door.

"Who is it?" she called, as the door swung open.

Tonia stood there, the cat carrier in her hand. She focused on Connor, saw the gun. Her dark eyes became huge. The cat carrier fell to the ground with a thud. An outraged yowl issued from it.

"Erin?" Tonia squeaked.

"It's OK, Tonia!" Erin whirled on Connor. "Put that thing away!"

He tucked the gun into the small of his back. An infuriated meow issued from the cat carrier, and Erin rushed to pick it up. "It's OK," she told the wary Tonia. "Really. It's fine. He's harmless. Come in."

"I thought you weren't getting back till this evening," Tonia said faintly. "I thought it would be better to bring back Edna and feed her here, since I have to work a double shift. I didn't mean to interrupt—"

"It's OK. You couldn't have known," Erin soothed her. "I'm so sorry Connor gave you a scare. He's kind of, ah, high-strung."

Connor looked disgusted. "High-strung?"

"That would be putting it charitably," she snapped.

"Connor?" Tonia's gaze raked him, up and down. "So this is the infamous Connor McCloud?"

His eyes were cool. "That would be me."

Tonia's sharp eyes swept over the apartment, taking in the disheveled bed, the quilt on the floor, the condoms scattered under the table. "You've been keeping things from me, you bad girl. You ended up with a bodyguard after all, didn't you? And something more besides."

Erin's face heated up. She opened the pet carrier door, and Edna bolted out and disappeared under the bed with a shriek. "I'm in for it," she said ruefully. "Emotional blackmail for a week at least."

"You've got to stop letting people make you feel guilty, honey. And you can start with your cat." Tonia stuck out her hand to Connor with a brilliant smile. "I'm Tonia Vasquez. Pleased to meet you."

He did not smile as he shook it. "Likewise."

Tonia turned to Erin. "Sorry I burst in on you, but I'm glad you're home. I was going to leave a note. Have you talked to your mom?"

"Not yet," Erin said. "I planned to run over there today. Why?"

"I tried to call you at the resort, but they told me that you never checked in." Her eyes flicked up to Connor's face. "Now I see why."

"Change of plans," Connor said.

"Why did you try to call me?" Erin asked. "What's going on?"

Tonia's eyes flicked to Connor, back to Erin.

"Don't worry," Erin said. "He knows what's happening. You can say anything in front of him."

"Is that so?" Tonia murmured. "Hmm. Well, the other night I was in the neighborhood and I thought I'd drop in and check on her. We've been pals ever since I helped you move, you know. I went there around eight, and the place was dark. So I pounded on the door for a while. Finally she came to the door, in her bathrobe. She was disoriented, as if she were heavily sedated. She didn't look good at all."

Erin pressed her arm against the empty, sucking feeling in her belly. "Oh, no."

"We made a pot of tea and chatted, and she kept saying she couldn't bear it anymore, seeing Eddie on the TV. Eddie's your dad, right? Was she referring to the media circus during the trial?"

"No," Erin said bleakly. "I doubt that's what she meant."

"She felt faint, but she wouldn't let me take her to the emergency room," Tonia went on. "She said she had a migraine. I ran upstairs to use the bathroom, and when I came down, I saw the photos." She paused dramatically, and shook her head.

Erin pressed her fingers against her mouth. "What about them?"

"The faces are gouged out with something sharp," Tonia said. "And then put neatly back into their frames and back on the wall. And the TV in the living room. This you will not believe. It's lying on its back with a fireplace poker sticking out of the smashed screen."

Connor's arms circled her from behind, pulling her tightly

against his warmth. She clutched his forearm with icy fingers. "Oh, God."

"Yeah. It creeped me out, big time. I was going crazy when I couldn't find you, girl. She needs help."

Erin forced herself to look into Tonia's sympathetic eyes. "Thanks for checking on her. And thanks for trying to get in touch with me."

"That's what friends are for," Tonia said briskly. She held out the keys to Erin. "I have to hustle if I want to get to work on time." She smiled at Connor. "Good to meet you. Sorry if I startled you."

He gave her an unsmiling nod. "No problem."

Tonia gave Erin a peck on the cheek and fluttered her fingers in an airy farewell. "See you, *chica*. Go check on your mom, quick."

"Of course," Erin said.

She stared blankly at the door after Tonia shut it. Connor nuzzled the top of her head, and she swayed in the warm circle of his arms. "I shouldn't have gone on that trip," she whispered.

"Don't start," he said gently. "It never helps."

She turned, and wrapped her arms around his waist, pressing her face against his chest. His hands moved gently over her back.

"What does your friend do for a living?" he asked.

"Tonia? Oh, she's a nurse."

His hand stopped moving. "A nurse? She was wearing three-inch heels. What nurse goes off to work a double shift in three-inch heels?"

"I think she's doing administrative work these days," Erin said. "I'm not sure. I've been absorbed in my own problems lately, and Tonia is one of those women who believes that one must suffer to be beautiful."

"I could see that."

His cool tone surprised her. "You didn't like her, did you?"

"I wasn't wild about her, no," he admitted. "Did you ask her to go check on your mom?"

"No. But she does know Mom. And she knew I was worried about leaving her for my trip," she said. "Why do you ask?"

"I didn't like the way she told her story."

She was puzzled. "What about it?"

Connor looked uncomfortable. "She was enjoying herself a little too much. Some people get off on being the bearer of bad news. Drama makes them feel important." His lip curled in distaste. "Like life isn't difficult enough."

"Oh, that's just her way," Erin assured him. "She's flamboyant by nature. She doesn't mean any harm."

"Hmph. When did you meet her?"

"About a year ago. She was working at a clinic where I went to visit a friend," she said. She kept her face pressed against his shirt and hoped that he wasn't doing his mind-reading routine. She was feeling shaky enough as it was without having to explain her obsessive clinic visits to him.

"She doesn't look like a nurse," he mused.

She let out a secret sigh of relief. "And just what is a nurse supposed to look like?"

"Not like her. Can't see her emptying bedpans and checking vitals. She doesn't look like the type that would stick it out all the way through nursing school."

She pulled away from him. "That is so cold and sexist and unfair! Just because she wears spike heels? You are such a—"

"Don't." He lifted his hands in surrender, grinning. "Sorry. You're right. That was an awful thing to say. Subject change, please. Do you want to go straight over to your mom's house?"

"As soon as I feed Edna." She pulled a can of cat food out of the cupboard. "But you going with me is not the most brilliant idea."

"Erin," he said, in a warning tone. "For God's sake, don't start."

She scooped the goopy stuff into Edna's bowl and started pulling the various dropper bottles, pills, and powders out of Edna's medicine bag. "I would really rather break this to her gently. You thought Nick's reaction was bad? It'll be nothing in comparison to Mom's."

He shrugged. "I'm not going to leave you alone just because I'm afraid of your mother. I can weather a tantrum, Erin. Sometimes you've just got to sacrifice yourself for love."

Erin let at least six extra drops of liquid Vitamin B plop onto Edna's wet food before her arm unfroze.

That was the first time the word had been spoken. Thirty-six hours of sexual involvement was pretty early to start thinking about love, at least from a man's standpoint. But there it was, dressed up as a casual, throwaway remark. She was probably making too much of it. She kept her hot face turned away as she laid Edna's dishes on the floor. "We better go," she said. "I hate leaving while Cindy might call."

Connor held out his cell phone. "Here. This is yours now."

She stared at it blankly. "But—"

"Nick's call soured me on carrying this thing around. You take it. We'll leave the number for Cindy on your outgoing message. I don't like doing that, but today's a special case."

"But if people call you?"

"Nobody but my brothers and my friend Seth have the number. And Nick. But I'm going to be with you twenty-four-seven until Novak's accounted for. They can still call me on it if they want."

At that moment, her telephone rang. She snatched it up. "Yes?"

"Erin?" Cindy's voice sounded soft and uncertain.

"Cindy? Oh, thank God. I've been so worried—"

"Look, Erin, don't give me a hard time, OK?"

Connor pushed the speakerphone button, and Cindy's anxious voice filled the room, high-pitched and fuzzy and distorted by the tiny speaker. "I've got enough problems without one of your lectures."

Erin suppressed a sharp reply. She couldn't afford for Cindy to hang up in a huff. "I won't give you a hard time," she said. "I just care about you. You scared me the last time you called, that's all."

Cindy sniffed. "Sorry. Um, what's up with Mom? I called her, and the phone was disconnected. And she's been so weird lately. Like, what is up with that?"

"I don't know yet," Erin said. "I'm trying to figure that out myself, and I could really use your help."

"Um, yeah. I guess. Look. Don't tell Mom about me and Billy and me being in the city, OK? She might wig out even more, you know?"

Connor shoved a piece of paper in front of her face with *ADDRESS?* scribbled on it.

"Where are you, Cin?" she asked.

"Um . . . I'm not really sure. I've never been here before last night. It's a big, fancy house with nice furniture and stuff, but all I can see outside the window are bushes. I don't know what neighborhood I'm in."

"You didn't notice when you arrived?"

"I was kind of out of it when we got here last night," Cindy admitted.

Erin struggled to stay calm. "Well, how about you look around for a magazine, or a piece of mail that might have an address on it?"

"I'm in the bedroom now. Billy's downstairs with Tasha. He'd be mad if he knew I was calling you."

Panic fluttered. "What's going on, Cindy? Are you scared of him?"

Cindy hesitated. "Um, I don't know," she said in a tiny voice. "It's weird. He's . . . he's different today."

"Different how?"

"Oh, I don't know. Cold, like he's impatient with me. He wasn't like that before. He made me feel stupid, because I didn't want to go out on another job tonight. He says I'm being a baby, and I guess I kind of am, but . . . I don't know. It's just so different today."

Erin's knees gave out like Jell-O. She slid down against the wall, her bottom connecting with the floor with a painful thump. "What job?"

Connor sank down into a crouch in front of her, listening intently. He laid his warm hand on her knee.

"Promise me you won't flip, because I swear it's no big deal, OK?"

Erin tried to swallow, but her throat was dry. "I promise."

"Well, I've been, um, dancing. Like exotic dancing, but not really, because I—"

"Oh, God, Cin."

"You promised, Erin. I only stripped to my thong. And it was for private parties, not at a club, and Billy's always with me, so I never—"

"Parties? Plural?"

"Yeah. We did three bachelor parties, me and another girl. We made six hundred dollars apiece. It's like, incredible money, and Billy said it was OK if I kept on my thong, since Tasha doesn't mind dancing totally nude, so . . . um, and Billy said he'll beat the shit out of anyone who touches us, so it's really no big deal. You know?"

Erin's voice had tightened to a squeaky thread. "Sweetie. Just tell me. Are you OK?"

Cindy paused. "I don't know," she whispered. "It's weird. Yesterday I was fine. Maybe I was just drunk. We did shots of Southern Comfort with Billy first, and it really loosened me up. I felt great when I was dancing, like a total goddess. I felt like the whole world loved me. But today . . . I have this monster headache, and it's all so different. Billy's different, I'm different. It's wild."

"And can't you just say you want to go home?" Erin demanded. "Just walk out the door?"

"I did," Cindy admitted. "I tried. But Billy said it was too late. He's already got the gigs lined up and he says I can't be a prima donna bitch baby and bail out on him now, because he's, like, a professional, so I have to be, too, and . . ." Cindy's voice degenerated into tears.

"Cin," Erin said desperately. "You've got to find out the address so I can come and get you."

"Wait. Oh, God. That's Billy on the stairs. I gotta go."

The connection broke. Cindy was gone.

Erin looked up at Connor, wild-eyed. "What is going on? I don't know what fire to put out first! What am I supposed to do?"

Connor's eyes were grim. He held out his hand. "Give me back that cell phone. Let's see what Sean's got for us."

He dialed. "Hey. So?" He listened intently for a moment. "Yeah. We just got a call from her. It's a bad scene. She's in a house she's never seen, doesn't know the address, and Fuckhead won't let her leave." He listened for a moment. "OK, fine. Jacey's Diner. We'll be there in twenty minutes."

Chapter

16

Connor surveyed the poorly lit, dirty stairwell with growing dislike. The place wasn't good enough for Erin. She wasn't safe here.

She'd be better off in his house.

The idea appeared fully formed in his mind, and stole his breath. He'd been living purely in the moment. This was the first time he'd dared, even for a moment, to project this thing he had with her into the future. He pushed open the front door, sweeping the block with suspicious eyes and taking note of everyone and everything he saw.

He made a mental note to call Seth and do something about her security. Or rather, her complete lack thereof. She might as well pitch a tent in a parking lot.

Erin fell into step beside him on the sidewalk, and he shortened his stride to match hers. There were haunted shadows under her eyes. He wanted to do something flashy and impressive to chase away those shadows. Slay a dragon, fight a duel, whatever it took.

He took hold of her hand. She glanced up, and her slender, chilly fingers curled trustingly around his. Her shy smile flashed out, like a flash of rainbow-split light from a crystal hung in a sunny window. *Wham,* all the colors that existed, in one bright, blinding rush.

And she was his lover now. His groin tightened at the thought.

"What is Sean doing at Jacey's?" she asked him. "That place is a health hazard."

"Stoking up on evil coffee and jelly doughnuts," Connor replied. "Sean has theories on how different types of coffee are appropriate for different activities. Hunting pimp assholes calls for gritty, hard-core Jacey's Diner coffee, something that's been sitting on the burner all night long. Starbucks is for nibbling a hazelnut scone, sipping a mocha latte, flirting with cute girls. It's the wrong vibe for serious business. Sean's kind of hyper, so coffee is his natural drug of choice."

He was rewarded for his nonsense by another smile, and it fired him up, made him famished for more of them.

"Speaking of drugs of choice." She shot him a curious glance. "You haven't touched your cigarettes in a long time."

He shrugged. "I must've been distracted by all the other mind-altering substances that my glands have been pumping into my bloodstream lately. You do a number on my endocrine system, baby."

She laughed. "How romantic. Have you smoked for a long time?"

His mouth opened up, and the words fell out. "Want me to quit?" He was making a lovesick ass of himself, but that was just too bad. He was hardwired for the grand romantic gesture.

Her eyes went wide with alarm. "Good Lord," she murmured. "Are you sure you want to?"

He fished the tobacco and the papers out of his coat pocket and held them over a Dumpster on the corner. "Say the word," he said. "I know I should quit. Everybody who smokes knows they should quit. I just never particularly cared before. Give me a good reason."

It was worth it ten times over, just for that fleeting moment that her face lost the haunted look and cute little dents appeared at the corners of her mouth. "OK," she said. "Quit, Connor."

He let go. The bag thudded into the Dumpster. "Quitting will be a piece of cake with you around," he told her. "I might have some nicotine fits, but I know exactly what to do about my oral fixation."

She giggled, and her fingers tightened around his.

"I have to call Seth today, after we take care of our other business," he said. "I want him to come check out your locks."

"Connor, you know that I can't afford to—"

"Even under normal circumstances, that place would be unsafe for you, Erin. And I'm going to have a talk with your landlord about the front door lock. Does he live in the building?"

"Are you kidding?" She looked worried. "Please, don't. I spent the whole month of January with no hot water because I had the bad judgment to complain about the bugs."

He scowled. "You should move out of that dump."

"To where? I can't afford anything better right now, and besides—"

"Move in with me," he said.

Her eyes went huge and scared. His heart sank like a stone.

He'd fucked up, evidently, but now he had to follow through to the grim finish. "It's a nice place," he said, trying to sound casual. "It's paid for. Two spare bedrooms. One can be your office. For your business."

Her mouth made an "oh" shape, but no sound came out.

He plodded grimly on. "I remodeled the kitchen a few years back. There's a yard for your cat. It's a quiet block. And I'm a pretty good cook. Ask Sean about my chili."

Yeah. Plenty of room in my king-sized bed every night. Underneath me, on top of me, all over me. That long hair spread out over my pillows.

They had arrived at the car. Connor unlocked her door. She got in and gazed up, her mouth forming and discarding words. "Uh . . . Connor? We've only been lovers for two days."

"I know what I like," he said.

She caught her soft lower lip between her teeth. "Maybe you should slow down," she said earnestly. "Before you make any more big pronouncements and sweeping gestures. It's incredibly sweet of you to offer, but it's just . . . it's . . . maybe you should think about it."

He gestured at the shapely ankle that still dangled outside the door. She pulled it inside. "I've been thinking about it for ten years," he said. He slammed her door shut by way of punctuation.

He was ashamed of himself by the time he got into the car. She stared into her lap as he started up the engine, her face hidden by the dark, thick fall of hair. "I'm sorry," he said. "I won't pressure you."

"OK. Thanks."

Hell. What technique. He might just as well have proposed marriage on the spot. He'd already invited her to have his baby. What was the perfect way to distract a woman from her personal problems?

Pile some brand new ones on top of them.

Erin was struck mute for the rest of the drive.

Connor pulled into the Jacey's Diner lot. He didn't take her hand as they walked toward the entrance. Her hand felt chilly and abandoned, swinging there on its own.

An astonishingly handsome young man with dark blond hair and a black leather jacket burst out of the diner. Erin took one look at his lean face and wide-set, tilted green eyes, the same glacial lake shade as Connor's, and knew he had to be Sean McCloud.

Sean's jaw sagged. "Holy shit. Look at you." A delighted grin spread over his face as he circled his brother. He poked

Connor's chest, palpated his shoulder, slapped his butt. "Only two days, and look at you! You've gained weight, you've got color. You've even shaved." He lifted a lock of Connor's hair. "And your hair doesn't look like it was chewed off by mice anymore." He sniffed the lock of hair. "Jesus. You're even perfumed. With girly stuff. Will wonders never cease."

He turned around and gave Erin an appraising look, which she returned without flinching. She'd been in training for two days with Connor. She knew how to stand up to intense male scrutiny by now.

Sean nodded, as if satisfied. "So you're Erin. The princess in the enchanted tower."

"Sean," Connor growled. "Don't."

"Don't what?" Sean stuck out his hand to her. "You see that shirt he's wearing?" he asked her. "I got him that shirt."

She shook his hand. "You, uh, have excellent taste," she offered.

"Yes, I know," Sean replied. "Lucky for him, or he'd be wearing nothing but thrift-store rejects. I love him, but he's a fashion disaster."

A big, black Ford pickup pulled up in front of them. A man got out who could only be the third McCloud brother; he was just as tall, but bigger and broader, thickly muscled beneath his fleece sweatshirt and jeans. His hair was close-cropped, his face craggy and hard, but he had the same strange, penetrating eyes as his two brothers.

He didn't say a word, just stared at Connor for a long moment. A huge grin cracked his face. "Hey, Con. Lookin' good."

"Hi, Davy," Connor said. "I didn't know you were in on this party."

"Didn't want to miss the fun." Davy turned his penetrating stare onto Erin. "So you're her, then."

"I'm who?" she asked cautiously.

Davy smiled and held out his hand. "You're good for him," he said calmly. "I like this. This works. Stick around."

"She doesn't have any choice," Connor said. "She's stuck with me until Novak's back in custody."

"And that's just how you like it, ain't it?" Sean turned his grin back upon Erin. "You know what? I could tell you stories about this pigheaded son of a bitch that would make your hair stand on end."

"But you won't," Connor broke in. "Because we've got other things to talk about today. Like Cindy."

"There'll be other opportunities." Sean gave him an evil grin. "Now that you have a girlfriend, you're going to be so self-conscious. Baiting you will be ten times the fun."

She giggled, in spite of Connor's scowl. "I can hardly wait. I would love to hear stories about Connor."

"But not today, thank God," Connor said sourly. "You're more manic than usual today, Sean, and that's really saying something."

"Give me a break. I just pulled an all-nighter in the stews of Seattle," Sean said. "I'm flying on caffeine and nerves."

"Did you meet anybody who knows Billy Vega?" Davy demanded.

"Oh, I did better than that," Sean said. "I met Miles." He knocked on the passenger door of a mud-spattered silver Jeep Cherokee. "Yo, Miles," he called. "Stop being a dweeb. Get out here and be sociable."

The Jeep door opened. A long, lanky figure slithered out and unfolded itself. Even hunched over like a vulture he was impossibly tall, thin and pallid, with long, snarled black hair and round glasses perched on his hooked nose. He was dressed in a dusty black Goth frock coat.

He lifted his shoulders, let them drop back down. "Hey."

Sean winked at Erin. "Miles doesn't get out much. He's been hiding in the basement for a little too long, but he's a great guy. Miles, let me introduce you to my brother Davy, my brother Connor, and his girlfriend, Erin. Who also happens to be Cindy's big sister."

Miles's dark eyes lit up. "Really? Cool. You're, like, almost as hot as Cindy." He realized what he'd just said, and his eyes froze open behind the magnifying lenses of his glasses. "Uh, that is, I didn't mean—"

"Thank you, Miles," she said gently. She held out her hand. "How sweet of you to say so."

He blinked rapidly as he shook it, as if unused to the light of day. Erin looked up at the three brothers. Meaningful glances and telepathic messages whizzed over her head. She turned back to Miles, who looked at least as bewildered as she felt. "Would somebody please explain to me what you gentlemen have been up to?"

"Let's get a booth," Sean said. "I was just in there, doing recon. It's perfect. There's a pissed-off waitress with big hair, and a tray full of surreal jelly doughnuts. And the coffee is a sure thing. Instant ulcer."

Erin looked around in trepidation as they filed in. "I should've brought my own cup," she murmured, sliding into the booth.

"Nah," Sean scoffed. "Get into it. The risk of food poisoning is part of the thrill."

Connor slid into the booth next to her, draping a possessive arm over her shoulders. The waitress flung menus onto the table, sloshed coffee into their cups, and flounced away without a backward glance.

"Excuse me, miss?" Sean called after her. "Doughnuts for everyone, please."

The waitress scowled back over her shoulder. Sean dimpled at her. She stopped, turned, did a double take, and smiled back at him.

"OK," Connor said. "So let's have it. What did you find out?"

"Well, I investigated the babe lair, and Lord, is that house ever pulsing with feminine pulchritude," Sean said. "They didn't have much hard info for me, but the blonde with the red thong undies suggested—"

"How did you know she had red thong undies?" Erin demanded.

Sean fluttered his lashes innocently over the rim of his cup. "Because she was wearing skin-tight white palazzo pants," he explained. "As I was saying, she suggested that I talk to the Vicious Rumors, Cindy's R&B band. She even tracked down their phone numbers for me, that sweet, helpful curly-haired cutie. What's her name again, Miles?"

"Victoria."

"Victoria. Yeah. Yum. Then there was the redhead with the eyebrow ring and the see-through black blouse. She was the one who—"

"See-through blouse? She came to the door in a see-through blouse, at Endicott Falls Christian College?" Erin was scandalized.

"Oh, she wasn't wearing the blouse when I arrived," Sean hastened to assure her. "She went upstairs and changed into it after I got there. Nice bra, too. I know it well. Victoria's Secret, spring collection. Black satin push-up demi bra. A good choice for the blouse."

Connor sighed. "You animal."

"Ignore him," Davy advised her. "He's just trying to impress you."

But Erin was already stifling helpless giggles, with both hands over her mouth. "Oh, God. I sent a wolf to a house full of lambs."

Sean snorted. "Lambs, my ass. Foxes is more like it. Don't worry, they're too young for me, but that's no reason not to ogle their underwear, now is it? But I stray from the point—"

"I'll say," Connor said.

"See-through blouse—what was her name?" Sean turned to Miles, snapping his fingers.

"Caitlin," Miles supplied.

"Caitlin, yeah. She told me about Miles, and the Rumors lead guitarist found his parents' address for me. And when I breached the basement fortress and saw Miles's screen saver, I knew he was my man."

"What screen saver?" Erin asked.

"A four-second video clip of Cindy, blowing a kiss. Over and over," Sean said. "It took my breath away."

Miles hunched down between his hulking shoulders. "Jeez. Don't tell people that stuff," he mumbled. "It's private."

"You tell him, Miles," Connor said.

Davy grunted. "He never listens, though, so what's the point?"

"Hey, we're all in this together," Sean protested. "Besides, my brother's not as high-tech as you, Miles, but he knows all about wanting an unattainable girl—"

"Shut up, Sean," Connor said wearily. "You're pissing me off today. I know you're fried, but one more crack like that—"

"OK. I'll focus. Chill out, Con," Sean soothed. "In any case, Miles was my big break. When we find your sister, she owes him a debt of passionate gratitude. You can tell her that I said so."

"I'll think about it," Erin said demurely. "Go on, please."

"Miles is the sound man for the Vicious Rumors, and Cindy's faithful admirer. You ever want to know what's going on with a girl? Ask a jealous man," Sean said. "Miles even provided me with the license number of the infamous Jag, which I passed promptly on to Davy."

Connor and Erin both turned to Davy. "And?"

"The car belongs to a guy named William Vaughn," Davy said. "A thieving, pimping dickhead with a rap sheet this long, which you may peruse"—he passed them a manila folder—"at your leisure. I checked out all the addresses I could find, but they're out of date. One of his ex-landladies told me she hasn't seen him in two years, and she hopes to God she never sees him again, even though he owes her money."

"I knew he was scum. From the start I knew it. I slashed the fucker's tires once." Miles's eyes flashed with vindictive heat. He hesitated, and shot a nervous look at Erin. "Uh, shit. Sorry."

"It's OK, Miles," she told him. "I'm glad you slashed his tires."

He hung his head bashfully and started ripping his napkin to shreds.

"Are you in Cindy's class?" she asked him.

"No, I graduated last year," Miles said. "Electronic engineering. I've just been hanging around to do sound for the Rumors, and . . ."

"And Cindy," Sean said.

Miles stared morosely into his coffee. There was an awkward silence, broken by the waitress, who eyed Sean hungrily as she flung a plate full of lurid-looking pastries into the middle of the table.

Sean seized a jelly doughnut, saluted the waitress with it, and took a huge bite. "Miles insisted on coming along, once I told him my strategy. He's got that hero mentality, just like you, Con."

Connor looked up from leafing through the rap sheet, smiled thinly, and jerked his chin for Sean to continue.

"So we took off on an all-night odyssey of squalid roadhouse dives, fueled by Miles's trusty flask of super-caffeinated Jolt Cola. We finally hit pay dirt when we got to the Rock Bottom Roadhouse, where we met LuAnn. Ah, the beautiful, strawberry blonde LuAnn."

"She's not as hot as Cindy," Miles said.

"Do we want to hear this, Sean?" Connor asked.

"Trust me, there's a thru-line. Turns out that LuAnn the barmaid knows Billy Vega by reputation. She used to dance in a club near Lynnwood. She told us that Billy comes across as a big-shot agent, but she knows girls who were recruited by him who spit on the ground at the mention of his name. So Miles and I abandoned the roadhouses and ventured out bravely into the wild world of the Seattle titty bars."

Erin covered her face with her hands. "Oh, God."

"Watch it, Sean," Connor said. "This is not for your entertainment."

Sean's smile faded. "I never thought that it was." He reached out and tapped Erin's wrist gently with his finger. "Hey. Sorry. I'm kind of wired right now, but I promise, I'm taking this thing dead serious. No matter what bullshit comes out of my mouth. OK?"

"Thanks." She gave him a wan smile. "I appreciate your help."

Connor grabbed a maple bar, eyed it with deep suspicion, and took a bite. "So that's why you've got that wild glitter in your eye," he said. "You always bounce off the walls when you're short on sleep."

"Sleep? How are we supposed to sleep if that scum-sucking piece of shit is with Cindy?" Miles asked the table at large. "I haven't slept in a month."

Sean slapped him on the back. Miles sputtered his coffee over the table. "Attaboy, Miles. You would not believe this man's concentration. We went to seven clubs full of naked dancing girls, and he might as well have been cruising the Christian Science Reading Room."

"They weren't as cute as Cindy," Miles repeated.

Sean shook his head. "He's a human laser beam," he said. "It's not normal. But anyhow, Miles and I cruised and schmoozed, nursed a few beers, and ingratiated ourselves with some of the young ladies present. Evidently Billy Vega is pretty well-known and generally disliked by the dancers. I passed my card around and let it be known that I was really, really interested in finding Billy Vega, and I would be glad to pass a real generous tip to anybody kind enough to find me a current address for him, or give me a call if he should show up in the club. Which reminds me. I have to make a trip to the bank machine. The slush fund's been blown on gasoline and beer."

"I'll cover it," Erin and Miles said in unison.

They looked at each other and smiled. It occurred to her

that Miles might actually have the potential to be attractive, in a wan, offbeat, undernourished sort of way. There was something sweet and unguarded about his face when he smiled. Like a vulnerable vampire.

"We'll work those details out later," Connor said.

"So what next?" Erin asked.

Sean ran his fingers through his spiky hair, and for an instant she saw a flash of weariness on his face. "Miles and I might drop by my condo, freshen up. I could use a shower. I hate stinking of smoke. This isn't the best hour to cruise girlie bars anyhow, so we should take advantage of the lull. Then we'll just head straight back into the fray."

"I want to keep looking," Miles announced.

"You could use a shower, too, buddy," Sean informed him. "You don't want your hair to look like that when we find Cindy."

Miles lifted a hand to his snarled, stringy dark mane. "What's wrong with my hair?"

Sean buried his face in his hands. "Why is it my karma to be the frustrated image guru for losers like you guys? Why don't you all just go buy a *Men's Health* magazine and learn how to groom yourselves?"

"I've got to get back to the gym," Davy said. "I've got to teach a karate and a kung fu class, and something tells me I'm going to be teaching your kickboxing class tonight, Sean. Again."

"Hey, that's what you get for being a responsible businessman and pillar of the community," Sean said. "You poor bastard."

"You're going to make up every class you miss," Davy warned. "I'll make you teach Tai Chi on Sunday mornings if you don't watch it."

Sean shuddered with distaste. "I hate Tai Chi. Too damn slow."

"It's good for you," Davy said. "It makes you concentrate."

"I concentrate just fine, in my own way," Sean snapped.

Connor signaled for the check. "We have to get going. Let me know if you get any calls from your dancing girls."

"Call me, too," Davy said. "I hate missing the fun."

"Where are you two heading?" Sean asked.

"Erin's mom's house," Connor said.

That announcement elicited a shocked, wide-eyed silence from both brothers. Davy's eyebrows climbed. "Whoa. That's quick work."

Sean whistled softly. "That's, uh, really brave of you, bro."

Connor gave them a fatalistic shrug. "Why waste time?"

Sean and Davy exchanged glances, and Sean stared down into his coffee, grinning. "That's what I love about you, Con," he said. "You're a human laser beam, too."

The waitress tossed the check on the table. Connor pulled a bill out of his wallet to cover it. "Let's get going."

Erin smiled at Sean, Davy, and Miles as they said good-bye in the parking lot. "I feel so much better now that you guys are helping," she told them. "Thank you. It makes all the difference in the world."

Davy grunted and looked away. Miles blushed and kicked the Jeep's muddy tires. Even Sean was at a total loss for a smart comeback for several seconds. "It's, uh, our pleasure, Erin," Sean said finally. "C'mon, Miles. Let's hit the road. Good luck with the mom, Con."

"Yeah. Watch yourself," Davy added.

The two cars pulled out and drove away. Connor laced his fingers through Erin's and tipped up her chin. Erin lifted her face for his kiss.

"So," he said. "The complete set of McCloud brothers for you."

"I like them," she said. "I like Miles, too. And I really like it that three smart people who give a damn are out there helping look for my little sister. Thank you for making that happen, Connor."

"Save the thanks for when we find her," he said brusquely.

"No." She kissed him again. "I'll thank you right now, no matter what happens. For being so sweet. For caring so much."

His arms tightened. "For God's sake, Erin. Don't get me all worked up in a public parking lot. It's embarrassing."

She smiled up through her eyelashes. "Does it excite you to be thanked, Connor?"

"Yeah." His voice was belligerent. "By you, it does. So sue me."

"Must go along with that hero mentality your brother was talking about," she murmured. "I'll remember. For future reference."

"Let's go. I don't like displaying my hard-on to the whole world."

The closer they got to her mother's house, the heavier Connor's silence became. "Are you nervous?" she asked.

He shot her an are-you-kidding look, turned the corner, and parked on her mother's block. They sat for a long, silent moment, and Connor let out a sharp sigh and shoved his door open. "Let's do it."

She got out of the car, marched up to him, and wrapped her arms around his waist. "Connor?"

"Yeah?" He sounded apprehensive.

"Just a detail I'd like to straighten up, before we go any further."

"Let's hear it."

"Your two brothers? They're both very good-looking. I might even go so far as to say extremely good-looking. But they are not more good-looking than you."

A radiant grin chased the tension out of his face, and he leaned his forehead gently against hers. "You're my girl-friend now," he said. "You have to say that kind of stuff. It's part of your job description."

"Oh, bullshit," she said. "You're such a—"

He cut her off with a kiss, pulling her close. She wound her arms around his neck and clung to him, wishing they were a million miles away from all her problems and worries, someplace where she could just wrap herself around his generous heat and strength and power, and soak it up like tropical sunshine. His lips moved over hers, sweet and coaxing and seductive, weakening her knees, making her—

"Erin? Honey? Is that you?"

They jerked apart with a gasp.

Barbara Riggs was standing on the porch in her bathrobe, squinting at them. "Who's that with you?" She fumbled in the pocket of her bathrobe, pulled out her glasses, and put them on.

"It's me, Mrs. Riggs." Connor's voice was flat and resigned. "Connor McCloud."

"You?" She gaped. "What are you doing with my daughter?"

Connor sighed. "I was kissing her, ma'am."

Barbara picked her way down the leaf-strewn steps in her slippers, her gaze horrified. "Honey? What is the meaning of this?"

Chapter

17

Connor braced himself to be martyred. His doom was averted when the next-door neighbor's front door popped open and a chubby gray-haired lady came out onto her porch. Her eyes were bright with curiosity. "Hi, Erin!" she called. "Well, well! Who's your young man?"

"Hi, Marlene," Erin said. "Um . . . Mom? Could we have this conversation inside the house?"

Barbara Riggs glanced up at her neighbor. "That might be best," she said icily. "Under the circumstances." She marched toward the house, head high, back straight, just like Erin when she was royally pissed. He followed. His doom was not averted. Just delayed.

He followed Erin's glance into the living room, saw it flinch away. Sure enough, the gutted TV lay there on its back like a dead bug in the gloom. A poker stuck out of its belly, just as Tonia had said. Ouch.

Barbara turned on the kitchen light and folded her arms over her chest. Her mouth was a flat, bloodless line of fury. Even as disheveled and haggard as she was, he could see where Erin's regal air came from.

"Well?" The single word was like a bolt from a crossbow.

He was terribly afraid that that was his cue, but he had no idea what to say. Everything felt like the wrong thing. He was on the verge of just opening his mouth and letting whatever happened to be lying there on top fall out of it, but Erin beat him to the punch.

"We're together, Mom," she said quietly. "He's my lover now."

A blotchy flush mottled the older woman's face. She let out a sharp, high-pitched sound. Her hand flashed out, toward Erin's face.

He caught the slap and held it suspended in midair. Her trembling wrist felt clammy and cold in his grip. "You don't want to do that, Mrs. Riggs," he said. "You can't take it back. And it's not worth it."

"Don't you dare preach to me. Let go of me."

"No hitting," he said.

Her chin jerked up. He decided to take that for an assent and let go. She snatched her hand back. Her eyes were glassy and feverish.

"You've been watching her since she was practically a child," she spat. "Waiting for your chance. I saw it in your face, so don't bother to deny it. And now that Ed's out of the way, you think the coast is clear."

Things couldn't get any worse, so there was no reason not to be brutally honest. "I would have gone after her anyway," he admitted. "That whole bad business was just a delay."

The flush burned purplish spots into her pallid face. "Just a delay? You call the ruin of my entire life just a delay? You have the nerve to come into my house and say that to me, after what you did?"

"I did my job, ma'am. I did my duty," he said, with steely calm. "Which is more than I can say for your husband."

"Get out of my house." Her voice vibrated with fury.

"No, Mom," Erin said. "You can't throw him out without throwing me, too. And you can't throw me out, because I won't let you."

Barbara's lips trembled with hurt and confusion. "What has come over you, honey? Are you punishing me for something?"

Erin grabbed her and hugged her tightly. "No. This is for me, Mom. Just me. For the first time, I am thinking only of myself, and you are going to have to swallow it. Because I've never called in a favor from you in my whole life."

"But you've always been such a good girl," Barbara whispered.

"Too good," Erin said. "I never misbehaved, I never made you wait up all night, I never put a foot wrong. I'm calling in all those points now, Mom. Remember those good behavior charts you made for us when we were kids? All those gold stars I got? This is my prize. And I picked it out all by myself."

Barbara's face convulsed. Her arms hung like sticks at her side in Erin's embrace. Slowly, they circled around her daughter's body.

Her eyes flicked up to Connor. He stoically endured it. It was no different than the way the respectable matrons of Endicott Falls had looked at him and his brothers in the old days whenever they came into town. A look that said, *Quick, lock up your daughters, here come Crazy Eamon's wild boys.* He'd gotten used to it. A person could get used to anything.

"Some prize," she said coldly. "Just how long have you been carrying on with my daughter behind my back?"

Connor thought about it, consulted his watch, and decided that those incendiary, mind-blowing kisses in the airport definitely counted. "Uh, forty-six hours and twenty-five minutes, ma'am."

Barbara closed her eyes and shook her head. "Dear God. Erin. Why didn't you tell me you were taking this man with you to the coast?"

"I didn't know at the time, Mom," she said gently. "It was

a surprise. He came along to guard me, and this just . . . happened."

"Guard you?" Her eyes sharpened. "From what?"

Connor stared at Erin in disbelief. "You mean you didn't tell her? No wonder she thinks I'm the Antichrist."

"Tell me what?" Barbara's voice rose steadily in pitch. "What in God's name is going on here?"

"You better sit down," he told her. "We've got stuff to talk about."

"I'll make a pot of tea," Erin said.

The only good thing about heaping shocking revelations onto Barbara Riggs was that it diverted some of her horror and distress from his own miserable self. Two pots of tea later, after endless hashing over the details of Novak and Luksch's escape and Cindy's involvement with Billy Vega, Barbara's face was still pale but the glazed look was gone from her eyes.

"I remember her calling last week sometime," she said. "I'd just taken a Vicodin, and I barely remember what she said. But it certainly wasn't anything about exotic dancing, or being held against her will by a horrible man. God, my poor baby."

"Mom, do you remember Tonia's visit?" Erin asked.

Barbara frowned. "Vaguely. Your nurse friend, the pretty dark-haired girl, right? Yes, she did come by recently. That girl talks very loudly. And she should've noticed that it was a bad time."

"She told me about the TV," Erin said. "And the photos."

Barbara flinched at the mention of the TV. Then she paused, and looked at Erin with blank puzzlement. "What photos, hon?"

"You don't remember?"

Barbara's brow knitted. "I remember having"—her eyes flicked to Connor's and quickly away—"a bad moment with the downstairs TV. But that's all."

Erin got up and left the kitchen. Barbara and Connor stared at each other over the kitchen table as they listened to her light footsteps creaking on the stairs.

"My life is falling apart," she said, in a conversational tone.

"I know exactly how that feels," he said.

"You are the very last person I would have wanted to witness it."

He shrugged. "Don't know what to tell you, ma'am."

"Don't you 'ma'am' me." Her voice was frosty.

He wanted very badly to say that it wasn't his fault, but that was debatable from several different points of view, so he kept his big mouth shut for once. Erin came back into the kitchen and spread out a bunch of photographs on the table. Connor leaned over and took a look.

Baby pictures, family shots, graduation portraits. All with the eyes and mouths gouged out.

Barbara lifted her hand to her mouth. She leaped to her feet and scrambled for the door that led off the kitchen. He glimpsed a utility sink, the corner of a washing machine, and heard a toilet lid flip up. Retching sounds came from the room. Erin moved to follow her, but Connor held up his hand.

"Give her a minute," he said quietly.

The toilet flushed. Water ran in the sink. Barbara Riggs appeared in the doorway a few minutes later, dabbing at her face with a hand towel. "Not me," she said. Her eyes darted wildly between Connor and Erin. "I did not do that. There are no circumstances under which I would deface a picture of my own children. I don't know what is going on here, but it was not me. I swear it."

Erin picked up a photograph of herself in elementary school, holding the toddler Cindy on her lap. Her hands were trembling. "Well, Mom. If you aren't doing it, someone else is. Any ideas?"

Seconds ticked by, stretched into minutes of awful silence. Barbara Riggs covered her mouth with the towel and shook her head.

Erin shoved her chair back. "I organized our negatives by year in the filing cabinet upstairs," she said. "I'm getting the negatives of these photos, and we'll get reprints made today. Every damn one of them."

"That's not going to solve our problem," Connor said.

"I don't care. It's something to do, and I'll make me feel better. Excuse me, please. I'll be right back."

And she left him all alone with her mother. Again. Dear God, what had he done to deserve this? It was like being roasted on a spit.

They eyed each other like boxers circling in the ring. "You've, uh, noticed no signs of forced entry?" he asked her.

She shook her head.

"And the alarm works? You always set it? You test it regularly?"

She nodded. "Of course. I always check the locks and set the alarm. Religiously. Sometimes I check them over and over."

"Who else knows the code?"

"My daughters and myself," Barbara said. "I had the codes changed after Eddie . . . left. And the locks, as well."

"Hmm."

"You must think I'm crazy," she said.

It was a statement, not a question, but he took it at face value and slipped into net-and-fish mode to consider it. He cast out the net and threw everything that was happening to the whole family into it.

Barbara's face swam in his gaze while he tried to feel the shape of the ugly pattern that was forming. There was something shifty and corrupt, but the source of it was not the woman sitting across the table from him. The words came out with total conviction. "No, I don't."

She looked almost offended. "Pardon?"

"I don't think you're crazy," he said.

There was a flash in her eyes, almost like hope. Her throat bobbed several times. "You don't?" she asked warily.

"No," he said. "I've dealt with crazy people before. I don't get that feeling from you. You strike me as stressed out, depressed, and afraid. At the end of your rope, maybe. But not crazy."

"Not yet, anyway," she said.

His mouth twitched. "Not yet," he agreed. "But if you're not, that means that somebody with a lot of resources is messing with you."

She pressed her hand against her mouth. "Novak?"

"He's my first choice," Connor said.

"But he was incarcerated until just a few days ago!"

"He's still my first choice. He has an obscene amount of money, a very long reach, a grudge against your husband. And he's crazy. This thing stinks of crazy."

"So somebody is trying to make me think that I'm insane?"

He shook his head. "No. I think somebody is trying to drive you genuinely insane. Like the porno video trick. That could be rigged, and controlled from the outside. It's crazy and improbable, but it's possible."

Her mouth tightened. "So Erin told you about that?"

"I'm not a techie, so I can't take apart your TV and tell you what they did to it," he went on. "But my friend Seth is an expert. I'll have him take a look, if you like."

"But it sounds so bizarre. Like aliens from outer space, or who killed JFK. Like a big . . . paranoid conspiracy theory."

"Yeah," he said. "I think that's the whole point."

She hesitated, eyes narrowed. "You must be paranoid yourself to even entertain these notions."

It sounded like an accusation.

He shoved down his anger and thought about the nightmare phone call in the hotel. Georg appearing out of nowhere in the phantom SUV. The coma. Jesse's death. Ed's betrayal.

"I was a cop, Mrs. Riggs. And you know exactly how that turned out for me," he said. "Can you blame me for being paranoid?"

She looked down into her teacup.

"You've got to trust your senses, and your instincts," he said, but he knew he was trying to convince himself as much as her. "They're all you've got. If you can't rely on them, then you're lost in the void."

Barbara's shoulders sagged. She nodded. "Yes, exactly. That's where I've been for the last few weeks," she said. "Lost in the void."

"Welcome back to the real world, Mrs. Riggs," he said.

She blinked, as if she had just woken up. "Ah . . . thank you."

The atmosphere was measurably less hostile than before, but he pushed on at the risk of ruining it. "How long ago was the first porno video joke played on you?"

She pursed her lips and thought. "A little over two months ago. Maybe two and a half, because at first I thought I was dreaming."

"Which would have been about the same time that Cindy started hanging out with this Billy Vega, according to her band members."

Barbara gulped. "You mean, you think it's all connected?"

He gave her a brief, tight smile. "You know us conspiracy theorists. We think everything's connected."

"You think Novak could have assigned this Billy to control Cindy, like he assigned Georg to Erin at Crystal Mountain?"

"Maybe. Although Billy Vega's rap sheet is nothing like Georg's. He's just a small-time thief, pimp, and con artist. Not a seasoned killer."

Barbara shuddered. "So . . . shouldn't we call the police?"

He thought about his latest conversation with Nick. "You know how it is with cops. They don't have the time or manpower to get worked up about things that might or could happen. They're too busy dealing with things that are happening or have already happened. Cindy's not a minor. Billy Vega hasn't done anything wrong yet that we know of, other than be an asshole. As far as the cops are concerned, we're talking about a girl having trouble with a no-good boyfriend."

Erin's light footsteps sounded over their heads as she bustled around, trying to tidy up chaos and madness, trying to make sense of a brutal nightmare. It pissed him off, to see her jerked around like that.

In fact, the whole thing was making him fucking furious.

"There's a down side to not being crazy, you know." His voice came out harder than he'd planned.

She looked puzzled. "What are you talking about?"

"If you're not crazy, then you've got no excuse for lying around in your bathrobe eating Vicodin and letting your daughter do everything for you."

She shot to her feet. Her chair pitched over and crashed to the floor. "How dare you speak to me like that?"

What the hell. Ingratiating himself with this woman was a lost cause anyway. It needed to be said, and nobody else was around to say it. He met her outraged eyes straight on, and let his statement stand.

"Mom? What's the matter? What's going on?"

Barbara's eyes shifted to Erin, who stood in the doorway clutching a manila folder. "Nothing, honey. I'm fine," she said crisply. "Excuse me for a moment. I'm going to run upstairs and get dressed."

She stalked out of the kitchen, head high. Erin stared after her, bewildered. "What happened? What did you say to her?"

Connor shrugged. "Nothing in particular. I guess some problems are just too scary to deal with in your bathrobe, that's all."

He paid through the nose for his snotty remark, all afternoon long. Barbara Riggs turned him into her combined slave, gofer, and whipping boy, and before he knew what hit him, he was taking out her garbage, fixing the drip in her upstairs bathroom, chauffeuring them to the phone center to get the phone turned back on. Then it was the grocery store, the photo shop, and the antique place, where he strained a muscle in his bum leg hauling that goddamn grandfather clock. But he didn't complain. It was all part of his martyrdom.

Back at the house, they argued about the dead TV. She wanted him to haul it away to the trash, and he wanted to leave it for Seth to dismantle. He won that dispute, but was forced to carry the damn thing out onto the back porch so she wouldn't have to look at it. Worst of all, she forced him to call Sean at ridiculously frequent intervals to check on his progress. Which meant that his wiseass little brother got to witness all this humiliation first hand.

"Mrs. Riggs," he protested wearily. "Please. He'll call us. He knows what to do if he gets news. Try to relax."

"Don't you dare tell me to relax! That's my baby we're talking about! Call him again!"

Sean picked up on the first ring. "Hey," he snapped. "Miles and I have not discovered anything in the three minutes that have elapsed since your last call. Would you please just take a pill?"

"It's not my fault," he muttered. "She made me call you."

"Mother-in-law's got you pussy-whipped, huh?"

He winced. "Jesus, Sean. Watch what you say."

"Listen up, dude. Next time, dial a fake number and have a fake conversation. You're distracting us."

"Bite me, bonehead," he hissed. He flipped the phone shut and dropped it into his pocket. "Nothing yet," he grumbled to Barbara.

And Erin was no goddamn help at all. If anything, she seemed faintly amused at his torment at her mother's hands, though she tried to hide it. At nightfall he escaped onto the back porch for a few minutes of blessed peace. He collapsed on the steps, rubbed his cramped, throbbing leg, and fished in his coat pocket for his tobacco.

He abruptly remembered that he was now a nonsmoker. The recollection did not make him happy.

He pulled out his cell phone and dialed Seth, who picked up with gratifying swiftness. "Hey, Con. What's up?"

"I need your help," he said.

"You got it," Seth said promptly. "They tell me you're in love. With another girl who's being stalked by Novak. It's the hot new thing."

"Can we skip the bullshit?" Connor asked. "I'm having a nicotine withdrawal fit. I can't take it right now."

Seth was unfazed. "No problem. So?"

"A couple of things. I need you to check out Erin's mom's house. Weird things are happening with the TV, and somebody's breached the locks and the alarms and vandalized the place. More than once."

"OK. How about day after tomorrow?" Seth asked.

"Why not tonight?"

"We're up at Stone Island. Raine's mom and stepdad are here. Tomorrow we're taking them out to cruise the San Juans, and then to dinner in Severin Bay. We put them on the plane back to London day after tomorrow. If I bag out on this, I'm dead meat."

Seth's lack of enthusiasm for his in-laws' visit was glaringly evident. A commiserating grin spread over Connor's face. He'd met Raine's mother, Alix, at Seth's wedding. She was a force of nature, unstoppable, like a huge mudslide. He didn't want to wait for his answers, but he also didn't want to subject the luckless Seth to domestic torture.

"I hope there's something left of you when she leaves," he said. "Alix will eat you alive and spit out your bones."

"Thanks for the encouragement. What else do you need?"

"I want to load X-Ray Specs onto my computer and get some of your transmitter beacons," he admitted. "For Erin."

Seth pondered this for a moment. "I thought you were sticking to that chick like white on rice."

"I am, but it's complicated. Erin's just humoring me. She doesn't really take me seriously. That makes me nervous. And I'm only one guy. I could get distracted, doze off, take a piss. I want technical backup."

"Gonna tell her?"

Connor hesitated, and peeked over his shoulder to make sure he was still alone on the porch. "Uh . . ."

"From personal experience? Women get pissed when you do shit like that. They think it means you don't trust them."

Seth's self-righteous tone made Connor laugh, knowing the guy the way he did. "Listen to yourself for a minute, you big hypocrite, and see if you can keep a straight face."

"I'm just trying to help," Seth protested. "I don't want you to fuck this up, if you really like the girl."

"She'd never go for it. And it's just until Novak's back in the bag, anyhow. Then it's like it never happened. She never needs to know."

Seth grunted his approval. "Good man. That's what I'd do."

"I know. You're as suspicious as I am."

"Oh, way, way more," Seth agreed cheerfully. "When it comes to suspicious, I kick your lily-white ass, McCloud. Come to the apartment and pick up whatever you need. You know where I keep all my stuff."

"Thanks. One more thing. Would you take a look at Erin's place, and see what you could do about security? It's a dump, but it's too soon to move her into my house yet. The lock in the lobby is broken. The door lock you could do with a credit card." Connor gave him the address, and glanced back over his shoulder. "I've got to get the hell off the phone. I'm waiting for Sean to call with news of the missing sister."

"Yeah, I heard. Wish I was there. Hunting assholes in titty bars with you guys would be more fun than fending off Alix in the middle of a hot flash. Hey, Con. Know what? It's good to hear you sound like this."

"Like what?" Connor snarled. "I just had the day from hell."

"Yeah, but you give a shit about it. That's what's different. You sound switched on." Seth was not given to deep analysis of emotions, neither his own nor anyone else's. He sounded surprised at himself.

"I'm glad somebody appreciates it. Later, Seth." He flipped the phone shut and stared morosely at the various picture windows up the length of the block. The screen door squeaked. He recognized Erin's light step, her scent. She sat down and scooted closer until their thighs touched. The contact sent a predictable stab of heat through him, as did her warm, tangy smell. The night breeze lifted a hank of her hair and blew it across his throat. He touched it with wondering fingers.

"Thanks for what you did for Mom," she said.

"For what? Getting my ass kicked around like a soccer ball all day? Thanks for sticking up for me, sweetheart. I sure appreciated it."

"Don't be silly. You handled her fine on your own. You didn't need my help. Besides, she's transformed. I don't know what you said to her, but I haven't seen her with this much energy since Dad was arrested."

She took his arm. He stared down at her small, soft hand, resting on his forearm. The skin of her inner arm was baby smooth and soft. Like he used to dream that clouds could be, if he could touch them. She cuddled closer. His heart thudded and his body sprang to attention.

"Your mom is in there, Erin," he muttered. "Don't do this to me."

"What did I do?" she asked. "Oh. Sorry, I forgot. I thanked you. Oops. Works like a charm, hmm?"

"Don't jerk me around," he said wearily. "It's no fun."

"I didn't do a single thing. I sat down next to you and took your arm. It's not my fault if you can't think about anything except for sex."

He was saved from replying by the cell phone's ring. Erin stiffened. Barbara Riggs burst onto the porch. It rang again.

"What are you waiting for?" Barbara snapped. "Answer it!"

Connor flipped it open and pushed TALK.

"Hey." Sean's voice was rough with excitement. "Just got a call from a fabulous, beautiful girl named Sable whom I will love forever. She told me Fuckhead just walked into a place called the Alley Cat Club, out toward Carlisle. He has two girls with him, one of whom fits Cindy's description. The Alley Cat was on LuAnn's list. I'm sending LuAnn a dozen long-stemmed roses."

"Not out of the slush fund, you're not," he growled.

"Cheap bastard," Sean said. "We're a little over a half hour away, if we speed. Davy just finished up the kickboxing class, but he's on his way, too. What do you say? Shall we go have some fun?"

"I'll meet you guys in the parking lot," he said.

Sean gave him directions. He stuck the phone in his pocket and stood up. "We got a lead," he told the two women.

Erin leaped to her feet. "I'm ready. Let's go."

"Let me get my purse." Barbara disappeared inside.

He stared at Erin, feeling trapped and dismayed. "Erin . . . uh, it's not—"

"Connor." Erin crossed her arms over her chest and gave him her most mysterious, mind-melting smile. "Don't tell me you're leaving us two defenseless women all alone while Novak and his goons circle around us like hungry sharks. Oh, no. Surely not."

"You don't fight fair," he told her.

Barbara burst out the door, her white purse swinging over her arm. "If you don't take me, I'll just get into my car and follow you," she said, voice ringing. "That's my little girl out there."

He grumbled and cursed as he shoved junk out of his backseat to make room. One of his canes was back there, the big one with the armrest and grip that he had used right after he got out of rehab. It had been buried and forgotten under a heap of newspapers and junk mail. "Throw that thing into the back window," he told Erin.

The Alley Cat Club was a long, squat dark building with a flashy animated LIVE GIRLS/COCKTAILS sign. Sean and Miles were standing in the parking lot, chomping at the bit. Davy was nowhere to be seen.

"About time you got here." Sean's jaw dropped as Barbara and Erin got out of the car. "Wow. I see you brought, ah, reinforcements."

"Sean, this is Mrs. Riggs, Erin's mom," he said, with stony politeness. "Mrs. Riggs, this is my younger brother Sean, and this is Miles, one of Cindy's friends who's been helping us look for her."

Barbara nodded stiffly. "Thank you for your help."

Sean's grin activated the automatic charm-o-rama function that was part of his basic wiring. "It's been a pleasure, ma'am. OK, you guys, listen up. I don't want to attract a lot of attention, so I'll just slip in there alone and look around for Sable. If she can lead us to Cindy, we'll whisk her off quietly, and that way we can be more relaxed and focused when we go back to have our talk with the Fuh—that is to say, with Billy. So—Mrs. Riggs? Mrs. Riggs! Wait!"

Barbara was marching toward the building. "My baby's in there."

Sean sprinted after her. He took her arm and started talking earnestly, but Barbara Riggs in full battle mode was a challenge, even for him. Connor left him to it and groped in the back window for the aluminum cane. It wasn't ideal as a weapon, since it was weighted all wrong, but it would do in a pinch. Bare hands were more fun, but whatever. The bum leg earned him a couple of pity points.

Sean had actually managed to collar Barbara right outside the entrance, the slick bastard. He smiled and kissed her hand, gave them a thumbs-up, and disappeared inside. Barbara waited by the door for them, clutching her purse to her chest with white-knuckled hands.

A couple minutes later Sean opened the door and gestured them in. The place was dark and loud. It smelled of spilled beer, smoke, and male sweat. Several nearly naked girls writhed around poles on a long stage that ran the entire length of the bar, lit with pulsing red lights.

Heads swiveled as Barbara Riggs walked through the room, wildly out of place in her pale pink pantsuit and her white purse, wide-eyed and tight-lipped. Sean shoved open an unmarked door. They crowded into a dingy corridor with an open door at the end of it. Light and noise spilled out. Two women dressed in skintight jeans came out, talking loudly. They shut up, painted eyes widening as they shimmied by the motley band that lurked in the corridor.

Connor turned to Erin and Barbara. He jerked his chin toward the door. "That's a dressing room. Go get her. Be quick. I want to get out of here." So far, this was going smoothly. Too smoothly. Not that he was complaining, but he had a nasty, prickling feeling behind his neck. No way could this play out so easily. Not the way his life was going.

Erin pushed her way into the crowded room, and Barbara followed close behind. The room was shrill with high-pitched voices. Brilliant light from the banks of makeup mirrors made Erin's eyes water. The smell of powder, hairspray, and cosmetics was heavy in the air.

She caught sight of Cindy in the back of the room. She was sitting on the floor with her knees drawn up to her chest. Her eyes looked dazed, and her mouth swollen and blurred. She was dressed in only a tank top and panties. A sharp-faced blond girl was bending over her, saying something to which Cindy was shaking her head.

"Cindy?" Erin called out.

Cindy struggled to her feet. "Erin? Mom?"

Cindy stumbled toward them and threw herself into her mother's arms, almost knocking her over backwards, and burst into noisy tears. The blond girl sidled past them and ran out of the room.

Oh, God. Now Mom was sobbing, too. As always, it was up to her to be the practical one. She was keenly aware of the men waiting out in the corridor for them, and the malevolent Billy lurking out there in the dark somewhere. "Cin? Help me out here! Where are your clothes, hon?"

Cindy looked around, glassy-eyed. "Um, I don't know."

A muscular redheaded woman handed Erin a pair of leggings. "Put these on her," she said. "I'm Sable. I'm the one who called that guy Sean, who was looking for Billy. Is that girl your friend?"

"She's my sister," Erin said. "Cin? Your shoes? Any idea where you put them?"

"I'm real glad you guys came to get her," Sable said. "She is, like, in orbit. I don't know what Billy's got her on, but she's not together enough to perform. No fuckin' way. She can't even stay on her feet, let alone dance. It is, like, incredibly unprofessional!"

"You are absolutely right," Erin agreed hastily. "And I'll be sure to tell her that you said so. Look, I have to find her some shoes—"

"Make sure she drinks a lot of water before she passes out," Sable advised. "And keep her away from Billy. He is pure, toxic scum." She thrust a pair of battered cloth slippers into Erin's hands.

"I will. Thanks a lot, Sable. You've been really kind to help—"

"Hurry. Go. Get her the hell out of here before there's trouble."

Cindy allowed herself to be dressed in the leggings and slippers, as unresisting as a doll. They hustled her out into the corridor. Miles took off his black frock coat and wrapped it around her, and the dusty black hem dragged on the ground behind her like a train. His dark eyes were fierce with anger behind his round glasses. "He hit you," he said.

Cindy squinted, stumbled, and finally focused on him. "Miles? Is that you? What are you doing here?"

"Looking for you. That bastard hit your face," he said. "He dies."

Cindy lifted her fingers to her mouth. "Oh. Yeah. I'm all right, though," she said faintly. "It doesn't hurt anymore."

"He dies," Miles repeated.

The three men formed a protective triangle around them as they pushed the shuffling Cindy through the crowded room. No one protested, no one barred their way. Erin held her breath and crossed her fingers. Out the door . . . sudden quiet and a blast of cool, bracing oxygen. Now just the length of the parking lot, and they were home free.

The door of the club swung open, and music blasted out. "Hey! You guys! Where the fuck do you think you're going with that girl?"

"Oh, thank God," Sean murmured. "Finally, some action."

Connor pressed his keys into Erin's hand. "Get your mom and sister into the car. Quick. We need to have a talk with that guy."

"But you—"

"Get them into that car and start it up. Now."

His tone left no room for argument. She bundled Mom and Cindy into the backseat, slammed the door shut, and leaped into the driver's side. Cindy sobbed in Mom's arms, and Mom was crooning comforting sounds. Neither of them seemed even remotely aware of the dangerous drama unfolding outside. She started up the car. Connor's phone was lying on the seat. She snatched it up and clutched it like a weapon.

Her heart beat so hard, it was about to burst out of her chest.

Chapter

18

Billy Vega swaggered out of the doorway. Connor drew a mental sigh of relief. He was a tall, dark guy, well dressed, with florid, sensual good looks and a gym rat's body: thick through the upper body, rigid through the midsection, over-developed shoulders hunched over, hammy fists dangling like an ape. No worries.

The blond girl who had pushed past them in the corridor darted out the door after Billy. More guys filed out, arraying themselves behind Billy: five, six, seven, eight . . . nine of them in all, counting Billy. With Sean at his side, the odds were still OK if nobody pulled a gun. He really, really didn't want to involve the gun, since that often necessitated shooting the gun, which was a fucking dangerous mess. He was still hoping to fly below the radar with this thing, but if bullets started to zing, he could kiss that fond hope good-bye.

He hefted the cane and wished that Davy or Seth were there.

"That girl was with me," Vega said. "Who the fuck are you guys?"

Sean nudged him. "Got any preference as to how we handle this?"

"Just make sure he's fit to talk afterwards," Connor replied softly. He addressed Billy. "Cindy told her sister that she wanted to go home. We're just here to give her a ride. We don't want any trouble."

"Hear that, guys? He doesn't want any trouble," Vega sneered. "Isn't that sweet. Too fuckin' bad, asshole, because you found some."

The loose battle formation started closing in on them. He and Sean sauntered closer. He made a big show of his limp as he scanned them for signs of weapons. Miles hesitated, and hurried after them.

Connor caught Sean's eye and flicked a questioning glance toward Miles. Sean gave him a who-knows? eyebrow twitch.

Too many unknowns. He wished he'd told Erin to gun the engine and drive straight home, but she probably wouldn't have obeyed him anyhow. There was no way out of this now except for through.

Billy's eyes narrowed when they landed on Miles. "I know you. You're that stupid band's autistic sound geek, huh? What's your name again, you big ugly fuck? Igor?"

"You hit her," Miles said. His voice was shaking.

"She was begging for it," Billy said. "The useless bitch."

Miles lowered his head like a bull and charged. Connor and Sean both hissed in anticipatory agony as Billy jerked aside, ducking the wild roundhouse punch, and rammed his fist up into Miles's belly. Miles doubled over, choking, and Billy followed up with a knee to Miles's face and a vicious elbow jammed down into his kidney. The kid went down like a felled tree. Shit. They should've coached him, but watching *X-Files* videos in the basement was no way to train for a street fight. Everybody had to learn the hard way. There were no shortcuts.

No time to fret, though, because Miles's opening gambit was the signal for the fun to begin. The goons closed in, and they got real busy, moving as if through unmeasurable slow-time, a state that he always slipped into in combat situations. Sean exploded into action at his side with a spinning kick that caught one of Billy's thugs in the teeth and sent him bouncing off the hood of a car. Flashy, as always.

Billy ran straight at him, bellowing. Connor flipped the cane up into guard. Billy lunged for the bait and gripped the cane, and Connor flip-twisted it, trapped Billy's wrist with his hand, and whipped it down until the bones in Billy's wrist snapped.

Billy lurched forward, sucking air. Connor tossed him away and spun to deal with the guy behind him. He parried the punch, sliced the heel of his hand down onto the bridge of the guy's nose, and kneed him smartly in the groin. A gurgling shriek; two down. Another attack; a sweep of the cane, a quick, judicious elbow jab to the throat, and he used the guy's own leftover momentum to fling him straight into his buddy, who was coming at Connor from behind. The two men crashed to the ground. The point of his boot to the kidney finished off the first guy, a forefinger stabbed into the soft pulse point under the ear finished off the second. Four down. Not bad, for a gimp.

Miles stumbled to his feet again and launched himself at Billy. Billy toppled, broke his fall with his broken wrist, and screamed. Miles started pummeling him. Good man. Connor left him to it. Out of the corner of his eye, he saw Sean smash one guy's kneecap and then spin through the air like a dervish as he went for the next attacker, but he couldn't pay real close attention; the last two guys were circling him warily and both of them had pulled out knives. He danced back, panting, and tried to keep both in his peripheral vision. His bad leg was trembling beneath him.

Darkness rippled, a flurry of movement. One of his opponents flew, shrieking, across the parking lot. He smashed into the grill of a big Chevy pickup truck and slid limply to the ground, twitching.

The other looked around himself, backed away, and fled.

"Hey, Davy," Connor called out.

Davy stepped out of the shadows, dressed in black. He tossed the blade he'd taken from the guy up into the air, and caught it, nodding his approval. "Nice balance," he said calmly. "Maybe I'll keep this one."

"Thanks," Connor said.

"You're welcome."

"But I could've taken them on my own," Connor added.

Davy looked amused. "You're still welcome."

Connor looked around. Eight guys were sprawled out in various attitudes of pain and penitence on the ground. Miles landed a wet-sounding punch in Billy's face and hauled off for another.

"Whoa. Miles! Hold off on him," he called out.

"He hit Cindy," Miles panted.

"So beat him to a pulp later. First let me interrogate him. OK?"

Miles subsided, and dragged himself to his feet. He was shaking so violently he could hardly stand. His mouth and jaw were covered with blood that streamed from his broken nose, and one of the lenses of his glasses was shattered. "I want to learn to fight like you guys."

The three of them exchanged wry glances. Miles had no idea what it cost to learn to fight like that. Their father had taught them hand-to-hand combat practically since they could walk, and lucky for them, since Crazy Eamon's wild boys were the target of every angry asshole spoiling for a fight in all of Endicott Falls and its environs. They would have gotten slaughtered regularly if they hadn't trained like commandos.

Eamon had been an expert in several disciplines, but as time went on, each brother developed his own preferences. Davy was drawn to the mystical stuff: kung fu, aikido, tai chi, and all the woo-woo philosophy that went with it. Connor preferred the angular, straightforward practicality of karate. Sean favored the acrobatic stuff, full of flying kicks and back flips. And that training had saved their asses. Many times. Just as their father had assured them that it would.

Crazy Eamon's legacy was a formidable one. Miles had no idea.

But the tenderhearted Sean just clapped Miles gently on the back. "Sure, man. Just be prepared to work your ass off for hours every day until every muscle screams for mercy and every inch of you drips with sweat. You'll get the hang of it."

Miles looked daunted, but he wiped blood from his mouth with his sleeve, nodding. "I don't want to ever get slammed like that again."

"No guarantees, buddy," Sean warned. "I've gotten slammed plenty of times. There's always some trick you don't know."

"Or they come at you six at a time," Davy said. "That's always a bitch. But training helps."

"Speaking of getting slammed," Connor said. "I saw you leave your balls wide open twice, Sean. Pull up your guard. It's not about looking good, it's about walking away in one piece. Show-off."

"None of those clowns could've gotten inside my guard if I'd given them a written invitation," Sean snapped. "And you're a fine one to talk about stupid risks with your track record, bozo. If you see me do it in a real fight, then you can give me hell. Until then, shut up."

Erin barreled into him and grabbed him. "Are you all right?"

The anxiety in her voice made him smile. "Miles got pounded pretty bad, but he's on his feet," he told her. "Nothing to worry about."

"Nothing to worry about? Nine against three? Is that what you call nothing to worry about? God, Connor! It happened so fast!"

He tried to put his arms around her, but she jerked away. "You didn't tell me that was going to happen!" she shouted.

"You didn't say one word about fighting with him! You said 'talk,' remember? Don't you ever, ever do that to me again, Connor McCloud! Do you hear me?"

"He started it," Connor protested. "And I didn't—"

"Don't even try!" she yelled. "Just shut up!"

He tried kissing her, but she was having none of it. "Look, babe," he soothed. "Why don't you go on back to the car and look after your mom and Cindy while we have a talk with Billy?"

"Let the little lady go and be good behind the scenes while the big manly men do their big manly thing, hmm?"

Erin's eyes were afire with anger. God, she was so red-hot when she was mad. It was making him hard just looking at her.

"Hey," Davy called. "You can spare yourself this argument, Con. Miles clobbered him." Davy crouched over Billy, touched his throat with his fingertip, peeked under his eyelids. "He's out of it for a while."

The rat-faced blonde ran over to Billy and flung herself across his limp form. "You killed Billy!" she shrilled. "Fuckin' murderers!"

Connor rubbed his aching leg, and visualized a cigarette with a sharp pang of longing. "Nobody's killed anybody, nor will they," he said wearily. "I guess we just have to wait for him to come around."

"The police will be here any minute," Erin said.

"Police?" Connor gaped, appalled. "What do you mean, police?"

Erin held up his cell phone. "Of course, the police!" she said tartly. "What do you expect? Nine guys attack you all at once, and what am I supposed to do? Twiddle my thumbs? Wave pom poms?"

"You were supposed to let me deal with it!" he snarled. "I don't want to talk to the police! The police cannot help me right now!"

"That's just tough!" she shot back. "You scared me to death! Now deal with the consequences!"

He glanced at Sean and Davy. "Let's get the fuck out of here. We can hunt down Billy some other time."

Sean turned to address the crowd of gawkers gathering around them. "Public service announcement, everybody! The cops will be here any minute, so start thinking about your witness statements now!"

The crowd melted away like magic.

The back door of the Cadillac was open, and Barbara Riggs was half in, half out, eyes frozen wide. He handed her his cane. "Would you throw that into the back window for me, Mrs. Riggs?" he asked. "Let's get going. I'm sure you want to get Cindy home."

He got into the car, and waited for the back door to swing shut. It did not. He followed Erin's startled gaze, and jerked his head around.

Barbara Riggs was marching across the parking lot, clutching his cane like a club. The evening, which could never have been called normal to begin with, was about to take a turn for the seriously weird.

"Which car is Billy's?" Barbara demanded.

Miles daubed at the fresh flow of blood from his nose with his gory sleeve and pointed across the lot, to where a low-slung silver Jaguar glowed softly in the dark, like a phosphorescent sea creature.

Connor ran to stop her, but it was too late. She lifted his cane high over her head and whipped it down over the Jag's windshield with admirable force. The glass crunched and sagged. Fault lines shivered through the entire gleaming surface. *Crash,* a blow to the other side of the windshield. *Smash,* out went the right headlight; *crash, tinkle,* there went the left. Driver's side window, *smash.* She whipped the cane down and managed to make a pretty decent dent in the roof. The white purse dangled and swung over her arm with each movement.

There was an awful, ponderous inevitability to it, like watching a wrecking ball taking down a brick building. She was drawing another crowd, too. It wasn't every day that you saw a middle-aged lady in a pale pink pantsuit bashing a hundred-thousand-dollar car to garbage.

"What's her problem?" a big, swag-bellied biker type asked him.

Connor shrugged helplessly. "He owes her money."

Pop, crash, crunch, the mayhem went on and on, until Erin's anxious voice penetrated the noise. "Mom? Mom! Listen to me, Mom!"

Barbara looked up, tears streaming down her face. "That son of a bitch hit my baby!"

"I know he did, Mom, but she's going to be OK. And the guys beat him up for you already, didn't you see?"

"Good," Barbara said viciously. Erin winced and covered her ears as the cane whistled down and shattered the back window. She put her arms around her mother's shoulders and hurried her back toward the car. Barbara went along without argument, the forgotten cane dragging behind her. The black rubber tip bumped over the asphalt.

Miles grinned through his gore. "You're a goddess, Mrs. Riggs!"

"I'm sure this is all very therapeutic, but can we leave?" Sean asked.

"Yeah, let's move. You and Miles come to my house," Davy said. "We need to clean that kid up. Hey, Con. I slipped one of Seth's beacons into Billy's cigarettes while your mother-in-law was trashing the Jag. We can track him down tomorrow, so take it easy tonight. If you can." Davy's sympathetic eyes flicked over to Connor's car, packed chock full of problematic Riggs females. "Good luck with them. And watch your back with Erin's mom. The woman is not to be fucked with."

"Yeah. Believe me, I've noticed," Connor grumbled.

This time Connor pried the cane out of Barbara's clammy grip with his own hands, closed the car door on her, and threw the cane into the trunk where it could do no more damage.

He pulled the car out onto the street and braced himself for absolutely anything.

"Mom?" Cindy quavered. "Are you wigging out on me?"

Barbara pulled Cindy into her arms. "Oh, no, baby. Not at all."

"I think you're going to be just fine, Mrs. Riggs," he said. "You certainly seem to have no problems expressing your anger."

Their eyes met in the rearview mirror. "You'd better start calling me Barbara, Connor," she said coolly. "I might as well get used to it."

"Gee. Thanks so much," he muttered.

"I really do feel much better," Barbara said, in a wondering voice. "Better than I have in ages."

"Oh, sure you do," Connor grunted. "Nothing like a little reckless destruction of private property to brighten up your mood."

Barbara blinked rapidly. "Oh, my. Do you think he might prosecute me? Oh dear. Wouldn't that be funny? If I had to send Eddie a letter . . . sorry, honey, but I can't make it in to see you on visiting day . . . I'm in jail, too! I'm a p-p-public menace!"

"That's not funny, Mom." Erin's voice sounded strangled.

"I know it's not, sweetie pie. So why are we laughing?"

All three of the women started laughing. Then they started bawling. Then it was a terrible mess. Connor just kept his head down, and his mouth shut, and drove the goddamn car.

This contract made Rolf Hauer very uneasy.

There was nothing wrong with the business end of things. The pay was excellent, the contact had been discreet and professional, the down payment had been delivered to Marseilles in American dollars, as promised. No problems at all there. Everything was in perfect order.

It was the details of this hit that bothered him. A list of nitpicking, grisly details, any of which, if not followed to the letter, rendered the contract null and void. Rolf prided himself on his professionalism, but if there was one thing this business had taught him, it was that there were always surprises. An artist needed room to improvise. There was no room in this job for improvisation. This one was skintight.

So was his hiding place in the goddamn garage closet. He'd been here for hours, and he was stiff and bored. He glanced at his watch. The targets should be arriving soon, if things went as the contact had assured him that they would. The explosives were in place. The list of instructions had the feel of a code. Not that he wanted to decipher it. The less he knew, the happier he was. He was only a pen, writing a message with fire and blood. He was paid to keep that ink flowing.

Ah, at last. The garage door rumbled up. Headlights glared into the garage under the secluded house. Adrenaline squirted into Rolf's body. He shifted into combat readiness, cracked the closet door, peered out. In his black ski mask, he was just another shadow in the dark.

The door of the van cracked open. Voices. A light flipped on. A man turned around, tall, round-shouldered, wearing a felt cap. He lit a cigarette. Yes. Double chin, big nose. Matthieu Rousse. His first target.

The passenger door opened, and a big, chunky woman got out. Helmet of gray hair. He didn't even need her to step into the light to identify that big jaw. She was the second target, Ingrid Nagy. She said something sharp to the man, in a guttural language Rolf didn't recognize. The man replied, sulkily, dropped his cigarette, and crushed it out. They went to the back of the Volvo van and opened the doors.

Rousse reappeared, carrying a limp, blanket-wrapped figure in his arms. Rolf caught sight of a slack, sallow face, balding brown hair. Target number three, the comatose man with no name.

Rousse carried him easily. The inert figure was as slight as a boy. Rolf watched silently as Nagy grabbed a metal valise and followed Rousse and Coma Boy into the house, bitching all the way.

He slithered up the stairs after them, toward what he knew was the kitchen, from his recon earlier that evening. Nagy was getting further, her scolding voice receding up the stairs. A woman chewing a man out sounded pretty much the same in any language, poor bastard. But pity was wasted on him. His pain was at an end.

Rousse was clattering down the stairs, probably heading back to the garage to get more gear from the van. The door at the top of the stairs burst open. Rousse didn't even have time to speak; just a surprised widening of the eyes, *pop, pop, pop* with the silenced Glock, and down he went. Thud. Eyes still open, in eternal surprise.

Nagy was still yelling from the upstairs. She wasn't moving toward him yet, but since Rousse wasn't going to respond any time soon, she would get pissed off and come looking for him soon enough. He followed her shrill voice up the stairs, toward the lit-up door at the end of the corridor. She charged out the door, and he took her out before she even finished winding up for her bellow of rage. *Pop, pop.* Dead before she saw him. That was how he liked it. So far, so good.

Now came the weird part. The part that made his flesh creep.

He walked into the room and stared down at Coma Boy. The open valise beside him was full of medical supplies. A plastic bag of glucose and what all lay beside him. A hypodermic needle. She must've been yelling for Rousse to bring her the IV rack. Coma Boy lay there, his head dropped to the side, mouth open, limp and helpless.

Rolf had been ordered to remove the plastic-coated adult diaper, to take the valise, needles, IV rack, stretcher, all evidence that Coma Boy was not a normal, healthy person. If any scrap were left, the contract was void. He did as he was instructed, glad of his leather gloves. Touching the man's limp body made his gorge rise. He searched through Nagy's pockets to make sure there were no clues there, bundled everything back in the valise, hauled it all back to the garage. The Volvo was full of machines to hook up to Coma Boy. He would dispose of them later.

He went back upstairs, stepping over Rousse and Nagy, and pulled out a knife to attend to the final details. His hand stopped.

Rolf was surprised at himself. Coma Boy wasn't going to weep and beg for mercy. Rolf would've almost preferred it if he had. It would've given him something to push against. It would've made sense.

This creature, so utterly passive, baffled him. Weakened him.

Rolf steeled himself, and used a trick that he'd thought he would never need again. He divided himself. There was a part of him that did not mind slicing off the first joint of Coma Boy's right index finger, and then the ring and pinky finger of the same hand. He'd been given a diagram explaining exactly how much of each finger to cut. He'd studied it carefully. Part of him did not balk at putting a bullet in Coma Boy's brain, and five more in his chest. *Pop, pop, pop, pop, pop, pop.* That strong part of him squeezed the trigger. The other part of him shrank away, like a snail into its shell.

He gathered up the fingers, put them in a plastic freezer bag he'd put in his pocket for that purpose. He tucked the bag into his jacket. He pulled out the small bottle of accelerant, and soaked the body with it.

The hard part was over. Now for the mopping up.

Rolf pulled up his rented vehicle from the hiding place in the shrubs, and got to work on the van. Not one scrap of medical equipment left in it, or the contract was void. He packed the machines and boxes and medicines into his own vehicle, and examined the Volvo inside and out with his flashlight. Clean and nice. He was done here.

Now the part he was looking forward to. He pulled away to a safe distance, took a deep breath, and pushed the detonator.

The house exploded. Rolf watched the expansion, the slow-motion fall of blazing debris, the licking flames, with dumb relief. Fire purified.

He drove to the cliff top he'd chosen the day before. The sea heaved and crashed below. He pitched the materials he had taken over the cliff. He threw the bloody Ziploc bag and its contents.

The terms of the contract were satisfied. But he didn't get into his car and drive away immediately, as he should have done. He stared out at the sea, thinking about what he had done. Always a mistake. He was a man of action. Not reflection.

All things considered, it was good that the pay was so high. Because after tonight, he was ready for a long vacation, someplace very far from here. The sky had begun to lighten before Rolf got into his car and headed back toward Marseilles.

Chapter

19

Erin was still buzzing with nervous energy hours later. It had been a long, trying evening. Her mother had insisted on taking Cindy to the emergency room, where the doctor had checked Cindy out, asked several probing questions, and sent them home with much the same advice as Sable had given to Erin: make Cindy drink a lot of water, sleep it off, and stay the hell away from whoever had gotten her into that condition. And drug counseling went without saying.

Mom and Cindy were finally asleep, in Mom's bedroom. Mom had pointedly not invited Connor to stay in the guest bedroom. He'd gotten the hint, and was outside in his car. She leaned against her bedroom window. The fog circle of her breath widened and shrank as she stared at the Cadillac parked outside. Banished from the house, and still he stuck by her, to guard her while she slept. So stubborn and gallant and sweet. Just thinking about it touched off that melting feeling again. She fought it down for fear she would start crying. She'd bawled all evening with Mom and Cindy. She was tired of it. Her sob muscles hurt.

She missed Connor. She started to pull on her jeans, and then looked down at her thin gauze summer nightgown with the embroidered pink flowers. She thought of his reaction to her baggy Victorian nightdress. "A calculated cocktease," he'd called it.

Hmm. Well, then. She would just have to see if he liked the skimpier version just as well. No one was awake to see but him.

She crept barefoot down the stairs, disarmed the alarm, and stepped out onto the porch. The night breeze was damp and chilly, whipping the thin fabric around her thighs. She felt Connor's eyes lock onto hers, through the car window, across the dark lawn. She was very conscious of her nipples, pressing against the thin fabric.

Connor pushed the passenger side door open and beckoned to her. She ran across the dew-soaked grass and slid into the Cadillac, scooting over on the slippery leather seat to press herself against his warmth. Her feet were covered with clinging blades of grass.

His arms went around her. "What the hell do you think you're doing out here? You're half naked!" His voice was sharp with outrage.

"I wanted to show you my nightgown," she said. "I wanted to see if you liked it."

"Oh, Christ." He flung his head back against the seat. "You're trying to kill me, aren't you?"

"I just missed you, that's all," she said. "I was watching you from my bedroom window. My brave, noble knight in the shining Cadillac."

He lifted her hand to his lips, kissed it tenderly front and back, and then pressed it against the hard, thick length of his erection. "I like your nightgown, babe," he said. "How noble is that?"

She stroked him from base to tip. Her fingers tightened appreciatively around his thick shaft. "Oh, very noble, Connor. Very."

He covered her hand, held it still. "Don't, Erin. That's enough."

"Why not? Everyone's asleep. Open your jeans for me and I'll practice some of my bad girl skills. I've never done anything in a car before. Except for when you kissed me at the airport. That counts."

"I think it does, too. But still, no."

Her fingers tightened, rubbed him, insisting. "Don't you want—"

"You know damn well how much I want it, but I'm not comfortable letting down my guard in a car parked out on the street. I'm wide open when you do your sex goddess routine on me."

"So come up to my room." She pressed her lips against his hot face, rubbed her cheek against the rasp of glinting beard stubble. "We'll lock the doors, set the alarms. We'll be as safe as it's possible to be."

He clapped his hand over his eyes. "Yeah, right. That'd go over great with your mom. You saw what she did to that Jag."

"Don't be silly," she said. "You're no Billy Vega, and besides, she already likes you." She rushed over his snort of derision. "My bedroom is in the attic, on the opposite side of the stairs from Mom's bedroom. They're asleep, Connor. They're exhausted. No one will ever know."

"You are lethal, sweetheart," he whispered. "Like Eve in the garden. Come on, baby, just one little nibble. See how shiny the apple is? Yum, yum."

She rubbed against him so that her neckline gaped low. "The apple is juicy and sweet, Connor," she said. "I promise, you'll love it."

His hand slid up over her hip, her waist, and cupped her breast. She arched against him. "Come upstairs, and you can take this nightgown off me and make love to me, Connor. I never sneaked a boy into my childhood bedroom, ever. I need to make up for lost time."

"I'm not a boy, Erin," he said. "I'm a man. That makes it different. That makes it kinky."

She cradled his face and kissed the frown line between his brows. "And I'm a woman," she said quietly. "Which makes it OK."

He stared into her eyes for a long moment. "Tell me what your bedroom looks like."

The odd question disoriented her. "Why don't you just come up and see for yourself?"

"Just tell me, so I can see if it's anything like my fantasies."

The longing in his voice silenced her, leaving her breathless. But only for a moment.

"Um . . . the wallpaper has a pattern of pink rosebuds," she began. "The bed is a maple four-poster, from my great-grandmother. There's a double wedding ring quilt in a million different shades of pink. Beneath it there's a dusty rose duvet. Dusty rose pillows with lace ruffles. There's a braided rag rug on the parquet floor, like the one in my apartment, but this one is in shades of peach and cream and pink. There's a washstand with a basin and pitcher. A maple dresser set and vanity, a matching armoire with beveled mirrors. Eyelet lace curtains. It's a very pretty room. I've always loved it."

His eyes glittered like a wolf's in the moonlight. "God, Erin. That just makes me want to explode."

She stifled a giggle. "Eyelet lace curtains turn you on?"

"No. You turn me on. You, in the middle of all that fluffy chick stuff. Lace and rosebuds. I could come in my pants just thinking about it."

"I have flower-scented candles," she offered. "And there's a jar of rose petal potpourri on the vanity. The whole room smells like roses."

"Any stuffed animals lying around?" he demanded. "Dolls? I'll feel like a sleaze if you've got dolls in there."

His suspicious tone made her giggle. "There are some antique dolls, but they don't bite. They just sit on the shelves and watch you."

"Yikes," he muttered. "That's creepy."

"I'll keep you too busy to notice them," she said. "I can even put on ankle socks, and do my hair in two braids, and suck on a striped lollipop, if you like. Just say the word."

"No thanks, Lolita," he said. "I like women, not little girls."

She put her arms around his neck and trailed soft, seductive kisses from his high, sharp cheekbone down to his rigid jaw. He was still resisting her, as hot and hard and eager as his body was.

Time to bring out the big guns.

"I'm naked underneath this nightgown," she whispered.

"Yeah, like I hadn't noticed," he said roughly. "I can see your nipples and your crotch right through that damn thing."

She tugged up the flounced skirt until it cleared her knees, then her thighs. She bunched it up under her breasts so that he could see her belly, her sex, the whorls of silky dark hair between her thighs. She opened her legs and lay her hand between them, brushing her fingertips against her labia. "Don't you want to touch me?"

"Goddamn it, Erin," he said hoarsely. "This isn't fair."

"I know," she whispered. "I can't help myself. I would never have dreamed of making a spectacle of myself to turn a man on before, but I'll do it for you. I want to drive you crazy." She slid her fingers into her cleft, tightened her thighs around the trembling ache of arousal.

He jerked her onto his lap. She almost sobbed in relief, and gave herself up to his strong hands, his ravenous mouth. His fingers slid inside her, and she whimpered and lifted her hips, desperate for the relief that only he could give. She had wanted to make him helpless with desire, but now she was the helpless one.

Connor's slow, seductive kisses made her lose all sense of gravity. His thrusting hand, his demanding mouth were her only points of reference. His fingers teased and caressed her until she splayed herself wide, shaking. Pushing herself against his hand in a silent demand for release. He withdrew his hand and set her down on the seat.

"OK. You win," he said. "You've got me right where you want me, but I've got you, too. Take me up to your room and fuck me, Erin."

She drew in a sobbing breath and got out of the car. Her legs shook so hard she could barely stand. "On the first flight of stairs, the fourth step creaks," she said breathlessly. "Be sure to skip it."

His eyes narrowed. "You realize, of course, that if your mother walks in on us, I will have a heart attack on the spot."

"There's a hook latch on the door," she told him. "Mom's not the type to kick in doors. Dad would have, but not Mom. She's the type to wait until later and then look at you with big, hurt eyes."

"Yeah, and then bash in my skull with a cast-iron skillet."

"Oh, don't be such a scaredy-cat," she chided.

They crept in the front door. Erin reset the house alarm, and beckoned him up the stairs. She listened for his footsteps, but she heard nothing, not even the brush of fabric against fabric. She turned, expecting to see him still at the foot of the stairs.

He was right behind her.

He smiled at her gasp of surprise and put his finger to his lips. He followed like a ghost, floating over the squeaky parquet floor to her attic bedroom. He closed and latched the door as she searched through a drawer for the matches.

She began to light her candles, and without conscious intent, the action took on a ceremonial reverence. She was gathering power, lighting an altar to love. Rose, lavender, hibiscus, and jasmine on the vanity. Heliotrope, lilac, lily of the valley, and vanilla on the dresser. Natural scents, not overpowering, but delicately effective. Candle flames reflected into the mirrors, dancing in the currents of subtly perfumed air that moved through the room.

She turned around to face him. She felt ridiculously shy, after all her seductive posturing. The room seemed to turn back time. It made her feel younger, more unsure. More vulnerable, if that were possible.

His eyes were soft with wonder. "You're straight out of a fairy tale, Erin. That perfect body, in silhouette, and the candles behind you that turn your nightgown into pure light. My enchanted princess."

"Princess?" She blushed rosy red. "Oh, please."

"That's how I've always thought of you," he said quietly. "A beautiful princess in a tower too high to climb. Wall of thorns, magical spells, dragons, the whole deal."

If he kept up with this sweet talk she was going to start crying again, she just knew it. She sniffled, and tried to laugh. "My tower was only so high because you were the only one I ever wanted to climb it."

The power games and seductive wiles and playful banter had evaporated. They had no place in the reverent hush. Time collapsed, and she was seventeen again, the first night she met him. She had lit her candles and lain awake for hours, tossing and turning. Troubled by sensual dreams and fantasies, by a restless ache in her body that sharpened, grew delicious and agonizing when she thought of his smile, his laugh. The shape of his hands. The breadth of his shoulders.

A crazy, fanciful thought began to form in her mind.

"Would you play out a fantasy for me?" she asked.

"I would do anything for you," he said.

The stark hunger in his eyes emboldened her. "I want to go back in time," she faltered. "I made a mistake once. I want to try and fix it."

He nodded in silent encouragement.

She gathered all her courage. "I picked the wrong man to lose my virginity to. I didn't have the guts to go after the man I really wanted."

"Oh, Erin—"

"It should've been you, the first time." She rushed on, desperate to get the thought out before it fragmented. "But it wasn't. And it was awful. It closed me down for years. I didn't even want to try to have sex again. Until I made love to you."

His fists clenched. "What did he do to you?"

The steely anger in his voice frightened her, and she shook her head quickly. "Oh, no, nothing like that," she assured him. "It wasn't his fault he was the wrong man. It wasn't his fault that I didn't love him, and I didn't really want him. It was more my mistake than his."

"I don't buy it, Erin," he said. "You have a real bad habit of taking responsibility for things that aren't your fault."

She threw up her hands. "Maybe, but so what? I don't want to think about that, or about him. Tonight, there's magic. Tonight, I think I could go back in time. Be nineteen again. And have the first time be with you. Beautiful and perfect. Even . . . holy."

He moved toward her, and took both her hands in his. "I love you, Erin." His voice was a fierce whisper.

She struggled to respond. Language had utterly deserted her.

"I didn't want to scare you off," he said. "I didn't want to say that too soon. But if you want me to make love to you like that, then it has to be said." He lifted her hands, kissed them reverently. "I love you."

"I love you, too," she burst out. "I always have, Connor. Always."

The truth was out, naked and stark and beautiful. Revelations unfolded inside the secret places in their hearts, like flowers blooming wide, releasing their sweetness to the wind.

"You know what this means, Erin," Connor said. "This is like our wedding night. You're mine, I'm yours. Forever."

Flickering shadows danced and swirled in her vision as tears welled up and flashed down her face. "Yes," she whispered.

Their lips met, in a solemn, reverent kiss. Not a kiss to coax or to conquer, but a kiss to seal a pact. A kiss to break an enchantment.

Or to unleash one.

Connor gave himself up to her fantasy, with all his longing and passion and generous tenderness. He pushed the nightgown off her shoulders, and followed its sliding path with his mouth and hands.

He made love to her with lips and tongue, with the soft warmth of his breath. He sank to his knees and tugged the nightgown over her hips until it pooled around her feet, and hid his face against her mound, worshiping her very essence. They were poised in perfect balance on a knife's edge of awe and bliss, suspended by grace. With no fear of falling.

Even the struggle to get his clothes off, the muffled laughter, was imbued with reverent wonder. They were as awkward as if it truly were the first time. Connor's fingers trembled so much that he dropped the condom. When Erin knelt to retrieve it for him, she got sidetracked, allured by his phallus: hot and smooth and hard to bursting, weeping delicious, salty drops of passionate need. All hers to caress and cherish. He gasped with agonized pleasure when she took him in her mouth, but after only a few tender, sliding strokes he pulled her back up.

"None of that, sweetheart. Tonight's all about you," he said. He rolled the condom over himself, pulled down the duvet and pressed her into the cool sheets. His body shook.

She stroked his hair. "Are you OK?" she asked.

"I'm scared." His voice was low and tense. "This has to be perfect for you. This sets the tone for the rest of forever. I think I'm entitled to be a little nervous."

She pulled him tighter. "But you can't go wrong," she assured him. "It's like you were made for me. Everything you do is perfect."

"God. You are such a sweetheart." He smiled at her. "The way you stroke my ego. Stroke away. Let it swell up like a hot air balloon. I love it. Can't get enough of it."

"But it's true, Connor," she protested. "Every time you kiss me, every time you touch me, I—oh, God . . ."

Her words choked off as he pushed her legs wider and nudged himself inside. "Are you ready?" he asked. "Do you want me now?"

Pleasure bloomed around his gentle invasion. Every point of contact glowed, incandescent. She wrapped her arms and legs around him as he pushed inside. The yielding rush of emotion was so strong, so sweet. It echoed in his eyes, reverberating between them until she wanted to cry out at the sheer beauty of it. Her man, her mate.

She reached up to brush away the hair that had fallen across his face. Her hand came away wet. She pulled his face to hers and kissed away his tears, moved beyond words. She tasted their hot, salty magic, and the spell was complete. They were bound for all eternity.

They began to move, rocking together in delicious, liquid accord.

He froze. "Oh, no. Not possible. This is so fucking cruel."

Her eyes popped open, alarmed. "What's not possible?"

"This bed squeaks!" He was outraged. "You didn't tell me you had a squeaky bed when you lured me up here with salacious promises!"

"I didn't know," she said defensively. "I've never had sex in this bed! How would I know? And what do we care?"

"Easy for you to say," he scoffed. "You're not the one who gets bludgeoned to death if your mom hears us."

She started to shake, with soft, helpless giggles that could melt into tears in an instant, and Connor clapped his hand over her mouth.

"I hate to put a damper on our romantic fantasy, because I was really getting off on it myself, but we have to make some modifications," he said. "Parental participation would seriously wreck the mood."

He pulled himself out of her clinging body with a groan of pleasure and slid off the bed. He tossed the comforter onto the rug, and arranged it into a soft, puffy nest. He grabbed a pillow and sank down onto his knees, holding out his hand to her. His smile was radiant and beautiful. "The floor doesn't squeak," he said. "Come here."

She scrambled into his arms. They both cried out with pleasure at the sweet shock of contact. She had no barriers at all, nor did he. He had offered his whole self to her with extravagant, childlike abandon, and it almost frightened her, how vulnerable he'd made himself, how enormous his trust. It was a vast responsibility, but she couldn't examine the thought. It exploded like a shower of sparks and gave way to the next wave of pure emotion.

"You want to be up or down?" he asked between kisses.

"Do I have to choose? Can't we do them all?"

"You're the enchanted princess. I am yours to command."

She leaned back against the pillows and pulled him down on top of her. "I want this, for now. I like your warmth, and your weight."

"Anything," he muttered, and he scooped her body up tightly against his, cradling her. He entered her again, and pulsed against her hips with lazy, sinuous skill until passion seized them and they heaved and writhed together, twining around each other like flames.

It was everything she could have desired. More than she had ever dreamed of. Each kiss, each worshipful caress and whispered word of love deepened their surrender to each other. They made love until she was limp and soft, her whole body one glowing smile.

She must have dozed at some point, although the whole night seemed like a sweet, feverish blur. She opened her eyes and found him gazing at her, a small piece of folded paper in his hands.

"You're not sleepy?" she asked.

"I can't sleep," he said, smiling at her. "I'm too happy."

"What's that you're doing?" she asked.

He made one careful, final adjustment, and handed it to her.

It was an origami unicorn. She gazed at its miniature, angular perfection, astonished. "It's beautiful. Where did you learn to do that?"

"Davy taught me, when I was recuperating. Davy goes for that slow, meditative stuff. Tai chi and meditation and cosmic harmony, yada yada. I was going nuts with boredom, so one day he comes in with some paper and a book on origami. He said hey, it's about time you learned to concentrate, Con. So I did. I had nothing better to do."

"It's so beautiful," she whispered. "I love it."

"It's yours," he offered. "I'd better go on out to the car."

She reached out in blind protest, but he blocked her words with a kiss. "This is all we get for tonight, sweetheart," he said. "It's almost five o'clock. God. I feel like a horny teenager, sneaking around like this. What's the password for the alarm?"

"It's katherine323jane," she said. "Katherine with a k, mind you. Those are our middle names. Mine and Cindy's."

He extricated himself from their tangled nest and scooped her up into his arms. "Erin Katherine," he murmured. "That's so pretty."

She was utterly limp and smiling as he carried her to the bed and tucked her in. "What's your middle name?" she asked.

He spread the duvet over her. "I don't have one," he said. "I'm just Connor. It was my mother's maiden name. Jeannie Connor."

He kissed her again like he couldn't bear to stop, sending diffuse ripples of pleasure through her exhausted body.

He pulled on his clothes, shrugged on his coat, bent over to blow out her candles. She hated to see him leave, but the second the door clicked shut behind him, something inside her finally let go.

Sleep rolled over her like a shadowy tide and carried her away.

The man who was no longer Novak hung up the phone, stared at it blankly, and went looking for Tamara. He could have summoned her to him, but he wanted to catch her unaware.

It was not every day that a man got news of his own death. He observed his feelings with detachment. The news did not elate him. He felt lost, drifting. The flip side of freedom. The price he must pay.

He found Tamara in her office, wearing a pair of glasses, of all things, as she peered into a computer screen. She gasped, whipped the glasses off, and assumed her most seductive expression. Obviously she thought she had fooled him. She could keep her illusions. They cost him nothing.

"I just got some news," he told her. "Kurt Novak is dead, together with his employees, Ingrid Nagle and Matthieu Rousse. They were murdered some hours ago, near Marseilles. The building was blown up. A crime lord, Pavel Novak's rival, striking a blow at him through his son, they say. Live by the sword and die by the sword, as they say."

Her sensual mouth opened, closed, opened again. "Oh . . . I'm not sure whether I should congratulate you or offer my condolences, boss."

He considered the question for a moment. "You may congratulate me, Tamara, by removing your clothing."

Fifteen sweaty minutes later, Tamara's office was in considerable disarray, and he was feeling somewhat better, for a man six hours dead.

Tamara slid down the wall onto the floor when he detached himself from her body. She started to say something, and stopped.

It piqued his curiosity. "What? Ask me anything," he urged.

She eyed him warily. "I was wondering . . . how you did it."

"Ah. My transformation into Claude Mueller, you mean." He sank down beside her, naked, and threaded his arm through hers. "I met him at the Sorbonne, years ago. He fell in love with me, and became tiresome, but he was so rich, I was sure he would come in handy one day, so I tolerated him. One night, when drunk, he confessed that he wanted to be me." He smiled at her. "And the idea was born. It's never too early to plan ahead."

Tamara was rapt. "You just . . . stole his life?"

"Claude was sickly, and naïve. He had no friends but me. It was easy to cut him off from his few social contacts. A doctor with a shady past was enlisted to make him ill, with the aid of a criminal cook. And then I arranged for his parents to be removed from the picture. No one seemed to care what happened to him then. He was weak-willed, forgettable to look at. When I finally put him into a coma, no one noticed. But I, posing as Claude, have become quite a personage on the Internet. Everyone knows of Claude's generosity, his passionate love for collecting. Everyone loves him and courts him."

"Brilliant," she murmured.

"Claude's wish has come true. He is me. And I will live his life for him. Far better than he ever could have lived it himself."

She was silent for so long that he turned and looked. Her eyes looked haunted. "What?" he demanded. "What is it?"

She swallowed several times before she answered, a sure sign that she was going to risk telling him the truth. "When you tell me so many details, I'm afraid that you're planning . . ." Her voice trailed off.

"That I plan to kill you?" He was touched by her honesty. "Every man needs someone with whom he can speak freely, no?"

"Of course," she said automatically. "But—is this wise? To risk this new identity, just to punish Connor McCloud for—"

"Do not question my wisdom ever again."

He got up and began to pull on his clothing. Tamara reached for her blouse. "No," he said. "Stay that way. I like to see you naked."

The blouse dropped silently from her trembling hand.

He glanced at her computer. "What were you doing, at this hour?"

"I was checkng McCloud's car," she said. "I got a call from Marc. The McCloud brothers descended upon Billy Vega tonight like avenging angels. They snatched Cindy and left Vega in a bloody heap."

He blinked. "Ah. That changes things."

"Yes. It also appears that McCloud has undermined what you were trying to accomplish with Barbara Riggs. She's rallied. To the point of smashing all the windows out of Vega's car with McCloud's cane."

He began to laugh. "You can't be serious."

"I promise, I am. He's at the Riggs house now. The house vidcams showed him creeping up the stairs, to play with Erin."

He stared out the window as he buttoned his shirt, letting his plans shift and flow into new patterns. Barbara and Cindy Riggs were doomed anyway, a few days more or less hardly mattered. But this news of Billy Vega's defeat gave him an amusing idea that could move the whole thing briskly forward. "Call Georg, Tamara," he said.

She rummaged on the devastated desk for her communicator, and pressed the button. "Georg? The boss wants you in my office, please." She clicked the line shut, and reached for her skirt.

"No," he said silkily. "Stay just as you are, please."

Her constant smile faltered. It was faltering quite often lately.

When Georg walked into the office, she gasped, so startled that she forgot her nudity. Georg had shaved his head and brows, and plucked out his eyelashes. Blue veins traced across his smooth skull; his blue eyes were feverish in deep, bruised pits. He seemed a ghoul, a misbegotten thing that had crawled out of a sewer. The man who was no longer Novak nodded in approval. "I see you have followed my instructions. Did you exfoliate?"

"Three times a day," Georg said. "Just as you said. I am ready."

He embraced Georg, and kissed him on both cheeks. "Excellent. You are a vicious, loyal hound, and tonight, you will taste fresh blood."

After Novak explained what was expected of him later that night, Georg turned to Tamara. Scarred lips drew back from his ruined teeth as he looked her up and down. "When I return, I will want sex," he said.

The man who was no longer Novak shrugged. "Obviously," he said. "You will be happy to oblige him, of course, Tamara?"

Tamara hesitated, longer than usual. He waited . . . ah, there it was. That bright smile, ever at the ready. "Of course," she said faintly.

He advanced upon her again once Georg departed. Tamara's smile was a challenge. She tried to hide behind it, but he knew how much she loathed being intimate with Georg. He knew that power and danger excited her, that she was testing her limits, that she was too intelligent not to sense how close she was to death. Layer upon layer of lies, and twisted motives. Her complexity aroused him.

He opened his clothing and availed himself of her body again. He wished to get past all of Tamara's layers, all the way to her tender, shrinking center before he added her to his legions of angels. She must be punished, for thinking she could hide her secrets behind a smile.

Punishment exalted. His angels knew this, and so would she. The Riggs family would learn it, the McCloud brothers would learn it.

Just as he had learned it. The day was always with him, frozen in his memory. The day that his father had strangled his mother. She had betrayed him. He had been five years old, too young to understand the nature of her betrayal, but not too young to understand empty eyes, slack limbs. He understood death. He understood punishment.

His father had not been a heartless man. He had wept, had cradled his dead wife's body in his arms and sobbed.

"Never betray me," he had begged his small son. "Never."

"*Never*," the little boy had whispered. "*Never*."

Someone was clutching, clawing at his hands. Wild-eyed. Red hair, green eyes, gasping mouth wide open. Tamara. He realized, with a start of surprise, that his hands were clamped around her slender neck.

He let go of her, and got to his feet. These odd fugue states occurred when he was under stress. But after all, he had died only six hours ago. That was a stressful event.

Tamara lay curled and gasping on the floor, clutching her throat.

He fastened his trousers. "Be ready for Georg when he returns," he said as he left the room.

Chapter

20

Connor sat on the porch and watched the sunrise turn the clouds a rosy pink. He was so happy, it terrified him. Anything that made him feel so open and soft had to be suspect.

Morning advanced, people came out of their houses dressed for work, herding their kids into car seats. It was a normal working day for the rest of the world. None of them knew that the universe had just shifted on its axis. Erin, the most beautiful girl in the world, was his future bride. He could barely breathe, he was so switched on.

The door opened behind him. He leaped up and turned. His foolish smile slipped a notch when he found himself face-to-face with Barbara Riggs's suspicious glare. He thought about the squeaky bed, and made sure she wasn't holding any blunt objects that could be utilized to bash his head in.

She looked different today. Nicely dressed, hair styled, made up. She looked like the old Barbara he remembered from before the fall.

"Uh, good morning," he ventured.

She gave him a curt nod. He wondered if he was supposed to make small talk. If so, too bad. He didn't have any to offer.

Finally she took pity on him and opened the door wider. "There's fresh coffee in the kitchen. You may have some, if you'd like."

Her tone implied that he didn't deserve a cup of fresh coffee, but he still forced himself to nod and smile. "Thanks, I would."

This, of course, meant following her into the kitchen, sitting down with a cup of coffee and confronting another screaming silence. All those years of deadly quiet meals with Eamon McCloud had not prepared him for the frigid quality of Barbara Riggs's silence.

Finally, he couldn't take it anymore. "Uh, how's Cindy?" he asked.

"Still sleeping," she said. "So is Erin."

"That's good," he said. "You all needed your rest."

"Yes," she agreed. "Are you hungry?"

Actually, he was ravenous, but her cool gaze made him feel self-conscious about it. As if being hungry were some sort of moral failing. "I'm fine," he said. "Don't worry about it."

She got up, with a martyred look. "I'll make you some breakfast."

Erin came downstairs some minutes later, dewy and fresh from a shower, and found him digging into his third stack of pancakes and link sausages. Her face colored a deep rose pink. "Good morning," she said.

There was no bra under that skimpy tank top, he noticed. His glance switched her brights on. They went hard and tight against the stretchy fabric. He could feel those raspberry-textured nubs against his face, his lips fastened around them, tongue swirling, suckling.

He looked down at his pancakes. "Uh, great breakfast, Barbara."

She shot him a narrow glance and turned to Erin. "Want some pancakes, hon?"

"Sure," Erin said. She poured herself some coffee and dosed it with milk. "What's on your agenda for the day, Connor?"

"I need to track down Billy Vega," he told her. "I don't like leaving you alone, but I'd rather do it on my own." She didn't need to know the rest of his plans. Which included planting microwave beacons in her stuff so he could keep tabs on her.

"You really think Novak might have hired him to control Cindy?" Barbara asked.

He gave her a noncommittal shrug. "Just ruling out possibilities. I want you all to stay right here with the doors locked. And I want you to keep that revolver while I'm not with you, Erin."

Erin winced. He braced himself for Barbara's disapproval, but Barbara nodded, a martial glint in her eye. "I have a gun, too," she said. "A Beretta 8000 Cougar. And I know how to use it, too. Eddie taught me. Anyone tries to touch my girls, and I will blow their heads right off."

Erin coughed and set her coffee down. "Good Lord, Mom."

Connor grinned his approval and raised his coffee mug in a toast to his future mother-in-law. "Excellent. This place is guarded by kick-ass Amazon warrior goddesses. I'm outclassed. Practically redundant."

Barbara passed Erin a plate of pancakes. "Hardly that," she said primly. She forked some sausage links onto Erin's plate, hesitated, and dumped the rest onto his own, a clear mark of favor. "You certainly made yourself useful last night. Your brothers, too." She pursed her lips, uncomfortable. "I, ah, haven't thanked you yet, for your help."

Erin hid her face behind her hair. Her shoulders shook. "Don't thank him, Mom," she said. "It has a very strange effect on him."

He choked on his coffee and kicked her under the table.

She covered her face and tried unsuccessfully to muffle her giggles.

Barbara regarded them with chilly hauteur. "When you two are finished chortling over your private joke, I don't suppose you'd care to explain what's so funny?"

"No," he said hastily. "She's just yanking my chain. You're more than welcome, Barbara. Anytime."

Barbara's lips twitched, as if she were suppressing a smile. "Eat your sausages before they get cold," she snapped.

He cheerfully obliged her, sneaking hungry glances at Erin as she tucked in her pancakes. She was so amazingly pretty. Gorgeous shoulders, cute rounded arms, all soft and luscious. And those tits, high and quivering against that tantalizing tank top. Her regal posture just did it to him: her head so high, her back so straight, shooting him secret, heated glances from under her eyelashes. It drove him nuts.

Erin dipped her fingers into pancake syrup and peeked to make sure that Barbara's back was turned. Her lips curved in a seductive smile as she licked her fingertip. She drew the next finger into her soft, rosy mouth and sucked it, circling her pink tongue around the tip.

Color flared in his face as if he were thirteen again. He stared down into his empty plate and scrambled for a diversion. "Uh, would you mind if I took the cell phone when I go?" he asked. "I want you to be able to reach me at all times."

"Of course," Erin said. "I charged it up last night."

He nodded his thanks and gulped down the rest of his coffee. "I guess I'd, uh, better get going, then."

"I'll miss you." Her smile made him want to fall to his knees.

"I'll come back as soon as I can." He fled the kitchen before he could start babbling, too flustered even to thank Barbara for breakfast.

Erin padded after him. "The cell phone is plugged into the outlet by the couch," she told him. "Let me get it for you."

She handed him the phone after he shrugged his coat on, and disarmed the alarm for him. They gazed at each other. There was so much to say, they were both speechless.

Connor touched her cheek with his fingertip. "Erin. Last night was really intense. I need to know if we're still, uh . . . I don't mean to pressure you, but I don't want to float around on cloud nine all day thinking it's a done deal if you've got second thoughts. If you need time, I'll back off. I won't like it, but I'll do it. So tell me if—"

"I love you, Connor." She went up on tiptoe and pulled his face down to hers. Her lips were so soft and sweet, his whole body was racked by a shudder of delight. "It's a done deal."

That was as much as he could take. He pulled her soft, pliant body against his. Her tits pressed against his chest, his hands were full of the satin richness of her hair, her mouth was a pool of honey and spices and juicy, sun-warmed fruit. She arched against him and—

"Ahem. Have a nice morning, Connor."

They sprang apart at Barbara's crisp tone. Connor twitched his coat shut. Erin hid her reddened mouth with her hand.

"Thanks, Barbara. I'll, uh, be on my way," he mumbled.

"I think that would be best," Barbara said.

He was almost to Seth and Raine's place before his jeans fit normally. He was so jazzed, he practically danced up the wooden steps that led to the side kitchen entrance. He disarmed Seth's high-tech security system with practiced ease and let himself in. For the first time, Seth and Raine's altar crammed with wedding and honeymoon photos didn't make his lip curl. The whole world should get so lucky. If everybody felt like this all the time, earth would be a paradise. No war, no crime. Everybody bouncing off the walls, singing all day long.

Connor had spent enough time in Seth's basement workshop arsenal to know his way around. He rifled through the disks until he found Seth's latest version of X-Ray Specs, and dug through the numbered drawers, pulling out a handful of beacons housed in little plastic envelopes. He filled his pockets with them, tucked one of the receivers under his arm, and scrawled a note of thanks, leaving it on Seth's computer keyboard.

Next stop, Erin's apartment.

Erin's cat presented him with the first of several moral dilemmas. The animal started yowling the moment he let himself in the door with the help of his ATM card. It twined around his feet, trotted to its food bowl, and sat down. Luminous golden eyes regarded him expectantly.

"But I can't feed you," he protested. "If I feed you, I'll be busted. Erin will know that I was here. I'll bring her over later and she can feed you then. A little patience. You're too fat, anyway."

The cat licked its chops, bared its fangs, and meowed. His conscience pricked him. "Maybe some dry food," he conceded. "Just a little to tide you over." He searched through the cupboards until he found a bag of cat food, and dumped a small amount into the bowl. The cat sniffed at it and gave him a you-have-got-to-be-kidding look.

"I told you," he explained. "No wet food. It's not my fault. I've got nothing against you personally."

The cat curled sulkily down over the bowl and began to crunch.

The second dilemma was actually more a practical one than a moral one. Planting beacons on one's girlfriend during warm weather was as difficult as it was morally iffy. It was easier to hide stuff in heavy outerwear, and her purse and wallet and tape recorder, which were his best bets, were all with her at her mother's house. The Mueller report would've been good, if she'd kept it in a briefcase, but it was just a manila folder full of loose papers and photos, no way to hide the thing. He tagged her organizer, stitched beacons randomly into her jackets and blazers. That was as much as he could do until he got a whack at her purse. He wished Seth were around. Seth was born devious.

His eyes kept returning to the small jewelry box that sat on the dresser. He opened it and poked around until he found a ring he'd seen once on her ring finger, a silver and topaz thing. He slipped it onto his little finger, memorized how far it came past the joint, and voila, he had a point of reference for the jeweler. What slender, tiny fingers she had.

The third moral dilemma stared him in the face when the phone rang and the message machine clicked, whirred, and began to play back its contents. Erin must be calling her machine. She hadn't invited him to listen to her private messages, yet here he was. He could hardly put his fingers in his ears. Besides, she was his future wife. Her phone messages were the least of what he had the right to know about her.

So he stood like a statue in the middle of the apartment while the cat crunched its snack, and let her messages flow by him.

Click, whirr. "Hello, Ms. Riggs, this is Tamara Julian from the Quicksilver Foundation. It's four on Monday afternoon, and I want to schedule a meeting with Mr. Mueller, who is arriving midday tomorrow. Call me as soon as possible, please. We have a narrow window of time in which to arrange this. Please call my mobile phone number." Tamara recited the number.

Click, whirr. "Hello, Erin, this is Lydia. My goodness, you have been playing with the big kids on the block, haven't you? I just talked with the people from Quicksilver, and they told me about your work on Mr. Mueller's Celtic collection and their plans for the Huppert. I'm so excited! Rachel and Fred and Wilhelm and I have called an emergency lunch meeting, and you must be there to help us strategize! And Erin, I do hope you won't hold what happened a few months ago against us. I had no choice in the matter, as you know. It was the board who insisted on your dismissal, not the four of us. We have nothing but admiration for your skill and your determination. Call me, Erin, right away. At home tonight, if you like. Any hour is fine, even if it's late. I'm sure I won't sleep a wink tonight. Buh-bye!"

"Two-faced bitch," Connor muttered. "Get stuffed."

Click, whirr. "Ms. Riggs, this is Tamara Julian again. It's seven on Monday evening. Call us, please." Click, whirr. "Ms. Riggs, this is Nigel Dobbs, hoping against hope to get in touch with you. You have the number." Click, whirr. "Erin, this is Nick Ward. I need to talk to you right away."

Cold ran through his body as he listened to Nick recite his phone number. His euphoria vanished. He looked around the room, the bed still in disarray, yesterday's breakfast dishes still on the table. His stomach clenched like a fist. He shouldn't have left her alone. He didn't want Nick to talk to her. Nothing Nick might say could possibly be to Connor's advantage. All Nick would do was create confusion.

He pulled out the cell phone and dialed the Riggs house. It was busy. He tried again once he got back out to the car. Still busy. Prickles crawled up his back. He dialed Sean, who picked up on the first ring.

"Something weird is going on," Connor said.

"I'll say." Sean's voice was tense, devoid of its usual ironic tone. "Miles and I are about a mile from Billy's house, and—"

"What the hell are you doing at Billy's house?"

"Davy's had X-Ray Specs running on his computer since the last time we were hunting Novak, Con. He just keyed in the beacon he planted in Billy's cigarettes last night. The house is in Bellevue."

"You knew damn well I wanted to be there when we—"

"You're too late, Con." Sean's voice was strangely heavy. "Nobody's going to be questioning Billy."

Unease prickled over Connor's skin. "What do you mean?"

"He's dead," Sean said bluntly. "I talked to a lady who lives down the block. She heard the screaming around six A.M. The place is seething with cops. Guess what else? Surprise, surprise. Nick's there."

"Oh, Christ," Connor muttered.

"Yeah. I saw him talking to that scrawny blond chick. Tasha."

"Did he see you?" Connor asked.

"I don't think so," Sean said wearily. "We got the hell out of there, lickety-split. I didn't know Billy rated the attention of the Feds. I thought he was a strictly small-time rodent."

They both pondered for a moment.

"This sucks," Sean said forcefully. "I was having fun until now."

"They're going to be knocking on our door," Connor said. "Tasha's fingered us for sure. And Nick's already called Erin."

Sean made a frustrated sound. "Probably this has nothing to do with Novak. Billy's lovely manners just earned him some enemies and last night one of them caught up with him. I can see it. It's credible."

"Sure, maybe," Connor said. "And maybe someone didn't want us or anybody else to talk to Billy. Maybe someone wants us distracted by finding out that we're suspects in a homicide investigation."

"Stop it, Con," Sean said sourly. "You're trying to make me into a conspiracy theorist, and I don't want to go there. It's not my scene."

"You think I'm doing this for fun?" Connor snarled. "Get out of here, Sean. Take Miles, and go back to Endicott Falls."

"Yeah, like I'd leave my big brother alone with all this weirdness."

"Goddamnit, Sean—"

"Talk to you later. I'm calling Davy." The connection broke.

He tried to call Erin again, but the line was still busy.

The cold weight of dread built inside him, swelling into panic.

*   *   *

Erin was dismayed by the messages on her machine. She paced back and forth next to the phone table, trying to sort out her thoughts. She didn't want to talk to Nick, that was for sure. She didn't want to talk to Lydia, either. And she really didn't want to confront the whole Mueller issue with Connor as nervous and overprotective as he currently was. The timing was just awful.

But this was the day. She had to have it out with him and be strong, no matter how upset he got. Her professional future depended on it. Anyone could see it. Connor was just going to have to see it, too.

She picked up the phone to dial Connor's cell number. It rang in her hand, and she was so startled, she almost dropped the thing.

She clicked the line open. "Hello?" she said cautiously.

"Hey, this is Erin, right? It's Nick. I'm glad I caught you. Is Connor there?"

"No," she said. "Call his cell phone if you want to talk to—"

"No, Erin. I don't want to talk to Connor. I want to talk to you."

Her knees wobbled in trepidation, and she sat down hard on the stairs, jolting her tailbone. "What about?"

"You were with him last night at the Alley Cat, right? When he and his brother pounded Billy Vega to a pulp?"

"No, Nick, I was there when he and his brother were surrounded by nine big guys who all proceeded to attack them at once, and who got exactly what they deserved. Why do you ask?"

"I'm not interested in the nine guys, Erin. I'm interested in Connor's interest in Billy Vega."

"That guy hurt my little sister, Nick. He hit her, and terrorized her, and God only knows what else. So don't ask me to feel sorry for—"

"Billy Vega is dead, Erin."

She froze, mouth agape. "Dead?"

"According to Tasha Needham, it happened a little before six A.M. Tasha took Billy to the emergency room, where they set his wrist. Then Tasha and Billy took a cab to his rental house, where they proceeded to get very stoned. Sometime in the early morning, the assailant entered the house and beat Billy to death with a blunt object. Tasha was vomiting in the bathroom at the time, which probably saved her life. But she told us all about the ninja monsters who kidnapped Cindy Riggs and beat up Billy earlier that evening. It wasn't much of a leap."

"My God," she whispered. "That's . . . that's so awful."

Nick waited a moment. "Was Connor with you last night?"

"Yes," she said, still dazed.

Then, like a splash of ice water, the implications of Nick's question hit her. "Nick, for God's sake. You can't be suggesting that—"

"For the whole night?"

She opened and closed her mouth like a fish out of water, and burst out, "Yes! Yes, of course he was!"

But her hesitation had betrayed her. Nick cursed softly into the phone. "This is getting ugly, Erin. I don't want you mixed up in it."

"But Connor would never—"

"You saw what he did to Georg Luksch," Nick said. "Connor is my friend, but he's wound up too tight, and he's finally snapped. This fantasy he's got, about Novak and Luksch gunning for you—"

"What do you mean, fantasy?" she demanded. "Are you saying that it's not true that they broke out of prison? He's just trying to protect me! He feels responsible because Dad's not around to do it."

Nick hesitated for a moment. When he spoke again, his voice was gentle. "Erin. There's no one to protect you from. Novak's dead."

She struggled to comprehend. The information didn't fit.

It rattled senselessly around in her mind, making noise. "When?" she whispered.

"Yesterday, in France. A *mafiya* hit. Territory war, they think. Rival crime lords. A building got blown up. Novak was inside. Dental records confirm it. The charred skeleton was missing three fingers on its right hand. They're working on the DNA, but they're sure."

Her mind whirled. "So Connor doesn't know?"

"I haven't told him yet, no, but he knew that Novak was back in France. Luksch, too. The police have been moving in on them for days. I told Connor, but he didn't share those details with you, did he?"

She started shivering.

"No," Nick said. "Of course not. It didn't fit his fantasy. He wanted to rescue you, so he created a bad guy to save you from. He sucked you in. I know this hurts, and I know you care about him, but you've got to be strong. You've got to drag yourself out of this dream world of his. You've got enough to cope with already. I'm really sorry, Erin."

She shook her head. "No," she whispered.

Not the man who was so in love with her that he blushed and stammered when she teased him at the breakfast table. Who had rescued her sister, and woken her mother from the ugly dream she'd been trapped in. Not the man who had made such sweet, passionate love to her all night long. Not her Connor. It was not possible.

The vortex was sucking at her, and this time there was no one to grab onto. No hero to rescue her.

"Erin? Erin!" Nick sounded as if he had repeated her name several times. "Are you there? Erin, I need to find him. If you know—"

"No." The word flew out of her mouth, flat and absolute. "I have no idea where he is, Nick. Not the faintest clue."

"It's for his own protection, Erin. We've got to stop this thing before it spins out of control. I swear, I'm on his side—"

"No. I won't do it."

"Goddamn it, Erin! If you really cared about him—"

"Fuck you. No," she hissed. She slammed the phone down. It started ringing seconds later. She wrenched the phone jack out of the wall and doubled over, gasping. Everything was spinning, going black.

Connor had made her feel so whole, so strong. Like she could bless the whole world with her happiness, just touch it and turn it to gold. For the first time, she had lost her fear of the vortex. Of chaos.

And Nick was telling her that her joy was rotten at the core.

"Erin? Honey? Are you OK?"

She looked up at her mother, who was gazing at her with anxious eyes, and pasted on the best smile she could. "Sure, Mom."

"Who was that on the phone?"

She hid the hand that was clutching the phone jack against her leg. "I was just talking to, ah, Lydia," she said.

"Lydia?" Barbara frowned. "From the museum? That cast-iron bitch who fired you?"

She nodded. "Mueller offered the museum a huge donation, but one of the conditions is that they take me back," she explained. She tried to sound excited about it, but her mother wasn't stupid.

Barbara sniffed. "Well, I think you should spit in their faces," she said. "The nerve! When it suits them, they snap their fingers and expect you to trot right back? I think not!"

"You have a point," Erin said. "But I think I'll go to that meeting today anyway, and see what it's all about. I can always spit in their faces after I see the terms they offer me."

"That's my smart, careful, thoughtful girl," her mother said. "Always hedging her bets, trying to do the right thing."

"Not always," she burst out. "Not always."

"I take it you're referring to Connor," Barbara said. "I must say, he's growing on me. He can be extremely rude, and his background leaves something to be desired, but I did like those brothers of his. Even if all three of those McClouds strike me as, well . . . kind of out there. But they got Cindy back. That won them lots of points. And it's plain to see that Connor's crazy about you, sweetheart."

She flinched at her mother's choice of words. "I know."

"And any man with the nerve to sneak into my house and seduce my daughter under my nose after what he saw me do to Billy Vega's car . . . well. All I can say is, he must be made of very stern stuff."

Erin's face flamed. "He didn't seduce me last night," she said. "I seduced him."

Her mother's lips flattened to a thin line. "That was more information than I needed, sweetheart."

"Sorry, Mom," she murmured.

Barbara's expression softened. "There's something you should know before you go to that lunch meeting, hon. I'm going to start looking for a job. And Cindy's going to learn how to pull her weight, too. You don't have to carry us. We'll be strong for ourselves, and for you, too. Do you get what I'm trying to say?"

Erin's lip began to tremble. "I think so," she said.

"You'll make it just fine without that trash at the museum. So if you want to spit in their faces, go right ahead. Don't think twice."

"Thanks, Mom. I'll keep that in mind."

"Follow your heart, honey. Don't compromise yourself."

"I'm trying." Her lips started trembling. "I swear, I'm trying, but I'd better get going now. I've got an incredibly busy day. I need to run home and feed Edna, and then dress for lunch with the museum heads. And I have to schedule a meeting with Mueller after that."

Barbara frowned. "You promised Connor you'd stay right here with us, where you're safe. And I agree one hundred percent that lying low is an excellent idea. At least until things calm down."

Erin kissed her mother's cheek. "I'll call him and explain. He's a sweetheart to be so protective, but I can't cower in a hole forever. I promise I'll take cabs everywhere, Mom. I'll be just fine."

Her mother still looked anxious, and Erin gave her another coaxing kiss. "We're going to be fine now. We got Cindy back, and now this big opportunity just falls into my lap. Things are looking up."

It took all the strength she had to keep the cheerful façade in place until the taxi arrived.

The traffic was a nightmare. Connor leaped out of his car when he finally arrived, bolted for the house, and beat on the door.

Barbara pulled the door open. "Connor, what on earth?"

"Is Erin here?"

She frowned. "Didn't she call you?"

"The phone's been busy for a half an hour," he snarled.

"She told me she would call you and . . ." Barbara's voice trailed off. "Oh, dear."

"What?" His voice cracked with fury. "She left? Alone? You're kidding me. Where the fuck did she go?"

Barbara bristled. "Don't you dare use that language—"

"Just tell me, Barbara. Tell me now."

The desperate urgency in his voice made the color drain from her face. "She got a call," she said faintly. "From the museum where she used to work, for a lunch meeting, and then—"

"And then?" he prompted.

"Then she has to meet with that Mueller fellow. She told me she was going to call you. She took a cab to her apartment so she could change. She left almost a half hour ago. She's probably home already."

He bolted for his car. The screen door burst open and

Barbara scurried after him. "Connor, I insist that you tell me what's going on!"

He wrenched his car door open. "Billy Vega was murdered this morning, before I ever had a chance to find him or talk to him. Strange, huh?"

Barbara's face went gray beneath her makeup. "Go," she said. "Hurry."

He ran lights, swerved in and out of lanes, screamed obscenities at slow motorists, but his most aggressive driving was nothing pitted against weekday Seattle traffic. He called her apartment while trapped at an interminable red light, and the machine picked up. "Erin, it's Connor. Pick up if you're there, please."

He waited, crossing his fingers. Nothing.

"Look, I just found out that Billy Vega's been killed," he went on. "I'm really wishing you hadn't broken your promise and left your mom's house. What were you thinking? Please pick up, Erin." The light went green. He dropped the phone and accelerated through it.

He double-parked, and took the stairs at the Kinsdale three at a time. No response to his knock. He used his ATM card again.

Erin was gone. The Mueller report was gone. Her perfume scented the air. She'd taken the time to make her bed, do her dishes, pick up her scattered clothes, feed her cat, and he'd still missed her. By so little that the animal was still crouched over its bowl, tail twitching for joy.

She had taken none of the items he had tagged with beacons, not even the goddamn organizer. He wanted to howl like a wolf, to break things, punch walls, smash furniture. He'd thought that she trusted him. He was bewildered, after the perfection of last night, that she would turn on him and disappear, with no warning, no explanation.

A sucker punch, right to the solar plexus.

He fished the phone number out of his freak memory, and dialed.

"Hello, you have reached the mobile number of the administrative offices of the Quicksilver Foundation," said Tamara Julian's melodious recorded voice. "Please leave us the date, time, and purpose of your call, and we will get back to you as soon as possible. Have a lovely day."

He grabbed the phone book and looked up the Huppert, wading through the voice mail menu until he heard the name Lydia.

"Lydia's out of the office right now," the secretary told him.

"I urgently need to get in touch with her," he said. "I know she has a lunch meeting. Do you know what restaurant? I could call her there."

"I'm sorry, I can't," the woman said. "I didn't make that reservation. She made it herself last night. I have no idea where they are.'"

He muttered an ungracious thanks, and slammed the phone down.

He ran down the stairs to let off steam, even though he had no place to run to. He tried throwing out the net for a pattern, a clue, any sort of jumping-off place, but his mind had to be soft and relaxed for that trick to work. This hurt was too sharp. It sank into his mind like claws, stabbing and rending, making him wild-eyed and stupid.

A door swung on the ground floor as he passed. An elderly lady with a shriveled apple-doll face and a lavender-tinted helmet of white curls peered out at him. "You're the fellow who's keeping company with that nice young lady on the sixth floor, eh?"

He stopped in his tracks. "Did you see her leave?"

"I see everything," the old lady said triumphantly. "She took a cab. Came in a cab, went away in a cab. Must've come into some money, because ever since her car got repossessed, she's been taking the bus."

"Was it a yellow cab? Or a private car service?"

The old lady cackled at his desperation. "Oh, it was a yellow cab. No telling where she's gone, no telling at all." Her voice was a sing-song taunt. "You're just going to have to sit that fine tight tush of yours down and wait for her. Young folks these days don't know the meaning of patience. The more she makes you wait, the better off you'll both be."

"This is a special case," he told her.

Her fearsome dentures gleamed. "Oh, they all think they're special."

The vindictive satisfaction in the lady's voice made him grit his teeth. "Thank you for the information, ma'am."

Her rheumy eyes blinked suspiciously. "Hmph. Pretty manners."

"I try," he said. "Sometimes. Have a nice day."

The old lady retracted her head like a turtle and slammed her door.

One last door to bang on. He groped for the phone and dialed Nick's number as he loped toward the car.

"Where are you?" Nick demanded.

"What the fuck did you say to Erin, Nick?"

"I told her the truth. It's time somebody did. You know about Billy Vega, right?" Nick waited. "Yeah," he said softly. "Of course you do."

Connor knew where this was going. "Nick—"

"I couldn't help but notice that the guy looked a whole lot like Georg Luksch looked after you were done working him over with your cane," Nick said. "Only difference was, Billy was dead. You're slipping."

Black spots danced in front of Connor's eyes. He leaned against his car. "You can't believe that. Come on, Nick. You know me."

"I thought I did," Nick said. "Novak is dead, Con. Blown up. Burned to a crisp. It's all over. All. Over. Am I getting through to you?"

Connor's head spun. The phone call. Georg, on the freeway. Billy Vega. "But that's not possible. I talked to him. And I saw Georg—"

"Don't bother," Nick said. "Georg's in France. Like I told you before. Novak's death is confirmed. Not that this changes anything for you, of course. You need a focus for your anger, and if you can't find one, you'll create one. Sure, Billy Vega was no big loss to the world, but I—"

"Don't be stupid, Nick," Connor said grimly.

"I deduced from my conversation with Erin that you don't have a real alibi for the hours of five A.M. to six A.M. this morning. I also deduced that she will lie to protect you. Is that what you want?"

"Fuck you, Nick," Connor said. "This is bullshit."

"We'll see. Get yourself a good lawyer. Because I'm all out of patience. I want this thing to end."

"You and me both." He hung up. His leg and head were both pounding now, a nauseous throbbing pain. He wrenched the door of the Cadillac open. He had to sit down. Quick, before he fell down.

Nick had been one of his best friends, once.

He dropped the phone into his pocket. If it weren't for Erin, he would throw the thing into the Dumpster right now.

Erin. Panic dug in its claws at the thought of her. His fight with Georg at Crystal Mountain began to play in his mind. The cane, rising and falling. Blood streaming from Georg's shattered nose, his broken teeth. The cane, smashing down onto the windshield of the Jag. Fault lines, running in every direction.

The cane. Something about the cane was tugging him. He checked the backseat, and then recalled prying the thing out of Barbara's fingers and throwing it into the trunk. He fished his keys out of his jacket pocket and walked around the car.

The back of his neck was prickling so much he already knew what he would find, even before the trunk light flooded into the dark interior.

The trunk was empty. The cane was gone.

Chapter

21

"Try a bite of my mousse, Erin. It's even better than the crème brûlée," Lydia urged.

Erin dabbed her mouth with a napkin and forced herself to smile. "Thanks, but no. I'm full."

"Of what?" Rachel complained. "You barely picked at your salad. You don't have to diet with that cute, curvy figure of yours, Erin. You've trimmed down some since you were at the Huppert. Good for you."

Erin coughed, and hid her mouth behind her napkin.

"Come on, Erin. You're as tight as a clam about how you landed Mueller. 'Fess up, now. We've been courting him for years, and all of a sudden we find him eating out of your hand!" Rachel gushed.

"I'm so excited. This donation puts us ahead by fifteen years," Lydia said. "You are just the one to spearhead our efforts, Erin. We need your innovative spirit to carry the Huppert into the new millennium!"

Erin didn't have the energy to hide her disgust, but it didn't matter, since none of them appeared to notice it.

"With a budget like this, Erin, you can name your own

salary," Fred boomed. "You're the belle of the ball! How does it feel?"

She got to her feet. "I'm afraid I have to go."

"Oh, really?" Lydia exchanged meaningful glances with the other three. "A hot date? Is that why you're saving your appetite?"

"Not at all. Just business," Erin said. "I'm meeting with Mr. Mueller to discuss some of his new acquisitions."

Lydia and Rachel waggled their eyebrows at each other. "I imagine you're having dinner with him this evening, too?" Rachel cooed.

Erin shrugged wearily. She could care less whether or with whom she ate dinner tonight. As queasy as she felt right now, it would be all she could do to get through the day without throwing up on anyone.

Wilhelm whistled. "So that's the way the wind blows."

"Hardly," she said sharply. "I have never even met Claude Mueller, Wilhelm, and I don't appreciate your insinuations."

"Oh, don't be so sensitive, Erin," Rachel purred. "We're all adults."

Lydia's smile was calculated and cold. "Have a lovely time this evening, Erin. Ah, youth is wasted on the young. Just wasted."

Erin fled the table and hurried out of the restaurant, gasping for fresh air. These people were awful. How could she ever have tolerated their falseness, their manipulative games? What had changed in her? She wanted to take a bath after lunch with those four.

She hailed a cab, gave the driver directions, and stared miserably out the window, pressing her hand against the sharp ache in her belly. It ate at her like acid, how bad Connor must feel: his anger and confusion and hurt. And his fear. His fear for her was very real to him. How well grounded it might be in outside reality she could not say, but that didn't make it any less painful for him. Or for her.

It felt so cruel, so incredibly wrong, to turn away from

him. But she had to break out of his hold on her. She needed some air, some distance, so she could figure out where she stood. What was real.

Connor's charisma was so powerful, he warped her reality into any shape he pleased. He was so intelligent and intense, his force of will so overwhelming. She couldn't think straight when he was near her. He swept her away every time, no matter how hard she tried to resist.

Her heart and her body and her love would always betray her.

The taxi pulled up at the curbside of a beautiful turn-of-the-century mansion on Heydon Terrace. The wrought iron gates yawned opened for her unbidden as she paid the cabbie. It was time to get jerked around by Mueller and his piles of money. Oh, goodie. She would have laughed, but she didn't dare shake up her unsteady stomach.

Tamara Julian was waiting for her in the palatial foyer. Erin greeted her with wary politeness after that odd episode at Silver Fork, but Tamara was warm and friendly.

"I'm so glad we got in touch with you in time," Tamara said. "Mr. Mueller is so anxious to meet you. Come with me, please. I have to show you something before I present you."

Present her, indeed. Good grief. As if she were being taken before royalty. She muffled silent, half-hysterical laughter behind her hand as she followed Tamara through the big, lavish rooms, up a sweeping flight of stairs, and down a corridor into a plush bedroom full of freshly cut flowers. Their odor was heavy and sickeningly sweet.

Tamara opened up a safe in the wall, and pulled out a flat black velvet case. She handed it to Erin. "Take a look at this," she said.

Erin opened the box, and let out a sigh of awe.

It was a golden torque, La Tene period, but far more sumptuous than any she had seen. And it was the same style as the jewelry excavated from the ancient burial mounds that she had studied in Wrothburn.

There were dragons with garnet eyes where the ends of the torque met, their claws raised in challenge. Their serpentine tails formed a lavish, swirling pattern that extended down over the wearer's chest. The piece was exquisite. It shimmered and glowed like trapped sunlight against the black velvet.

"This is Mr. Mueller's latest acquisition," Tamara said. "He's been negotiating for it for months. This is the reason he had to rush off to Hong Kong the other day."

"It's incredible," she breathed. "Perfect. Would you show me the provenance information?"

Tamara smiled. "I could, but I won't. Not tonight, Erin. This is not for you to study. Put it on."

"God, no!" She held out the box, appalled. "That's ridiculous!"

Tamara gently pushed it back. "Why do you think I brought you up here? Mr. Mueller has a very special request of you today. He wants you to wear the dragon torque when you meet with him."

She looked down at her simple navy suit, her high-necked white silk blouse. "But I . . . I can't. I—I—"

"I understand perfectly," Tamara said briskly. "You need something different as a backdrop. Mr. Mueller and I anticipated this problem. We've arranged for several different gowns to be delivered this afternoon. Size eight, right?" Erin nodded. "Thought so," Tamara went on. "They're all stunning, and believe me, I'm fussy. We'll find something you'll like."

"Oh, no. It's not that," she protested. "But it's not—"

"Proper?" Tamara's laugh rang out, full and rich and beautiful. She kissed Erin's cheek. "That's priceless. I love it. You are a work in progress, Erin Riggs, but you'll be a masterpiece before you're through."

Erin shook her head. "I can't."

"Why?" Tamara demanded.

Erin closed her eyes against Tamara's probing gaze and tried to breathe deeply. She was too stressed and confused to come up with the cutting retort that she needed to fend the woman off. All she could think of was Connor's certain reaction to Mueller's request. His outraged pride.

"Don't you like playing dress-up, Erin?" Tamara's tone was lightly teasing. "It's just a harmless game. Mr. McCloud is nowhere in sight, and we're certainly not going to tell on you."

The taunt stung. "I do not need permission from anyone," Erin snapped. "I'm just uncomfortable with the idea. That's all."

Tamara's face fell. "I see. I was hoping you might indulge him. Mr. Mueller's health has been very fragile lately, and he's been reclusive and quite lonely. He's allowing himself to be fanciful, and that's rare for him. It gave him such a lift, to plan this surprise for you. He sees it as a gift, you see. To honor you. A way of thanking you for all your hard work."

Erin held the velvet box out to Tamara, almost desperately. "But I . . . it's so inappropriate. I don't even know—"

"Mr. Mueller just wants to share his delight in the torque with someone who appreciates it as much as he does," Tamara coaxed. "He's fascinated with you. He has been for months. And you should learn to make the most of your looks anyway. I can help you with that. You have such incredible potential. That hair, that skin, those eyes."

"Thanks, but I don't need a fashion consultant," Erin said tightly.

"No, you don't," Tamara agreed. "You look perfectly fine. You're a very pretty girl. But if you wanted, you could cause car accidents when you walked down the sidewalk."

Erin recoiled. "Good Lord! Why on earth would I want to do that?"

Tamara laughed at her. "Power, Erin. It's useful. Believe me."

Erin shook her head. "I don't need that kind of power," she said quietly. "I don't want it. It's not my style."

"We all need it." Tamara's voice was hard. "What a shame

McCloud has you under his thumb. Now you don't even have the nerve to try on a five-thousand-dollar evening gown, just for fun. Some lessons in female power might do you good."

Erin bristled. "Don't you dare try to manipulate me."

Tamara tilted her head to the side and contemplated her next tactic. "I just want to play," she wheedled. "Try on the gowns, Erin. They're beautiful, and so are you. Let me show you how exciting it is to be truly glamorous. It's a kind of magic. And it's fun. Just look at this beautiful thing. I don't even want to tell you how much money he spent for it. And it's perfect for your looks. As if it were made just for you."

Erin stared down at the inherent tension and violence in the torque's stunning design. The two dragons were locked in a state of mortal challenge. Their garnet eyes glowed red with rage. The design tricked the eye into the illusion that the twisting serpentine tails were flipping and writhing. The thing practically hummed in her hands.

She'd always privately considered this style of jewelry to be the most beautiful and evocative that existed. Sensual and savage, the designs echoed with the blood and dust and noise of ancient history. She loved Celtic artifacts exactly because they were a tangible point of contact with that mysterious culture. They made her dream, set her imagination on fire. They called to her across the ages.

A high-ranking Celtic noblewoman had worn this torque around her neck well over two thousand years ago. She had lived her everyday life in it, waking and eating and breathing and loving. If Erin put on that torque, history would fold over on itself. She could reach back in time and almost touch that woman. The torque had made her real.

It was utterly seductive. She was so tempted, her hands shook.

"Mr. Mueller did this to please and flatter you, Erin," Tamara said softly. "Humor him. And indulge yourself. Mc-Cloud will never know, because it's all . . . between . . . us."

Erin broke eye contact. She was on the brink of tears again, for God's sake. What a wreck. Tamara was right. The very thought of Connor's anger made her weepy and unsure of herself.

This indulgence would be her own secret. And maybe it would serve as a liberation. She was her own woman, who made her own choices. Her passion for ancient history was all hers. It had nothing to do with Connor. He would never understand it.

But Claude Mueller might. "All right," she said.

She was instantly sorry. She knew the moment the words left her mouth that she had made a big mistake, but it was too late. Tamara was thrilled, smiling, leading her by the hand into another bedroom, the bed of which was covered with boxes and bags. "I'll show you the lingerie and the shoes, first," Tamara said.

"Lingerie?" she echoed faintly.

"Of course." Tamara rolled her eyes. "You can't show panty lines under these gowns. And I ordered stockings to match, of course."

A half hour later, Tamara closed the cold weight of the golden dragon torque around Erin's neck and turned her around to face the mirror. "Look at yourself. If Connor McCloud could see you now, he would kneel and beg for mercy."

Guilt and pain stabbed through her. "Please, don't."

"Trouble in paradise?" Tamara asked. She laughed and held up her hand at the look in Erin's eyes. "Sorry. Forgive me for asking. Curiosity is one of my little vices. Don't hate me for it. I don't mean any harm."

"You don't know me well enough to speak to me like that."

"No, but I would like to." Tamara flashed her a quirky, disarming smile. "I find you very interesting, Erin Riggs. Now take a look at yourself. Are you a knockout, or are you a knockout?"

Erin turned to the mirror, and stopped breathing for a moment.

It wasn't that she looked all that different. She was still herself, but a glowing golden haze hovered around her. Her eyes seemed bigger, more deeply colored, more shadowy. Her lips were fuller and redder, her skin glowed with earthy golden tints. Even her hair seemed glossier.

The dress that Tamara had helped her choose was a simple gown of gleaming bronze bias-cut silk with a sheer chiffon overdress. It was tight in the bodice, fluttering out in a deep, voluptuously flared skirt. The plunging neckline was designed to show off both the torque and her cleavage. The dress was off the shoulder, so no bra could be worn, but the bodice was reinforced, and snug enough to hike up her full bosom, offering it up to the eye like a gift.

The dragon torque was cold against her skin, but she felt its strange, ancient energy pulsating against her skin. Her hair flowed around her, unbound. Tamara had brushed out her French twist and run her fingers through Erin's waist-length hair with a murmur of approval. "This doesn't need any help. You're done."

Erin stared at herself in the mirror. She felt vulnerable and exposed, with her femininity, her sexuality, showcased for an unknown man's enjoyment. The heavy, sensual gold torque seemed to exaggerate her looks. Maybe it was enchanted, and she was under a glamorous spell. Certainly she'd never looked like this in her entire life.

She'd been a fool to fall for this, but she'd agreed. It would be silly to be difficult about it now. Now that she thought about it, that had been her exact reasoning when she'd gone to bed with her first lover. She'd forced herself to endure what had happened out of politeness, out of fear of looking silly, of being rude and childish and undignified. She had to learn to accept the consequences of her decisions without whining—that was what it meant to be grown-up, but oh, God, sometimes she felt like she'd been grown-up since the day she was born.

"Are you all right, Erin?" Tamara asked gently.

Erin started to say that she was fine. The impulse petered away into silence. She closed her eyes and shook her head. When she opened them, they were swimming with tears.

Tamara was ready with a tissue. She carefully blotted Erin's tears without smearing her makeup, and rested a cool hand on Erin's shoulder. "At least you look fabulous," she offered. "That's a powerful weapon to carry into battle, no matter what problems you might have."

Erin let out a soggy laugh. They smiled at each other. Tamara embraced her briefly. "Are you ready to go? Do you need a minute?"

Erin straightened her shoulders. "I'm ready."

She wobbled on the spike heels until she found her stride. Five different sizes of designer shoes had been delivered along with the dresses. A staggering extravagance for a rich man's whim.

Tamara led her down the corridor, past the stairs and into another wing. She flung open the door into a huge, airy salon with floor to ceiling windows, many of them open. Diaphanous white curtains billowed in the breeze. The room was lit up with slanting golden beams of sunset light. Erin was dazzled by the sensation of light and vaulted space as she followed Tamara in.

And of cold. The room was oddly chilly. As if it were refrigerated.

A slender man of medium height stood with his back to them, gazing out the window. He turned slowly as they entered. The gesture looked staged, like an ad for European luxury cars. She brushed the thought away as silly and unworthy.

Claude Mueller smiled. He was an attractive olive-skinned man, his dark hair cut severely short, and receding over his temples. His smile was dimpled and charming, and his eyes were electric blue, striking against his tanned skin. He wore a casually elegant dove gray linen suit.

"Mr. Mueller. At last, the elusive Ms. Riggs," Tamara announced.

He glided toward her, took her outstretched hand, and bowed over it. For a dreadful moment she was afraid he was going to kiss it, but he stopped short, his eyes flicking up as if he sensed her alarm.

"Ms. Riggs," he said. "Thank you for humoring me in the matter of the torque, and the dress. I know it was a great deal to ask of you, but the result is breathtaking. Nigel and Tamara told me you were beautiful, but words are insufficient. You put the torque to shame."

He gazed into her eyes, lifted her hand, and pressed it deliberately against his smiling lips. The contact gave her a sharp, buzzing shock. For a split second, it was as if a veil before her eyes became transparent, and the luxurious room seemed as cold and hard as an ice sculpture, leached of color and life. She tugged at her trembling hand.

He did not release it. "Thank you, Tamara," he said, still holding Erin's gaze. "You may leave us now."

Erin felt abandoned as the door shut behind Tamara. The woman was her last link to the warm world of the living, and now she was all alone, in a cold, beautiful tomb. What a ridiculous notion, she told herself. Absurd. She had to get a grip, but her heart raced with sickening panic. She had that falling away feeling, as if she were about to faint. God forbid. She would never recover from the embarrassment.

She forced herself to smile, and thought about Connor.

Thinking about him hurt, but the pain grounded her. The part of her that was bonded with him was earthy and elemental, rooted in her deepest feelings. She clung to it, and the rising swirl of panic subsided.

"I'm glad to meet you at last," she said. "Thank you for the privilege of wearing such a beautiful thing. I'll treasure the memory."

"The dragon torque will remember you, too. Since I began collecting artifacts, I've begun to think that they, too, have memories of where they once were. Of the people who used them. The torque is eager to lie against the bosom of a beautiful woman again. To warm itself with her vital heat, after millennia of isolation in a tomb."

She had absolutely nothing to say to that. Her mind had gone blank. She stared stupidly into his hypnotic eyes, her mouth working.

She finally managed to break eye contact, and groped randomly for something, anything, to say. "Um, I'm really sorry, but I haven't had time to complete my report on the pieces I examined in Silver Fork," she said. "I've had some pressing personal difficulties, so I—"

"It's just as well," he cut in smoothly. "I have another three items for you to assess anyway. You may as well include them in the report."

Her mind seized gratefully onto the thought of a job to do. "Do you want me to look at them now? I don't have my tape recorder, or my—"

"No, thank you. The pieces will not be delivered until tomorrow afternoon. I'm afraid you must return, my dear. Tomorrow at five o'clock, if that is convenient for you."

Her head jerked, like a puppet on a string. "That's fine," she said. "But . . . then why did you invite me here tonight?"

He lifted his shoulders, smiling. "Tonight is not for work," he said. "Tonight is for the pleasure of getting acquainted, exploring our common ground. May I get you a drink? A glass of champagne?"

The hypnotized marionette who had taken over her body jerked her head up and down in assent. She didn't even like champagne.

Mueller poured the bubbling liquid into a crystal flute and handed it to her. "I wished to secure as much of your time as possible before I go back to Paris. I leave day after tomorrow. Managing a fund the size of the Quicksilver is a tyrannical undertaking. One becomes a slave to it."

She sipped her champagne and thought of her own devastated bank account. "I wouldn't know about that," she muttered.

His eyes flashed at the hint of irony in her voice. "Did that strike you as a tactless comment, Ms. Riggs?"

"Not at all. And please call me Erin," she said politely.

"Then you must call me Claude. I speak freely of money because I have reason to believe that your financial difficulties are at an end."

"Oh." She had never met anyone who made her feel so empty-headed. She'd been tongue-tied with Connor, but there had always been millions of things she wanted to say to him. A lifetime of things.

With Mueller, her mind felt wiped clean. As if a voracious computer virus were eating everything on the hard drive of her brain.

"Have you given any thought to my offer regarding the Huppert?"

That, at least, was something she was clear about. "Yes, as a matter of fact, I have," she said. "I'm afraid I have to decline."

She watched the bubbles rise as she waited for his reaction, until curiosity compelled her to look up at him again.

He was half-smiling, as if she amused him. "May I ask how you came to this decision?" he inquired.

She set her champagne glass down. She was shivering in the chilly room, and all too aware of the effect that had upon her nipples, covered only by a fragile layer of silk and chiffon. "I can't bear the falseness," she admitted. "I know I'm being childish. I'll find it everywhere I turn, in every work environment. But I can't go back there and pretend everything's fine when it's rotten inside. I won't do it. Not for anyone. Not for any sum of money."

He chuckled, and poured himself a glass of champagne. He lifted it to her in a silent, smiling toast, and took a sip.

She was bewildered. "What? Did I say something funny?"

"Not at all," he said. "You said exactly what I hoped you would say. This was a test, Erin. A test that you have passed."

She shivered, and wrapped her arms around herself tightly.

"So you've just been playing with me? Is this all a game to you?"

He sipped his champagne, regarding her keenly over the rim of his glass. "No. The offer was a real one. But I was wondering if you would refuse it on principle. I wanted to see what you were made of. Only if you passed this test would you know what lay beyond the initial offer."

She reached for her glass, and took a gulp, coughing as the bubbles burned down her throat. The torque felt as heavy around her neck as a hangman's noose. "And what does lie beyond it?" she asked.

His lips curved. "An infinity of other possibilities. If you have the courage to embrace them."

"Please be more clear and direct." She'd grown accustomed to Connor's blunt honesty. She had no patience for talking in circles.

"Very well," he said. "Come to Paris with me."

She almost dropped her glass. His hand flashed out and steadied it, his fingers closing over hers. The delicate stem wobbled. Bright drops of liquid splashed out onto his hand, glittering like gems.

He lifted his hand to his lips and licked the drops away.

The calculated sensuality of the gesture repelled her. The room felt glacial, the billowing curtains were ghosts that fluttered around her, wringing their hands in frantic warning. She could almost hear their voices, whispering in her head.

"Paris?" she whispered.

He nodded. "Yes. I did not plan this. I am not an impulsive man by nature. But now that I have seen you, I have never been so serious in my life. Come to Paris with me, Erin."

Erin took a cautious step back. "Ah . . . and do what?"

This panic was so silly. Men flirted with her on a regular basis. Not as extravagantly as this, perhaps, but it was not an unknown occurrence in her life. And yet she wanted to turn and run. She wanted to cover up that plunging neckline that exposed her chest, her breasts, her heart to his gaze. She wanted a woolen greatcoat, a suit of chain mail. A six-foot reinforced concrete wall. Claude Mueller scared her. There was no earthly reason for it, but he scared her to death.

"And do what?" he repeated softly. "Ah, we'll discover that as we go. Some things can't be planned. They must be lived, in the ever-changing flow of the moment. But we have so much in common, Erin. I, too, have been wounded by falseness. I am repelled by what is venal and rotten. I am intrigued by your refusal to compromise. I am moved by authenticity. I sense it in you. I know how rare it is. I crave it. Like a drug."

She forced her mouth to close, forced herself to swallow. "You don't know me," she said stiffly. "You don't know anything about me."

He reached out his hand, and traced the sensual outline of the dragon torque. His forefinger was very cold against her skin. "I know all I need to know," he said.

She forced herself not to recoil, not to be abrupt and rude, but Connor's face blazed in her mind as she stared down at Mueller's hand against her body. The love in Connor's eyes the night before, when he had kissed her hands and offered her his heart.

Her perception shifted, and she saw herself, a tiny, lonely figure standing on a wind-whipped arctic ice floe that bobbed in dark, icy cold sea water. She was dressed only in the fragile golden gown. The icy white sky above was reflected in Claude Mueller's hungry eyes.

She thought of Novak.

No. Enough of that. Novak was dead, far away in Europe. Nick had said so. It was confirmed. Besides, this man did not look anything like the pictures she'd seen of Kurt Novak. This man was dark-haired, blue-eyed, with two normal hands, a different face. She would not be sucked into a paranoid fantasy. She refused to be controlled by irrational fear.

Follow your heart, her mother had said. In this frozen, arctic landscape, her heart was all she had to follow. Everything else was hidden by cold, blinding light. She thought of her heart. Her warm, red, beating heart, which could not be commanded or fooled. Her heart, which had made its immutable choice years ago: Connor.

She put her glass down and gave in to the impulse to raise her hands to her bosom, shielding her vulnerable heart from his gaze. "I'm, ah, very flattered by your interest, but I'm not free."

His face hardened. "You refer to the gentleman who accompanied you to Silver Fork? Tamara and Nigel described the scene to me. I was sorry to have missed it. McCloud is his name, no?"

She nodded.

"My timing is wretched." He turned and set his glass down sharply on the table behind him. "You were not yet involved with him when you came to Santa Fe, correct? Or San Diego?"

"No," she admitted.

"No. Of course not." He dug his hands into his trouser pockets, his back still turned to her. "From what Nigel and Tamara said, it does not sound as if you were made for each other. Mr. McCloud mistrusts the quality in you that I would treasure the most. You are tragically wasted on a man like him."

She drifted slowly, imperceptibly away from him on her bobbing ice floe. "You are entitled to your opinion," she said.

He gave her a small, self-deprecating smile. "Forgive me. I take it back. I had no right."

"It's all right," she murmured.

He stepped forward impulsively and seized her hand. "Forget it. And forget my offer, if it makes you uneasy. Dine with me, Erin. We will talk of beauty and authenticity in a squalid world. A meeting of minds on a higher plane. It will be our secret, my dear. Your nervous, jealous gentleman friend need never know."

His words pulled it all into focus. Mueller was driving a wedge between the two of them, widening the gap that was already there. She could feel Connor's fear and longing, reaching out across space, tugging at her. The tug unraveled her unnatural calm. Black dots danced in her eyes. Her heart raced wildly.

She had to find Connor. Right now. This minute. She jerked her hand out of Mueller's grip. She didn't give a damn if she seemed abrupt, or rude or childish. She had to get the hell out of here and find Connor.

"I'm sorry." She backed away. "I can't. I have to go. Right now."

His eyes narrowed to cold blue slits. "So soon?"

"I have to go," she repeated. "Sorry. Really. I don't mean to be rude. I'll come back tomorrow to look at your new pieces if you like—"

"How kind." His voice was heavy with irony. "It would seem to be the least that you can do."

She rushed out of the room and down the corridor, running on the balls of her feet so that the heels would not trip her. Tamara looked up from the foot of the stairs, alarmed. "Erin? Are you all right?"

"I need my purse. I need my clothes. I need a cab. Please, Tamara. Help me. I have to get out of here," she said desperately. "This minute."

Tamara lifted a device strapped to her wrist, and pressed a button. "Silvio? A car for Ms. Riggs out front immediately, please."

She looked back up at Erin, frowning in concern. "Silvio will take you anywhere you wish to go. I'll get your things. Wait just a moment."

They were, in fact, only moments, but they felt like hours. Erin seized her clothes, shoes, and purse from Tamara and backed toward the entrance. "I'm sorry, but I can't take the time to change," she babbled. "I'll bring the dress back tomorrow when I come to assess the other—"

"The dress is yours, Erin."

"Heavens, no. I can't possibly accept it. I have to—oh, dear God. I almost forgot. Please, take this thing away." She pried the torque off her neck and handed the thing to Tamara. Immediately she could breathe more easily. "I'm sorry, Tamara. I don't know what's come over me. I feel like—like I'm out of my mind."

Tamara's eyes were somber. "Go, then. The car is waiting."

Erin got in and gasped out her address to the driver. She could not wait to get out of this hellish dress. She could not wait to call Connor, to hear his voice, assure herself that he was all right.

She needed it with a frantic desperation that felt almost crazy. If he was crazy, too, then fine and good. It meant they were a matched pair.

Tamara watched the taillights disappear into the dusk, and then continued to stare, her eyes straining in the gloom, but for what she was not sure. Something about that girl moved her. She would like to help Erin Riggs, if she could, but she was no longer sure if she could even help herself. If there ever had been a chance to change her mind and run, it was long past. She was alone in a boat with no oar, a wild current pulling her toward a huge waterfall. She could almost hear its thundering roar, almost feel the cold, white, foaming water, the blinding force. The sharp rocks that awaited her at its foot like teeth.

The quality of the air changed, chilly currents swirling around her as her employer joined her on the steps. He pulled his maimed hand out of his pocket and touched her face. He had taken off the prosthetic, as he always did when they were alone together and he wanted to touch her. He moved his hand until the thumb and the one entire middle finger that remained encircled her throat, pushing aside the high Chinese collar of the satin dress she'd chosen to hide the bruises on her throat. The tip of his finger found her pulse, felt it quicken. Danger had always been her most potent aphrodisiac, but this quickening no longer resembled sexual excitement. This had passed far beyond. Deep into the toxic, barren wasteland of pure fear.

"Everything is in place, of course." It was not a question. If the answer had been no, her life would already be forfeit.

She nodded. "The transponder on McCloud's car shows it parked in a garage near her apartment building. He's waiting for her there."

"And she left wearing the gown. Costumed for high drama. A special bonus. Delicious. This episode should be even more piquant than I had imagined. Do you care to watch the show with me?"

She heard the implacable command beneath the polite phrasing. "Of course," she murmured. "How could I resist?"

How indeed. Voices inside the barricaded part of her howled with bitter amusement. She'd been asking herself that question all week.

"Come," he said. He removed his hand from her throat, and gestured for her to precede him down the corridor to the viewing room.

He never turned his back on her, never. It was uncanny. He must sense that she wanted to kill him, and yet he had confided all his most perilous secrets to her. She wondered why he hadn't killed her yet.

Maybe he was saving her for something special.

They entered the viewing room, with its huge wall screen. Novak sat on the couch before it, on the side with the mouse pad, and clicked on the icons until the dim, silent interior of Erin Riggs's tiny apartment filled the screen. "It's almost a waste," he mused.

"What's a waste?" She was quick to give him openings to hold forth. He loved the sound of his own voice.

"She's rare. So genuinely innocent. I'm surprised that a

worthless specimen such as Edward Riggs ever managed to spawn such an unusual daughter. More beautiful than I had expected, too, though I expect that is partly the result of your genius, my dear."

"I try to be useful," she said.

"Do you?" he said. "Come here, Tamara. Be useful."

She sat next to him. "She's very intelligent. She senses a trap."

"But she doesn't recognize the source of her panic," her employee said. "She doesn't trust her instincts. She is ruled by her own code of conduct. She persists in thinking that the world follows rules that she can understand, and therefore, she'll be back tomorrow, right on time, like the conscientious professional that she is. If she were free of the prison in her mind, she would change her name and run."

"But it wouldn't do any good," Tamara said, to flatter him.

He smiled as he touched her face with his ruined index finger. His teeth seemed incredibly sharp. "I'm tempted to take her to Paris for real," he said. His hand trailed lower, touching her throat, her breasts. "I would like to have sex with her. It would be stimulating, I think, to plunder all that radiant, sensual innocence."

He seized her hand, placed it on the bulge in his trousers. She forced herself to smile. She was in for it now. Erin had aroused his most sadistic instincts. She hastened to divert him.

"She never would have gone with you willingly," she said. "She's already bonded with McCloud. You would've had to lure her before their affair caught fire. And once she saw your hand . . ." Her voice trailed off. Sometimes her employee appreciated honesty. In other moods, it could be a deadly miscalculation.

"You are right," he said. "We're committed to this course of action. It would be a shame to waste all this planning, anyway. Every detail is falling into place. Even the ones I did not anticipate. The sacrifice is acceptable in the eyes of the gods."

"I don't believe in gods," Tamara said boldly. "Any gods."

His eyes pinned her, like a snake mesmerizing its prey. Their luminous glow probed ceaselessly for weaknesses, secrets.

"No? What a treasure you are. A woman who is not afraid of anything. Not even fear." He pulled out a pocketknife from his trousers. The blade whicked out. He lifted the gleaming point to her larynx, and pressed. If she swallowed, it would break the skin.

The blade moved down, feather light. The dark, lapis-colored satin of her dress silently gave way to the preternatural sharpness of the blade. Her body was naked beneath it, only a pair of high, lace-topped black stockings. She wore no panties. She never did. On principle.

She closed her eyes and held herself still as the blade skimmed over her skin, tracing patterns like letters, but an unspeakably alien script. An evil enchantment, to pull her deeper into his thrall.

The blade grazed over her chest, pausing over her racing heart as if drawn to its frantic energy. It trailed lower, over the vulnerable hollow of her belly. He dug the tip into her navel, but she dared not gasp from the pain. One breath, and it would sink into her vitals.

He drew the knife lower, tickling it over her hipbone. The point dug into the skin over the femoral artery in her groin. It brushed tenderly over her mound. "Open your legs, Tamara." His voice was silky soft.

She couldn't move. She was transfixed with terror. She'd gone too far, missed her chance, overshot, fallen short. What an ignominious end. She, who had always hoped for a bold, glorious death.

The level of light in the room suddenly augmented. The video screen flickered into motion. Erin was home. The show had begun.

She gestured toward the screen. "Don't you want to watch?"

He snapped the blade shut, slipped it into his pocket. A reprieve.

"We watch, Tamara," he said. "And then we play."

She barely saw what was happening on the screen, she was so conscious of his mangled hand, burning against her naked thigh.

Chapter

22

Erin burst through the doors of the Kinsdale and bolted for the stairwell. As soon as she'd torn off that hellish dress and showered off the soiled feeling that Mueller's touch had given her, she would call Connor and apologize for running away. She had to start following her heart. It was that, or watch it break into a million pieces.

Connor was sitting on the staircase, waiting for her.

She reeled back at the foot of the stairs. Her purse, her shoes, her clothes, thudded to the floor. She teetered on the heels and braced herself against the wall, horribly aware of her bosom practically falling out of the bodice, and her eyes, smudged from the tears she'd been blotting away in the car. "Connor?" she whispered.

His hard gaze raked her from head to foot. "My, my," he said softly. "Don't . . . you . . . look . . . special."

"Connor, I—"

"Check you out, babe." He rose to his feet, looming over her. "No bra. And I've never seen you wear makeup before, at least not like that. It changes your whole look. Wow. What a wild woman."

She shrank back against the wall at his soft, deadly tone.

She'd seen him angry, but never like this. "Connor, I was on my way to—"

"What does it say to me, this new look?" His voice was a mocking parody of playfulness. "It says, the party's over and I've had too much champagne, so take me home and fuck me hard."

Anger jolted her upright. "Don't you dare speak to me like that!"

He advanced upon her. She stumbled away until her bare back was pressed against the tiles. "Did you have fun today, Erin?" he asked.

She lifted her chin. "No, I did not, as a matter of fact," she said. "Connor, don't do this."

He seized her shoulders and pinned her against the wall. "Where the *fuck* did that dress come from?"

The fury in his voice snapped like a whip against her raw nerves. She struggled wildly in his grip, but he just pressed her harder against the wall with his lower body and cupped her breasts in his hands. "This thing shows your tits off to a really great advantage. Did Mueller like the view? Is this what you meant when you said you were a bad girl now?"

She slapped his hands away from her breasts. "Don't speak to me like that! I did absolutely nothing wrong."

"You lied to me, and you broke your promise. And you're dressed up like a high-priced whore to kiss some rich man's ass. Did you fuck him, too?"

Her hand flashed out. He caught it, lightning quick. "None of that, Erin," he snarled. "It's a valid question. Just look at yourself."

"I would never do a thing like that, and you damn well know it. You owe me an apology."

He let out a crack of bitter laughter. "Don't hold your breath. I've had a really shitty day. I don't feel very apologetic right now."

"Erin? Is that you, dear?"

Their heads jerked around in tandem. Mrs. Hathaway, her

nosy ground-floor neighbor, was hunched over her cane in the doorway of the stairwell. Her curls glowed in the fluorescent light like a violet halo, and her face was a fierce snarl of wrinkles. She brandished her gold-tipped cane. "Is this fellow giving you trouble? Because if he is, I'll just call the police this minute! Terrorizing a young lady on her stairs. The nerve!"

Connor's eyes were fierce with challenge. "So, Erin? Am I too scary for you? You want to call the guys in the white coats to come haul me away?"

"Stop it," she hissed.

"Better yet, take this." He pulled out his cell phone and punched in a number. He pressed it into her trembling hand. "Call Nick. It's faster than nine-one-one, and he's hot to arrest me anyway. Go on, call him. Put a stop to this whole fucking mess once and for all."

Her mouth hung open, aghast. He jerked his chin at the phone and took a step back. His Adam's apple bobbed. "Do it," he said savagely. "Just push the green button and make it end."

The bleak, tight mask of hurt on his face made her heart twist and burn. She snapped the phone shut. "Go to hell," she said.

"You tell him, missy," Mrs. Hathaway said. "I say call the cops."

Erin tried to smile at her. "Don't worry, Mrs. Hathaway. We're just having a disagreement, and we had the bad taste to have it in public instead of in private."

"He's trouble," Mrs. Hathaway warned. "I can tell."

"I have the situation under control," Erin soothed. "But I really appreciate your concern. You're a good neighbor."

Mrs. Hathaway looked disappointed. She rounded on Connor. "I don't like your kind." She punctuated every word with a vicious stab of her cane in Connor's direction. "That long hair and those dangerous eyes, and that filthy dirty mouth on you. Swearing like a stevedore in front of a nice young lady. Men like you are pure trouble and nothing but."

"Yes, ma'am," Connor said patiently. "That's what they tell me."

"Think you're so smart, hmm?"

Connor rolled his eyes. "Hardly," he muttered.

She jabbed her cane toward Erin. "You watch yourself, missy. He mouths off to you again, you let me know. Don't you ever let a man swear at you. They just think it's a license to take liberties. Every time."

"Don't worry," Erin said again. "Really. Have a nice evening."

Mrs. Hathaway stumped back toward her open apartment door, muttering. They waited until the door had shut on the flickering blue TV light and the canned laughter before they dared to look at each other. She held out the phone to him. He shook his head.

"Keep it," he said. "I don't want to talk to anybody."

She dropped it into her purse, for lack of anything better to do with it. They stared at each other warily, both afraid to breathe.

"Want to take this fight upstairs and have it in the privacy of your apartment?" His voice was still hard, but the terrifying edge of his fury was blunted.

She nodded, and knelt down to gather her things up against her chest. Her clumsy fingers kept dropping things. Six flights were a long journey with Connor seething behind her. She felt his gaze burning into her back. Staring up at her body in that insubstantial dress.

She fished her keys out of her purse. As usual, he took them from her and pulled out his gun. She waited patiently through the whole familiar ritual until he waved her in, and locked and bolted the door.

She flipped her floor lamp on as he shrugged off his coat, flung it over a chair. He planted his feet wide and folded his arms over his chest. "So?" His voice was flat. "Let's hear it, Erin."

She dropped her things on the floor. Covered her breasts

with her arms, and dropped them again, in an agony of embarrassment. She gathered up handfuls of her skirt and searched for a starting place.

"When I got to Mueller's place, Tamara met me at the door," she began. "She showed me a Celtic gold torque, in the shape of two fighting dragons. A new acquisition. Extremely beautiful."

He nodded for her to continue. "OK. And?"

"Mueller had requested that I model it for him. I tried to excuse my way out of it, told her I was dressed wrong. She said they had already ordered several gowns to set off the torque for me to choose from. She pressured me and . . . and so I—"

"And so you did it. You took off your clothes in that man's house and put on a dress that he bought for you." Fiercely controlled anger vibrated through his words. "Jesus, Erin. What were you thinking?"

She squeezed her eyes shut against his gaze. "I wasn't," she admitted. "I wish I hadn't done it. It was embarrassing and awful, and I will never, ever do anything so stupid again in my life, I promise. Please don't make such a big thing of it, Connor. It's just . . . a dress."

He seized her upper arms, so suddenly that she gasped in alarm, and pulled her over to the standing mirror, the only antique piece that she had allowed herself in the tiny apartment. The rosy light from the basket lampshade painted her body with garish reddish streaks of light and shadow. His arm beneath her breasts pulled the décolletage lower, so that the aureoles of her nipples peeped over it. Her lips were stained red with Tamara's cosmetics. Her eyes looked huge and frightened.

Connor stared at her in the mirror. His eyes were dilated with dark fascination. "Look at yourself," he said. "Maybe this is just a dress on some other woman, but not on your body. On you, it's something straight out of a hard-core wet dream." He pressed his erection against her bottom. "Last night you said you were my woman." His low voice took on a soft, hypnotic quality. "This morning you said it again. Did you mean it? Or were you lying to me?"

"I meant it." Her voice was very small.

He slid his hands down and gripped her waist. "Then I'm going to keep this real simple. We'll just forget our many other complicated issues, and concentrate on basic ground rules. Things that I thought should be obvious."

"Connor, you don't have to—"

"It is not OK with me that my woman should go to a strange man's private home unaccompanied," he said. "It is not OK with me that she should model priceless ancient jewelry for his enjoyment. And it is really, *really* not OK with me that she should strip naked in his house, paint her face, and put on sexy clothes that this other man bought for her. A man makes that kind of move when he means to fuck you, Erin. A woman agrees to it when she's willing."

She shook her head. "It wasn't like that. I'd never even met the man, Connor, and I—"

"Bullshit it wasn't. Are you telling me that he didn't come onto you? In that dress? The way you look? Because I'll never believe it."

She hesitated, and licked her dry, trembling lips. "He didn't force himself on me," she said cautiously.

That wild, scary look began to burn in his eyes again. His fingers dug painfully into her waist. "Ah. Now there's a nice distinction for me to chew on," he said. "What did he offer for your favors, sweetheart? Ropes of pearls? Paris by moonlight?"

She gulped at the fiendish, pinpoint accuracy of his guess. He felt it, and yanked her back against him, hard and possessive. "Shit," he hissed. "He did. Didn't he? That fucking bastard. He actually did!"

"Don't," she pleaded. "It doesn't matter anyway, since I refused."

"Ah. That's comforting. Must have confused the hell out of the poor guy. Talk about mixed signals."

She shoved against his implacable grip. "Be reasonable," she snapped. "That's enough of this macho power trip, please."

"Oh, I have not even begun the macho power trip yet, babe," he said. "This is all just the buildup." He cupped her breasts, tugging the fabric down until her taut brown nipples peeked out.

His skillful fingers caressed her breasts, and his unexpected gentleness made her vibrate with startled pleasure. She flung her head back, shivering. Completely unprepared for him to seize the neckline of the dress and tear it straight down the front with one vicious wrench.

She cried out. He held her struggling body fast, and ripped it again, baring her breasts. Another rending rip, and her belly was bare. She twisted against him, frantic. "Good God, Connor! What are you doing?"

He wrenched until the dress gave way around her waist. "This is called nonverbal communication. I want you to understand how strongly I feel about this. I want you to take me very, very seriously."

"I get the message, for heaven's sake! There's no need to—"

"I also want to make absolutely sure that you will never wear this goddamn thing. Ever again. I want"—he tore the skirt wide open—"to be dead certain." He let the ruined thing drop to the ground around her feet and stared at the black lace thong, the thigh-high sheer black stockings. The spike-heeled black shoes.

He plucked at the sheer lace of the panties. "You don't have lingerie like that in your underwear drawer, Erin," he said. "You haven't been a bad girl for long enough. This is Mueller's stuff. Right?"

She pressed her quivering lips together. "I was wearing regular old cotton briefs when I went. Panty lines. A huge fashion don't. Tamara had ordered these for me, along with the dresses, and the stockings. And . . . the shoes." She braced herself for another explosion.

It didn't come. She opened her eyes. He was staring at her body.

"Take them off," he said. He let go of her, and stepped back.

She slid her fingers beneath the strip of lace, tugged it slowly down over her hips, and let it drop to join the discarded heap of golden fabric.

"Just look at you," he said hoarsely. "I want to fuck you right now. With the stockings and the shoes and the slutty makeup. Turn around, Erin. Slowly. Give me the full treatment."

Her heart quickened, her breath along with it, with primal female caution. Her body responded to his hunger, no matter how volatile the brew of passion was tonight: a wild alchemy of lust and possessive fury. She wanted to drink deep of that dangerous potion. No matter the cost.

She straightened her spine, and turned around for him.

She lifted up her hair over her head, arched her back so that her breasts jutted out. She spun on the balls of her feet in the fragile, sexy shoes, undulating for him. She flung her hair back so that the ends of it tickled her bottom. The air she moved through felt as thick as honey.

Connor unbuckled his belt. He wrenched the buttons of his jeans open and pulled his stiff, flushed penis loose of the constricting fabric. "Come here," he said.

Challenge followed escalating challenge. The feverish glow in his eyes sharpened the liquid ache of yearning that started between her thighs, rippling down her legs, up into her belly, her chest. Taking him in her mouth had always made her feel powerful. She started to sink to her knees, but he grabbed her shoulders.

"Wait." He shifted back so that his thick boots were planted squarely in the middle of the heap of torn golden fabric, and pulled her toward him. "Kneel on top of this dress. And suck on my cock."

Startled alarm jolted her out of her sensual dream. "Good Lord, Connor. What are you trying to prove by—"

"You know damn well. Me and my macho power trips."

He shoved her down in front of him. The fabric was slippery and insubstantial between her knees and the cold, scarred linoleum. His penis jutted in her face, his hands dug into her hair. Protests formed and dissolved in her mind as she looked up into his ruthless face.

She'd never taken him into her mouth in this position, him on his feet, her on her knees. She'd never imagined doing this when he was angry with her. This was going too far, beyond the realm of games. This threatened the shining tenderness and trust that they had forged together. He could push her past passion, into fear and shame.

She was scared of it. It was up to her to put her foot down, to make him stop, but this was too big to stop. Too strong.

"This is what I want, Erin," His soft voice challenged her. "Prove to me that you're my woman. Show me that you know that I'm your man."

"But you're angry," she said unsteadily. "You're—you're—"

"Furious," he agreed. "I'm so angry I think my dick is about to explode. Suck on me, Erin."

He pushed himself against her lips, made her taste his salty heat.

She was too aroused to resist him. She clutched his hips and drew his hot, smooth member deep into her mouth. She bathed him with hot, wet, suckling tenderness, with the swirl and flutter of her tongue.

She forgot the dress, forgot Mueller, forgot everything except this raw, elemental dance of lust and longing, and amazingly, she found her power over him again in his harsh, sobbing breaths, in the desperate way he thrust himself against her. She gripped him in her hands, exulted when she felt his climax gather, tighten, about to burst—

He flung his head back, gasping, and pulled her head away from his penis. The pulsations of the orgasm that he had denied himself throbbed heavily against her gripping, sliding hands.

She looked up at him. "Connor? Why—"

"No," he said. "I don't want to come yet. I want to fuck you first."

He jerked her up to her feet and dragged her close to him, sliding his hand beneath the curve of her bottom and into her cleft, seeking out the liquid excitement hidden there. "I won't force you if you don't want me," he said. "But I don't scare you, do I, Erin? You're sopping wet. I want to bend you over and fuck you hard. Do you want it?"

She had no words, no strength to resist this dark tide of passion. Her thighs clenched around his hand, silently begging for more.

"Oh, yeah." He set his teeth delicately against her throat and licked away the sheen of sweat on her skin. "I take that as a yes. Tell me if I'm wrong. Tell me quick, because in a few seconds it's going to be too late."

Her voice was locked in her throat. She craved his strength and passion, she craved the savage, conquering warrior behind his mask. She moved against his hand, seized his penis, and gave it a long, slow, swirling caress. A sensual demand he could not misunderstand.

That was all the answer he needed.

He exploded into movement. She spun through the dim room, dazzled by hot red streaks of light and darkness. Always before, her rustic basket lamp had struck her as homey and cozy. Now the effect was as voluptuous as an erotic dream set in a Victorian bordello.

He bent her over, shoving her face down onto the table. The teapot and the vase of dried flowers toppled, rolled, and shattered on the floor. The sugar bowl tipped and spilled sugar across the table. Scattered granules glinted in the reddish light like snow at sunset. Connor shoved her hair out of her face. She saw his shirt fly off behind him out of the corner of her eye. He thrust his legs between hers, kicked them open.

She was desperate for intimacy with him, but this incoherent, furious sexual energy separated them as much as it aroused them. The room was silent but for their harsh breathing. He pressed against her and thrust inside, too hard. It hurt, deep inside. She let out a sharp cry.

He stopped moving instantly. She hadn't softened enough yet for such a total invasion. Tension gripped her. An awful, shrinking fear that this could turn really bad. That he might punish her with his body.

He did not. He curved himself over her in mute, trembling apology and petted her, soothing her with his hands. His fingers silently begged her forgiveness as they slid around her hips and into her damp thatch, seeking her clitoris. They coaxed and sought her pleasure with tireless, tender persistence. When she relaxed and moved herself against him, he finally began to rock inside her, gliding in tender, careful thrusts.

He pressed his face against her throat, an animal gesture, nuzzling its mate. "You are so goddamn beautiful, Erin," he said roughly.

Her throat began to shake. His thrusts deepened. Tears wet her face, pressed hard against the spilled sugar on the table. Salt and sweet against her open, panting mouth. No matter how angry he was, he could not bear to hurt her.

Connor sucked in a deep breath, concentrating until the drum roll of impending ejaculation had receded. He didn't want this to finish quickly. He wanted it to be extremely memorable for her. He wanted to lay his claim, put his stamp on her, no matter how futile the effort.

He stared down at their joined bodies. His cock gleamed as it emerged from the slick, clinging recesses of her body. Her delicious scent was a humid, intoxicating cloud. Her flushed face was turned to the side, eyes squeezed shut, hair a dark tangle against the table. Her rosy buttocks quivered, and the tight folds of her cunt clasped around him. She was beautiful and red-hot, and she was his.

Goddamn it, she was *his*.

He'd started out with every intention of being hard and selfish with her, but it happened again, like it always did. She surrounded him with her heat and her scent and her softness, and bam, he'd already coalesced into one writhing entity, totally fused with her. Tuning into her feelings so he could find just the angle, just that perfect pressure that would stoke the hot glow deep inside her that he sensed, like a burning coal in his mind. The table rocked on its wobbly legs with every slap of flesh against flesh, with every gasping pant. She was dripping, whimpering, her sheath so softened that he could finally dare to let go, and fuck her as deep and hard as he longed to without hurting her.

She convulsed around him, wailing. The clutching pulses of her climax almost pulled him over the top with her, but he dragged himself back. Just barely. The table was about to collapse. He pulled her, stumbling, to the bed, and tumbled her facedown onto the quilt.

She rolled over to face him before he could pin her down from behind. Not good. He wanted to lose himself in pounding oblivion. What he absolutely did not want was for her to stare up into his face with those big dark eyes that saw so much, that stripped him bare.

Then he saw her hair tangled over the pillow, her plump breasts heaving, legs splayed open, cunt glistening. A sheen of sweat made her body gleam like a pearl in the red whorehouse light.

He trembled as he stared down at her. He'd never seen the point of kinky sex props and accoutrements before, but those black stockings, those fuck-me shoes, that smeared mascara, drove him out of his skull, like whips snapping at him, stinging him into a blind red chaos of lust and fury. The goddamn bed was too narrow to push her legs wide. He wrenched it away from the wall. He wrenched off his boots, his jeans.

He had no secrets, no masks with her anyway. He would

take her from the front, and to hell with what she saw in his face.

Connor's expression did not soften as he mounted her. She flinched and braced herself, grasping his shoulders. It was so different like this. None of the warmth and tenderness of last night. None of the joy. Just hunger and need and hard anger. It made her feel alone and desolate, even while he overwhelmed her with his big body.

She pressed her hands against his chest, feeling the muscles shift and move beneath the hot softness of his skin as his hips pumped heavily against her. "I don't want it like this between us," she said.

He bore her down under his weight, pinning her to the bed. "This is the way it has to be," he said. "I couldn't pretend to feel anything else tonight, even if I wanted to. Which I don't. What would be the point?"

"I'm not asking you to pretend," she said. "I'm asking you to trust me. I'm asking you to remember. Last night, you said that we—"

"Last night you hadn't lied to me and jerked me around. Last night you hadn't driven me out of my skull with jealousy. The world was real different last night, sweetheart." He folded her legs up high and thrust, hard enough to make her gasp. "And you were the one who changed things. Not me. So take responsibility."

His words kindled a spark of anger that glowed and flared brighter every second that passed. "I always take responsibility," she shot back. "Always. All my life. For every single goddamn thing. But this time, I won't do it." She slapped at his chest, and struggled beneath him. "This time, it's not my fault, Connor! This thing is *not . . . my . . . fault!*"

He grabbed her flailing wrists and gazed down at her with narrowed eyes. "So are you saying that it's my fault, then?"

"I don't know! I don't understand what's happening to us.

It's like we're under an evil spell. But I do know that I love you, Connor! I love you!" She grabbed his shoulders and pulled him down against her.

"Damn it. No. I don't want to—damn it, Erin!" He swore viciously and fought her, but she hung on to him with all her strength. He would have to hurt her to make her let go, and she knew he couldn't bear to.

She persisted, pulling on him until he collapsed on top of her with a harsh sob. He hid his face in the pillow and pumped himself against her, painfully hard. He let out a muffled shout. The paroxysm that wrenched through him seemed almost more like pain than pleasure.

His heart thundered against her bosom. She cradled his trembling, sweaty body and tried to pull his face to hers so she could kiss him.

He utterly refused to turn. He just shook his head and kept his face stubbornly buried in the pillow. She petted his damp hair, searching for words, but there were no words that could make the wall between them disappear. It felt as thick and cold and implacable as stone.

Connor finally pushed himself up and off her body, letting his hair veil his face. She knew that trick. She'd been using it all her life.

She reached to push his hair back. His hand flashed out and clamped over her wrist, blocking it. He shook his head, and let go.

He turned his back on her and started to pull on his jeans.

She stood up on unsteady legs, and realized that they hadn't used a condom. Scalding liquid trickled down her thigh.

She unbuckled the fragile, ridiculous shoes. Stripped off the ruined stockings. Her mind couldn't encompass it all. She could only handle little bits at a time. Connor's back to her, rigid with unspoken pain and fury. Mueller's icy attempt at seduction. Nick's revelations. Novak's death by fire. The golden dress, rent in two. Connor's seed, trickling down her thigh. The seams of her life had all burst.

She stumbled into her bathroom, and closed and locked the door.

Connor got dressed and waited, his head in his hands, for her to come out. It was a long wait. At one point, Erin's cat poked its head out cautiously from under one of the chairs. It picked its way daintily out into the middle of the ravaged room, sat down on its haunches, and regarded him. There was a cool, judgmental gleam in its golden eyes.

"Who the hell do you think you're looking at?" he asked it wearily.

The bathroom door finally opened. Erin walked out, still naked, but damp and smelling of her shower gel. Her face was severely innocent of makeup, her hair smoothed back into a tight, gleaming wet braid.

She headed to the chest of drawers next to the bed, pretending he wasn't right there, at arm's length, staring at her. She pulled out white cotton briefs that looked like they came three in a pack from Kmart. She pulled on a pair of baggy sweatpants. An oversized T-shirt. A fleece pullover. She tugged thick white athletic socks onto her feet.

She was trying to look sexless. What a joke. He would have laughed, but if he let himself laugh he might start to cry again, and he couldn't risk it. He waited until he could trust his voice to be steady.

"Nick called you this morning. That's why you broke your promise." He tried to make his tone neutral, but it came out accusatory anyway.

She nodded, and padded across the room to the kitchen nook. She rummaged in a drawer until she came up with a garbage bag.

"What did he tell you? That I'm crazy? Delusional?"

She struggled with the bag until it opened, and went to the table, still ignoring him. She scooped spilled sugar off the tabletop and into the bag with her hand. She gathered up the crushed dried flowers.

Tension built inside him. "Answer me, Erin. What did he tell you?"

She let out a long, shaky sigh, sank down onto her knees, and began to gather up the shards of the ceramic teapot and the vase. "He told me Novak was dead. That you knew that he'd been spotted in France. That the police there have been moving in on him for days."

"Sure, he told me, but I didn't believe it. Novak is—"

"Was. Novak *was*. He is dead, Connor. Blown up. They're sure it's him, based on dental records, the missing fingers. The DNA tests will follow, but they're just to confirm it. He's dead. It's over."

He shook his head. "No way. Too many things don't fit."

"That's what Nick told me you would say," Erin said.

He forced himself to say it, and the words came out rough and halting. "Did he tell you that I'm a murderer, too?"

"He said you were a suspect," she corrected. "Not a murderer."

"And do you think I did it?"

She shook her head, unhesitating. "Not in a million years."

She tossed all the broken crockery into the bag, and reached under the sink for a dustpan and whisk broom. Every gesture was brisk and efficient. Trying as always to make order out of chaos.

But this time, he was the chaos.

"What else did he tell you, Erin?" he demanded.

Erin dragged the plastic bag over to the ruined dress and stuffed it inside. "He told me I should keep my distance from you. So that I wouldn't get hurt. But surprise, surprise. I couldn't."

"I would never hurt you," he said.

"You already have." She dragged the clinking garbage bag behind her, and knelt in front of him, flinging the balled up stockings into it. She flung the shoes in after them, jerked the neck of the bag up, knotted it. "In any case, it's over. This whole bodyguard trip of yours, I mean. Try to see it from my point of view, Connor. I truly do believe that your intentions were good, but—"

"Do . . . not . . . pity . . . me." He bit the words out.

She threw her head back and dashed away angry tears with the back of her hand. "OK, fine. No pity, no mercy, no masks. I'm going back to Mueller's tomorrow to appraise some new acquisitions for him. Since we're being so pitiless and all, I thought you should know."

He was on his feet and clutching her shoulders in an instant. "No. Erin. You can't! You can't go back there!"

"Why not?" she yelled. "He's just a guy who likes Celtic relics! He also happens to be attracted to me. Big deal, Connor! This may come as a shock to you, but he's not the first man who has ever shown an interest in me. I've said no to quite a few men in my lifetime. Who cares? Get over it!" She wrenched herself out of his grip.

There was no reasoning with this breathless, clawing panic. This went beyond jealousy. This was flat-out nuts. "But I've seen things that I can't explain any other way," he pleaded. "Someone is stalking your family, Erin. I'm convinced of it, and if you would just—"

"No! I have had enough!" She backed away, holding up her hands. "I can't stand this anymore. I do not need your protection. I love you, and I appreciate what you did for Cindy, but I do not need you to save me! If you keep insisting on this, you're going to drive me crazy, too!"

Her words reverberated in the sudden silence. He saw from her face that she regretted them the instant they left her mouth. "Oh, God, Connor. I'm sorry. I didn't mean that you . . . I don't think you're—"

"Crazy," he said heavily. "Too late. You said it. I heard it. You can't take it back. If that's really what you think of me, then . . . then there's nothing more to say."

Tears slid down her face. She covered her mouth with her hands. Her shoulders shook. "Oh, God. This is awful."

"Yeah," he agreed. He grabbed his coat and tried to move towards the door. His feet were made of lead. "Uh, Erin."

"What?" Her voice was a wary thread of sound.

"If you ever have cared about me at all, do me one favor. Please."

She nodded.

"Take someone you trust with you when you go to Mueller's house. Don't go there alone. Please."

"Connor, please. I—"

"I know that you won't let me go with you, but take someone. Do this one thing for me, and that's it. That's all I'll ever ask of you."

She opened her mouth to argue, and closed it. She nodded.

"Swear it," he said. "On something important."

"I swear it on my honor," she said quietly.

He knew that was his cue, but he was still rooted to the floor.

She picked up her phone and dialed. "Hello, Tonia? It's Erin . . . yeah, I'm fine. It's been a very strange time . . . can't talk right now, though . . . no, just tired. Look, I have a favor to ask. Tomorrow's your day off, right? I was wondering if you would go along with me on a job tomorrow afternoon. To Mueller's . . . it's a long story. I promised Connor I wouldn't go alone . . . yes, I know, but I promised . . . Really? Oh, great. It shouldn't take long. I'll buy you dinner after, if you're free . . . See you tomorrow afternoon. You're an angel, Ton. Thanks. 'Bye, then."

She lay the phone down. "Done," she said. "As promised."

The silence after her words had a horrible, echoing finality to it.

She'd cut him loose. There was nothing left to say, nothing more that he could do. Maybe she was right, and he really had gone crazy.

He hardly cared. Ghosts, monsters, bring them on. He would welcome them, if they would only agree to put him out of his misery. In any case, he'd better get the hell out of there, to someplace where no one could see his face, because total meltdown was only seconds away.

"OK," he said. "I'll, uh, just get the fuck out of your way, then."

Chapter

23

"I can't tell you how much I appreciate this," Barbara said into the phone. "I'll be there first thing Monday. This is exactly what I needed."

"I'm sorry it's only a temporary position, Mrs. Riggs, while the office manager is out on maternity leave," Ann Marie said. "But you know the organization so well after all those years of volunteering. We'll all put our heads together and come up with something else when she comes back. Everyone will be so happy to see you. We've missed you."

"I've missed you all, too. See you next week, then. 'Bye, now!"

She hung up the phone, floating with relief. Things were moving again. Her girls were safe, that horrible Novak was burned to a crisp, and Billy Vega was dead too, thank goodness. She was shedding no tears for him. She wasn't having those awful spells, and Erin's life was shaping up nicely. All was looking orderly and positive.

The doorbell buzzed, and she peered out the peephole. Erin's pretty little nurse friend, Tonia. At this hour, on a weekday. How odd. She opened the door. "Hello there, Tonia."

"Hi, Mrs. Riggs. I hope I'm not disturbing you."

"Not at all," Barbara said. "Come on in. Let's make some tea. You're just in time to help me celebrate. I just got a job! I'm so excited."

"That's so fabulous," Tonia said. "Where?"

"The literacy center where I used to volunteer. It's just temporary, but it's perfect to start with. Their office manager is about to have a baby. It's been a while since I've done much typing, but I can practice on their computers after closing time. I'll catch on."

"That'll be so great for you." Tonia followed her into the kitchen. "Look, Mrs. Riggs, I can't stay long, but there was something I wanted to talk to you about. I'm meeting Erin later on this afternoon."

"Oh, really?" She filled the kettle and put it on the stove.

"Yes. Connor made her promise not to go to Mueller's home unaccompanied." Tonia rolled her eyes. "Silly, if you think of it. Not that I mind. But for heaven's sake. She is a grown-up, after all."

"Yes, Connor is very protective," Barbara said. And that suited her just fine, she thought privately. Protection looked very good to her right now. Particularly for her precious girls. She was all for it.

"That's what I wanted to talk to you about, Mrs. Riggs. Connor's protectiveness. If you can call it that."

The edge in Tonia's voice made Barbara uneasy. She finished rinsing the teapot and set it down. "Yes, dear? What about it?"

Tonia hesitated. "Connor makes me nervous," she blurted. "He's so jealous and possessive. He's even hostile and suspicious of me."

"Ah, I see," Barbara said cautiously.

Tonia's blood-red fingernails flashed as she gesticulated. "I've seen women get involved with men like that. That's always the first sign of trouble, when a guy cuts a woman off from her girlfriends. It's a classic technique of abusive, controlling men."

Barbara opened her mouth, but nothing came out.

"Family's the next step," Tonia went on. "Snip, snip, and voila, she's totally isolated and in his thrall. Then he gets to work breaking down her self-esteem. Making her think she's nothing without him."

"Oh, my goodness. Really, Tonia, I don't think that Connor—"

"The problem is, she's smitten with him, and I can see why. He's a very attractive man. Handsome, charismatic, compelling. And I mean that literally. Compelling, Mrs. Riggs. He thinks she belongs to him."

Barbara's spine stiffened. "Ah. I see. Well. If he thinks that, he is very, very wrong."

"And it makes me nervous, to think of how angry he must be at your husband," Tonia said. "Sorry to bring up a painful topic, but I'm sure you don't want Erin to pay the price for that."

"Oh, but Connor would never take that out on Erin," Barbara said faintly. "He seems to really care about her. That's the impression I got."

The teapot was whistling. Tonia smoothly shouldered her out of the way and seized the kettle. "Here, let me. Sure he cares about her." She poured boiling water into the teapot. "He's obsessed with her. Did you know that he practically kidnapped her at the airport last weekend?"

Barbara sank down into a chair and frowned, bewildered. "Erin told me he went with her, but she didn't say anything about—"

"She didn't tell you all of it, and I'm not surprised," Tonia said. "He just showed up at the Portland airport, where she was supposed to meet Mueller's limo driver. She never got the chance. Connor dragged her to his car, drove her to a motel, and . . . well, you see the results, hmm? He got exactly what he wanted, didn't he?"

Barbara stared at her, horrified. "Erin's such a sweetheart," she whispered. "She can't bear to disappoint anyone.

I hate to imagine, if she were all alone, and pressured by someone forceful and . . ."

"Compelling," Tonia supplied.

"Compelling." Barbara shuddered. "Oh, God. I hate to think of it."

"Exactly," Tonia said. "I see we're on the same wavelength, Mrs. Riggs. Maybe you should call around to other family members and friends, and Connor's former colleagues. Make everybody aware of the situation. Discreetly. Did you know that Connor has a family history of mental illness? His father. A sad, awful story. Paranoia, delusions, social alienation. He raised his sons up in the hills, in total isolation. No one knows for sure what happened to the mother."

"Dear God."

"Heaven only knows what that crazy man did to those poor boys," Tonia went on. "Or maybe it's better not to imagine."

"I was always nervous about his background, but I had no idea—oh, God. I have to talk to Erin. I have to call her. Right away."

"Be careful." Tonia poured Barbara a cup of tea. "She's under his spell. Don't be direct, or you'll just create resistance. We need to act quietly. Activate a support network for Erin. Soon. Like, right now."

"Yes, you are so right," Barbara said. "I'll get right on it. This instant. Thank goodness you told me this. I had no idea."

Tonia smiled broadly and raised her cup. She clinked it against the one Barbara held in her trembling hand. Barbara's cup wobbled, and tea splashed out onto the tablecloth. "Go, Mom," Tonia said. "Erin's lucky to have a mother like you."

Barbara thought of the last few months. Her mouth tightened. "Hardly," she said. "But I'll do my very best for her from now on."

The doorbell rang again. Her cup clattered into the saucer,

sloshing yet another brown wave of tea onto the table. "Who on earth?"

"I'll get it," Tonia offered. "You stay comfortable."

"No, that's all right."

Tonia followed right on Barbara's heels as she went to the door. Curious as a cat, that girl. Barbara had noticed that the first time she'd met her. She peered out the peephole. It was Connor's brother, Sean, and Cindy's strange-looking friend Miles, burdened with shopping bags.

She opened the door. Sean's grin coaxed an instant smile out of her. "Hi, Mrs. Riggs. I'm a taxi service for Miles, here," Sean said. "He was hoping to visit with Cindy. She doing OK?"

"Oh yes, she's much better, thank you," Barbara said. "She's upstairs. I'll call her. Come on in."

Miles's face was purpled with bruises, and he had a white bandage over the bridge of his nose. He was carrying a paper shopping bag full of videos, a saxophone case, and a big, dripping bunch of freshly picked wildflowers, mud dripping copiously from their roots. "I, uh, brought Cindy some stuff," he said. "*X-Files* videos, and flowers. And her sax. If she wants to, you know, like, practice." He held out the flowers to her.

Barbara smiled at him. "That's sweet, Miles. I'll call Cindy." She turned up the stairs. "Cindy? Hon? Come downstairs. You have guests!"

She turned back to Tonia. "Tonia, this is Connor's brother, Sean McCloud, and Cindy's friend, Miles. Sean, this young lady is Erin's friend, Tonia . . . I don't remember your last name, dear."

"Vasquez," Tonia said, sticking out her hand to Miles, and then Sean in turn. "I'm glad to meet you."

Sean held her hand for a moment, and his face went thoughtful. "Wait a minute. I know you."

Tonia dimpled. "Oh, no. I'm sure I would remember."

"No, really. I never forget a face. Particularly not a cute one. None of us McCloud guys can. It's a weird family trait. One of the many. Hold on . . . it's coming to me." He scowled up at the ceiling, snapping his fingers. "Bingo!" he exclaimed. "You're a nurse! At the clinic. Right?"

Tonia blinked at him, her mouth dangling open. It was the first time Barbara had ever seen her at a total loss.

"What clinic?" Barbara asked.

Sean shot her a wry glance. "The clinic where my brother spent two months in a coma, remember? That clinic."

Cindy saved her the embarrassment of a reply by appearing at the top of the stairs in a baggy sweatsuit, rubbing her fist in her reddened eyes like a little girl. She stumbled down the stairs, shy and hesitant.

"Miles brought you flowers," Barbara said. "Isn't that sweet?"

Cindy gave Miles a wan smile. "Thanks. They're really pretty."

Miles gazed up adoringly. "I, uh, brought you some, uh, other stuff, too," he stammered. "Some vids. Your sax. You know. Stuff."

"That's cool," Cindy said. "You want to come up to my room?"

"Uh, yeah, sure." He looked around at the rest of them. " 'Scuse me," he mumbled. He bolted up the stairs after Cindy.

Sean turned back to Tonia. "I know I saw you at the clinic a couple of times. That uniform actually looked good on you."

Tonia's laugh sounded forced. "Thanks. You have to forgive me for not remembering you. It was a long time ago."

"A year and two months," Sean said. "To be precise."

"I thought Erin said you worked at Highpoint," Barbara said.

"I do," Tonia said. "I'm sort of a butterfly. I flit from job to job. Well, um . . . I'd better be on my way. And that matter we discussed, Mrs. Riggs? Really, it's urgent. Get right on it, please."

"Oh, I will," Barbara said fervently. "Thanks for stopping by."

"Lovely to meet you," she called back over her shoulder. " 'Bye."

There was a long silence after Tonia left. Sean's green eyes were so much like his brother's. Bright, direct . . . compelling. Dark, fluttering panic threatened to unravel her. She steadied herself against the wall.

"Hey, Mrs. Riggs. Are you OK?"

How ironic, an offer of help from one of the few people on earth she could not share her problem with. "I'm fine, thanks."

"You sure? Can I help you out with anything? Anything at all."

The concern in his face made her feel ashamed for lying to him. She forced herself to smile. "Just dandy, and thanks for asking."

"OK, then. I'd better be on my way, too. Things to do. Glad that Cindy's doing better. You take care, now."

"Thank you, I will," she said.

Sean bounded down the walk and got into his mud-splattered Jeep. Barbara reset the alarm and stumbled back into the kitchen. She grabbed the cordless phone, sat down, and stared at it.

Both of her girls had been threatened by violent men. Erin six months ago by Novak and Luksch. Cindy by Billy Vega. And now her innocent, eager-to-please Erin had been swept off her feet by an unbalanced, controlling man with a family history of mental illness.

Her sweet girl who tried so hard, who deserved the very best.

It was unendurable. She was done with sitting around and doing nothing. It was up to her to protect her children, in any way she could think of. And Tonia's suggestion was a damn good place to start.

She dialed a number she had thought she would never dial again.

"Would you please beep Nick Ward for me?" she asked the switchboard operator. "It's urgent."

The slam of a car door jerked Connor out of his stupor. He twitched open the kitchen curtain to make sure it was one of his brothers. Not many people knew how to find the ramshackle, hand-built house out in the hills that Eamon had left to his sons, and the McCloud brothers liked it that way. It was a sure refuge from the weirdness of the world. Only their closest friends knew where it was.

It was Sean. This was going to be exhausting. He looked down at the bottle of Scotch on the table. His attempt to drown his sorrows in alcohol was as much of a failure as the rest of his life currently was. Instead of blunting emotions, like liquor was supposed to do, it had just blurred his capacity to think clearly. The emotions had partied right on.

He didn't need Sean to scold him for sulking. He was already scolding himself, but there wasn't enough oomph behind it to break his paralysis. The kitchen door creaked open. He didn't bother to turn.

Sean's distinctive smell wafted into the room. Expensive citrus aftershave and well-tended leather. God, his brother was vain. But he loved him, even when Sean drove him nuts. The whiskey was making him maudlin. He buried his face in his hands and braced himself.

"I've been looking for you all morning." Sean's tone was accusing.

"You found me," he replied.

Sean was silent for an unnaturally long time. "I went by your house. Did you know that you left it unlocked? It's not a bad neighborhood, but you did get robbed a few months ago, remember?"

He gestured carelessly with his scarred hand. "If somebody wants my stuff, they're welcome to it."

Sean made a sharp sound under his breath. "Oh, Christ, not again. What bug has crawled up your ass this time?"

"Leave me alone, Sean."

"I tried Erin's place, but no one was home. And I tried to call you, but the phone's off, of course. Why should today be any different."

"I gave the phone to Erin."

Sean sighed in frustration. "I don't know why you keep getting rid of them. You know we're just going to get you a new one."

Connor shrugged. "Where's your faithful sidekick?"

"Miles? I left him down in the city. He wanted to worship at Cindy's shrine. He's fried. It hurts my heart to see it." Sean circled the table, studying his brother. "Miles is a good guy," he went on. "I'm thinking of hiring him. He could deal with the techno-nerd side of my business, and leave me free for the fun stuff."

"Good idea." Connor tried to sound enthusiastic.

"I think so, too. Only condition is, I have to teach him how to fight."

Connor made a neutral sound.

"I know," Sean said. "It's going to be a job. His muscle tone is about on par with Puffy the Marshmallow Man." He pulled out a chair, sat down and waited. "Out with it."

Connor rubbed his stinging eyes. "Novak is dead, they say. Blown up yesterday. Someplace near Marseilles."

Sean tapped his fingers, waiting. "Am I missing something?" he asked. "Is that not what we were praying for? It that any reason to sit alone in the dark with a bottle of scotch?"

"It's great news for Erin and the rest of the world," he said wearily. "It's only bad news for me."

"Why?"

Connor winced at his brother's sharp tone. A headache was gathering like storm clouds in the back of his skull. "Because it means I'm seeing and hearing shit that's not there," he said. "I saw Georg on that highway. I heard Novak's voice on the telephone. Now Billy Vega gets beaten to death, my cane disappears out of the trunk of my car, and you know what? I've got this really scary feeling that it's going to turn up somewhere with Billy Vega's blood all over it. I am up shit creek without even a fucking boat, let alone a paddle. And they tell me Novak's dead. What do you say, Sean? What's wrong with this picture?"

Sean's face was rigid. "They can't pin Billy Vega on you. No way."

"Sure they can. If Novak's dead, I'm looking at several unpleasant possibilities. Brain damage from the head injury that they didn't notice before they cut me loose, that's the most appetizing of the lot. Worst case scenario? I've snapped. I really am going nuts. Like Dad."

"Don't say that." Sean's voice shook. "Don't even say the words. You are nothing like Dad. Nothing."

"Who knows? Maybe I did kill Billy and I don't remember doing it," Connor said wearily. "Anything's possible."

"You didn't even know his address, asshole!" Sean yelled. "We never told you! You were too busy dealing with your girlfriend's family!"

Connor shook his head. "Maybe if I'm lucky, I can plead insanity and end up in a padded cell instead of—oof!"

Sean grabbed him by his shirtfront, hauled him up off his chair and slammed him hard against the kitchen wall. Kevin's drawing of a waterfall fell to the floor. The glass in the frame shattered.

"That's not going to happen," Sean said.

Connor blinked into his younger brother's eyes, shocked out of his own despair by the stark fear he sensed behind

Sean's fury. He tried to put his arms around his brother. "Hey. Sean. Chill. It's not—"

"Don't you dare say that to me! Not after two months of hell when you were in the coma. I almost lost you, Con. I can't go through it again. Not after losing Kevin."

"OK, Sean," he soothed. "Let me loose. Relax."

"You are not crazy!" Sean's fist pressed painfully hard against Connor's windpipe. "You are just a depressed, melodramatic dickhead!"

"OK!" Connor yelled. "Whatever you say. I'm a dickhead. Stop strangling me. I don't want to have to hit you."

"Yeah, like you could get in a punch at me, in the state you're in. Listen, Con. Get this straight. Nobody's going to lock you up. Because if anybody tries to hurt you, I will kill them."

The bone-deep sincerity in Sean's voice chilled him. Connor dug his hands into his brother's spiky blond hair and cradled his head.

"No, Sean. You're not going to kill anybody, so don't talk like that. Calm down." He used the same mellow, hypnotic tone he and Davy had used to talk Sean down from his freakouts back when Sean had been a hyper little kid bouncing off the walls. "You're flying off the handle, buddy. You can't do this anymore. You're a grown-up now."

Sean let Connor drop from his tiptoes down onto his feet. His shoulders slumped. "I'm not going to say I'm sorry," he warned.

Connor rubbed his sore neck. "Too bad. I forgive you anyway. Snot-nosed punk."

"You provoked me. Talking like you don't care if they lock you up. Fuck you, Con. Maybe you don't care, but I do."

"I won't say it again," Connor said quietly. He retrieved the waterfall drawing, and picked shards of glass out of the frame. "I promise."

"I'm not just acting out to get attention, like the old days.

I'm dead serious. You, in a cage? Not an option. No way. You get my drift?"

"Sean, you can't talk like that. This isn't the Wild West—"

"Davy's going to feel the same way," Sean said. "Davy makes like he's Mr. Cool, but he'd slit the throat of anybody who hurt you. Without even blinking. So would Seth, for that matter."

Connor laid the picture down. "You're scaring me, Sean."

"I'm just telling you how it is. It's not just you alone on your white horse riding into the sunset, asshole. You get hurt, we get hurt. Got it?"

Connor nodded obediently and dropped into the chair. His knees were trembling. "Uh, you want a shot of whiskey? It'll mellow you out."

Sean frowned. "Things are too weird right now," he said. "We need to sharpen up, not chill out. I want coffee. You could use some, too, from the looks of you. And a shower, and a fresh shirt. You have a girlfriend now. You've got to make more of an effort."

The look on Connor's face made Sean freeze as he reached up for the coffeepot. His face tightened. "Oh, no. What's up with Erin?"

"Nothing," Connor muttered.

"What kind of nothing?" Sean persisted.

The memory of last night replayed in his mind in one cold, hard, sickening whoosh, like a punch to the gut.

"The bad kind," he admitted. "The worst kind."

Sean grabbed the coffeepot. "That sucks," he said grimly. "We're in for it now. What happened?"

Connor suppressed a sharp retort. Sean was on edge today, and he didn't have the energy to cope with another outburst. "Nick told her I was nuts. He told her I was a murder suspect. And she doesn't appreciate getting dragged into what she sees as a wacko paranoid fantasy. Christ, who could blame her. She's got enough problems."

Sean measured coffee into the espresso pot. He flipped on the gas and turned his hard gaze onto his brother. "So? That's it? End of story?"

Talking about it left a bitter, metallic taste in his mouth. "She told me to get lost, Sean. She thinks I'm mentally unbalanced."

"And that means you're going to give up? Just like that?"

Connor looked at him, and threw up his hands in silent eloquence.

Sean paced restlessly around the kitchen. "You know what, Con? I remember the night you first met that girl."

Connor knew his brother too well not to mistrust that light, casual tone. "Do you, now?" he said warily.

"I sure do. It wasn't long after you got recruited into the undercover unit. Back when you were still starry-eyed and heavy into the mystique of your new job. A year or so after Kevin was killed. Davy was just about to ship out for Desert Storm."

"Your memory is freaky," Connor commented.

"Yeah, just like yours, except that yours is selective. Let me finish my story. So you come back from dinner at Ed's house one night, all bug-eyed and quiet. And when I ragged you to find out what was up, you said, hey, leave me alone. It's a big day. I just met my future bride."

Connor went cold. "I said that?"

"Yeah, you said that," Sean said. "It knocked me on my ass. You said, Ed Riggs's daughter is so pretty, I can't even believe the stupid shit I said. Probably Riggs's wife thinks I'm a retard. Only problem is, she's seventeen years old."

"You're making this up," Connor said.

"Cross my heart," Sean said. "This scene is engraved in stone in my memory. So I say to you, You filthy perv. That's going to go over real good at your new job, lusting after your colleague's teenage daughter. And you know what you said to me?"

Connor braced himself. "What did I say?"

"You said, No problem, man. I'll wait for her." Sean glared at him.

"I said that?" Connor said numbly.

"Yeah! You said that! And I thought you were joking! But you weren't! You fucking weren't joking!"

The coffeepot began to gurgle and hiss, but Sean was locked in his indignant pose. Connor reached past him and shut off the gas. "Don't blow this all out of proportion," he muttered. "It's not like I kept myself pure for ten years, for God's sake."

"Oh, yes, you did." Sean put a sharp, vicious emphasis on every word. "Sure, you fucked some other women now and then, but that's as far as it went. Am I right? Answer me, goddamn it!"

Connor thought about all the times he'd gently broken things off whenever the woman he was seeing started talking about the future.

Ouch. Not much point in denying it. "Calm down, Sean," he said. "I don't have the energy for another big scene right now."

"Don't tell me to calm down! Don't tell me that you've dreamed about this girl for a decade, you save her from a fate worse than death, you survive her conniving asshole of a father, you rescue her sister from the Fuckhead, you win over the homicidal mother-in-law, you finagle your way into her bed, and you're giving up now?"

"She thinks I'm nuts, Sean!" Connor yelled.

"So convince her that you're not!" Sean bellowed back. "You are never going to be happy if you let this go, and I hate it! I can't stand to watch you waste away again!"

Their furious gazes locked. Connor was the first to look away. "I've got to make sure I'm not crazy for real before I get near her again," he said heavily. "I've created enough chaos in her life. I don't want to pile something like that on her shoulders, too. That would be cruel."

Sean's mouth tightened. He poured the coffee and handed

Connor a cup. "Weren't you with Erin when Vega got whacked?"

"No. I was with her until around five A.M. Then I sneaked outside."

"Why the hell did you do that?" Sean demanded.

"I was afraid of her mother," Connor admitted. "You saw that Jag. Can you blame me? I came back in around eight for breakfast."

Sean stared out the window, scowling. "Can't she just say you were with her? What does it matter, if you're innocent anyway?"

"I'm sure she would, if I asked her to," Connor said softly. "But it wouldn't be right. I don't want anything with her that's built on lies."

Sean slammed his cup down onto the counter. Scalding coffee splashed over his hand. He lunged for the sink and ran cold water over it. "Built on lies, my ass! Brainless, self-righteous idiot!"

Connor winced and covered his ears. "Please don't break anything else," he pleaded. "My head hurts. I can't stand the noise."

"You've got to shake this thing off of you, goddamnit! And you've got to get that girl, too. And do you know why?"

Connor sank back into his chair, resigned. Evidently today's histrionics weren't over yet. "OK. Tell me why, Sean."

"Because you deserve it. You're a righteous dude. You're like . . . noble or something. With your code of honor. Your marching orders. That's why Davy and I tease you about the hero complex. It's a soft spot that can't be shielded. It leaves you wide open."

Connor sighed. "That is such a crock—"

"You're a good guy, Con," Sean trampled over his protests. "More so than Davy or me. More than anyone I know, except for maybe Jesse, and look what happened to him. You can't bend, you can't cut bait and run. You can't compromise. It's like, you don't even know how."

Connor stared down into his coffee and tried not to think about Jesse. He felt bad enough already. "Dad was like that," he pointed out. "He didn't know how to bend. So he broke."

Silence fell. The dour ghost of Eamon's memory weighed upon them. Eamon had been a good and honorable man, but he had been profoundly disillusioned by the violent insults that life had dealt him. Grief and anger had chipped away at his sanity until it was totally gone.

"You're not like Dad, Con." Sean's voice vibrated with suppressed emotion. "You're stronger than Dad was. And you're kinder, too."

Connor took a gulp of his coffee and groped around for a change of subject. The coffee itself was always a handy culprit. "Christ, Sean, how did you make this stuff so strong? It's corroding my gut."

"That's the scotch, bozo, not my coffee. Let's coat it with some food," Sean said. "Go shower while I make you some lunch."

"Don't coddle me," Connor snapped. "I can take care of my—"

"Take a shower, and put on one of my shirts. None of your limp, faded crap. You want the world to think you're sane and well-balanced? Start by shaving and combing your hair."

When Connor came back down to the kitchen, he was freshly shaven and dressed in a crisp denim shirt he'd found in Sean's closet. His brother ran a critical eye over him, and nodded. "You'll do."

Connor grunted and sat down. They honored a tacit agreement not to tear open any more raw, unspeakable topics, and since there was nothing to talk about except madness, murder, love, heartbreak, and God only knew what else, they concentrated on chewing and swallowing Sean's grilled ham and cheese sandwiches in silence.

Sean shrugged on his leather jacket afterwards. "I cooked, so you do the dishes," he announced. "I'm going to go track down Davy. We have to start turning over some rocks about that murder rap."

"Stay out of it," Connor snapped, as he followed him out to the car.

Sean dug for his keys. "Yeah, sure. As if. You should find Erin, now that you've shaved. Talk to her. Lay on that old McCloud charm."

"Charm, my ass. I sprout hair on the back of my hands whenever I get near her. Besides, she's busy with the filthy rich art fiend who wants to drape her in jewels and take her to Paris."

Sean's jaw sagged in dismay. "What? And you just let her go? Where do you keep your brains, Con? In a box under your bed?"

"She wouldn't let me go with her," Connor snarled. "Get it through your thick skull! She doesn't want me, so I can't follow her around. It's against the rules. It's called stalking. Crazy guys stalk women. I'm making a big effort not to act crazy right now. Do you follow me?"

Sean looked pained. "Yeah, but letting her go see a guy who's waving tickets to Paris? Jesus, Con. That calls for desperate measures."

"Don't get me started," he growled. "I've been going over it all night. At least she's not alone, for all the good that does. Tonia would probably cheer Mueller on. Hell, she'd probably propose a threesome."

"Tonia Vasquez, you mean? Erin's bodacious nurse friend?"

Connor stared at him, startled. "How do you know about Tonia the bodacious nurse? I never told you about her."

"I met her this morning when I dropped off Miles. She was talking to Erin's mom. Beautiful tits. I recognized her, you know."

"From where?"

"From the clinic." Sean gave him a funny look, as if it should be obvious. "She was a nurse there when you were in your coma. You know I never forget a face. Or a chest, for that matter."

"The clinic? Tonia worked at the clinic?" The net started to widen in Connor's mind, scooping up shifting, darting thoughts. Sifting and sorting, searching for patterns.

Sean's eyes narrowed as he recognized the look on his brother's face. "Hold everything. What's going on? What's with that look, bro?"

"Erin met her about a year ago," Connor said slowly. "What a coincidence, huh?"

"Uh . . . wait a sec. Are we still freaked out about Novak? Didn't you tell me Luksch is in Europe, and Novak got blown sky-high yesterday? Have we turned that page, or what?"

"Don't start with me, Sean."

"I'm not!" Sean protested. "Just help me out here! I need to know where we stand before I can figure out what to do."

"I know that, goddamn it!" Connor exploded. "That's been my problem from the start! I don't know where I stand! I don't know what's real anymore! I can't trust my eyes, my ears, my instincts, nothing!"

"OK. I had my tantrum, and you're entitled to yours," Sean soothed. "I'm going to talk to Davy and Seth. You just sit tight. Try not to think. You always fuck up when you think too much. If you see any apparitions from beyond the grave, call me. And stay out of trouble."

Connor tried to laugh. "That's my line. To you."

Sean got into his Jeep and rolled down the window. "Yeah. It's weird to be the one to say it to you for a change. Later, bro."

He watched the Jeep leap down the rutted driveway. The bit of data that Sean had dropped so casually echoed through his head.

Hell of a coincidence, that a nurse who worked at the clinic while he was in his coma should strike up a bosom friendship with Erin. There was no connection that made sense. No one had any reason to know a year ago how interested he was in Erin Riggs. Her mother had guessed it, his brothers had known it. No one else.

His skin prickled. He felt it happening. Marching orders taking form inside his mind from an authority he couldn't gainsay. He was going back to the clinic, to find out more about this Tonia. Now.

He was Crazy Eamon's boy, flesh and blood and bone. If this meant he was nuts, so be it. It would drive him even more crazy to resist that inner force. He couldn't go against his own nature.

He ran into the house. He was trembling with wild energy. He strapped on his ankle holster with the .22, stuck the SIG-Sauer into his pants. He threw on his coat and bolted for the car.

He was going to catch hell for not washing the lunch dishes. It was a cardinal rule to leave the kitchen clean, but this was a special case. The Cadillac wallowed and fishtailed in the gravel. It finally leaped into action, bouncing heavily over the ruts.

He was diving headfirst straight back into his paranoid fantasy, and anybody who didn't like it could go fuck himself.

Chapter

24

"I cannot believe it," Tonia scolded. "I simply cannot believe you are dressed like that to go to Mueller's house. You're as white as a ghost, and even if you weren't, that washed-out gray is all wrong for you. And your hair. Save me. The scraped-back peeled-onion look is too severe for your face. What is wrong with you?"

Erin stared down at her lap, too tired to react. "Don't bug me, Tonia. I had a really bad night. I don't want to look pretty. I was shooting for respectable when I got dressed. That's all I ask of myself."

"You should have called me! I would have come over and done an emergency salvage job," Tonia fussed. "Nothing raises the spirits better than a quickie makeover, *chica*. Some magic eye gel, some cover-up, some foundation, a little blush—"

"I'm not interested in Mueller. I don't want him to be interested in me. There is no reason for me to make a fuss over my looks today."

Tonia shot her a cold glance. "Well! Excuse me."

"Sorry," Erin said miserably. "I didn't mean to snap."

"What's happening with your boyfriend?" Tonia demanded. "Is he the reason you're so pissy?"

Erin's jaw began to shake. "I think it's over."

"Who dumped who?"

Tonia's harsh choice of words made Erin flinch. "I think . . . I think that I dumped him."

"You think?" Tonia rolled her eyes. "Oh, please. You're not sure?"

Erin pressed her mouth against her hand. "I can't talk about it."

"Oh. That bad, huh? Frankly, I'm relieved. The guy was way, way too intense for my tastes. I mean, the first time I met him he was holding a gun on me, for God's sake."

"Maybe so." She dashed away stray tears and thanked heaven she'd done without mascara. "But let's have this conversation some other time. Like, six months to a year from now might be better."

Tonia sniffed. "God, you're sensitive. So what's wrong with Mueller? Is he repulsive or something?"

Erin held her eyes wide open, hoping they would dry out. "Not at all," she said dully. "He's pleasant. Nice looking, intelligent, cultured. There's nothing wrong with him. Nothing that I can put my finger on."

"He's just not Connor McCloud. That's his only flaw, right?"

Erin closed her eyes. "Tonia. Please. Could you just this once give me a break? I'm begging you. On my knees."

"I'm not saying this to bug you!" Tonia protested. "I'm just trying to get to the bottom of this! Mueller is such a big break for you, Erin. It drives me crazy that you're not taking advantage of—"

"I don't care about Mueller!" Erin yelled. "I don't give a damn about his collection, or his donation, or the museum! I could give a shit! About any of it! It's all just a stupid, meaningless game!"

"Ah. Well. Excuse me for caring," Tonia said. Her voice was clipped and chilly. "If you feel this way, why are we going to Mueller's house at all? I do have other things to do with my time, you know."

Erin dragged a Kleenex out of her purse and blew her nose. "Because I said I would." Her voice was flat and colorless. "And no other reason. I've got nothing else left to steer by. Everything's breaking down, falling apart. All I've got left is my word. So I'll by God keep it."

Tonia snorted. "Oh, spare me the melodrama, please."

Tonia's derisive tone was the final blow. Erin's face crumpled.

Tonia swerved into a gas station parking lot to the angry blare of several horns, and killed the engine. She pulled Erin into her arms. "Oh, come down off your high horse for a minute," she soothed.

"I feel so bad. I can't stand much more of this, Tonia."

"I know you can't." Tonia's voice was soft and hypnotic. "Of course you can't. And you won't. You'll see."

Erin didn't want her goopy nose to leak over Tonia's white linen suit, but when she tried to pull away, Tonia just pulled her back down.

"You know what this means, don't you?" Tonia said. "This means I get to fix your face. No matter what you think of Mueller, you've got to go in there with your head high. You've got to show some attitude."

"Whatever," Erin said wearily. "Fix my face. Do your worst."

Tonia started pulling hairpins out of Erin's bun. "We'll start with the hairdo," she said briskly. "It's hateful, and it must go."

Erin sniffled and tried to laugh. "Thanks, Tonia."

Tonia pulled her into an embrace so tight, the back of one of Erin's stud earrings stabbed into her neck. She gasped at the sharp pain, and tried to extricate herself from Tonia's grip.

Tonia hung on. "It'll be over soon, Erin," she crooned. "I promise."

* * *

Connor shoved the glass doors open and strode over to the clinic's front desk. He had to struggle to control the trapped feeling that came over him. There had been times when he would've gladly chewed off a limb to get out of this place. Not that the staff wasn't great. They'd all done their best for him. And oh, good, there was Brenda, one of his favorites. A heavyset lady in her fifties was behind the reception desk, peering at a computer through gold-rimmed half-glasses.

"Hi, Brenda," he said.

She looked up at him blankly, and then her eyes lit up. "Connor McCloud! Why, look at you!" She scurried out from behind the desk and gave his face a maternal pat. "You're looking good, honey! What brings you in here? Just come by to say hello? I'll have to call your PTs. JoAnn and Pat worked with you, right?" She reached for the phone. "I'll just buzz them and—"

"Actually, I'm not here to visit. I'm in a hurry." He was sorry to cut her off, but he was too edgy to shoot the breeze with the clinic staff. "I came for some information. You'll have to tell JoAnn and Pat hi for me. I'll drop by to see them sometime. I'm doing pretty good. Those months of torture paid off."

"They sure did, you handsome devil. What did you need to know?"

"I'm looking for information on a nurse who worked here during the period I was in the coma," he said. "Her name is Tonia Vasquez."

"Hmm. Doesn't ring a bell, but this is a big place. Tell you what. I'll buzz Annette. She does admissions up there. Maybe she'll recognize the name." Brenda dialed. "Hi, Annette, it's Brenda. Guess who I have standing in front of me? Remember Sleeping Beauty? . . . Yep, in the flesh. Cute as can be. He's got a question for you. Could you pop down, or should I send him up? . . . OK . . . Yeah, tell me about it, honey. I'll send him on up, then. Thanks a bunch."

She hung up and waved Connor toward the elevator banks. "Third floor, left out of the elevator, then take the first left again, and you'll find her in the glassed-in internal office."

"Thanks, Brenda," he said fervently.

Annette's office wasn't hard to find. He knocked at the open door. A tall, smiling black woman in her forties hurried over to greet him. "Well, hey! Connor McCloud! Looking good!"

He shook her hand, smiled, and did as much of the chitchat routine as his nerves could handle before he blurted out his question.

Annette's brow furrowed. "I don't remember anybody of that name, but I'll beep Geoffrey. He's in staffing. He knows everybody in the clinic, and their great-aunt's birthday, too." She punched the number into the phone. "If anybody will know, it's Geoffrey."

Conversation lagged while they waited for Geoffrey to respond. Annette gave him a cheery smile." And how's your lovely girlfriend doing?"

He was frozen into total immobility. "Excuse me? My *what?*"

Annette hesitated, wide-eyed and wary of a gaffe. "I was just asking about your, ah . . . girlfriend."

"I don't have a girlfriend. I sure as hell didn't have one then."

Annette blinked. "She came so often, I just assumed—"

"Who came to see me?" he barked. "What was her name?"

Annette's face stiffened. "I don't recall her name. And I don't appreciate being spoken to in that manner."

He let out a long, slow breath through clenched teeth. "I'm sorry, Annette," he said carefully. "Forgive me for snapping at you. I shouldn't have. Could you describe this girl to me, please?"

Annette was mollified, but still suspicious. "She had long brown hair and a lovely smile. She was always dressed in a suit. She came on her lunch hour and read books to you. She signed in every day. I suppose I could look for some old registers, if you're so curious—"

"Please," he said. "Please, Annette."

She went into an adjoining room and rustled around for a minute. She came back out burdened with two thick three-ring binders and dumped them on the desk in front of him. "There you go. Be my guest."

He opened the book at random. The name practically leaped out into his face. Erin Riggs.

He turned the page. There she was again. He flipped over another page. Every time, his eye fell right onto her graceful cursive script, as if pulled by a magnet. Erin Riggs, Erin Riggs, Erin Riggs. His heart was galloping. He riffled through the pages rapidly.

Every goddamned day.

"Did you find what you're looking for?" Annette asked.

He looked up at her. Something naked and desperate in his eyes made the frosty hauteur fade out of her face, to be replaced by cautious concern. "Yes," he said. "More than I was looking for."

A chubby young man with a receding hairline swept into the room in a cloud of flowery aftershave. "Hello, beautiful! I saw your number on my pager, but since I was headed here anyway, I thought I'd just—"

"Do you remember Tonia Vasquez?" Connor demanded.

Geoffrey gave him a blank look. "Who are you?"

"Connor was one of our patients a while back," Annette explained. "He's looking for a nurse who worked here sixteen months ago. I thought you might remember her. That's why I beeped you."

Geoffrey exchanged quick glances and nods with Annette. "Tonia Vasquez? Yes, of course I remember Tonia. You said sixteen months, though? Wait a second." He leaned over the computer. "Can I close out of this document and access the database, Annette, o light of my life?"

"*Mi* computer *es tu* computer, cupcake," she responded.

Geoffrey typed with blinding speed, tapping and scrolling. "Here we go. Very strange. Her employee status is still current, but it shouldn't be, because Tonia moved down to San Jose over three years ago. She wanted to be closer to her daughter and her grandchildren."

"Grandchildren? No way! This woman is in her twenties!"

Geoffrey shook his head. "The only Tonia Vasquez who ever worked for us was pushing sixty. Lovely woman. Odd about the employee status. Must be a glitch in the system. I wonder if she's still getting paychecks. Wouldn't that be a howl? I'll have to call payroll and check it out right away."

"Uh, yeah," Connor said.

Somehow he managed to shake hands and thank them for their help. He sprinted down the hall, knees wobbling. He'd thrown out his net, and instead of darting fish, a writhing sea monster had boiled up out of the depths. And Erin had chosen Tonia to accompany her to Mueller's lair. No, Novak's lair. He was convinced. There was no time for the luxury of self-doubt. Erin's life was on the line.

He ran past the slow elevator. He would take his chances with the stairs. He groped for his phone, but there was nothing in his pocket.

Of course. He'd given the phone to Erin, she'd turned it off, and he didn't know where she was. Again. God. It was like a bad joke.

There was a pay phone in the stairwell. He dug for change, and plugged it in with shaking fingers. He tried Erin, for the hell of it. In vain. He was the last person on earth she wanted to talk to.

But she'd come to see him during the coma. Every goddamn day.

He pushed it away. Later for that. No time to process mind-boggling revelations right now. He dialed Seth.

"Who the hell is this?" Seth snapped.

"It's me. Look, Seth, I've got an emergency—"

"Why is your phone turned off? And why are you calling me from a land line? I can't scramble you on a land line!"

"I don't have time for this, Seth. Listen to me. Novak's not dead."

Seth was silent for a moment. "Uh . . . I heard it was confirmed," he said cautiously. "How do you figure?"

"Erin's best buddy Tonia posed as a nurse at the clinic when I was in the coma. She must've used the employee ID of a real nurse who retired three years ago. I'm at the clinic now. I just found out."

Seth grunted. "OK. Whatever. I'll buy it. I'd rather hunt Novak with you again than have you be crazy. You got a plan?"

"No," Connor said desperately. "I don't know where she is. She went to the millionaire art collector's house today. Mueller is Novak. I would bet my life on it. And I never got the chance to tag her stuff."

"Huh. Well, I've got some info for you, too. Remember when you told me to check out your girlfriend's apartment?"

"She's not my girlfriend," Connor said harshly.

There was a delicate pause. "Uh . . . .that sucks. But anyhow, I just left the place, and I found something really weird—"

"I don't have time for this, Seth!"

"Bear with me. It's relevant." Seth's tone was hard. "There was a vidcam mounted behind the wall paneling. Rigged with a short-range remote transmitter. Probably the receiver and recorder are in the same building. The setup is crude. Looks homemade."

Connor swallowed, hard. "Holy shit. That is weird."

"Oh, I haven't even gotten to the weird part yet," Seth said. "About that vidcam, uh . . . you don't know anything about it, do you, Con?"

"What the hell are you talking about? Why would I? What is it about the goddamn vidcam? Spit it out, Seth!"

"It's yours," Seth said bluntly. "I sold it to Davy, and he passed it on to you. It's the one that got stolen in that burglary at your house a few months ago. I know it's yours. Because I marked it."

Connor tried to find space in his mind for that piece of info. His brain refused to accommodate it. "Huh?"

"Is there something you're not telling me, Con?"

Seth's voice had a cold, suspicious edge to it that Connor had never heard, at least not directed toward him. Panic jolted through him, at the thought that even Seth might abandon him.

"Fuck, no!" he burst out. "I didn't plant that thing. Not me!"

"Good." Seth's relief was palpable. "That's sort of what I figured. A hidden vidcam in a girl's bedroom isn't your style. It's more like something I would do. You're too much of a tight-ass Dudley Do-Right for a dirty trick like that."

"Thanks for your touching faith in me," Connor said.

"Anytime, man, anytime. The first thing you need to do is to turn on your phone so I can scramble you. It makes me nervous to talk—"

"I don't have the phone," Connor said. "I gave it to Erin."

"You gave the phone to Erin?" Seth repeated slowly.

"Yes! I did!" he yelled. "Will you guys please stop giving me shit about the fucking phone?"

"And she has it on her now?" Seth persisted.

"How the hell should I know? She put it in her purse last night. I assume she has it. Why shouldn't she?"

Seth started to laugh.

"What is so goddamn funny?"

"You just solved all our problems in one blow," Seth said. "We'll use the phone to find her."

Connor's hand tightened on the phone. "Come again?"

"There's a beacon in your phone. It feeds off the battery, so if it's been charged recently, it should be transmitting."

"You planted a beacon on me? Why?" he demanded.

"You never know when you might need to find your friends

in a hurry." Seth's voice was defensive. "I put 'em in Davy's and Sean's phones, too, so don't take it personally. Besides, you get your ass in a sling on a regular basis. I felt more than justified."

Connor started to grin. "I'm gonna pound you when this is all over for planting shit on me," he warned.

"Yeah, but right now, when I'm useful, you love me and I'm golden. I've heard that tune before. I'll head home and key the code into my computer. Get over here, and we'll mobilize."

"Call Sean and Davy for me," Connor said.

"Watch yourself," Seth said.

Connor bounded down the remaining two flights like his feet were on springs. It was beautiful, it was amazing, it was awesome, that his pathologically sneaky gearhead friend had actually had the brilliant good sense to plant a bug in his phone. He dodged and spun around gurneys and wheelchairs, leaving shouts of furious protest behind him. He sped toward the parking garage and dug out his keys.

The door of the gray SUV with tinted windows parked next to his car swung opened, and discharged a tall, black-clad bald man.

Connor reeled back with a gasp. The guy was a hideous apparition: pallid and hairless, blue eyes burning out of dark pits, a scarred, grotesque face. A gap-toothed leer.

Georg Luksch.

Georg's arm flashed up, took aim. Connor heard a popping sound, felt a stab of pain, an explosion of helpless fury. A dart was poking out of his chest. He fought it, but he was already sagging onto the asphalt.

Shadows overtook him. The world melted into formless darkness.

"Punctual, as always," Tamara murmured, when she met them at the door. "And who is this?"

"This is my friend Tonia Vasquez," Erin said. "Tonia, this is Tamara Julian. I told you about her."

"How do you do? What a fabulous outfit," Tonia gushed.

Tamara gave her a lofty smile. "How kind of you to say so."

Tamara was dressed in black, a severe high-necked jacket paired with a billowing black taffeta skirt. The heels of her shiny, pointy-toed boots clicked over the dizzying swirls of antique tile on the mosaic floor. She glanced back over her shoulder. "I'm relieved that you made it. Mr. Mueller was distressed when you ran away last night. He was afraid he'd offended you. We weren't sure you'd be back."

Tonia slanted her an odd glance. "Ran away? What's this?"

"It's a long story," Erin said stiffly. "It had nothing to do with Mr. Mueller, though. He needn't have worried."

"I see." Tamara's face looked pale and drawn beneath her flawless makeup. Her emerald eyes looked haunted and shadowy.

Or maybe it was just Erin's own bleak perceptions, reading ominous portents into every innocuous thing. The dread in her belly got heavier. Flutters of the panic that had mastered her the day before stirred inside her, and she clamped down on them ruthlessly. She would get through this job, close this chapter gracefully, and that was all she would ask of herself. Professional suicide or not, once she delivered that report, she would be politely unavailable to Claude Mueller forevermore. She would refer him to other experts who would all fall over their feet in their eagerness to consult for him. In the meantime, she would be taking typing tests, filling out W-4 forms for temp secretary and paralegal jobs. And she would be cheerful about it if it killed her. Yippee. What a joy. You shape your own reality, she reminded herself.

Unless you allow other people to shape it for you. The thought flitted through her mind like a bat's shadow, almost too quick to catch.

God, how she hated this house. It seemed to give her a

constant, low-level electrical charge, just enough to feel nauseous and dizzy, and determination alone wasn't enough to manage it. She'd bolted out of the place in a full-blown panic attack last night, like Cinderella fleeing the ball as the clock tolled midnight. But here she was again, putting one foot in front of the other, cold sweat trickling down between her shoulder blades. Trying to act like a grown-up.

Tamara stopped in front of the door to the salon. The heavy, ornate door was like the mouth of some monstrous creature, gaping wide to swallow her whole. Erin stomped down on the childish, queasy surge of panic, and tightened her belly into tempered steel.

Mueller was staring out the window, as he'd been the day before, the deep-in-thought-aristocrat pose. He turned, and smiled as he came forward to greet her. "Ah, excellent. I wasn't sure I would see you again," he said. "I am sorry if I upset you yesterday. You look pale."

"I'm fine, thanks." *See? Polite, pleasant, nothing wrong with this picture. Novak is dead, on the other side of the planet. Everything here is perfectly normal. I will not let someone else's fear control me.* It raced through her mind in the blink of an eye. "I'm so sorry about that. I don't know what came over me."

His teeth looked so sharp when he smiled. "And who is your lovely companion?"

"Tonia Vasquez. Glad to meet you," Tonia said, when Erin took too long to reply. "I'm Erin's shadow today. I hope I'm not in the way."

"Not at all. Any friend of Ms. Riggs is welcome. One can never have too many beautiful women in one place."

"That depends," Tonia purred, "on the circumstances."

So Tonia was going to flirt with him. Fine. It made her flesh creep, but if it diverted his attention from her own unhappy self, she could weep for gratitude. Soon this would be over, and she could retreat to her dingy mouse hole at the Kinsdale and lick her wounds in the dark.

And maybe she was being unfair, but it was going to be a very long time before she called Tonia again. If ever.

"Can I get started?" Her voice came out so sharp that Tonia and Mueller stopped their bantering and stared at her, startled.

"Of course." Mueller indicated a table at the far end of the room.

The sooner I get this over with, the sooner I can get out of this hellish place. Her mind repeated the thought like a mantra.

Three items lay on the gleaming dark wood table. The folders of provenance papers lay beside them. She dug out her recorder, and grimly disposed her mind to concentrate. Grown-up. Professional.

The first item was a bronze dagger and sheath. The provenance papers placed it as La Tene, 200 B.C.E., dredged out of a river in Wales in the 1890s, but the blade seemed much older to her. The guard, grip, and pommel had been made of some organic material that had rotted away, but the wasp-waisted, leaf-shaped sweep of the blade was still beautiful. It had the reinforcing ridges, grooves, and finger notching that she had seen on many bronze Celtic swords from 1000 B.C.E.

The next piece was a stone statuette, eighteen inches high, of a hideous beast holding out its arms. Huge, thick claws sank into the forehead of two severed heads. An arm dangled out of its fanged, gaping jaws. La Tarasque, very like the Gallo-Roman limestone statue she had studied in Avignon on her junior year abroad in France and Scotland.

She flinched away from it. It was a rare and beautiful piece, but she felt too wretched to cope with bloodthirsty man-eating monsters, unprofessional or not. Later for that one.

The third item was a bronze flagon, decorated in the vegetal swirls and spirals of late La Tene style. It was embossed with several mythical creatures, but the ones that caught her eye first were the two dragons.

Fiery red garnet eyes glared at each other. They were symmetrical, a perfectly balanced pose of eternal mortal challenge. Like the torque. Serpentine tails coiled beneath them, blending into the intricate, flowering tendril design that decorated the whole piece.

The realization crept up on her so slowly, the way a headache gathered force until it had to be acknowledged by the conscious mind. A puzzle she hadn't known she was trying to solve slipped into place. The provenance papers cited the flagon as discovered near Salzburg in 1867 by a gentleman explorer and tomb raider from the nineteenth century, and subsequently sold in the 1950s to a rich Austrian industrialist.

But this flagon was not from Salzburg. It was from the Wrothburn cemetery. As was the dragon torque. And the Silver Fork torques, too.

She felt it in her skin. Her instincts were never wrong. Every hair on her body was on end. The wrongness deepened, widened.

She forced the words out. "Mr. Mueller. I'm sorry to tell you this, but I believe that the provenance papers for this flagon are falsified."

The murmur of conversation from the other side of the room stopped. "I beg your pardon?" Mueller's voice was gentle, puzzled.

"The distinctive designs show it to be almost certainly from the grave mounds in Wrothburn, which were only discovered three years ago. I suspect that the dragon torques, and at least two of the torques I saw in Silver Fork, are from Wrothburn, too. These pieces were looted. They belong to the people of Scotland."

She didn't have the courage to face him. Dread held her body in a paralyzing grip. She heard a dry, whispery chuckle, like a snake sliding through dead leaves. She knew. She turned, slowly.

Mueller's eyes were no longer electric blue. They were a

luminous white-green, a cold, dead color. He lifted his hand and waggled his index and middle fingers. The blue discs of his colored contacts clung to the ends of them. "Congratulations, Erin."

"It's you," she whispered. "You're Novak. Connor was right."

His smile widened. "Yes. He was. Poor, mad Connor."

She wondered how anything so alien could have masked itself as human for so long. Then she thought of Tonia, with a shock of guilt and horror. She had dragged poor, unsuspecting Tonia into a world of hurt.

Her anguished eyes met Tonia's—and her heart skipped a beat.

Tonia was smiling. She reached into her white Prada bag, and leveled a small silver revolver at Erin with casual skill. "I'm sorry about this, Erin. I genuinely did like you. You seemed like such a priss when I met you at the clinic, but you're actually smarter than I thought." She shook her head. "But not quite smart enough."

Outrage held the creeping horror temporarily at bay. "You vicious, lying, heinous bitch!" Erin hissed.

"I am impressed with you, my dear," Novak said. "You exceeded my wildest hopes. Not only did you come to the right conclusion in record time, but your first impulse was to uphold the rules. You win the grand prize, Erin. Tamara, show her what she's won."

There was no taunting glitter in Tamara's eyes this time, no smile on her pale lips. She opened the library door. A tall, pale, hairless man stepped inside, grinning. Erin cried out before she could stop herself.

Georg. She knew him, even shaven bald, with the missing teeth. His eye was distorted by the drooping lid. One side of his mouth was thickened and twisted. Crimson weals marred his pallid cheeks.

He leered, his eyes dragging hungrily over her body. "Hello, Erin," he said. "I am happy to see you. You look very pretty."

She backed away. The table bumped painfully hard into her hip. "It really was you in that SUV last Sunday, wasn't it?"

His grin widened, became triumphant. "Yes."

"Georg's usefulness to me was much reduced by your lover's beating," Novak said. "He was once so beautiful, remember? And prison was very hard for Georg. He is very angry. Are you angry, Georg?"

"Yes." Georg's good eye was bright with venomous hatred. "Very."

"He suffered permanent nerve damage to his face, you know," Novak said. "In thanks for all of his pain and sacrifice, Georg shall be the one to execute my plans for you. He lives for this promise."

"No," Erin said. She sidled along the table. "No."

Tonia clucked her tongue in warning. "Don't move, please."

"It is a beautiful plan," Novak said. "Prison gives one time for a great deal of reflection, you see. I'm sure your father finds it to be so."

"So this is all just to get back at Dad?" She hardly cared what he answered. Her words were just a desperate bid for time.

He laughed. "No, Erin. I'm getting back at everyone. Tonia, did you do as you were told this morning?"

"Yes, Mr. Mueller." Her smile was smug. "Barbara Riggs is in a tizzy. Phones are buzzing about McCloud's family history of mental illness, his delusions, his persecution complex. His obsessive pursuit and seduction, and let me add rape, of Erin Riggs—"

"That's ridiculous! No one will ever believe that! My mother saw me with him! She saw how he—"

"When the video footage of last night's tryst is found in his house, she may well take a different view," Novak said. "McCloud couldn't have behaved more perfectly for my purposes if I had given him orders. I loved it when he tore your dress and bent you over the table."

She covered her shaking mouth with her hand. "Video footage?"

"Indeed. You both surprised me last night, my dear. I had no idea that McCloud could be so . . . raw."

"I had a conversation with your neighbor Mrs. Hathaway today." Tonia was enjoying herself. "She can't wait to tell what she saw last night in the stairwell. It's common knowledge that McCloud killed Billy Vega. A massive manhunt is already underway."

"And they will find him," Novak said. "They will find you, too, but alas, it will be too late. Let me explain the sad sequence of events for you, my dear. After McCloud killed Billy Vega, his mental imbalance escalated, faster than anyone could have anticipated. Brought on by mad jealousy, no doubt. Ah, love is a dangerous thing."

"But that's ridiculous! No one would believe that Connor would kill Billy Vega. He had no reason to—"

"Georg left no trace of himself at Billy's house," Novak said smugly. "But the forensics team have found the hairs from McCloud's comb. The bloody cane is in McCloud's basement. A clear sign that he wanted to be stopped. A subconscious cry for help, if you will. We mounted McCloud's camera in your wall, we used tapes that were covered with his fingerprints. The camera was reported stolen months ago, so it will be obvious that he has been stalking you for some time. I'm sure the police will enjoy the spicy episodes from your affair. Maybe they will even turn up on the Internet. Like father, like daughter."

"Oh, God," she whispered.

"It was about time something happened in that wretched apartment of yours," he said. "The people who monitored you almost expired from boredom. Georg, turn on the video monitor, if you please."

She hadn't even noticed the wide-screen flat monitor mounted on the wall. The image that appeared on it made her knees turn to water.

Connor was tied spread-eagled on the bed, blindfolded.

"He will wake up shortly." Novak's tone was gleeful. "Then the real entertainment begins. He will watch while Georg performs the dreadful acts for which he will bear the blame. Then he will apparently come to his senses, realize what he has done, and commit suicide with his own gun, in an agony of guilt and horror."

She stared into the monitor. Connor looked so still and vulnerable. "It will never work," she said desperately. "Forensics—"

"No, I promise, I have thought of everything. Is he awake, Tamara?"

She peered into the monitor. "Could be. Hard to say."

"Tamara will see to it that the bodily fluids upon your ravaged body are the genetically correct ones. Tamara could extract bodily fluids from a stone statue, couldn't you, my seductive beauty?"

Tamara gave him a wide, empty smile. "Oh, yes, boss."

Novak clapped his hands together. For the first time, she noticed the prosthetic fingers. He followed her gaze and held them up, waggling them playfully. "You never checked, Erin. You were so convinced that the world behaves like you do. Now we shall watch Tamara and McCloud on the video monitor. Would you enjoy that?" He gave her an encouraging smile, as if offering a special treat to a child.

"No," Erin said.

"What a poor sport," he chided. "Making Riggs women watch their men with other women is something of a hobby of mine."

"Mom's TV," she whispered. "It was you."

"Oh, yes. I was sorry when McCloud put a stop to it. He spoiled my plans for Cindy, too. I had planned for your mother to commit suicide, you see, and for Cindy to begin the long slide into addiction. Those Riggs women just cannot choose good men. But no matter. Your death will finish them off nicely. Tamara, it's time. See to it," he ordered.

Tamara left the room. There was a heavy silence. Everyone was looking at her, as if waiting for something.

"It won't work," she said flatly. "Connor is a noble, honorable person. Too many people know this. But you couldn't be expected to understand that. You're just a squirming thing that feeds on death."

Georg pulled a pair of thick rubber gloves out of a box on the table, and put them on. He glanced at Novak. Novak nodded.

Georg seized her by the hair and struck her in the face.

Erin spun around, crashed against the wall, and slid down to the floor. There was blood in her mouth. No one had ever hit her in her entire life. Her mind reeled with pain and shock, fought to orient itself.

"Georg must cover himself with plastic, of course, before he touches you," Novak said, as if nothing had happened. He took a step closer, and chuckled as she shrank away. "Oh, I have no intention of hurting you," he assured her. "I will only watch this time. Nothing must threaten my new identity. Only Connor's blood and hair and semen will be found upon your ravaged body. His skin, beneath your fingernails."

"No one would believe that Connor could ever do such a thing. No one who knows him." Her voice shook with furious conviction.

"No? Picture it. He will be found dead, his pistol in his mouth, not far from your body. Half naked, scratched to ribbons. Once the sex tapes are found, the case will be closed, my dear. Everyone already thinks he has lost his grip. Everyone. Even you thought so, remember?"

She pushed away the guilt and shame his words provoked, and struggled up onto her knees. "They will come looking for you." She threw the words at him. "My mother knew that I was coming—"

"But you never made it, Erin. I called your mother right before I buzzed you." Tonia's voice took on a taunting, singsong quality. "Mrs. Riggs, is Erin with you, by any chance? I had an appointment with her to go to Mueller's, but she's not home! How odd! It's so unlike her!"

Erin stared at her, stunned. "You are so incredibly cruel."

"Yes. And now that I am dead, no one will bother me," Novak said smugly. "I should have arranged my own death years ago, but I was too attached to my raffish identity. Ego, you know. Gets you every time."

"How did you turn yourself into Mueller?" Erin demanded.

"Tempting my ego? It's difficult not to boast. I stole Claude's life fourteen years ago, which is not so great a crime as you might think, since he wasn't really living it anyway. I needed his live DNA to exchange for my own in the databanks, so I kept him in a drug induced coma. One last stint with the plastic surgeons and I can show myself to the world without a care. Perhaps I will give that donation to the Huppert after all, on the condition that they name the new wing after you. In memoriam. Wouldn't that be touching?"

"You are a demon," she said.

He looked hurt. "Not at all. I have a very tender heart. I used to visit Claude from time to time, back when my life was less complicated. I would hold his hand, tell him of my various doings. They say comatose people understand on some deep level. But you know that already."

She struggled up into a sitting position. "You've been watching me ever since Connor was in the clinic. All this time."

"Your devotion gave me the idea," Novak said. "McCloud gave me another when he brutalized Georg. The two of you were destined to destroy each other. Your mother—pah, too easy. Cindy, too. Like your father. But you, Erin. You are the key to that whole family. All that moral fiber and self-control. All that rigorous effort."

She had slipped into a state of surreal calm. "So this is to punish Dad, for failing you, and the McClouds for catching you? That's all?

"Ah, yes, the McCloud brothers. Connor's death and disgrace will set them on the road to ruin, and I will pick them off at my leisure. There are Seth Mackey and his bride to think of, too, but no hurry. Everyone who has dared to affront me will be punished. And not a trace will lead back to me, because I no longer exist. I am transfigured."

"So you have nothing against me personally," she persisted.

"No," he said. "You couldn't cross me. It's not in your nature."

"My nature is changing." Erin struggled up onto wobbling legs, supporting herself against the wall. "I've loosened up quite a bit. I've been leaving my bed unmade, the dishes unwashed. Losing my temper. Using swear words. My tolerance for chaos has risen sharply lately."

Novak laughed at her. "Bravado in the face of doom. It almost moves me to pity." His eyes flicked to Georg. "Almost."

Erin's mind was strangely lucid. Novak was the embodiment of her nightmares, the goad behind her ceaseless efforts to control her world and keep chaos at bay. And all her struggles had led her straight here, into this monster's grasp.

The fear of chaos had controlled her all her life. She may have just a few minutes left to live, but she would be free in them. She would create her own reality for as long as she had the power. She drew herself up as tall as possible. "Your plan is inherently flawed," she said.

Novak looked slightly startled, as if a doll had come to life and criticized him. He gestured politely for her to explain herself.

"You studied everyone's strengths and weaknesses, but you forgot one thing," she said. "Real people grow. They change. But for you, everything is already dead. Inanimate objects for you to move around. Because you're dead inside, Novak. You can't grow. That's why you hate us all so much. If I were a saint, maybe I would pity you, but I'm not. You miserable, twisted, dead thing."

Novak blinked. He looked at Georg. "Hit her again."

Georg lifted his arm. Erin cringed against the table and braced herself.

The lamps flicked off. The image of Connor on the video screen collapsed into a pinpoint of light and vanished into a flat gray void.

Chapter

25

Someone was slapping him. Saying something urgent. Yelling. He wanted to tell them to stop, but his tongue and lips and teeth couldn't figure out the choreography of speech. A haze of black and red and white swam in his vision. It coalesced into a white oval. A face. Emerald eyes. Lips, teeth, moving soundlessly.

Slap, slap. The green-eyed bitch wouldn't leave him alone.

Icy water splashed his face. He gasped into wakefulness. "What?"

"Wake up, you idiot! We don't have much time. Once they get the power back on, they'll be on to me."

He squeezed his eyes shut, opened them. "What the fuck—"

"It's Tamara. You're Connor McCloud. Novak's got you tied to a bed, and Erin at gunpoint. Does that ring a bell?"

"Erin? Novak?" He surged up, and was jerked back by the duct tape that held him to the bed. "Where is Erin?"

"Excellent. Much better," Tamara said. "Now listen carefully. We don't have much time. I'm going to untie you, and give you a weapon. Then you are going to help me kill Kurt Novak. Are you up for it?"

He nodded, bemused, as she pulled a knife out of a seam

in her skirt and set to work on the tape that bound him. One arm came loose, then the other, numb from being pulled so tightly. Her full skirt rustled as she hurried around the bed and started on his feet.

He struggled into a sitting position. "Are you an undercover cop?"

She laughed abruptly. "Hah. Far from it. It's a personal thing."

"What did Novak do to you?" A foot sprang loose, swathed in gray tape. He still couldn't feel it.

"He murdered my favorite lover." Tamara's voice was matter-of-fact. She slashed his other foot free. "Nobody touches my stuff."

"Oh." His brain was so squishy and soft from the drug they'd pumped into him that the pattern just leaped out of the net and broadsided him. "Tamara . . . Mara! From Stone Island! You were Victor Lazar's mistress. I remember now. I saw you on the vid clips. But you were a brunette. You've changed your nose. And your eyes were . . ."

"Topaz, smart boy," she said. "Yellow cat eyes. Lucky for both of us you weren't smart enough to figure that out at Silver Fork. You would have gotten your throat slit. Maybe mine, too. Come on, now. On your feet. Move. Get that blood pumping."

He staggered around the bed, catching himself on the bedpost when his knees buckled. His head throbbed with every heartbeat. He fought back the humiliating urge to vomit. It reminded him of his days in physical therapy. "Why are you helping me?"

"Actually, I'm not. It's you that's helping me," she said crisply. "Rescuing you wasn't part of my agenda. I've been trolling for a chance to kill that bastard all week, but he's too smart, and too suspicious, and I'm in over my head, and I think he's about to kill me."

"Oh," he said inanely. "Uh . . . why didn't you just turn him in?"

"Oh, yeah. Like that worked so well the last time," she mocked. "Besides, I have my own reasons to avoid the law. I wasn't expecting things to move so fast with you two, but it's just as well. I'm tired of being that monster's concubine. It's stressful. And the rape and murder plans for you and your girlfriend, well . . . yuck. I have a very strong stomach, but everybody's got to draw the line somewhere."

"Thanks," he said. "That's awfully nice of you."

"You're welcome." His irony was completely lost on her. "I'm glad for some backup. I would like to live through this. Can you walk? The drug should be wearing off by now. I loaded that dart myself."

He stumbled down onto his knees with a gasp. Tamara yanked him back up, her long, vicious nails digging into his arm. "I cut the power, so he won't see us on the surveillance screens for a few more minutes," she said. "He'll send Nigel to check on it any minute now. He'll be livid if he thinks he won't get to see the sex show."

"Sex show?" He gave her a wary glance. "What sex show?"

"Don't ask. Oh, but speaking of sex shows—goddamn it, *move* your ass, McCloud! The one bright spot in my week has been watching you and your girlfriend get it on. Very entertaining. And that's a high compliment, from me. I hate to be bored."

"Oh, Christ." He stumbled onto his knees again. "Don't tell me."

She yanked him back up. "You're good, big boy," she taunted. "Keep treating her right, or the next time we meet I won't be so friendly."

She was trying to piss him off, to help him throw off the effects of the drug. It was a nice effort, and he appreciated the thought, but it was all he could do not to pass out or barf. He didn't have the strength for anger. Tamara yanked the door open. He wiped cold sweat off his brow. His sleeve came away dark with dried blood. He swayed, and caught himself on the doorjamb. "In James Bond flicks, there are always at least two beautiful girls," he panted. "A good one and a bad one."

She gave him a catlike smile. "I'm the bad one."

"Don't confuse me. It's hard to take this in when I'm stoned."

"Flexibility is the true measure of intelligence. Novak told me you were relatively intelligent. Don't disappoint me now. OK, listen. This is the story. You got free somehow, clobbered me, took my gun, and forced me to show you where Erin is. We burst in, you using me as a shield—"

"Forget it." Connor splayed his hand against the corridor wall and stumbled doggedly after her. "He doesn't care if I kill you. We know it, he knows we know it. He might shoot you just to prove a point."

Tamara's perfect eyebrows snapped together. "Got a better idea?"

"How about you tell me where they are, and then run like hell and get help?" he suggested. "I'll just go in and do what I can."

She sniffed derisively. "Oh, please. You and Erin are dead meat if you go in alone, and so am I when he comes after me later. If I go in with you, it's two to three. Sort of. Tonia's stupid and slow, but Novak and Georg each count for two apiece."

"Three to three," he said.

"You're counting Erin?" She sounded amused.

"Hell, yes," he said. "Erin is an Amazon."

"An unarmed Amazon," Tamara said wryly.

"Three to three," he insisted.

"Whatever. We're getting close. Shut up, and think fast."

He struggled behind her for a second, and tapped her shoulder. "One thing," he asked. "Why are you avenging Lazar? He was a—"

"Criminal? Corrupt? Greedy? Ruthless? Sure. He was complicated. I like complicated men. I'm a greedy, ruthless criminal myself. And Victor was the only man who ever gave me what I needed."

He tried not to ask, with all his strength, but she'd set him up, and now he had to know. "Uh . . . so what do you need, anyway?"

She yanked up her skirt and pulled his SIG Sauer out of a pouch beneath it. She flung it at him, nodding her cool approval as he caught it one-handed.

"None of your fucking business, little boy," she said. "Let's move."

"Stop," Novak said.

Georg's raised arm froze in mid-air. He and Novak exchanged looks. Erin reached out behind herself. Her stiff, cold fingers slid along the surface of the table, groping. They brushed the sharp tip of an object that spun around at her touch.

The bronze dagger.

They were all still looking away from her. She slid the tip of the dagger into her sleeve, trembling at her own daring. She scooped it up and wrapped that arm across her chest. She pressed her other arm over it in a shrinking, defensive pose. It didn't take much acting.

Novak barked out something in a language she didn't recognize. Georg made a brief, sullen reply. Novak pressed a button on his watch and snarled into it in the same language. He held a conversation with the person who replied. A long, heavy silence followed.

Novak paced back and forth across the room. He scowled at Erin as if the power outage were her fault. "I do not like surprises at this stage of the game." He spoke into his watch. "Tamara?" He waited. No reply. He turned to Tonia. "Check on her. I will leave nothing to chance. If I cannot watch them on video, I will watch them in this room."

Georg leered at her. "We watch them, and then he watches us."

She recoiled. The dagger slid up into her sleeve, all the

way to her elbow. It was very cold against the skin of her arm.

Tonia opened the door. She leaped back with a shriek and leveled her gun. Guns appeared in the hands of Novak and Georg.

"Relax, everyone," said Tamara's light, amused voice. "I have the situation under control."

She walked into the room. Connor staggered in beside her, his arms fastened behind his back, his head bent over at an awkward angle. Tamara clutched a handful of his hair. Her pistol was shoved under his chin. "When I saw the power outage, I assumed you'd want a change of plans, boss," she said. "I know how much this means to you."

Novak's eyes narrowed. "You should not take initiatives of this kind without consulting me. He might have over-powered you."

Tamara looked contrite. "I'm so sorry. I was overly eager to please you," she said. "Forgive me. As you can see, I managed him easily."

Connor's eyes sought hers across the room. He was so beautiful, and so pale. His chiseled face was bruised and streaked with blood. The blaze of love in his eyes was like a blow against her heart.

Tamara jerked her chin at Georg. "He has to be restrained for this. Help me cuff him to the radiator."

Georg shot Novak a questioning look.

"Get on with it," Novak said curtly. "It's getting late, and we're already behind schedule."

Tamara let go of Connor's hair and eased away from him, her gun still trained on his face. "Down on the floor," she said. "Sit. Right there."

Connor crouched down, and slowly did as she asked.

Georg advanced, flexing his plastic-covered hands. "I want to beat you with your cane," he hissed. "But it will be beautiful to have her"—he jerked his chin at Erin—"in front of you. And then you will die."

He leaped onto Connor with an animal snarl and bore him to the ground. Connor twisted under him. A gun went off. Georg arched back, gurgling. Tonia screamed. Tamara whirled, kicked her in the face.

The gun in Novak's arm rose, taking aim at Connor. Erin exploded out of her shocked paralysis. She flung herself against Novak and let the dagger slip from her sleeve into her hand. She jarred him, and stumbled back. His shot went wide. A window shattered.

Novak let out a shriek of inhuman fury and leaped at her.

Erin brought the bronze dagger up, clutched tight in both hands. It met his own furious momentum. The blade bit deep into his throat.

His pale eyes went wide. Black-red arterial blood gushed out over spotless white linen. The gun dropped from his hand. His arms encircled her as he fell forward. His blood had a meaty, metallic smell.

He was taking her down with him, into the steaming pits of hell.

She heard another gun blast, then another, but they came from very far away. The table caught the back of her head as she fell, but it was some other person who suffered that awful pain. She was falling into the vortex that had always waited for her. Fading into the dark.

"Erin? Goddamn it, Erin, wake up! Talk to me!"

Connor's voice sounded terrified. She wanted to comfort him, but she'd lost contact with the part of herself that knew speech. Everything was so far away. She was so small. Lost in a huge, echoing void.

"She's covered with blood." Connor's voice shook. Rough hands wrenched her blouse open. "I can't tell if—"

"Not hers," said Tamara's voice. "It's his. Relax."

Erin's eyes fluttered open. Staggering pain filled her head. She struggled to focus. "Connor?"

"Erin? Are you OK?"

"Don't know. Am I?"

His hands slid over her body, searching for injuries. He let out a long, unsteady sigh of relief when he found none. He slipped his arm behind her shoulder and pulled her up. "God, you scared me."

"My head." Erin tried to lift her hand up to her head, but her arm was made of lead. Connor's long, gentle fingers slid into her hair and explored. She hissed in pain.

"You've got a bump, but it didn't break the skin," he said. "We'll have it checked out."

"Novak?" she asked.

He jerked his chin to the left of them. She glanced, and looked quickly away from the still, blood-drenched thing next to them. Her gorge rose. She squeezed her eyes shut. "He's really dead this time?"

"Very dead," Tamara said. "Thanks to you."

She looked up, startled. Tamara was crouched next to her. "Me?"

"You took him out with the neck wound." Her approval was clear. "It would have taken a minute, but it was a sure thing. You hit an artery, girl. Blood's all over the wall. Looks like a slaughterhouse in here."

Erin closed her eyes before she could see the gore-spattered walls. "I heard all those gunshots," she said.

"We were just making dead sure," Tamara said. "Connor said you were an Amazon. He was right. I'm impressed." Tamara was pressing hard on her upper arm, her fingers wet with blood.

"You're wounded," Connor said to her. "Let me see."

"Tonia grazed me," she said. "The bitch always did have lousy aim. No big deal. I've taken worse than this and then gone out dancing."

The world widened into vast, echoing emptiness again. Erin heard their voices, but she could not take in what they were saying. Connor's hand was warm against her face. "Erin? Babe? Anybody home?"

"I'm not dead," was all that came out. What she wanted to say was too complicated, a million desperate things all struggling for precedence. "I'm not dead," she repeated stupidly.

"No, you're not, sweetheart. Thank God."

Connor's head dropped onto her blood-soaked shoulder. She smelled his warm, tangled hair against her face. He loved her, but he couldn't follow her to that frozen wasteland. No one could. She didn't know the way back to where he waited, warm and gentle, and needing something from her that she was too destroyed to give.

"It's all chaos," she whispered. "That's it. That's all there ever was. Anything else is just a lie. Just a mask."

Connor smoothed her hair back, frowning. "I think you've got a concussion, baby."

"I think she's telling you something important," Tamara said. She tilted Erin's chin up gently with a blood-streaked hand. "You know what? You've got the makings of an excellent professional bad girl."

That was so bizarre, it actually penetrated the haze and pulled her back to the room. She focused on Tamara, blinking. "Really?"

Tamara smiled. "Sure. You've got all the prerequisites. The looks, the brains, the nerve, the flexible attitude. You need a little help with the style, but that's no biggie."

Connor pulled her back against the warmth of his chest. "That's very kind of you, but it's not her scene."

"Let Erin speak for herself," Tamara mocked. "Today's a big day. Her first kill. It's all chaos, right? I've known that all along, you see. It's made me what I am today."

Connor's body was rigid. "Hey. Forget it. Erin isn't a—"

"I owe you one, beautiful," Tamara told her. "If you ever need help with something scary, leave me a message at the

Honey Pot sex toy shop down in Pioneer Square. Scary things are my specialty."

"Scary like this?" Connor asked harshly. "Jesus. That's kinky."

"This situation was pretty much my outer limit," she admitted. "I plan to be very mellow for a while. Unless Erin needs me, of course."

Connor's arms tightened jealously. "Thanks, but I can help her with anything scary that comes up."

Tamara stroked Erin's cheek with a long red fingernail. There was a glittering silver lightning bolt appliquéd onto it. "Men may come and men may go, but sisters look out for each other," she murmured.

Erin let out a bitter laugh. "Like Tonia?"

Tamara dismissed Tonia with a flick of her bloodstained hand. "Tonia is trash," she said. "What you lost in her, you gained in me . . . and then some." She leaned forward and kissed Erin's mouth. Her lips were soft and lingering. "Keep that in mind, girlfriend."

Connor made a rumbling sound in his chest. "Hey. I appreciate your help, and this eternal sisterhood stuff is touching, but it's been a tough day. You can stop fucking with my head anytime now. Anytime."

Tamara laughed in his face and poked him with her lightning bolt fingernail. "Toughen up, McCloud," she said. "You're such an easy mark." She rose and hiked up her skirt to holster her gun. "This place is going to be full of cops in a while, so I'll just be on my way. Cops make me itch. Except for you, of course, big boy."

"I'm not a cop anymore," he said.

Tamara's eyebrows lifted. "Once a cop, always a cop. I'm out of here." She smiled at Erin. *"Ciao,* beautiful. It's been intense."

"Any other goons to worry about?" Connor demanded.

She shook her head. "He was keeping a very low profile. The only ones in the house were Silvio and Nigel. They probably bolted when they heard the gunshots. The rest are scattered around the city. They'll evaporate soon." She dug her toe into Tonia's buttock as she passed. "Stop sniveling, you stupid cow. You won't bleed to death. Apply direct pressure with the heel of your hand and shut up."

"Tamara?" Erin called.

Tamara turned at the door.

"Thank you," Erin said. "I owe you one, too. You know how to find me if you need me."

Tamara's brilliant smile flashed. "Till later, then."

She vanished into the dark. The two of them huddled together in the dim room between two blood-soaked corpses. Tonia's miserable whimpering grated on her raw nerves. Connor was saying something. Repeating it. She wrenched her mind into focus.

". . . still got that cell phone on you someplace, sweetheart?"

"In my purse." Her teeth chattered. "Around here somewhere."

"I'll find it," he said.

She started to shiver uncontrollably when he took his warmth away to search for it. She heard his voice, getting further and further away. "Hey. Nick. It's me . . . yeah. Shut up and let me talk. I need an ambulance. I've got Novak and Luksch . . . come see for yourself. They're dead. You can ID them at your leisure, and then you can arrest me, if you still want to. There's a woman down with a gunshot wound to the thigh, one of Novak's . . . hell, I don't know. I was unconscious when they brought me here. Hold on." He crouched down in front of Erin, and patted her face. "Baby, what's the address of this place?"

She gasped it out through chattering teeth. Connor repeated it to Nick. "Hurry," he said into the phone. "Erin's going into shock."

He tossed the phone aside and peeled off her blood-drenched blouse. He took off his own shirt, wrapped her in it, and pulled her onto his lap, hunching his warm body around hers.

She felt the fear in his fierce, tight embrace. Part of her longed to comfort him, to tell him how sorry she was for not believing him. How grateful that he'd come to save her anyway, against all hope. He was heroic and beautiful, and she loved him.

She couldn't say it. She was shaking apart. She vibrated in his arms, teeth rattling. All the horrors that could have happened coexisted in her mind, an explosion of dreadful time lines radiating out from one crushing blow like the cracks in a shattered windshield.

Something inside her was screaming, and could not stop.

That was how Connor's two brothers and his friend Seth found them. They glided like silent shadows into the room and looked around, speechless at the carnage. They pried Connor's arms away from her and draped her in a man's leather jacket, still radiating heat. Connor pulled her into his arms again. She huddled there with her eyes shut.

The lights came on, the room filled with people, noise, a hum of activity. She could've cared less. Connor carried her out of the place.

She was turning inward, coiling up tight in total silence. Bright lights, the sting of a needle. A wailing siren. Then nothing.

Chapter

26

Connor parked the car, killed the engine, and sat there aching for a cigarette. There was no good reason not to just go buy himself some tobacco and some rolling papers. He'd given them up to please Erin, but he wasn't her boyfriend or her husband, or even her bodyguard, so what the hell? He wasn't her anything. Damn. That called for a smoke.

But he couldn't, as if that promise were the last tenuous bond he had left with her. Lighting up a cigarette would be admitting that he was never going to have her. He couldn't face that. Not quite yet.

Erin hadn't made a move toward him since the bloodbath, over a week ago. She'd dumped him very definitively before that, so he figured the ball was in her court. But he wasn't going to be able to wait much longer. Carrying an engagement ring around was wearing down his nerves. He felt like he had a bomb ticking in his pants pocket.

He got out of the car, rubbing the muscle in his thigh that cramped whenever he was stressed, which was pretty much all the time these days. He gazed up at the grim bulk of the state prison. The place made him tense, in much the same way that hospitals did. He guessed that was probably the whole point.

It was a long, tedious wait. He'd stuck a few scraps of paper into his pocket to fold into origami animals, a vain effort to keep his mind too busy to dwell on the dumb-ass thing he was doing. How much false, useless hope he might be pinning on it.

Finally his name was called. He had a sickly, nervous feeling in his stomach, almost like he was going to see a doctor or a dentist.

He met Ed Riggs's dark eyes through the heavy panes of glass. He was limping more than usual. He forced himself to walk more smoothly.

Erin had gotten her wide-set brown eyes from him. Weird, to see those eyes, so similar and yet so different on Ed's stone-hard face. Riggs picked up his phone and waited.

Connor picked up on his side. "Hi, Riggs."

Riggs's gaze was grim. "McCloud."

There were many ways to approach it. All of them sounded stupid.

Riggs grunted impatiently. "They don't give you much time, so if you've got something to say to me, spit it out."

He took a deep breath. "I'm going to ask Erin to marry me."

Riggs's eyes went blank. He stared through the glass at the younger man. "Why are you telling me this?" he asked slowly.

There it was. The million-dollar question. He'd been trying to answer it for himself for days, ever since the marching orders to go talk to Riggs had come over him. "I'm not sure," he admitted. "To clear the air, I guess. You're her father. I wanted you to hear it from me."

Riggs let out a bark of bitter laughter. "Man to man, huh? Are you here to ask for my permission?"

Anger twisted and burned, the sour, familiar pain of betrayal corroding his gut. He breathed it out and let it go. "I don't need your goddamn permission," he said. "And neither does she."

Riggs shook his head. "You self-righteous son of a bitch. You always did piss me off."

Connor shrugged. "There's a limited amount of pissing off that I can do to you through a telephone and bullet-proof glass. Look on the bright side. You're never going to have to drink beer and talk football with me over the barbecue."

Riggs's mouth twitched. "Fuck you, McCloud."

"Fuck you, too, Riggs," he replied.

They were silent, eyes locked. Seconds ticked by. Riggs's eyes flicked away. His shoulders slumped. "Barbara was in here last week. She told me what happened. What you did for Erin and Cindy."

Connor waited. Riggs leaned his face in his hands. When he looked up, the frustration of a trapped animal burned in his eyes. "Damn it, McCloud, what do you want? You want me to thank you? You want an apology? Forget it. This place is punishment enough."

"No, I don't want that," Connor said.

"I couldn't protect them, but you can, is that what you're here to tell me? You want to puff out your chest and gloat? Go ahead. Yay for you, asshole. You did good. You win. You get the grand prize."

"That's what I'm hoping for," he said.

Riggs's eyes narrowed. "Oh, yeah? You think you deserve her, because of this? You think you've earned her? You think—"

"No," he cut in. "Erin decides. What I deserve or don't deserve doesn't mean shit."

"Then what the fuck are you doing here?" Riggs hissed.

Connor looked away from him. "I was hoping you would wish me luck," he said quietly.

He braced himself for a vicious retort. Silence greeted his words.

When he raised his eyes again, the flush of anger was gone from Riggs's face. It was bleak and gray under the fluorescent light. "You are so fucking strange," he said heavily. "I always thought so."

Connor lifted his shoulders. "I know. But what can you do."

"You ask a lot."

"You owe me a lot," Connor said. "And I really want this."

Riggs's mouth flattened, like he was tasting something bitter. "Oh, what the hell," he muttered. "Good luck, then. For what it's worth."

Connor let out a long, shaky breath. "Uh . . . thanks."

"Don't thank me yet," Riggs warned. "Consider the source. Good luck from me might be a curse."

"I'll risk it," Connor said.

"Time's up," said a disembodied voice over a ceiling intercom.

He nodded at Riggs and put down his phone. Riggs gestured for him to pick it up again. Connor put it back to his ear. "What?"

"You keep protecting her, McCloud," Riggs said. "You take good care of her."

"Hell, yes. If she'll let me," he promised. "I was born for it."

Riggs let the phone drop. He got up, turned, and marched away.

The apartment looked even more forlorn now that the pictures and hangings she'd used to cover the stains in the wall were packed away. Miles ducked into the door and headed for the standing mirror.

"Be careful, please," she begged. "It's extremely old."

"I'm always careful," he assured her. He wiped the sweat off his forehead, grabbed the mirror, and galumphed out the door.

Her mother bustled in. "That's all that will fit in the van for now, hon. A couple more armfuls of clothes, and you're out of this place."

Erin tried to smile. "Cindy's still guarding the van?"

"Yes. Let's take down this load, and then we'll go grab a bite."

"I'm not hungry, Mom. I'll just do some last-minute cleaning."

"Cleaning? This place is cleaner than it deserves to be, honey! If you clean it any more, it'll disintegrate into grit!"

"I just need some quiet time," Erin insisted. "Don't worry."

Her mother saw the steely look on Erin's face, and pressed her lips together. "Whatever." She yanked an armful of plastic-wrapped clothes out of the closet and marched out the door, her back stiff.

Erin stood in the middle of the apartment. Her legs trembled from all those trips up and down the six flights of stairs. The elevator, of course, was still broken. Soon that would no longer be her problem.

Her real problem was that something inside her felt broken, too.

She sank down onto the floor in the middle of the room and hugged herself, shivering. It was a warm day, she was sweating, but she still felt cold when she thought of what had happened. Even though Connor had saved her. Disaster had been averted. She hadn't been hurt, and yet she was bleeding inside.

And Connor had not called.

God. What did she expect? What did she want from the guy, anyway? He'd tried so hard to protect her. She had fought him, and undermined him, and finally turned against him, along with the rest of the world. She wouldn't blame him if he never wanted to see her again. He must be disgusted with her. She was disgusted with herself.

And yet, he'd risked his life for her. He had carried her

out of that charnel house in his arms. And then he had melted away like fog.

The first few days after Mom brought her home from the hospital, she'd barely cared if she lived or died. She was frozen stiff. She had no feelings at all. She just lay in her bed and stared at the wallpaper until Cindy and her mother were frantic. She didn't care. It was their turn to chew their nails, to tear out their hair, to be the grown-ups. Let them sweat.

Then one day, she'd been lying on her stomach, hand dangling to the floor, and her fingers had brushed over a scrap of folded paper.

Connor's origami unicorn.

Feelings had roared through the ruined landscape of her heart, and she'd remembered. She had realized what had been taken from her. That magical night of perfect trust and love. Her gallant knight errant, tender and passionate and brave. It had cracked her wide open.

She pressed her hand against her belly and stared at the scarred linoleum. The memory of that night with him still stabbed like a knife.

It hadn't gotten any better in a week of endless days and sleepless nights, but every time she picked up the phone to call him, she stopped. She had so little to offer him. Just herself, and she felt so small right now. Such a sorry prize. And if he rejected her, that would be it. She would shrivel up like a dead flower and crumble into dust.

Not knowing was preferable to dreadful certainty. Every day, she dropped the phone back into the cradle, and she thought, tomorrow. Tomorrow I'll have more nerve.

Well, there were no tomorrows left. She had to call him today. Her contingency plan was ready. If he said no, she would leave tomorrow. Her friend Sasha lived in a group house in Portland that had a free bedroom. Just like her college days. It would be a step backwards in time, but it was all she could afford, and the noise and bustle of a house full of busy young women would be good for her. She could temp in Portland while she sent out resumes. There was nothing holding her in the Northwest now, if . . . if the answer to the big question was no. Mom was working, and loving it. Miles was tutoring Cindy through summer school. They didn't need her to take care of them, and lucky for them, because she was all tapped out. She would be lucky if she managed to take care of herself.

"Honey? I decided to get one last load. Let's go down together."

Erin smiled up at her mother's anxious face and scrambled to her feet. She grabbed the final armful of clothes from the closet and followed Barbara down the stairs. She kicked the lobby door open.

She stopped, as if she'd been turned to stone.

Connor was lounging against his car. His long, rangy body was dressed in battered khaki cargo pants and an olive drab T-shirt. His hair was loose, blowing around his shoulders. His face was grim. Wary.

Plastic-wrapped clothing slid out of her arms and scattered every which way over the steps.

"Well!" Mom said. "You took your own sweet time showing up!"

Cindy gave her mother a horrified look and scrambled to gather up Erin's fallen clothes. "Mom! Don't make it worse!"

"Worse? How could it possibly be worse? Stabbing villains to death? Gouts of blood? Threats of rape, torture, and murder? She can't sleep, she won't eat! Don't talk to me about worse!"

Connor's face softened. He almost smiled. "Nice to see you again, too, Barbara."

"Don't you get smart with me, Connor McCloud. I am very annoyed with you, and I've had a bad week."

"Me, too," he admitted. He turned his gaze up to Erin.

Her mother flung the clothes into the van. Erin was still

transfixed. The silence dragged on. It reached deafening proportions.

"Hi, Erin," he said gently.

The simple, innocuous words released a tide of emotion. It swept over her, made her body quake and shudder. "Hi," she whispered.

Connor glanced over at Barbara, Miles, and Cindy. "I was hoping to get Erin to go for a ride with me," he said. "You all mind?"

"Ask her, not us." Barbara jerked her chin in Erin's direction. "She's the one who's been holding her breath for a week."

"Mom!" Cindy moaned. "Stop! You'll ruin it!"

Connor looked at Erin. "Erin? Will you come for a ride with me?"

Somehow, she unlocked her muscles enough to nod.

"We'll get out of your hair, then," Mom said. "I'm sure you have a lot to talk about. Connor, she hasn't eaten yet. See to it that she does."

Cindy shot her a hopeful thumbs-up as she slid the van door shut. Miles folded his impossibly long self into the passenger seat. Barbara yanked the driver's side door open, and hesitated.

She stalked over to Connor, grabbed him around the waist, and gave him a fierce, stiff hug. Then she took a step back and swatted him on the chest, hard enough to make him wince and leap back.

"Ouch!" He rubbed the spot, indignant. "What the hell?"

She made a frustrated sound.

Connor leaped between her and his car and held out his arms protectively. "Don't you dare touch my car, Barbara. I love this car."

"Idiot," she muttered. She glanced at Erin as she hurried to the van. "Call me," she said. "Don't make me worry, whatever you end up doing. I just can't handle it right now."

"OK," Erin said faintly.

They waited until the van turned the corner and was lost to sight.

Connor rubbed his chest. "I'm going to have a bruise. Christ. That woman is dangerous."

"Mom's dealing with a lot of conflicted emotions right now."

"Huh. Aren't we all," he grumbled. "As long as she doesn't come to terms with them using a tire iron, we'll be fine."

It was time to move her legs, but if she bent them, the starch might just go right out of her, and she would fall flat on her face.

Which, now that she thought of it, was exactly where she'd been for the past week. She unlocked her knees, a smidgen at a time. She took a step, then another. She made it to the car without falling.

He held open the car door for her like a perfect gentleman. Not sweeping her into his arms or covering her with kisses or anything great and reassuring like that. No, he politely opened the door for her as if she were his eighty-year-old maiden aunt.

She slid into the car with a murmur of thanks.

Connor drove the car, and she searched through the database of her mind for one of the zillion prepared speeches she had made. They were nowhere to be found. She could only stare at his chiseled profile, at the beautiful line of his jaw. Scratches and bruises were still fading on his face. She wanted to kiss every last one of them.

"Looks like you were moving," he said.

His voice was so neutral. She could deduce nothing from it. "Yes," she said. "I'm putting most of my stuff in Mom's attic. Just taking a couple of suitcases with me."

"Where are you headed?"

She echoed his casual tone. "Portland, to start with. A friend of mine lives in a group house there. I figured I'd temp while I send my resume around, see who bites. Just for a change of air. It'll be fun to live with girlfriends again."

"A change of air," he repeated.

"Yeah, it's time," she faltered. "I have to get going on my career. Cindy and Mom are going to be fine now, so I'm free to . . . to—"

"Free to go," he finished. "Good thing I came by when I did. I might have missed you completely."

"Oh, no," she said hastily. "I meant to call you before I left."

"Just to say good-bye." His voice was hard.

He parked the car in front of a white two-story house with a deep, wraparound porch surrounded by rosebushes and hydrangeas.

"Where are we?" she asked.

He looked at her silently for a long moment. "This is my house."

Her gaze skittered away from his. "Oh. It's, ah, very nice."

"Come on up," he said.

She followed him up the walk through a green, lush lawn and peeked around herself as she followed him in.

The place was simple and tidy. Starkly furnished, but with warm colors. Parquet floors, a rust-colored rug in front of a navy blue couch. A fireplace. State-of-the-art speakers and sound system. A few carefully placed pictures on the walls, mostly charcoal landscapes.

"Come on into the kitchen," he invited her. "Your mom said you hadn't eaten. Can I fix you some lunch?"

"No, thank you," she said.

"A drink, then? I've got cold beer in the fridge. Or iced tea."

"A beer would be fine," she said.

Connor pulled two long-necked bottles out of the refrigerator. He popped them open with his key chain, grabbed her a glass from the drain board. He pulled out a chair for her. For the first time, she saw past her own anxiety and noticed that his face looked strained.

He sat down across from her. "Why didn't you call me, Erin?"

The question lay between them, heavy and important. She poured out a glassful of beer, stared into it, and told him the simple truth. "I felt too awful," she said. "About not believing you."

"Don't feel bad about that," he said. "I wouldn't have believed me either. No one would have. It was so bizarre, I barely believed myself."

She shook her head. "All that violence and malice and hatred. It made me feel . . . small. Squished out of existence."

"Your mom said you're not sleeping. Nightmares?"

She nodded.

"They'll pass," he said. "You're very strong."

Tears prickled her eyes at his quiet comprehension. She tried to reply, but the words tangled into a burning knot in her throat.

"You know how I figured it out, in the end?" he asked.

She dug for her Kleenex and gestured for him to go on.

"I went to the clinic," he said. "Sean saw Tonia there when I was in the coma. I checked it out. The only Tonia Vasquez who had ever worked there was in her sixties, and retired years before."

"Oh," she said. "I see."

"And that wasn't all. They showed me the guest register."

Erin covered her face and braced herself.

"I found your name there, Erin. Every single day that I was in that coma, you came in to see me."

She peeked through her fingers at him, and tried to smile. "Whoops," she whispered. "Busted."

He did not smile back. He just waited.

Erin let her hands drop. "I heard somewhere that it can help people in a coma, if you sing to them or talk to them or read to them," she said. "I can't sing, and I had never been able to think of anything to say to you even when you were conscious, let alone in a coma. But I can read. I remembered once you said you liked thrillers. I bought a Dean Koontz novel, *Fear Nothing.* I picked it out for the title. Then I got *Seize the Night,* since it was the sequel."

She paused. He just waited, eyes averted. His face was as still as if it were carved out of granite.

"At the end of *Seize the Night,* the hero, Chris, proposes to his girlfriend," she said. "It made me cry. I closed the book, and I started to talk to you. For the first time, I just held your hand and talked."

He let out a jerky sigh, and rubbed his face. "What did you say?"

Tears were running down her face. She dug a Kleenex out of her pocket and mopped them up. "I told you how I felt about you. How much I wanted you to wake up. How badly I hoped that someday we could be together. That was the last time I came."

His head jerked around. "Why?" he demanded.

"Because that night, you woke up," she said.

He looked baffled. "Why? Why stop, after all that? Why didn't you come to see me anymore?"

She blew her nose. "Oh, please. There you were, barely conscious, in terrible pain, just finding out that your partner had been murdered. I thought some silly, crushed-out girl demanding your attention was the last thing you needed. I was embarrassed. I didn't want to bother you."

He stood up, so suddenly his chair shot back and crashed against the wall behind him. "Bother me? Jesus, Erin. Is that why you didn't call this week? You were embarrassed? You didn't want to *bother* me?"

"Connor, I—"

"Why the hell do you think I woke up?" he asked furiously. "Did it ever occur to you to ask yourself that question?"

She pressed her hands over her mouth and shook her head.

He threw his hands up. His face was tight with pain. "I would've come back from the dead if I heard you say you wanted me."

He stalked out of the kitchen.

She lunged for him and grabbed his arm. "Connor?"

He spun around. It was impossible to tell who grabbed who. They fell toward each other, giving in to the immense, inevitable force of gravity. They came together in a wild, desperate, clinging kiss.

Somehow they ended up in a trembling knot on his living room carpet. She scrambled on top of him and twined herself around his body, shoving his T-shirt up. She was starving for the sumptuous details of his beautiful body, every dip and curve, every bulge of hard muscle, every sensitive hollow, every silky tuft of hair. He was real, he wanted her, and she craved every salty, earthy, delicious inch of him.

He grabbed her wrist. "Wait. Slow down."

"No?" She rubbed the glow of heat between her thighs against him. "No?"

"No more playing around," he said flatly. "I want it all. I'm not putting out again until my ring is on your finger. So don't even start with that sex goddess stuff." His bright eyes challenged her to object.

A smile started, deep inside her, in the secret place where blushes and tears were born. A joy so deep and explosive, her body shone with it, expanding into infinite space. "You're serious?"

"No ring, no sex," he said sternly.

"You are kidding, right? You couldn't deny me. I won't allow it. I'll use all my powers to seduce you. It's a matter of pride."

He propped himself up onto his elbows. "Forget it. I'm no fool. I know how this works. Why buy the cow if you get the milk for free?"

She laughed, but her eyes were overflowing. "That's so crass."

Connor pushed himself up, dug into a tattered pocket on his cargo pants. He handed her a small black velvet box, and looked away quickly. "I've been carrying this around with me for more than a week," he said. "If you don't like it, we can look for something else."

She jammed her soggy tissue against her nose and flipped it open.

It was an antique ring. A faceted oval aquamarine, rich with shifting shades of pale, milky blue and green, was suspended within a filigreed circle of platinum. It was ethereal, unique. Exquisite.

The colors in the stone swam and blended in her eyes, into a swirl of green, blue and white light. Her throat was too tight to speak.

"I didn't figure you for the traditional diamond type," he said warily. "This, well . . . it fit my fantasy of something you might like."

"Your fantasy fits me fine," she whispered. "It's so beautiful."

He took the box from her and pulled the ring out. He looked into her eyes. "Will you wear it?"

She held out her left hand without hesitation. "Yes."

He slipped it onto her finger. He pressed her hand against his mouth, and held it against his cheek. "Oh, God," he said shakily. "That was really scary. And I got through it. Look at me. I'm still alive."

The ring glowed on her hand, as if light were shining behind it. "It fits perfectly," she said softly. "We don't even have to size it."

"I already sized it. I tried on one of your rings. It came to right here, on my smallest finger. I just told that to the jeweler."

She was staggered. "You were already convinced? Back then?"

"Hell, yes. God favors those who are prepared. That's what my crazy daddy used to say, as he taught us how to build a bomb or perform an emergency tracheotomy."

She laughed, and wrapped her arms around his neck. "I love you, Connor. I'm sorry for every time I wasn't brave enough to tell you so."

He kissed her tears away. "Do you trust me, Erin?"

The longing in his voice made her heart ache. She pressed her forehead to his. "With my life, with my heart. With everything. Forever."

A shudder went through his body, as if he were shaking off the shadow of some old lingering fear. "Will you come upstairs with me?"

"I would go anywhere with you," she said.

They scrambled to their feet, and he took her hand. She followed him up the stairs and into a big, sparsely furnished bedroom. Golden afternoon sun slanted through bamboo shades. Simple white walls, an antique dresser, a king-sized bed with a rough, textured coverlet of silvery charcoal fabric. There was a long handmade chest beneath the window. It was plain, almost medieval in its simplicity.

He watched her look around his room. Each step they went through felt like a holy ceremony. A series of doorways that led them ever deeper into the most secret and tender parts of each other.

"I love your room," she said gently. "It suits you."

"I've dreamed of luring you in here for so long," he said. "I even changed the sheets this morning. For luck."

Erin tugged her T-shirt over her head, unhooked her bra, kicked off her sneakers. "God favors those who are prepared?"

"Yeah." His cheeks flushed as he stared at her. He laughed at himself and rubbed his hand over his face. "Jesus. How do you do this to me?" he said, in a wondering voice. "I feel like I'm thirteen, again."

She shimmied out of her jeans and panties, and shoved

his chest. He sat down on the bed as if his knees were too weak to hold him.

"So?" she teased. "I'm wearing your ring, Connor. Nothing else. I held up my side of the deal. What are you going to do with me now?"

He wrapped his arms around her waist and pressed his hot face against her belly. "Everything," he said. "Everything you want. Anything you can dream of. For the rest of our lives."

She buried her nose in his fragrant hair. His lips moved against her skin, his hands moved over her body. He knew her so well, all the ways to make her quiver and go soft and wet and desperate for him. He slid his clever fingers between her legs, stroking her with loving skill.

She swayed, her knees buckling, and grabbed his shirt.

"Enough teasing." She yanked it up over his head. "It's been ten days, and I want you. So get ready to put out, Connor McCloud."

She shoved him down onto the bed and attacked his belt. He laughed up at her in pure delight. "But we just got engaged," he protested. "I thought that a tender, romantic vibe would be more—"

"Think again." She yanked the cargo pants off and stared down at his sleek, powerful body with hungry eyes. "You can be tender and romantic afterwards. When I'm tired."

"OK," he said cheerfully. He lunged for the bedside stand and rummaged in the drawer until he found an unopened box of condoms. She loved the way the muscles in his arms and back and belly flexed and rippled. He rolled the condom onto himself, jerked her down on top of him, and rolled her over.

It was delicious, exactly what she craved, to curl herself around his lithe, hot, muscular body. Everything she wanted to do with him, all the pleasures she wanted to bestow upon him crowded through her mind at once. She resented the constraints of time and space that forced her to do one thing at a time. She wiggled into the position she wanted. She was one hot, aching glow of need, her sheath throbbing with each pulse of her heart. "Now," she begged. "Please."

He filled her with himself, and the first wave of pleasure broke over her then and there, before he even began to move.

She fell apart in his arms, in a cleansing, healing storm of tears.

"Oh, Erin," he murmured. He cradled her face, kissed her tears away.

She moved beneath him, still weeping, and finally understood the nature of the truth she had faced in Novak's house of horrors. Chaos did rule. But love had lifted away the shadow of Novak's twisted loathing from that truth. Love had exalted it.

Love was chaos, too. She couldn't control it and didn't want to try. Everything beautiful and wild and free was part of that chaos. She finally caught a glimpse of the rich, beautiful design that underlaid it. She would never resist it again: surprises and wonder, heat and light and laughter, blazing color and raucous noise. Messes and mistakes, change and growth and risk. Magic, and love.

Everything that made life sweet, that gave it meaning.

Connor lifted his face from hers. "Come to Vegas with me," he said. "Let's get married tomorrow."

"But I . . . but we—"

"I want it nailed down. I want my wedding night with my beautiful bride, and I want it now."

She laughed. "But it's a sure thing. We just have to wait until—"

"I've waited long enough."

"That's a dirty trick," she told him sternly. "And this isn't the first time you've played it on me."

"What trick?" He fluttered his lashes, all innocence.

"You know. Springing something big on me while we're making love. When you're inside me. It gives you an unfair advantage."

She could feel his smile against her mouth as he kissed her. "It goes both ways, you know," he said. "You have the same advantage that I do. You just haven't used it yet. Come on, sweetheart. Take a road trip with me. It's the perfect time. We're still unemployed, but probably not for long. I have some money left. We'll get a honeymoon suite at a cheesy casino hotel with a Jacuzzi tub and a vibrating bed. We'll order out for room service. I'll buy you an evening dress. On our way back, we can explore the desert together. Ever see the sun set in the desert?"

She rubbed against him, so that her sensitive nipples brushed against his chest. The contact was a rippling thrill. "My mother would never forgive you if you cheated her out of planning our wedding."

"Who says she needs to know? We'll do it again for her benefit. Another wedding night, another honeymoon? I'm all for it."

He was grinning, glowing with happiness. So gorgeous, her heart was going to explode with tenderness. She pulled his face to hers and kissed him. "Persuade me," she ordered. "Go on. Do your worst."

"Huh?" He looked baffled, but intrigued.

"Go on. Bend me to your will. Overwhelm me with your masterful charisma. Sweep me off my feet. You know I love it."

"You're already on your back," he observed.

"Well, then. You have a head start," she said. "Lucky you."

His smile grooves carved themselves deep into his lean face, and she sighed with delight. She was going to be dazzled by that gorgeous grin for as many years as luck would grant her.

"OK, fine," he said. "This is how it's going to be. I'm going to make passionate love to you until I reduce you to a puddle of sated bliss. Then I'll carry you out to my car. When you wake up, we'll be speeding through the middle of a beautiful nowhere. Mountains, deserts, who knows what. The sun will just be coming up, turning everything pink. If you give me any trouble, I'll pull off the road, lay you out on the hood of my car, and go down on you while you stare up at the morning star, glowing in that huge, open sky. Just you and me and one lonely eagle circling up there to watch us. What do you say? Sound like a plan?"

She pulled him closer. "Oh, God, I love you. I love this."

He hugged her so close, their hearts thudded in unison. "I love you, too. But what about my plan? Is it masterful enough? Will you be swept away and overwhelmed? Or do I need to fine-tune?"

"It sounds pretty great," she assured him. "But what about the part where I spread you out on the hood of the car under that big open sky? Fair's fair, right?"

They gazed into each other's eyes. Connor shook his head. "Wow, sweetheart," he said softly. "This is going to be one hell of a road trip."

Hot suspense. Hotter men ...

Looking for a romance that *really* sizzles? Available now: BEHIND CLOSED DOORS, the prequel to STANDING IN THE SHADOWS, from Kensington Romantic Suspense!

Surveillance expert Seth Mackey knows everything about the women his millionaire boss Victor Lazar toys with—and tosses aside. But Lazar's latest plaything, Raine Cameron, is different. Beautiful. Vulnerable. And innocent. Just looking at her stirs a white-hot passion he can barely control as, night after night, he watches her on a dozen different video screens. Raine is pure temptation, but Seth can't slip up: he's convinced Lazar had his half-brother murdered. His secret investigation—and his life—are on the line. But then he finds out that Raine may be Lazar's next victim ...

Next, head down the highway with BAD BOYS NEXT EXIT, a Brava Romance anthology featuring a super-sexy, smoldering hero that only Shannon McKenna could write—available now!

All Jane Duvall wants is to bag another big account for her headhunting firm, even if it means stealing a key employee right out from under sexy hotel CEO Michael McNamara's gorgeous nose. But Mac can tell that the luscious, elusive Jane is up to no good. He has to find out what game she's playing—even if it involves giving her a very private tour of the hotel's finest suite, where she can take whatever she wants from him—and he'll give her everything he's got in the process ...

And here's a scorching sneak peek at her latest Brava, on sale now! RETURN TO ME ... Bad boy Simon Reilly comes home at last—to a woman he couldn't forget—and the demons of his past ...

"Excuse me, miss. I'm looking for El Kent." The low, quiet voice came from the swinging door that led to the dining room.

Ellen spun around with a gasp. The eggs flew into the air, and splattered on the floor. No one called her El. No one except for—

The sight of him knocked her back. God. So tall. So big. All over. The long, skinny body she remembered was filled out with hard, lean muscle. His white T-shirt showed off broad shoulders, sinewy arms. Faded jeans clung with careless grace to the perfect lines of his narrow hips, his long legs. She looked up into the focused intensity of his dark eyes, and a rush of hot and cold shivered through her body.

The exotic perfection of his face was harder now. Seasoned by sun and wind and time. She drank in the details: golden skin, narrow hawk nose, hollows beneath his prominent cheekbones, the sharp angle of his jaw, shaded with a few days' growth of dark beard stubble. A silvery scar sliced through the dark slash of his left eyebrow. His gleaming hair was wet, combed straight back from his square forehead into a ponytail. Tightly leashed power hummed around him.

The hairs on her arms lifted in response.

His eyes flicked over her body. His teeth flashed white against his tan. "Damn. I'll run to the store to replace those eggs for you, miss."

Miss? He didn't even recognize her. Her face was starting to shake again. Seventeen years of worrying about him, and he just checked out her body, like he might scope any woman he saw on the street.

He waited patiently for her to respond to his apology. She peeked up at his face again. One eyebrow was tilted up in a gesture so achingly familiar, it brought tears to her eyes. She clapped her hand over her trembling lips. She would not cry. She would not.

"I'm real sorry I startled you," he tried again. "I was wondering if you could tell me where I might find—" His voice trailed off. His smile faded. He sucked in a gulp of air. "Holy shit," he whispered. "El?"

The gesture tipped him off. He recognized her the instant she covered her mouth and peeked over her hand, but he had to struggle to superimpose his memories of El onto the knockout blonde in the kitchen. He remembered a skinny girl with big, startled eyes peeking up from beneath heavy bangs. A mouth too big for her bit of a face.

This woman was nothing like that awkward girl. She'd filled out, with a fine, round ass that had immediately caught his eye as she bent into the fridge. And what she had down there was nicely balanced by what she had up top. High, full tits, bouncing and soft. A tender, lavish mouthful and then some, just how he liked them.

Her hand dropped, and revealed her wide, soft mouth. Her dark eyebrows no longer met across the bridge of her nose. Spots of pink stained her delicate cheekbones. She'd grown into her eyes and mouth. Her hair was a wavy curtain of gold-streaked bronze that reached down to her ass. El Kent had turned beautiful. Mouth-falling-open, mind-going-blank beautiful. The images locked seamlessly together, and he wondered how he could've not recognized her, even for an instant.

<u>BOOK YOUR PLACE ON OUR WEBSITE</u> <u>AND MAKE THE</u> <u>READING CONNECTION!</u>

We've created a customized website just for our very special readers, where you can get the inside scoop on everything that's going on with Zebra, Pinnacle and Kensington books.

When you come online, you'll have the exciting opportunity to:

- View covers of upcoming books
- Read sample chapters
- Learn about our future publishing schedule (listed by publication month *and author*)
- Find out when your favorite authors will be visiting a city near you
- Search for and order backlist books from our online catalog
- Check out author bios and background information
- Send e-mail to your favorite authors
- Meet the Kensington staff online
- Join us in weekly chats with authors, readers and other guests
- Get writing guidelines
- AND MUCH MORE!

**Visit our website at
http://www.kensingtonbooks.com**